The History of Lucy's Love Life in Ten and a Half Chapters

Deborah Wright

D1428552

sphere

SPHERE

First published in Great Britain as a paperback original
in 2006 by Sphere

Copyright © Deborah Wright 2006

A CIP catalogue record for this book
is available from the British Library.

ISBN-13: 978-0-7515-3703-1
ISBN-10: 0-7515-3703-9

Typeset in Plantin by M Rules
Printed and bound in Great Britain by
Clays Ltd, St Ives plc

Sphere
An imprint of
Little, Brown Book Group
Brettenham House
Lancaster Place
London WC2E 7EN

A Member of the Hachette Livre Group of Companies

www.littlebrown.co.uk
www.letsgetintoatimemachineandgotobedwith.com

This book is
for
S.L.K.
With all my love

Acknowledgements

Thanks to all my friends and family, especially Mum and Dad, Lewis, David, Tristan, Victoria, Jessica and Alexander.

Thank you to Germaine Greer and Andrew Motion for their kind permission to feature in my book!

Thanks to my wonderful agent, Simon Trewin, and my lovely editor, Jo Dickinson. Thanks also to everyone else at Little, Brown, especially Kerry Chapple, Sheena-Margot Lavelle and Jenny Fry.

A note to my readers: like my heroine Lucy, I have, at times, broken the rules of time. I have tried to be historically accurate but I have taken the odd liberty here and there – any fan of Byron, for example, will know that he met Shelley a little later than 1813 – so readers must forgive me for cheating a little and compressing time for the purposes of a good yarn.

Prologue

Sometimes when I can't sleep, I lie in bed and pose the question: *if you could spend one night with any man in the world – just one man – who would it be?* It's certainly a good deal more interesting than counting sheep.

That night – before everything changed – I woke up at 3.30 a.m. and lay staring at the amber streetlamp streaks patterned on my wall. I yawned, feeling heavy and irritated. My full bladder pulsed but I couldn't be bothered to get up. I rolled over on to my left side. Then my right side. Then my back. Then my front again. None of them helped. I thought of a Sylvia Plath poem I had learnt and loved at school: *He suffers his desert pillow, sleeplessness / Stretching its fine, irritating sand in all directions.* How horrible this is, I thought. I'd never suffered from insomnia before, so why did I seem to be making a habit of it over the last few weeks? It wasn't as though I had anything to worry about. I had a good job working as a PA for a scientist who was mad enough not to notice I could only type at a speed of eight words per two fingers per minute. I had a pleasant boyfriend, a nice flat in Primrose Hill, a playful cat, wonderful friends, all my limbs and teeth still intact, etc. Maybe that was the problem. My mother used to say, 'You're not happy unless you have something to worry about in life, Lucy.' Maybe I was just bored.

At the bottom of my bed, my cat stretched out in a mottled arch of pleasure, utterly smug in her deep sleep.

OK, I thought, time to play the going-to-bed game.

I composed a short-list in my head . . .

1. Lord Byron
2. George Clooney
3. The gorgeous guy in the newsagent who I buy my *Daily Telegraph* from every morning

I mulled over the possibilities with my cat, Lyra. 'Lord Byron is obvious. He was the best poet of all time. He was handsome. And – the most important thing in a man – he was brainy. I must have a man who can make me think, who in postcoital chats can discuss politics alongside positions, Ovid alongside orgasms.'

Eight times out of ten, Byron would win the game. But tonight I felt like a change. Byron was too unattainable.

Mind you, the same went for George Clooney. And he had a pet pig whom he was reputed to share his bed with. I liked animals, so the pig might be fun – but how would the pig get on with my cat? What if I woke up one morning to find Clooney's pig with a porky smile on its face and a frayed white tail hanging out of the corner of its mouth? Then again, my cat was fairly psychotic . . . but I had a feeling Clooney might kick me out of bed if I was responsible for the death of Mr Pig.

'So, *not* Clooney,' I mused to Lyra, who stretched languidly and curled her head under her paw. 'How about the gorgeous guy I buy my *Daily Telegraph* from?'

I smiled deliciously. Every morning the dull routine of getting out at Embankment Tube station and surging up the escalators in a flow and flood of commuters into a ragged, grey dawn is brightened considerably by him: six feet tall, slender, chocolate-brown eyes that crinkle into wings as I pass him my money. I always worry that my lust will leave an invisible imprint on the coins, too warm and damp from being curled in my hand, caressed and flipped by my fingers for much of my journey. Over a six-month period, we've progressed from shy 'hi's to 'How are you doing today?'. He knows my job and I know his age, but that's about it so far. There is something so sexy about his down-to-earthness, his cheery 'Cheers!' when I pass him the coins (perhaps because I spend much of the day with my scientist boss posing questions such as 'Surely there is nothing in the world more *thrilling* than imaginary numbers – don't you agree?'). But th   e detail about him that

2

really gets me is the grubby black smudges on his hands. His fingers are as fragile as a violinist's and the incongruous smudges look dirty and sexy. Sometimes I even fantasise about making love to him not on a bed of roses but on a bundle of newspaper sheets, the print smearing our bodies so that we become, literally, yesterday's news.

That night I fantasised about buying the paper from him and being drawn into a back alley, shutting London and the commuters out. I pictured him pushing me up against a graffiti-covered wall and sharing hot kisses, his hands delving into my blouse . . .

That is the trouble with my game. If you play with too much enthusiasm, it may only increase insomnia. Still, like I said, better than counting sheep.

Sheep. Funny things. Sheep-shagging even funnier. For a moment I was distracted by how and why men bother (another problem with the game – if you're tired, your mind may have a tendency to wander down weird, irrelevant avenues . . .). Then I started laughing and shook myself. Back to the game. Time to decide.

Not George Clooney, I thought. Not unless he agreed to roast the pig.

'So it's either Lord Byron or my *Daily Telegraph* guy,' I said to Lyra, whose tongue was rasping against her tail. 'And I think it's going to be . . . oh God, how predictable . . .'

Lord Byron. I just melted at the thought of his soft Romantic locks, his brown eyes, his haughty tipped-up chin, but at the same time I felt a bit sad and exasperated with myself. Lord Byron was thirty in the year 1818; I wouldn't be thirty till the year 2006. It didn't really bode well for a love match.

And there was another worry.

I hadn't included Anthony in my going-to-bed game. Anthony has been my boyfriend for the last two years and yet he didn't even scrape the top four. Don't get me wrong. Anthony is fine in bed. He is handsome. Sweet. Quite wealthy – he is head of a computer firm. He has a wonderful sense of humour, and doesn't mind when I make jokes about sheep. He buys me chocolate and flowers. He makes me laugh. I can phone him any time and tell him whatever teeny thing is on my mind, even if it's something utterly stupid, like what I should wear to work or my lunchtime what-to-have-in-my-sandwich dilemma or what underwear I'm wearing (he is particularly helpful when discussing the latter).

So why had I recently had to start faking my orgasms? And why, the last time we met, did I pretend I had my period? I thought the fizz was meant to go out of relationships after eighteen years of marriage. If I couldn't even manage two years without getting bored, what hope was there for me?

I pictured myself breaking up with Anthony, walking around the idea uneasily and giving it the odd nervous prod. I pictured the look of devastation on his face. Anthony's mother had left him when he was five years old, and though he was confident on the outside, in more vulnerable moments I'd seen the fear it had left in his heart. After making love, he never rolled over and went to sleep. He clung to me tightly and sometimes woke me in the night and whispered, 'You won't ever leave me, will you?' and I'd kiss him and hug him and say, 'Never – I promise – you're not only my boyfriend but the best friend I've ever had.' And we'd fall asleep, nose to nose, wrapped in loyalty and intimacy, a silent pact between us that we would always be there for each other: it was us against the world.

The thought of breaking up with him suddenly made me feel like crying. I quickly went back to thinking of Lord B.

Eventually I slipped into the quicksand of sleep and dreamt of chasing Lord Byron through London all night, unable to ever quite catch him . . .

Of course, I had no idea then that in less than three days' time I was going to actually end up in bed with Lord Byron.

But – thank God – life never fails to surprise us.

Just when you think you have everything in place, it will creep up on you when you least expect it . . .

Chapter One

Anthony Brown

In rivers, the water you touch is the last of what has passed and the first of what is to come; so with present time.

LEONARDO DA VINCI

i) Late

By the next morning, Lord Byron was forgotten. I overslept and Lyra, ever an unreliable alarm clock, woke me by swishing her tail over my face. As I blearily opened my sleepy-dust-sticky eyes, she retreated to the bottom of my bed, all purrs and wide emerald eyes, as if to say: 'Oh, I'm *so* sorry, I seem to have accidentally woken you.' I rolled over and saw that it was nine o'clock – the exact time I was meant to be in the office. I jumped out of bed and threw on my suit, which I had fortunately ironed and hung over my chair the night before.

Friday was normally a hair-washing morning, but there was no time for that. I forked out a plate of tuna for Lyra, locked up and hurried to the lift. Just as the doors were about to close, a group bundled in: Mrs Evans from next door with her two children, and Dave, the guy who lived in the flat below me.

Dave was a nice enough neighbour. He was twenty-three years old and loved computers; his flat was simply full of them. On my first night in the block, he'd invited me in for a drink and had drunkenly confessed he was a virgin, which I thought was rather sweet.

'Hey, I heard you last night!' Dave cried.

'So did I,' Mrs Evans muttered.

'I'm sorry?' I flushed. Oh God. After my going-to-bed game had failed to induce sleep, I'd been practising my fake orgasms so I'd be all ready for my date with Anthony this evening. I kept forgetting how thin the walls were. Whoops.

'Those vocal exercises!' Dave cried. 'I mean, they did keep me up, but you have a great voice.'

'Oh, oh, right. Yes.' I ignored Mrs Evans' grimace and shrugged lightly, as though Pavarotti was my middle name. 'I just find that "o" sound really loosens the tongue, and . . . ah.' The lift, thank God, pinged. 'Well, I can't stop, I'm *really* late for work.'

7

By the time I reached the Tube it was nine thirty. I managed to squeeze into the last untaken seat. Commuters with newspapers ruffled them, frowning; those without stared at their shoes.

Getting off the Tube, I checked my watch. Nine fifty. Oh shit, oh bugger, oh bogger, oh clogger. Time to do some running.

I worked in a very odd-looking building. It had only been built a year ago, a huge skyscraper with a hundred or so silver-plated windows that gleamed like mirrors. I know this may sound overly romantic, but I secretly found those mirror-windows rather fairy-tale-ish, as though godmothers and witches and Cinderellas might secretly hover in the lifts practising magic, or a window on the twentieth floor might one day open to let out a long Rapunzel plait.

It was its outrageously priapic shape that had deterred a lot of serious businesses from taking up leases. Most of the floors had curling 'TO LET' signs in the windows and my boss rented two rooms on the otherwise empty third floor. As I dashed up the stairs, I nearly collided with a delivery man struggling with a parcel: a huge cube covered with brown paper and string like some monstrosity a Father Christmas on drugs might have conjured up. Seeing my boss hovering furiously in the background, I hastily offered to help him with the parcel, ignoring his gentlemanly protests. We heaved it up and into the main office; my boss looked incensed. She was a rather terrifying woman – tall, built like a Viking warrior, her face ugly and yet rather beautiful in a noble, intelligent way, framed by a fizz of strawberry-blonde curls. The delivery man handed her a clip-board, saying, 'Please sign for this.'

'What the hell is this? Did you order this, Lucy? Did you, Lucy-who-also-happens-to-be-an-hour-late?'

'No!'

She was *always* doing this. She would come into my office in a flap asking me to order a long-arm stapler or a back issue of *New Scientist* from March 1787 or whatever; then by the time they arrived she'd forget she'd ever asked and blame me.

'It's from a Dr Schwartzman in Stockholm,' said the delivery man.

'Oh. Oh, fine, then,' she snapped, scrawling her flamboyant signature across the page: *Dr Kay Merrick,* her 'k's flying like kites across the page. 'Lucy, this is the third time you've been late in a fortnight. I have already given you one warning.'

'I know,' I quavered. As the delivery man left, he gave me a sympathetic wink, as if to say, 'My boss is just as bad,' and I felt a little cheered and winked back. 'It's just – there was a problem with the Tube.'

'Then leave earlier!'

'I know, but I've been having trouble sleeping – I'm really sorry . . .'

'Well take some sleeping pills!' she roared.

'But—'

'No, Lucy. No more buts. You've had one warning as it is. Get your notepad and come into my office. *Now!*' And she disappeared with a terrific slam of the door, the glass tinkling in the frame.

Right. Notepad. I went to my desk, searching through its ravaged landscape, its undulations of in and out trays, its oceans of paper and islands of paperclips and pens. My hands were shaking slightly. If she'd asked me to bring in my notepad, then surely she wasn't going to fire me? I finally found an HB pencil with a reasonable point and a pad half detached from its spiralled teeth. Then, in a flash of horror, I remembered hearing the story of how she had fired her last PA, by inviting her into her office and then dictating her own letter of dismissal in order to save time and money.

In a panic, I procrastinated. The green light of my answerphone was winking. I must listen to my messages, I told myself, they might be utterly urgent.

Unfortunately, they weren't. Just one from Anthony confirming he was taking me out to dinner tonight and telling me to wear something extra nice.

I sidled into Kay's office, praying hard.

'Was there anything on the answerphone from Alain Botson?' she snapped.

Alain Botson was a TV presenter with his own popular science programme. He had a hoary beard and wore heavy glasses, but he'd

9

become a bit of a sex symbol with older women. Apparently he got sacks of knickers sent to him daily.

'I . . .' I paused. 'Er, yes,' I gibbered. 'He called and said he wants to give you a quote to put on the cover of your book *Exploring Unified Field Theory: A Radical Reinterpretation of Superstring Theory and the Lagrangian of the Superstring*. He said he wants to say, um . . . how did he put it, "This is the most exciting book I've read in years – I stayed up all night turning the pages in a frenzy."'

A change came over my boss's face. Her tight, budded mouth unfurled into a sweet rose. Her eyes glimmered behind her glasses.

'Well,' she said, a smile catching in her voice, 'then we must write him a kind reply. "Dear Alain, Thank you so much for your kind offer of a quote. I do hope that I can repay the favour by taking you out to dinner sometime . . ."'

Lucy, a cross voice said inside my head, *why did you lie? Now what's going to happen if Alain sends a letter with a polite fuck-off: this book is a load of crap and I'd rather use it as a bonfire than give it a quote?*

Then I looked up and saw the dreamy look on her face. She was staring into the distance, no doubt picturing moonlit walks involving intense discussions about the elasticity of time; bedroom frolics where they explored equilateral triangles. Love was a funny thing, I thought. Here was Dr Merrick, with zillions of letters tap-dancing after her name, a member of Mensa, regular science columnist in the *Guardian,* acting like a teenage girl at a pop concert. I wondered if I ought to tell her that I'd recently read in a *Sunday Times* supplement that Alain was married. Soon my guilt was overridden by laughter tickling my stomach. I kept trying to bite it back, but it poured up my throat.

'What?' She broke off in surprise.

'Sorry – I'm just . . . I was thinking about the package,' I improvised. 'I'm dying to know what's in it, aren't you? I'm getting so excited!'

'Lucy, really, do try to concentrate,' she tutted, but after we had finished the letter and had a chat over coffee (it was amazing the way she could threaten to fire me one minute and act like I was her favourite daughter the next), she suggested we open the parcel.

So, like little kids with a Christmas present, we set to work. Peels of brown paper rippled across the floor like flat fish. Finally we were left with a large corrugated-cardboard box with *BRACKLIG!* stamped all over it. I'm good at languages and I was used to eccentric packages, so I knew that was Swedish for 'FRAGILE'. Kay used her Stanley knife to cut away the thick swadges of brown sticky tape sealing it and we pulled back the flaps. Beneath the cellophane wrapping were lots of parts, many encased in green plastic. It looked worryingly like one of those wardrobe kits from MFI.

'What the fuck . . .?' she muttered, and we exchanged bemused smiles.

'Here's an envelope,' I said. She opened it, drawing out a wodge of papers and photocopies and journals, with a letter pinned to the top.

'It's a time machine,' she said carelessly, passing the papers over to me. 'Read up on this, will you, and type up a summary and a reply thanking him.'

'But . . .' I spluttered back giggles.

'Remember that only a hundred years ago people thought that the idea of the earth revolving around the sun was poppycock. Perhaps in another hundred years' time people will look back on us and laugh at our inability to escape from the present,' she said crisply, but there was a twinkle in her eye too.

After she had gone, however, I remembered Stephen Hawking's thoughts on time travel – perhaps the most simple and sensible I had heard: 'I do not think time travel is possible, otherwise we would have been visited by people from the future.' Dr Schwartzman, I concluded, was probably just insane.

As I made my boss a cup of coffee, I wondered if, like Eskimos and their huge range of words for snow, someone ought to invent a new language for people working in offices defining 100 words for boredom.

Borecoffedom – for the boredom of making your boss a coffee.

Or *borfiredom* – for the boredom of hoping you will get fired and then panicking when you nearly do and then feeling disappointed when you don't.

BorewhatthefuckamIdoingheredom – for what the fuck am I doing here?

Here is a brief history of my life, with key dates highlighted:

19 November 1960: My mother meets my father at a Beach Boys concert; my dad gives up his wild ways and gets a job in computing; ten years later my sister is born.

3 January 1976: I am born in hospital after an easy labour. My mum and dad have a big fight over my name. Dad wants to call me Lucinda; Mum likes Pam, so they end up with a compromise.

19 September 1980: I begin school. My dad is promoted to manager at work. The teachers say I am intelligent for my age, which Dad declares is due to my genes. Mum gets excited and tries to buy me a place in Mensa in advance.

3 January 1989: I turn thirteen and for my birthday am given a copy of *Wuthering Heights*. I fall in love with Heathcliff and his ruthless masculinity. Hence, when Jason across the road gives my friend a note for me saying *Would you like to (a) arm wrestle with me (b) kiss me (c) watch* The Simpsons *with me (d) spit at me*, I tick the last one.

3 January 1991: I turn fifteen and discover Lord Byron. When my friends ask me if I feel left out because I haven't even kissed a boy yet, I declare that I prefer to fantasise about Byron than put up with spotty schoolboys.

17 January 1992: At a school disco I finally cave in and dance with a spotty schoolboy called Dave. I endure my first kiss. I decide I prefer reading about good kissing to suffering real-life bad ones.

21 January 1992: I hold a sleepover at my house and my oh-so-knowledgeable friend Val, the only non-virgin among us, shows us how to give a blow job using a Flake. But when I test this out in the back of a car with Dave, the screams can be heard for three miles. How am I supposed to know you're not meant to bite down hard? Back home, I take solace in Byron and decide I never want to lose my virginity, ever.

18 August 1994: I get three A's at A level in English, Latin and Economics (funnily enough, history was never my subject).

20 September 1994: I go to York University to study English. To my surprise, I get a nice boyfriend. I lose my virginity to him. Then I get bored and we break up.

2 July 1996: My dad has a mid-life crisis and announces that he is leaving my mother for a woman half his age. My mum is 75 per cent devastated, 25 per cent relieved.

14 September 1996: Infuriated by my dad's betrayal, I lap up *The Female Eunuch* and become inspired by a bunch of feminists who, declaring that all language is masculine and all writing involves the rape of the male Muses, produce a book consisting of sixty blank pages, though when I try this with my essays, my tutor is unimpressed. I begin dating a guy called Ralph. He is good-natured and laughs at my feminist rants.

24 December 1996: Dad tries to move back in with Mum, repenting his mistake. After telling my mum never to take him back, I see the sadness in his eyes and wish she would. But it's not a question of forgiveness; she says simply: 'I'm enjoying myself. I don't have to iron shirts or cook meals any more. I'm happy being on my own.' They begin divorce proceedings.

18 July 1997: I graduate with a first-class degree. All my friends have careers, have direction, but I don't know what I want to do. Ralph asks me to move in with him. I do. Then he proposes. And I can't say yes. I can't say yes because somehow it all feels a bit too . . . *perfect*. Ralph is nice, his flat is nice, I am nice. We'll die of boredom by the end of the honeymoon.

19 September 1997: I leave Ralph. I feel terrible to have broken his heart, but I know I need to *live* before I settle down. So I go off travelling.

16 August 2001: After four years of wandering the globe, I realise I need a job. So I get a job I am deeply overqualified for, reasoning that I can do it whilst working out what I really want out of life. I am the PA to a scientist called Dr Kay Merrick. She is a lunatic.

15 April 2003: I have reached a point of such deep loathing for my job that on Monday mornings I regularly stand on the Tube platform and contemplate chucking myself under the train. I am about to resign and go travelling again when I meet Anthony. And then I decide to stick around. And two years or so on, I'm still sticking around.

Which brings me up to here and now – a great boyfriend and a crap job. A life that seesaws between fulfilment and boredom, only now I'm worried that it's beginning to tip the wrong way. Or perhaps it's been tipping the wrong way for quite a while and I've only noticed now it's about to hit the ground.

I came out of my life-crisis reverie as my mobile beeped. It was a message from Anthony:

Tonight when we hve dinner I have a surprise 4 u.

I'd only got a mobile phone last year, relatively late in life (most people seem to acquire one at about twelve). I didn't even want it. I hated the idea of people being able to track me down wherever I was, and my social conscience was sickened by the idea of phone masts. But Anthony said: 'I'm fed up with having an affair with your answerphone, so I'm going to buy you one whether you like it or not', and that was that. Within a week I was utterly addicted, despite the image that kept creeping into my mind of squiggly green rays beaming into my brain and gobbling up cells.

As for texting, the first week Anthony and I exchanged fifty a day. Then, when we realised we were in danger of getting the sack or, worse, RSI, we settled on a more sensible five a day, bouncing back texts like ping-pong balls; we even had text pet names for each other; I called him Valmont, after *Les Liaisons Dangereuses* (specifically, I was thinking of John Malkovich in the film version), whilst he called me Catwoman (specifically, I think he was thinking of Michelle Pfeiffer in *Batman)*. But gradually we had run out of steam, until two years on we were reduced to the odd joke cribbed from a magazine or *Hi, I am bored – u?*

I looked at Anthony's text and sighed, trying to think of a reply that was more witty than *What?* But I couldn't, so in the end I didn't bother.

14

ii) A brief history of Anthony and me

I met Anthony on a transatlantic flight, New York to London. I had been to the wedding of an old school friend and now I was going home with a hangover.

I have never liked flying. I am not a nervous flyer; I am a paranoid flyer. I am paranoid about everything, and my specific aviation fears are silly little things that on the day of the journey will buzz in my brain like hyperactive flies. I worry that when the check-in attendant asks, 'Could anyone have tampered with your luggage or given you anything to add to your luggage?' I will discover that, though I have not let my case out of my sight for one second, somehow someone has stashed a load of drugs in my face cream and it will be sniffed out by the black security hounds and I will end up spending the rest of my life in jail. I worry that the benign balding man next to me who keeps scratching his M&S patterned socks has secretly lodged a knife in them and is about to whip it out at any minute.

There were no suspicious ankle-scratchers on this plane, but actually something far worse. I had been given a seat in between a young couple. The girl was by the window, her boyfriend on the aisle. He introduced himself as Dominic and kept flirting with me; he was mad, sad and boring to know. I kept trying to give his girlfriend reassuring 'Isn't he a wanker?' smiles, but her grimaces showed she was clearly interpreting them as 'Oh, your boyfriend fancies me, how smug am I?' smirks. I had offered to swap seats but Dominic quickly refused, ignoring his girlfriend's enraged grimace.

Several times I got up and went to the toilet. Each time I returned I hoped the girl might have moved into my seat, but she was in a total strop now, arms crossed, shoulders hunched towards the window.

As I made my fifth escape trip, I noticed the guy who was sitting in the seat behind me. I had been vaguely aware that he was attractive, but when he happened to glance up, I felt quite breathless. Dark-haired and handsome, eyes the colour of olives. Lightly tanned. Possibly Spanish. An expensive coat was draped across the empty seat next to him, and he was squinting tiredly at his laptop. He smiled at me, an eye-crinkling, soft, sexy smile. I felt the blood beating in my cheeks and hurried to the toilet, silently cursing and close to tears. *Why?* I wanted to yell. *Why does fate do this? I get sandwiched between the couple from hell when behind me the most gorgeous guy in the world is surrounded by empty seats. And now I have to spend the rest of the flight – another five hours – stuck with Adonis behind me and Moronis beside me.*

But for once fate decided to be nice to me.

I was just going back up the aisle to hear Dominic muttering, 'That girl sure does have a weak bladder – I'm not sure if I could cope with that in the long term,' when the gorgeous guy looked up again.

'Melanie!' he exclaimed. To my surprise, his accent was not Mediterranean but Anglo-American.

Melanie? Was he mistaken? Then he winked at me and cocked his head at Dominic, and I twigged. I was being saved by a knight in cashmere, armed with a Toshiba. A true gentleman.

'Oh God, Rufus – I haven't seen you for ages!' I cried.

'How long's it been? Six years since we . . .'

'Met at the bowling rink,' I concluded.

He patted the seat next to him. In front of us Dominic huffed audibly. We giggled.

'Thanks,' I whispered.

'No problem,' he whispered back.

Once our euphoria had faded, an awkward silence arose. It struck me that he might have saved me just to be nice but regarded conversation as a burden, an irritating distraction from his work. So I opened up my *Marie Claire*. He flicked me a quick glance and reopened his laptop. It hummed elegantly. As he tapped, I noticed his long fingers. I've always had a thing for violinist's fingers. I began to fantasise that he was a world-famous musician.

'Does that really work?' he asked.

'Sorry?'

'That.' He nodded at my magazine. 'Ten Ways To Get A Ring On His Finger.'

Oh, why had I turned to that? Why not 'My Sister Slept With My Boyfriend and His Dog'? Even 'Do You Ever Feel Itchy Around

16

Your Vagina?' would have been less blush-inducing. And I could hardly tell him that I hadn't read a word of it because I'd been staring at his fingers.

I went on the defensive. 'As a matter of fact, I think it's crap.'

'Really?' He raised his eyebrows. 'So men don't interest you, then?'

'Men do interest me, but not much.' Did that sound bisexual? 'What I mean is – I shall never, ever marry, for as long as I live. The thought terrifies me and I don't think I'm going to change as I get older. I mean, I am only twenty-seven, but still. And I don't think I'm the only woman about who's scared of marriage. Men are the ones who want rings on fingers, not women. After all, you're the ones who propose!'

'So we are.'

'I think there's a conspiracy about, mostly perpetuated by Jane Austen, that any young, single woman must want to finish her story with a man ready to walk her down the aisle – The End. But actually, I was reading a survey the other day, and do you know what it said?'

'What *did* it say?'

'It said that the happiest people in society are young, single women in their early twenties. *Single* women. I even think it may have said that young men in their early twenties are the most unhappy. Men need us more than we need them.' I broke off, realising that I sounded like Germaine Greer. 'I do like men,' I said, more softly. 'I like them very much. I just . . .'

'You're a fellow commitment-phobe?'

'You're a commitment-phobe?' I asked excitedly.

'Oh yes. When I was in New York, I dated about twenty women in the space of a year.'

'That's fabulous.' I wanted to shake his hand. Then I became suspicious. 'Why are you a commitment-phobe? Are you an evil womaniser?'

'I'm a womaniser, maybe, but not an evil one. I don't hate women, if that's what you mean. I *love* women. I think they're the superior sex. I just . . . just find it hard to . . . I don't know . . . tie myself down.'

This was music to my ears.

'Why are *you* a commitment-phobe?' he asked.

I set about trying to give him a brief history of my love life in ten and a half minutes. My first kiss, losing my virginity, Ralph, my string of boring relationships with nice men who wanted to settle down with me.

'You know, Lucy,' he said, 'there are plenty of bastards out there. My sister is forever calling me up and wailing about them. Maybe you're lucky.'

'I'm not, I'm not . . . OK, you're right,' I conceded. 'But the problem is, men always seem to fall into two categories: bastards or nice guys. You either get excitement and pain, or niceness and boredom. I admit I go for the nice guys because I have some self-respect and I like to treat people well myself. But I'm beginning to feel as though my love life is the most boring ever. I mean, I've travelled the bloody world and I haven't even had a one-night stand!'

'Hang on, why not?' he asked, with such interest and intensity that I blushed. 'Did you go to Italy?'

'Yes.'

'And you didn't have a one-night stand with an Italian?'

'I tried to.'

'What d'you mean, you tried to?' He smiled, raising an eyebrow.

'I tried to, and then he kept coming back and asking to see me again.'

'You're hopeless,' he sighed. 'You obviously just drive men wild and they don't want to leave you.'

'Ha, ha,' I said, sighing. 'If only. I think it's just human nature. I think we like to chase what we haven't got. I think when we have something, maybe it's . . . maybe it's too easy to stop appreciating it . . .'

'But you've never had a one-night stand. A proper goodbye-never-see-you-again, one-night stand?'

'No.'

His eyes gleamed and held mine.

'Well, you could always break the trend.'

I was taken aback by his directness; my mouth formed an 'O'.

'I'm sorry,' he said quickly, flushing boyishly, and I felt a flood of desire and affection for him. 'I didn't mean—'

18

'Oh, but I'd like—'

'You . . .' He trailed off.

'I'd . . . yes, I mean.' Our cheeks were both competing to burn the brightest. We looked at each other with hot eyes and then smiled nervously. As though taken aback by our own brazenness, we quickly changed the subject, chatting about brothers and sisters, jobs and travels, aeroplane horror stories. But beneath the chit-chat, our eyes spoke so many more words, zinging and sparkling with lustful anticipation.

By the time the plane touched down in London, we had a pact. We got into a taxi and went to the Langham Hilton. We were as nervous and giggly as a pair of teenagers and thought it might be amusing to check in as Mr and Mrs Smith, just like the movies. Then the girl behind the desk pointed out that she couldn't accept his credit card as it didn't have *Mr Smith* on it and we sobered up.

I deliberately didn't check out his signature. I didn't want to discover his real name, burst the fantasy bubble. I wanted him to remain Rufus, womaniser, modern-day Byron, greatest violinist in the world.

Upstairs in the hotel room, we pulled the cream curtains shut and then sat on the bed and rather shakily drew up the rules and conditions of our forthcoming union. Our verbal treaty stated that we were to spend only one night together, and his weapons of mass destruction were only to be deployed on this one night, though he could deploy them as many times as he wanted. Though, in a moment of weakness, we added an additional clause declaring that we were allowed to exchange mobile numbers and contact each other – but no sooner than one year's time.

And then we stopped talking and stared at our feet. Suddenly fantasy had become reality and I was swirling with doubts. What if he was an axe murderer? Did I really want to let this complete stranger use and abuse me and then discard me?

We were just about to kiss when he said, 'D'you need to go to the toilet? After all,' he imitated the dreadful Dominic, 'you do have a weak bladder.'

I laughed very loudly and so did he, and then I realised that he was just as petrified as I was and that his jokes were a frantic form of delaying. I relaxed and kissed him, very softly, on the lips, to let him know it was safe. And he kissed me back just as carefully, playing the gentleman and letting me take the lead . . .

Afterwards, we raided the mini-bar and fed each other Maltesers and swigs of vodka and laughed and kissed and burst a few bubbles.

'I'm Anthony,' he said.

'I'm Lucy.'

'I work in computing.' Seeing my face, he added, 'You look disappointed. Just as well this is only a one-night stand, hey?'

'No – I didn't mean . . . so tell me why you're in England,' I said hastily, kissing his shoulder. He smiled and stroked a strand of hair from my face.

'I'm actually just moving back. I was born here, but I moved to America with my dad when I was about ten.'

So that explained his accent, with its mix of New York and London.

'Oh, oh, right. So where are you moving to?' I asked.

'Er – I'm going to have a flat in Mayfair,' he said. 'I'm pretty nervous, to tell you the truth. It's a work thing – they've set up a London office and I'm going to head it up.'

We kissed some more, and then, in that dreamy, hazy way postcoital chats can leap from subject to subject, he asked me what my favourite thing in the world was.

'Chocolate,' I said, without hesitation.

'I know a place where they make *the* best chocolate in the world,' he said. 'I flew there once on a business trip.'

'The best in the world?' I mocked him, secretly wide-eyed.

'I'm serious. It's this place in Paris. When I'm next there on business I'll pick some up, and then you'll be eating your words . . .' He caught himself. 'Only you won't, will you, because this is just a . . .'

A long silence.

Suddenly he got up and unzipped his briefcase. I tensed, panicked: this is where I find out he's a weirdo, I thought. There was a video and a TV in the corner of the room, and he switched them on and slotted a video in.

'I want you to know I'm not just a boring computer guy,' he said edgily. 'I don't want you to remember your one and only one-night stand like that. I want you to see my hobby.'

'Uh huh,' I said, hardly daring to breathe, convinced the fuzzy screen was about to transform into an image of a pneumatic blonde sharing a bed with three well-endowed men.

And then: a ball of sun rising slowly above a loch.

'I like photography and videoing things,' said Anthony. 'You know – just capturing life, beauty. I was in Scotland last year and I got up every morning and videoed the dawns.' I was too surprised and moved to speak, so I just reached out and clutched his hand and we sat and watched different types of dawn – fiery dawns rippling red across water; dawns creeping up slowly like a child wanting to surprise the world with a sudden flash of brilliance; sad watercolour dawns with tearful yellows and pinks that wept from the clouds – and he squeezed my hand tight and then we were kissing again and the dawns rose without us . . .

'What a terrible morning,' I observed the next day, in a jerky voice. 'You wouldn't have wanted to video this.'

We had put on rumpled, jetlagged clothes and were standing outside the hotel. The sky was gloomy, tendrilled with grey. We kissed one last goodbye on the cold pavement. I was about to go when he pulled me oh-so-tight and rubbed his stubbled cheek against the top of my head and whispered, 'That was the best one-night stand I ever had . . .'

Back in my flat, I lay down on the bed, feeling too exhausted and exhilarated to sleep. I could still taste his kisses, feel the echo of his touch on my body. I needed a shower, but I couldn't bear to wash away the sheen of his presence that seemed to have formed over my body like a fragile, translucent skin. *I'll never see him again*, I kept telling myself, dropping the expression into my heart like a stone into a well. *And that's why it's so perfect. If I ever do marry, in twenty years' time I'll be bored and fat and grey and I'll remember this night always.* Then, hazy with tiredness, I began to play the 'If you

21

had to *marry* any man in the world, who would it be?' game, and Anthony, surprisingly, won. Not that I would ever marry, of course. But in a parallel universe, where I did want to marry, and it was a law that all women had to marry by the age of thirty, then he would do.

The next day I moped through work as though I had flu, and when I came home there was a message on my answerphone politely asking if I would like to meet him for another one-night stand.

'This really, really has to be the last time,' Anthony insisted, the moment we met.

I agreed: 'Two commitment-phobics like us can't start building habits.'

Even so, our second one-night stand was even more rapturous than the first.

For our third one-night stand, he took me out for a meal at the deliciously expensive Odins, where we got drunk and became gigglingly romantic and he annoyed the waiters by asking for all the lights to be turned down. Our fourth, fifth, sixth and seventh one-night stands took place on a romantic long weekend in Barcelona; our eighth was in his flat, a glorious three-bedroomed, spotlessly clean apartment in Mayfair. Our ninth was to celebrate his birthday, following a meal with his adorable, debonair father, a high-flying film producer; our tenth followed his cousin's wedding, where I met the rest of his family (well, everyone except for his mother, whom he refused to speak to). Our eleventh one-night stand was make-up sex, after a row where he had said, 'Lucy, you're so contrary; whatever I say, you have to disagree with it.' Our twelfth was to prove I was right and never contrary and our thirteenth to explore my favourite position. Our fourteenth was a lovely surprise, for Anthony bought me a little white kitten, and after making love under the stars we decided to call her Lyra, after the constellation. On our twenty-third one-night stand we made a pact during our postcoital chat that when we got to twenty-six that really would be the limit, but we got to twenty-six and thought, Why end a good thing? and soon we reached our ninety-ninth one-night stand, and oh, that was the best.

One-night stand number ninety-nine took place in Paris.

The day had not begun well, as Anthony dragged me through the city in determined pursuit of the world's best chocolate. I was tired and fed up, and by the time we entered Patisserie Marie I felt close to tears. He picked up a truffle, a dark, succulent ball dusted with icing sugar, and gently slid it between my lips. I bit down. Beautiful, shocking, harsh flavours exploded into my mouth. My taste buds were close to weeping. I was too euphoric to speak. He gently leaned in and brushed his lips against mine, picking up a chocolate smear. We stayed there for a beat, our noses touching, breath mingling, and then he whispered, 'I love you.'

While I stood there, stunned, he smiled a funny smile and went to pay for the world's best chocolate: a snip at seventy-five euros.

For the rest of the day, I was convinced that I needed a hearing aid. I *must* have misheard him. All day I calculated different permutations: I like you. I lust you. I've heard a dove coo. I've booed you. He started to sulk, and I felt even more confused. We ate dinner in silence and went back to our hotel. We made love, and for the first time he switched the light off, so we couldn't see each other's faces. In the elderberry darkness, our one-night stand was frantic, a little desperate. As he clung to me, sweat-damp, I took the plunge. I whispered, 'I love you.'

'What did you say?'

'I said I heard a dove coo.'

'You said *I love you*,' he whispered. 'Didn't you?'

'Maybe,' I said in a small voice, burying my face in the pillow. And then I heard him laugh like a little boy and pull me up. He kissed my nose and said joyously, 'I love you,' and I said it again, and so did he, and we decided to make love again – just to celebrate.

That was the night he confessed everything to me about the roots of his commitment-phobia. He told me how his parents had got divorced when he was five and how his mother had walked out on him. He told me that I was teaching him to trust again, that I had given him back his faith in women, in love, in life.

★

After our two hundredth or so one-night stand, we realised that a year had passed and we began to discuss moving in together. For the first time I felt a kick of commitment-phobia in my stomach. After all, Anthony had claimed, rather grandly, that he was a total cad. But he seemed to be turning into a rather nice and dependable boyfriend – which really wasn't what I'd been expecting.

'Let's not live together,' I said. 'It might spoil things. I mean, what we have is so good.' I don't know why, but I was beginning to perpetually fret that things might go wrong. It was as though our relationship was like a precious statue, and one mistake would shatter it into a thousand tinkly smithereens. In irrational moments I feared that some sort of bad karma from my previous relationships was about to come bouncing back at me; Anthony would move in and then get bored and meet another woman and desert me. Worse, we might move in together and not feel bored; we might fall deeper in love, we might drown in it, and then what if it went wrong? I might spend the rest of my life feeling as though I was filled with salt water, struggling to reach the surface, never able to swim happily and freely again.

'I don't think we should live together because, you know, we have different routines. You like going to bed early and I like going to bed late. I'm messy and you're tidy. You like watching sitcoms and I like nature programmes and documentaries. We might grate against each other,' I improvised, flustered, 'and then, you know . . .'

'Do I?' Anthony sighed. 'OK.'

But I feared he was going to bring it up again. And I'd wake up in the middle of the night feeling as though I was screaming inside, as though I wanted to kick him out of bed and go rent a cottage on some island and just be alone for a while. Or sometimes I would find myself looking in the mirror and, without thinking, adopting one of his facial expressions, or hear an Anglo-American tinge slipping into my accent, as though our identities were seeping into each other, and I'd freak. People talk all the time about becoming one with somebody; I wanted to be in a relationship, but still be a two, a separate Lucy and Anthony, not a LucyandAnthony or worse a Lucyanthony. The thought of losing my identity, my sense of me, my independence, terrified me.

Which was why, from time to time, I found myself flirting with other people. It was only ever meant to be safe flirting, just a bit of banter to add some sparkle to life, to make me feel better. At least that was what I told myself.

iii) The Daily Telegraph guy

At lunchtime I didn't feel at all hungry, so I finished off a game of Solitaire on my computer, then almost rang Anthony but couldn't quite summon the energy. Then – *ding!* – a thought came to me. I would go to the newsagent's and see my *Daily Telegraph* guy! There was nothing like a good flirt to brighten the day.

Before leaving, I found myself putting on a bit of make-up.

Outside, I felt cheered by the optimistic sky. The sun was pale but leaking gold through the clouds. I was enjoying the spring before the weather got too hot; in truth I've always preferred winter to summer. Perhaps it was because with my pale skin the sun always scorched me and brain-baked me into severe headaches. I remember sketching pictures of winter and summer as a kid. Summer was a hot fiery beast, winter a whiskered old man with a kindly face. Perhaps it was no wonder I was always getting told off for daydreaming and the phrase 'Lucy, your head is in the clouds!' was bandied about a lot.

As I reached the Tube station, butterflies began to stir in my stomach. *He probably won't be there,* I told myself.

But he was. He was, he was, he was.

Unfortunately, it was very crowded, with people coming in to buy bottles of Volvic or quick lunchtime sandwiches. I went to the lottery ticket stand and chose my numbers, carefully not looking at him once. Every so often I heard his cheery voice talking to a customer and felt myself burn.

I picked up my *Daily Telegraph* and joined the queue.

I stood on tiptoe and tried to peer over the top of the people in front of me, catching my first proper glimpse of him. Despite his cheery manner, he was looking tired, his eyes puffy, and I fretted that perhaps he'd had a late night with another girl. Then he noticed me, and I saw emotions flit across his face in just the right order: recognition, surprise, pleasure, delight.

Then I was at the front of the queue, and it was as though an hourglass had been turned upside down and the sand was sliding through so quickly . . .

'Hi, how are you?' he said as I passed over my money. I'd given him a twenty-pound note, hoping it would delay things (rummaging around, having to open plastic bags of fresh coins, etc.), but, sadly, his till was crammed full of change.

'Well, thanks. You?'

'Great. Nice to see you.'

'So you've, erm, moved from the stall outside?'

'Yep. I'm climbing the corporate ladder. Maybe eventually I'll be put in charge of ordering the Marlboros.' He laughed, and I laughed too.

Behind us, the queue rippled with impatience. I bit my lip; I had to grab the moment, before the last few grains of sand sealed my fate.

'Erm – I was wondering if I could, er, order a specialist magazine,' I burst out. It was all I could think of on the spur of the moment.

'Sure. Ron!' he called out to the back. 'I need to take an order, can you come and do some serving?' He turned back to me. 'What was it you wanted?'

'Er . . .' I needed to think up something really obscure, something they wouldn't have readily available in the shop. 'Er, *Knitting Monthly*.'

'Uh, sure.' To his credit, he didn't blink. 'I'll just need to take your name.'

'I'm Lucy,' I said.

'Hi, Lucy, I'm Nigel.'

Nigel? What sort of name was that? I know that a rose called by any other name is meant to smell as sweet, but let's face it, if roses were called snot-plants, nobody would buy them on Valentines', and men called Nigel were not meant to be charming and handsome. In my fantasies, I had pictured him as a Matt, or a Harrison, or at least a Steve. Still.

26

'Now, Lucy, I need your—'

'For God's sake!' The man in the suit behind me finally snapped. 'Just bloody well organise your shag and let me pay for my paper! Oh, sod it – keep the change!' He flung a coin down on the counter and walked off.

We both looked at each other and laughed blushingly.

'Well, er, maybe you could come over to discuss the order at my place,' I suggested, taking a deep plunge. For one terrified moment I feared it was all a mistake; his smiles had just been smiles, not invitations, and he was going to call the police and I'd never be able to buy another paper again without crying. But he said, 'Sure,' and winked at me playfully and that wink made my heart skip a beat. I tore off a corner of my *Daily Telegraph* and scribbled my details on it, and as I passed it over our fingers touched, and we caught our breath and then looked at each other and laughed.

Back in the office, I couldn't type, couldn't take calls, couldn't think.

How many times, I pondered dreamily, have I longed for this to happen? For my fantasies to become reality? Like those moments where you're on a train and you see a stranger sitting opposite and he's oh-so-handsome and he smiles at you and you wish, just wish you had the courage to be bold, to say *hi* and strike up conversation and take his number, only you never do, you just get off at your stop and go home full of erotic dreams and dampened frustrations and sighing what-ifs.

Only now, Lucy, it's happened! You've got your stranger, and your fantasy can be reality: you can have dinner and amazing sex and—

Lucy, a stern voice cut in furiously, *have you forgotten you have a boyfriend?*

Oh yes.

A very nice boyfriend who is funny, handsome, loving . . .

Yes yes yes.

My excitement cooled off and I began to feel distinctly sheepish. *OK, Lucy,* I told myself sternly, *you have to blow the* Daily

Telegraph *guy. I mean, blow out the* Daily Telegraph *guy.* I tutted at my filthy mind and told it off several times, then promised myself, seriously, cross my heart and hope to die, that I wouldn't betray Anthony, not while we were still going out.

iv) Dinner

I was three-quarters dressed for dinner when the doorbell rang.

'Bugger!' One stocking was fully on but the other was a tan pool on the floor. I had put on mascara but no lipstick and my toothbrush was sticking out of my foaming mouth.

The doorbell rang again. Anthony didn't anger easily, but waiting on doorsteps made him very peevish.

'Hi.' He kissed my cheek and waggled the end of my toothbrush. This was a minor disaster: a trickle of white foam ran down my chin and – ah! – was about to hit my little black dress—

I caught it in my palm just in time, glaring at him.

'Sorry,' he said meekly.

Why is it, I wondered, that these tiny, harmless little things he does make me feel so cross?

Anthony went off to say hello to Lyra. I retreated to the bathroom, where I rinsed my mouth and applied lipstick. I found myself yawning, still gritty from insomnia, and thought hazily: *Wish I didn't have to go out tonight. Wish I could just stay in and have an early night and a long bath and read Emily Brontë and nibble on some chocolates. Maybe we can escape early, but then Anthony will want sex, won't he? It'll probably be gone midnight by the time I can slip between the sheets . . .*

In the mirror I saw the door opening and Anthony snuck in. I busied myself with lipliner while he started fiddling about with the bottles on the shelf. Both his flat and mine had sets of his 'n' hers bathroom paraphernalia. But while Anthony's shelves were made of sparkling, pristine glass, his bottles lined up neatly on the left, my Body Shop concoctions on the right, my bathroom shelf was complete chaos. Bottles oozed shampoo; lipstick-stained tissues trailed like kites through clouds of used cotton wool. Anthony, as

28

usual, had started cleaning up. Irritation prickled my stomach. We'd had numerous rows about tidiness; we'd both fought hard to preserve our habits, and after a lot of negotiation I had agreed to try to be good when I stayed at his place. But this was *my* place, and I wanted it to be messy. Messy was my middle name; messy was *me*.

I tried to stamp my irritation down. I didn't want to row just before dinner and ruin the whole night.

Then, as he wiped a sticky blue trail from a shampoo bottle, I noticed his hands were shaking slightly. I frowned and flicked him another sidelong glance, my antennae prickling. There was definitely something a bit shifty about him, something on his mind that he was keeping secret.

'So where are we going tonight?'

'Oh, just The House.'

The House was *the* new restaurant in town. All the celebs were being snapped there. The waiting list was meant to be something like five years and meals cost something like a million pounds.

'Wow,' I said breathlessly. 'I mean – that's amazing. Thanks.'

'That's OK.' He laughed thinly.

Suddenly my previous irritation felt mean and petty. After all, he was only trying to help clean up. That was Anthony – always so considerate.

'Are you all right, honey?' I asked, touching his cheek.

'Sure, why wouldn't I be?' He came up behind me and gently kissed the back of my neck. I waited for the icicle-down-the-spine shiver, but all I could feel was . . . actually, I felt as though soggy ice cream was being trickled down my spine. I shuddered and closed my eyes, fiercely telling myself to find a better metaphor. I was bandying about hopeless images involving snowballs and feathers when fortunately he moved on from my neck, turning me round and kissing me on the lips. His hand slid up my skirt.

'I've only just got dressed,' I whispered.

'Well I'll help you put it all back on again afterwards,' he whispered back.

We carried on kissing. I closed my eyes again. I knew that at this stage my hands should be sliding towards his trouser belt, but I kept them on his back. I was searching for a flicker in my stomach,

29

holding out my desire like kindling, desperately hoping for it to be set alight, but it was useless. His hand slid a little further up my skirt and I had to bunch mine into a fist to stop myself from pushing him away. Tell him you have a headache, I told myself frantically. I mean, for goodness' sake, having sex with a man when you don't want to have sex with him is basically a lazy form of rape. You've read all the books! It's your body! What would Germaine say if she could see you now!

But he's your boyfriend, a small voice pointed out, *and you're supposed to want to have sex with him.*

So just keep going, I concluded. Sex had been hit and miss over the last few months and sometimes I had found myself taking a long while to get going. Just hang in there, I instructed myself, and it will come – so to speak.

I squeezed my eyes very tightly. Still not even a pulse. I pointed out to myself that I was thinking too much. Sex required the unbridling of the mind from thought; I needed to allow my senses to take over, to become abstract. I let my hands flow up through his hair and it struck me that the thickness was just how I'd imagined the *Daily Telegraph* guy's would feel. Suddenly I pictured him, Nigel, kissing me, and desire flared in a blue flame. I ran my hands down to Anthony's trousers, caressing him, only to find that he was entirely flat. I wondered idly how big the *Daily Telegraph* guy might be by comparison . . .

Lucy, a voice that sounded like my mother's berated me, *what are you thinking?*

'Er, maybe we should wait till after dinner. Wouldn't want to miss our booking.' Anthony breathed out and pulled away. 'I'd better, ah, go and feed Lyra.'

I saw the shame on his face and realised with alarm that his Flat Stanley was something he was very conscious of. He left his anxiety behind him like steam in the air. I reapplied my lipstick and now it was my hands that were shaking. What if he had been thinking the same as me? What if it had all been a chore for him too? I couldn't remember a time ever when he hadn't been instantly hard from just a kiss. What if he had been touching me and thinking, '*Oh God, Lucy is such a foul kisser, and she really is so flat-chested – how come I never noticed before? And God, I just want to get this over now before dinner so I don't have to sit through my meal thinking about the hassle of it later on . . .?'*

Or, worse, what if he had been fantasising about another girl? During the early stages of our relationship, Anthony had surprised and touched me with his emphasis on loyalty. 'I might have been a cad in the past, but I'm not now. I'd never, *ever* cheat on you,' he'd reassure me, also warning me, with fierce passion, that if I ever strayed from him, he would never speak to me again as long as he lived.

And so, unlike some of my girlfriends, I'd never had to worry. When Anthony told me he was working late at the office, I knew he was working late. I never had to speculate about some gorgeous blonde secretary, because he always hired old boots to avoid temptation.

And yet. Before he had met me, he had been a cad. He had told me I had changed his ways – but what if he was sliding back to them? What if he had been kissing me and picturing some girl he sat opposite on the Tube on the way to work?

What awful thoughts.

That was the trouble with infidelity – you became more suspicious. If you couldn't even trust yourself, how could you trust anyone else?

We took a taxi to The House and got caught in the rush-hour traffic. At least all the honking filled our long silences. We both yawned a lot, as though emphasising how tired we were. When we got to the restaurant, we found they'd lost our booking.

Anthony is naturally very good-natured and patient, but everyone has their flaws, their weak points. And if there is one thing that makes him mad, it's bad restaurant behaviour. It seems to act as some sort of trigger for a Jekyll to Hyde transformation which normally terrifies waiters into giving us the best table in the restaurant and a meal for free.

But this waitress – a thin Taiwanese girl with a tired, unsmiling face – shrugged at Anthony's ranting. She was a tough case; clearly underpaid and overworked, with an aura of 'I don't really give a fuck if the customer is right – I wish you'd just give me a big fat tip and go away.'

31

'You can wait in the bar and we'll have a table in an hour,' she said.

'We'll want free drinks,' Anthony said sharply.

We got half-price drinks.

We sat down on an uncomfortable piece of grey cushion and sipped green concoctions from cocktail glasses. It was so noisy we had to shout at each other to be heard, so we gave up and just surveyed the room. I watched the couples and wondered idly if they were all as happy as they looked? Then I became aware of the girl at the bar surreptitiously eyeing up Anthony. It struck me that two years ago I would have been both jealous and proud to be seen with him. Now I just thought it was vaguely amusing.

Anthony wasn't amused.

After half an hour of waiting, he hauled me up and decided we ought to storm out. And then things went from bad to worse.

During my Latin A level, I'd learnt about the Fates: Clotho, who wove life together, Lachesis, who measured it, and Atropos, who cut the thread, a trio who perpetually laughed at humans' feeble attempts to evade them. Well, it looked as though we had offended Clotho big-time, because after catching a sweaty Tube to Baker Street to try Odins, we found they were full too. By now Anthony was spitting. I suggested Pizza Express and he refused; then I threw a strop and he retaliated, saying he'd wanted to take me somewhere nice and what was the point of getting dressed up in suits and little black dresses if we were going to eat sophisticated cheese on toast, and I pointed out that the tartufo ice cream made it all worthwhile but he still couldn't be persuaded. Then we compromised and decided on the New Blues Jazz Café. We took the Tube to Chalk Farm, only to find a glass door looking into a room littered with junk and paper. The nice man next door helpfully informed us that the owners owed some heavies a lot of money and had fled to Mexico, but a chippie was going to be opening soon.

By now it was nearly 9.30. I'd barely eaten all day, saving myself for tonight, and my stomach was howling. A few spots of drizzle landed on my nose. I saw Anthony looking longingly across the road and followed his gaze.

'Oh sod it!' I cried. 'Let's just go there!'

'We can't,' he said despairingly. 'I haven't eaten there since I was twelve.'

'The evening is doomed and I'm so hungry I'm going to start pulling things out of the litter bin. Please, Anthony, *please* . . .'

Anthony put on a brave face and steeled himself.

And so we entered the bright, shiny yellow doors of Burger King, bypassing a table of twelve-year-olds having an ice-cream fight to find a cosy table in the corner. To be honest, I really enjoyed my fish burger. It was all good greasy, yummy fun. Soon I was stealing Anthony's fries.

'So how was work today?' Anthony asked, trying to inject some cheer into his voice. 'What did you do? Let me guess. Arranged your paperclips into colour-coordinated piles?'

'No,' I cried hotly. 'Of course not! My job does require a certain amount of intelligence, you know.'

'I'm just joking,' said Anthony.

I realised I had overreacted and frowned, wondering at the shortness of my temper.

'Sorry,' I said. I injected a bright eagerness into my voice. 'Actually, a time machine arrived.'

'Really?' Anthony laughed loudly, and I laughed too, and we were glad for the relief of tension. 'But that's crazy.'

'I know. It was sent by one of Kay's ex-lovers. The letter that came with it was so gooey, but really rather sweet. He said he'd spent the last ten years making the machine in the hope that she would be so impressed that she'd come back to him. He said that he'd been tempted to use the machine to go into the past and change their relationship so that they'd end up married, but that he wanted it to be real, not the result of any manipulation, and he hoped his gift would be enough.'

'I'm surprised at you, Lucy. I thought you told me you were a cynic.'

'I am.' But like all cynics, I was a romantic at heart; I thought he knew that by now. I frowned. We'd been together all this time, but perhaps we didn't really know each other at all.

Anthony carried on eating, quiet again. There were dark circles under his eyes from all those long days in the office, and a raindrop was still quivering on one of his eyebrows. I felt a sudden surge of emotion. It was perverse that that tenderness, that love, caused me to say what I said next.

'I – I think we should, er, you know . . . maybe take a break from, well, us,' I said quietly.

Anthony paused in mid-bite, mayonnaise smeared across his lips. 'Because I took you to Burger King?'

'No . . . no. I . . .' I started to laugh, and he laughed too, and there was a moment of slack relief which instantly tightened up again, taut and painful. 'I just . . . I . . . you know . . . it's . . .' I circled my finger on the table. 'We've . . . you know . . . been together for a while and . . .' The words seemed to be stuck in my stomach, curdling along with my burger. Was this the hardest thing I had ever done? 'I . . . you know . . . I do really, really love you, I want you to know that, and I'll always love you, but I just feel . . . we need a break . . . things are a bit flat and . . .' I looked into his eyes, searching for emotion, but it was like looking into the eyes of a dead person. I saw the mayonnaise still on his lips and I folded a napkin and tenderly wiped it off; he recoiled, pushing my hand away so violently I felt tears in my eyes.

Silence. I picked off tiny flecks of sesame seed from my burger bun, dropping them into the polystyrene container.

'I think it's great,' he said at last.

'Huh?' My head shot up.

'Well . . . come on, we can still be friends.'

'We can?' I felt as though I had been clenching my heart tight, like a closed fist, and now I shakily uncurled it. 'You won't hate me for ever and make effigies of me and do voodoo magic?'

'No – I feel completely the same,' he said in a high voice. 'I mean, that was exactly what I'd been planning to say tonight too . . . and . . .'

'Really?' I gasped.

'Well, I mean, it just seems like we've reached a natural conclusion. We always said it would just last one night, and our one night has lasted over two years and now it's over.'

'Oh.' I couldn't help feeling indignant. Hang on, I kept thinking, I'm the one who is meant to be doing the dumping. Because if you're dumping me, then this really is it. I can't wake up tomorrow and pretend it was exhaustion or PMT or work pressure and beg you to come back.

34

'Hang on,' I cried suspiciously. 'So this was the surprise you mentioned in your text? You were going to take me to the most expensive restaurant in town and then *dump* me?'

'Well,' he smiled shakily, 'I just thought it would be a nice way to do it . . . you know . . . a nice way to say goodbye. . .'

I was so upset and outraged, I burst out laughing. He laughed too, and we sat there holding hands and laughing, tears burning our eyes.

Back in my flat, I got ready for bed in a numb state of shock. My bedroom is normally a comfort zone, full of gorgeous pleasures to calm me down after a tough day at work; after any emotional crisis I retreat into it like a cocoon. The bed is thick with big, fat, fluffy pillows, and on the bedside table there is a tea-making set with little Earl Grey tea bags and honey, as well as a packet of chocolate digestives, a box of Godiva mints, and a pile of well-thumbed paperbacks: Brontë and Hardy and Eliot and Ovid and Byron.

Tonight, however, I couldn't bring myself to eat or read. My body felt dead, my eyes tired, my heart shrivelled. I lay under the covers and realised I had forgotten to clean my teeth, but the thought of getting up seemed exhausting. I lay in the dark, curtains billowing, watching the night shift through different shades of black. I had forgotten my hot-water bottle, and cold started to crawl over me, but my emotions were so abstract that I found the pain – teeth chattering, and goose pimples and, finally, violent shivering – satisfying.

I tossed and turned until one o'clock and then finally fell asleep.

I dreamt about Anthony. I dreamt that he proposed to me, only he had lost the ring and it was all my fault, and however hard we looked it couldn't be found. I woke up crying, and wept into my pillow until the cotton was saturated with salt. *What have I done?* I sobbed. *What have I done?* Longing filled me until I felt sick. I reached out, hand pressed on to the receiver, dying to call him and tell him it was all a mistake. But then I remembered him saying, 'It just seems like we've reached a natural conclusion . . .' For another hour I took our relationship apart ruthlessly. How long had he been planning to dump me? When had been the exact point when he had thought, this is enough, Lucy no longer delights me, she repels me? Had he been seeing another woman? The more I searched through our relationship, the more I unpicked it, the more panicked I became. As I held up each patchwork square, the cloth seemed to dissolve in my hands; butterfly memories of love and delight curled up their wings and wriggled back into their chrysalises, sticky and dull and asleep. Had he ever loved me? Did love even really exist? I felt as though my heart had aged ten years in ten minutes and turned to dust.

At around three o'clock the phone rang.

'Hello?' I said in a neutral voice, heart hammering.

'Hi, it's me.'

'Hi.'

'I can't sleep.'

'Neither can I.'

A beat. We hung in the darkness, breathless, waiting. Finally I gave in.

'Are you reading?' I said.

'No, I'm eating toast with marmite and jam. What are you doing?'

'I'm reading *Wuthering Heights*. I've just got to the bit where Cathy's dying.'

'Lucy . . .' he began, a catch in his voice.

'Yes?'

'I guess we should sleep,' he said at last.

'Yes.'

'I'm glad we . . . said what we said. It's good, it's for the best.'

'Yes.'

'So.'

'Good night.'

'Night.'

I put the phone down and curled up in bed, hugging Lyra to my chest. I felt as though a poisoned arrow was slowly stabbing in and out of my heart, a pain too excruciating for tears.

I tried to play a game where I listed all the things I didn't like about him. I remembered the time I'd asked him, 'If you could sleep with any woman in the world who would you choose?' and he'd said, 1) Catherine Zeta Jones, 2) Liz Hurley and 3) Jordan. Choice number 3 had nearly precipitated our break-up there and then (despite his protests, 'It's a fantasy game, Lucy, not real life!'). But no matter how much I told myself that I didn't like him, all I could think of was how I much I liked him and that night, when I played the going-to-bed game myself, for the first time in a long time, Anthony won.

I barely slept another wink, and the next morning I went to work and got fired.

v) Wormholes

But let's rewind time a little bit.

Before I managed to get fired, the day didn't begin too badly. I felt like absolute shit as I slunk into the office, but for once I was only three minutes late. And to my relief I didn't get shouted at, because Dr Merrick was out. She had left a bundle of papers and a dictaphone on my desk, with a yellow Post-it that informed me she would be back just before lunch so could I have the letters ready to sign by then. Great – just what I was in the mood for. At the bottom of the Post-it she had added, *Have you replied to Dr Schwartzman yet? Plse thank him for the time m. and say I am away on business but will be in touch soon – or he may start ringing the office in his persistent manner. And plse sort the time m. out.*

Well, I figured that getting on with things would help me to blot out Anthony and hide from reality. I found the letter that had come with the machine and reread the first page:

My dear Kay,
    As you know, ten years ago people laughed at me when I first proposed that I would be able to build a time machine that worked. You were one of the few professionals who defended me at that dreadful conference in Berlin (oh Kay, I have not forgotten the week we spent there!) and saved me from losing my tenure. Now, ten years on, the fools are

37

finally coming round. But they ought to have come round fifty years ago. It is simply absurd that they should stick to their outdated Newtonian beliefs that time is straight and uniform and never deviates and always flows at the same rate. For God's sake – Einstein pointed out that this is quite untrue: time meanders, speeds up and slows down around stars and galaxies. And in 1937 W.J. Stockum took an infinitely long cylinder that was spinning like a maypole and found that if you danced around it you would come back before you had left . . .

As the letter went on, it became more and more technical, with references to wormholes and negative energy and collapsing plates causing zero energy, not to mention the pages and pages of equations that followed, interspersed here and there with romantic remarks such as 'Oh, kiss me, Kay' or 'How I long for your rosebud lips', which was rather incongruous but touching all the same.

The time machine box was still taking up a huge patch of space on the other side of the room. I went over to it, curiously pulling out the parts.

As a child, I had always enjoyed doing puzzles, and on the Tube home I regularly tackled the *Daily Telegraph* crossword. There is something satisfying about solving puzzles – everything resolved by logic, not too much patience required, and the joy of a neat conclusion: order created from disorder. Now I spread the instructions on the carpet and laid out all the pieces around me, feeling a little like a mechanic about to work on a car.

Hours must have passed, and finally it was assembled.

It certainly didn't look how I had imagined a time machine should look. Nothing *Dr Who* about it. Nor was it like the machines in movie adaptations of H.G. Wells' book: huge, grand, gold-plated things with wings and fancy gadgets. In terms of gadgets, this was pretty shabby: a digital timer where you punched in the date which looked as if it had been detached from a large egg-timer; and a gear shift which had once lived in a Ford Fiesta. As had the leather seat, with its detachable sheepskin cover. I couldn't help thinking that as a whole the machine looked like one of those buggies old people rumble about in – small, squat, cream-coloured, with rather thin perspex glass. Still. Don't judge a book by its cover and all that.

I heard approaching footsteps and jumped. I suddenly realised that the whole morning had gone by and Dr Merrick was back. I also realised – with a sinking of my heart – that I had managed to forget Anthony. Now my grief returned in a fresh wash of grey.

'Well, Lucy, have you finished those letters—' Dr Merrick stopped short. 'Goodness. Well, goodness me. This isn't *quite* what I was expecting,' she added, but her tone was intrigued.

'D'you think it could really work?' I cried. 'I mean – the letter was quite convincing, though I'm still not sure if I can make out what a wormhole is.'

'A wormhole is a term used by physicists,' Dr Merrick murmured, inspecting the machine closely. 'A mathematician called Rob Kerr found that a spinning black hole collapses into a ring of compressed matter, not into a dot as you would expect.'

'Er, yes.'

'If you were to fall through the ring, you'd end up going backwards in time – or even in another universe.'

'Really? Wow. So it *could* work.'

'Well, I'm not sure if there any wormholes to speak of in this office,' Kay said doubtfully. 'But then again . . . Well, go on then, Lucy.'

'Me?' I'd hoped that she would be the one to test it. I wondered if I could get compensation if it all went horribly wrong.

I sat down in the machine and blinked at the keyboard.

'Well, type in a date, Lucy,' Dr Merrick said, in a typically patronising tone. As though a time machine was a perfectly straightforward thing to use, like typing your PIN into a cashpoint.

'OK, I'll pick ten minutes back from now,' I said, rolling my eyes. 'In which case I'll step out of the machine and you won't be here.'

I typed in the date and the time. There was a green button which clearly indicated 'GO'. I pressed it gingerly.

Now, I have to admit that at this point I did feel rather nervous. I kept thinking about *Charlie and the Chocolate Factory,* my favourite novel as a child, and how the boy who is obsessed with TV ends up getting transported into one and shrinking a million times smaller in size. What if, in the process of being transported backwards, all my particles and atoms and what-not ended up getting muddled about and distorted? I'd end up needing plastic surgery. I closed my eyes, heart hammering, gripping the seat tightly.

When I opened my eyes, nothing seemed to have changed. I stepped out of the machine. Dr Merrick was standing there with her arms folded, a smile on her lips.

'Well,' she said briskly, 'it didn't work. There's a surprise. Now, could you pack it up and put it out with the rubbish?'

'But you can't just throw it out,' I cried. 'I mean, you can't . . .'

'Nor can I have it cluttering up my office,' she snapped, heading for her room. 'If you want to keep it, Lucy, you can take it home. You have forty-eight hours to remove it.'

'OK – I'll take it,' I called after her back. Then I felt slightly foolish. My flat was rather small – just where would it *go*? Still, it could be a kind of cool and kitsch thing to have. And if the worst came to the worst, I could sell it on eBay as a novelty. I might well need the money, now I had broken up with Anthony.

My lovely flat, you see, belonged to Anthony. It had been his sweet suggestion after our thirty-fourth one-night stand. On my crappy PA salary I'd only been able to afford a flatshare in Balham. Since arriving in England, Anthony had been making even more money buying properties on the side. One of them was a studio flat in Primrose Hill, and instead of renting it out to some young city boy for £2,000 a month, he had let me have it for a measly £500. I was convinced that with the mortgage he was actually making a loss, but he insisted he was breaking even – just.

Now I would have to move out. It was bad enough having to suffer the pain of the break-up without having to worry about where I was going to live.

The rest of the afternoon went relatively smoothly. I packed the machine back into the box, ready to be somehow transported to my flat. I shut Anthony out of my mind and heart by throwing myself into work, typing out letter after letter until my fingers ached. In fact, it was ironic that on the day I worked the hardest I've ever worked for Dr Merrick, she decided to sack me.

vi) The Daily Telegraph guy

After I was fired, I felt there was only one place to go. I went to Victoria Station and caught the train to Horsham, where I walked down Woodley Park Road, sniffling in the drizzle. As I rounded the final corner of the cul-de-sac, I saw the same sight I used to experience on my way home from school, from the age of eleven to eighteen: the blue door, the wisteria clinging to the peeling porch, the overgrown rose bush hanging over the grey stone wall. Home. I walked up the cracked path to the front door, and my frantic heart felt softened and swaddled with the comfort of familiarity before I'd even rung the bell and my mum had hugged me and bustled me into the kitchen and sat me down at the scarred oak table and offered me a cup of PG Tips.

She wasn't too upset when I told her I'd been fired.

'I was doing well – and then she found out about the fake quote,' I confessed, blushing at my lies. 'She wrote to Alain asking him out for dinner to thank him for the quote, and he called back asking what on earth she was talking about, he'd never even *seen* the book. She said it was the most embarrassing thing that's ever happened to her, and she just snapped and said enough was enough and that she was also sick of me being late every morning.'

'Well, Lucy,' Mum tutted, 'you always were hopeless about getting up. I remember having to tickle your feet in the mornings to get you out of bed for school. What about that alarm clock I bought you for Christmas? Didn't you use that?'

The said alarm clock had been a garish Mickey Mouse design. I didn't like to tell her I'd sold it on eBay for £3.50.

When I told her about Anthony, however, she totally flipped.

'What d'you mean, you've broken up with Anthony? Why? Why?'

'Well, I was bored,' I said in a small voice. I felt as though I was thirteen years old again and had just brought home a report card saying, *Lucy must stop day-dreaming and learn to focus!*

She became so agitated that she couldn't sit still. She had to get up and start tidying, banging pots and pans and slamming washed-up things into cupboards.

'Honestly, Lucy, I thought you said he was the one . . . I thought

41

you were going to marry him . . . You're nearly thirty now. Now you know I've always said you needn't worry about marriage and it doesn't always work out, but unlike your bloody father, Anthony was *nice*. He was good to you. I mean, in my day we weren't so picky. By your age I was married and pregnant with your sister. We didn't expect things. How can you get better than Anthony? I mean, Lucy, you ought to hear about Mavis from next door, her man beats her up . . . And what about your flat? What will you do if Anthony turfs you out? I'm sure he has every right to. If I was him, I certainly would.'

'Mum, I can't just date Anthony for the flat, that's mean and mercenary!' I cried. Though she did have a point. 'Anyway, I didn't just break up with him, he broke up with me too – at the same time. He might even have another woman, he might want to give her the flat,' I said painfully.

'Well perhaps she's a bit more grateful than you.'

As she made another cup of tea with an awful lot of sugar, I sat and pondered. For the past twenty-four hours, my mind had been boomeranging back to the subject of a possible other woman. There was something, some niggling little memory that kept pinching me, some hint of a suspicion I'd had a while back . . . but when I tried to focus on it, my memory was nothing but a blur.

We were interrupted by the doorbell and the sound of muted cries. Mum opened the door and my six-year-old nephew entered the kitchen, tugging my sister behind him as though he was taking her for a walk.

'Oh God, it's a nightmare, I've just had it up to here with everything,' my sister was ranting. Then she saw me. 'Oh, hi! Aren't you supposed to be at work?'

'Hmmm,' I said and pulled my nephew, Adam, on to my lap, kissing the top of his head and breathing in that milky, innocent scent that all children seem to possess. I let him play with the beads on my bracelet and he calmed down for two minutes, which gave me a chance to observe my sister. I didn't get to see Sally much these days, and when I did I was always struck by how much she had changed.

The old Sally, the Sally she'd been before getting married, had been utterly glamorous, with long blonde hair as straight as a ruler, and an endless string of boyfriends. She used to coolly dispense advice to me on how to twist a man around my little finger.

These days she looked ten years older than her thirty-five years, her fair hair stringy as dried beans, her face pinched with stress, all her poise blown away in the stress of juggling a demanding job in marketing, a demanding kid with hyperactive problems, and a demanding husband who still thought housework was for women only.

'If you think you have problems,' my mum interrupted Sally's moaning, 'you ought to hear what Lucy's been up to.' She pointed her finger at me accusingly.

I was saved by the shrill of my mobile. Adam bounced on my lap in excitement.

'Hi,' said a sexy, strangely familiar voice. At first I thought it was Anthony. Then I twigged.

'Oh. Hi. It's you.'

The *Daily Telegraph* guy, aka Nigel.

'I was wondering if you fancied going out for a drink tonight . . .' he said.

'Er . . . well . . . yes . . . only . . .' I had visions of sitting in a pub and Anthony, by horrible coincidence, walking in and seeing us. 'Why don't you come over to my place? Seven-ish. I'll cook something.' I gave him my address.

'So what are we going to do at your place?' he asked.

'Um, play Scrabble?'

He laughed, such a dirty laugh that a blush swept across my cheeks. When I hung up, I saw my sister and mum looking at me accusingly. There was no point in lying; their feminine antennae had been tweaked and they *knew*.

'And you've only just got rid of Anthony twelve hours ago,' said Mum, shaking her head. 'Honestly, Lucy, I don't know what's got into you.'

Neither did I.

Not long after Nigel's call, Anthony rang. In a shaky voice I told him the story about me being fired.

'Well, you were much too intelligent for the job,' he said in a cross voice. I fell silent; any compliments he gave me now made me feel strangely guilty. He offered to go and collect my stuff from the office so I wouldn't have to face Dr Merrick, and though I kept saying no, no, he really didn't have to, not now we had . . .

'OK, so we've broken up,' he said, even more crossly, 'but we *are* friends, right?'

'Of course,' I said, in relief.

He was meant to come by at five-thirty, after work, but he sent me a text saying he had a work crisis and would be there at six. I had to get ready for the *Daily Telegraph* guy. I felt excited as I shaved my legs and tweaked my eyebrows and splashed on make-up and scent. But I also felt uneasy. Anthony never minded if I hadn't had time to wash my hair or if there was stubble on my legs. Our relationship had nestled around me like a swaddling; now I felt naked and vulnerable.

Six o'clock passed and I began to fret. I could see the scene: Anthony arriving just as Nigel turned up. Oh God. I'd wanted to lay the table with candles and fancy cutlery, but I couldn't now: I had to make do with setting it out in the kitchen.

To my relief, Anthony turned up at six-thirty. He was struggling with an enormous box; he'd had to get Dave from upstairs to help him haul it into the lift.

'The time machine,' said Anthony breathlessly. 'Your boss said you'd like it as a memento.'

'The cheek of her! She said it was filling up her office and decided to dump it on me more like,' I cried. 'Anyway, it's so kind of you to do this, Anthony . . .'

We stared at each other, our eyes bright with pain. Then Anthony dropped his gaze, sweeping it over me, assessing my make-up and sexy clothes. He opened his mouth to say something, and then closed it.

'No worries,' he said. 'I'll just get the rest of the stuff. A cup of tea would be nice, Lucy.'

'Of course.'

He brought in the rest of my boxes and followed me into the kitchen. And then it happened. Disaster. There was all the cutlery for tonight; crystal glasses, candles, bottle of wine. Unmistakably romantic.

44

I followed Anthony's gaze, opened my mouth to speak, but he got there first.

'I see,' he said, and walked out.

'Anthony! Wait! Look, I do have a friend coming over tonight.'

'Female or male?'

'Male—'

'I see.' He opened the front door.

'Look, I haven't been having an affair, if that's what you think. I'm just—'

'Just?'

'Moving on.'

'We only broke up last night!' He turned on his heel and stormed out, ignoring my pleas to talk.

Oh God, I thought, now he'll think I was having an affair all the way through our relationship. I watched him drive away angrily, and my heart felt as though it was a precious ornament I had just dropped on the floor, smashing and tinkling into thousands of tiny pieces.

I wanted to cancel the *Daily Telegraph* guy but I felt too shaken to even pick up the phone. I locked myself in the bathroom and watched myself crying in the mirror with a strange detachment. Then I washed my face and gave myself a fierce pep talk. I told myself that I was going to enjoy the evening. I had, after all, broken up with Anthony for this: for fun, for freedom, for danger, for adventure. I had an almost hysterical determination that the evening had to be brilliant to make the sacrifice feel worthwhile, to prove to myself that I had made the right decision.

The doorbell rang. It was him.

'Hi,' he grinned. He was looking utterly woof-woof in a casual, scruffy I've-just-got-out-of-bed way: jeans ripped at the knees, old scuffed boots, and a red Coca-Cola T-shirt. And though he clearly hadn't washed his clothes, he had washed his hair, which hung in a sexy fringe, brown and shiny as conkers.

'How are you?' he said.

'Oh, fine. You?' I gulped.

'Very well, not so bad. I've bought some stuff,' he said, coming into the hall swinging an Asda carrier bag.

'Oh, wow, thanks,' I exclaimed, taking the bag. Inside was a four-pack of Tennants Extra and a packet of Wrigley's chewing gum.

'It was just some stuff I grabbed from the shop.'

'Oh, sure, it's great,' I enthused, putting the Tennants pack down on the table alongside my bottles of spirits and the chewing gum next to the plate of little Belgian chocolate Florentines.

'Well . . .' he said, stuffing his hands in his pockets. 'So – how are you?'

'Oh, great. Yep. Er – I've got vegetable risotto on the go – is that OK?' I didn't add that it was all out of an M&S packet; there was no way I was going to risk cooking it myself.

'Uh, yeah, sure. I had a big roast for lunch, so something light will be fine.'

Something light?

'I'm a vegetarian,' I said, and his face assumed an 'oh dear' expression. 'Well, anyway, it'll be ready in about ten minutes.'

'Oh, good.'

His past manner had always seemed so cocky and cheeky that his nerves took me quite by surprise. Just watching him walking about, picking things up and putting them down in the manner of an alien making notes for a thesis on human living habits was getting me jittery. I tried to look relaxed by sitting on the sofa. Eventually he joined me, though as far away as possible, a gulf of cream cloth between us. I couldn't help feeling disappointed. I'd been half fantasising about him walking into the house, tearing off my clothes in the hallway with helpless passion and making love to me on the stairs. At this rate it would take six months for us to have a one-night stand, which sort of defeated the object a bit.

He broke the silence. 'D'you mind if I smoke?'

Oh God. I loathed smoking.

'No, sure,' I said.

He grabbed the African pot on my table, mistaking it for an ashtray, and lit up a Silk Cut. I tried to hold my breath. He leaned forward, sifting through the pile of magazines and books on my table. I felt a bit more cheered up when I noticed his fingers were still looking deliciously grubby.

'So who's this weird-looking bloke then?' he asked.

'What?' I frowned. He was holding up a copy of *Don Juan*. Byron was looking at his most dewy on the cover.

'Lord Byron, of course,' I said.

'Oh, right, who's he then?' He took a puff and looked up, and he must have seen the look on my face because his smile faded and he hunched his shoulders defensively. 'Well, look, I never bothered with school – I had crap teachers, and so reading isn't exactly my cup of tea.'

'Sorry – I'm not some big snotty snob, if that's what you're thinking. I'm just a bit obsessed with Byron, and so I kind of go around thinking everyone else must be.'

He looked guilty for making me feel guilty.

'So tell me about him,' he asked.

'Well,' I said, smiling, 'I think he was the greatest poet of all time.'

'Wow,' he said, and for a moment I thought he was being sarcastic, but he grinned and I carried on, relieved to have something to talk about.

'Well, he interested a lot of people because he was so handsome . . .'

He looked at the cover doubtfully.

'. . . but he was born with a club foot, so he had a limp. It didn't stop him being irresistible to women, though.' I used to hate those TV adaptations about historic figures which were full of rose-tinted bedroom scenes with perhaps one stale breadcrumb of poetry tossed in, as if to say yeah-we-know-history-isn't-*all*-about-shagging. But I found myself doing just the same, committing the sin of sensationalism. 'His father, Mad Jack, was an alcoholic and a gambler, and when he was only eleven, his Scottish nurse, May Grey, initiated him into the pleasures of sex . . .'

'*Eleven!*'

'Yep. When he was eighteen, he went to Cambridge. He was a bit of a rebel – the college rules forbade him to keep a dog, so he kept a bear instead! He lived a life of such dissipation that by the end of the first term he was a thousand pounds in debt. After he left, he wrote some outrageous pieces of poetry, like *English Bards and Scotch Reviewers*, where he slagged off just about every contemporary. It'd be a bit like a Booker Prize winner today writing a prologue to his next novel with rhyming couplets declaring all his contemporaries are a bunch of tossers – unlikely, I guess – but an entertaining thought. *Childe Harold* was the poem that got him noticed. He found himself famous overnight and wanted at every party. That was how he came to have his famous love affair with Caroline Lamb, who called him "mad, bad and dangerous to know".'

'So how many women did he have altogether?'

'Oh, hundreds. Boys too.'

Silence.

'He went travelling around Italy. That's when he wrote his masterpiece, *Don Juan*. What else? Oh . . . er . . . and he had a love affair with his half-sister, Augusta.'

Suddenly Nigel woke up.

'Half-sister? You're kidding! But in those days surely you'd get hung, drawn and quartered for that sort of thing?'

'Well, yes – and it was made even more awkward by the fact that Augusta was married. There was a massive scandal, and in the end it was one of the reasons he left England in exile. He died at the aged of thirty-six. All the Romantic poets died young. Keats, Chatterton, Shelley. It was the fashion, really. When they did an autopsy on Byron, they found that the sutures of his skull were fused together, which is normally a sign of old age. He really had lived life to the full.'

'God, it makes me feel as if my life is so boring,' Nigel said glumly, and I smiled in sympathy.

The risotto was ready.

We ate dinner and gradually the conversation dwindled. Feeling self-conscious, I suggested we skip dessert and have coffee; he shrugged sheepishly.

Coffee was a little more intimate. We sat down next to each other on the sofa. Close, this time. I couldn't help feeling guilty, as though I was being unfaithful to Anthony. I reminded myself that I was free and single, but doubt still writhed in my stomach. That's the trouble with fantasies coming true: reality is always slightly frightening. Anticipation intensifies and enriches emotions, but reality seems to smooth them out into a kind of blank bewilderment. Then I saw the desire in Nigel's eyes and Anthony was forgotten.

Well, for a minute, anyway. As he kissed me, I felt taken aback by his style. Anthony and I had always shared soft butterfly kisses which deepened into something more sensual. Nigel was strong and forceful, grabbing the back of my neck and pulling me in close. I closed my eyes and something clicked and I sank into the mood. I ran my hands through his hair and it was just as luscious as I'd imagined.

Beep-ding-a-dong-a-ding, his mobile sang.

He broke off and said, 'Hello?'

I watched, breathless and indignant. Couldn't he switch the damn thing off?

'OK . . . yeah . . . sure . . . right . . . I'm sure she's fine . . . lovely . . . come on, be good . . . OK.' He put it down and rolled his eyes and cupped my face.

'Who was it?' I asked suspiciously.

'Nobody.'

He cupped my face in his hands and carried on kissing me.

Five minutes later, his mobile rang again.

'Oh, Jamie – for God's sake! OK . . . yes, yes . . .' I was taken aback by the emotion in his voice. 'Sure, I'll come home, I'll come home right now. OK, sure, Daddy's coming . . . yep, OK.' He pressed the red button. 'Sorry, I have to go.'

'Back to your wife and kids?' I said furiously.

'No – there is no wife. Just a kid, from my last girlfriend. He's four. It's a bit complicated. I got him a babysitter tonight, but he hates them . . .' He looked tired – the way he had done the morning I had asked him out – and suddenly a lot of things fell into place. He let out a sound that was somewhere between a sigh and a sob of frustration and buried his face in his palms. My heart went out to him.

'It's OK,' I said. 'We can meet another night. Don't worry, it's cool . . . I understand . . . it's fine . . .'

'It's not fine. It's crap. I bet you'll never buy a *Daily Telegraph* off me again. I bet you'll upgrade to *The Times* from that fat geezer across the road,' he said, shooting me a sidelong glance, and we both laughed.

Out in the hall, he tried to kiss me goodbye, but it felt strange, so I turned it into a peck on the cheek. He looked hurt, but I said another warm goodbye and 'I'll see you again,' even though I knew that I wouldn't. Somehow it just didn't seem like it was meant to be.

After Nigel had gone, I sat staring at the dinner table, watching the candle melt into a disfigured stump, dripping fat wax tears on to the lacy cloth. I was so upset, I barely even noticed Lyra jumping on to the table, whiskers bristling excitedly. I felt utterly flat with disappointment. I'd been expecting a night of wild passion, a perfect rebound fling, but reality had given me a sharp slap around the face, slamming me back down to earth. Why couldn't life be like the movies for once? I thought indignantly. Why couldn't it end in fulfilment and a sensual, low-lit bedroom scene and then happy ever after? Why did it always have to be full of cross-purposes and anticlimaxes and plot threads left dangling, never to be tied up?

I got up, shoving away my chair, and went to the window, gazing out at the London skyline, a necklace of amber lights hanging in the indigo sky. An aeroplane sparkled a gold trail through the dark. I felt envy burn in my heart as I imagined people with lives a hundred times more glamorous and exciting than mine travelling to exotic places I might never see before I died. Or maybe I was just being overly romantic again; maybe they were on a package holiday to the Costa del Sol and would end up in a cheap hotel, getting drunk and sunburnt, before returning to the same old jobs, marriages and mid-life crises.

I was definitely having a crisis. I just wanted some excitement, some adventure, some danger, something. I'd spent much of the last decade feeling as though there was something special around the corner – a wonderful man, a career opportunity, a spiritual epiphany – but the corner seemed to be forever out of reach.

I realised just how much I missed Anthony. I wanted to call him up and tell him all of this. I wanted him to hold me tight and tell me everything would be all right. But it wouldn't be all right. Even if I asked him to come back, would he say yes? I had lacerated his heart today, and those wounds were going to take a long time to heal; perhaps we couldn't even hope to be friends.

'Hey!' I turned suddenly to see Lyra devouring the dessert, whiskers splattered with cream. I picked her up and cuddled her against my chest, sighing.

Maybe I just needed to stop waiting for fate to solve my problems and make the change myself. Maybe I should move abroad, start afresh. Maybe I should . . . maybe maybe maybe. I felt my head was going to explode with confusion. I thought longingly of my bed, of the comforting blankness of sleep.

I looked round guiltily at the mess in my flat, telling myself I'd clear up in the morning. Matters weren't helped by that ridiculously large and stupid time machine box in the corner. I gave it an angry kick as I walked out.

vii) Fiddling with the time machine

I finally fell asleep around one a.m. and by two I had woken again, my temples pounding. I tried to play the bed game, but after a half-hour toss-up between Will Self, Orlando Bloom and Anthony, Lord Byron somehow won – which demonstrates just how scrambled my brains were. I thought of some more lines from Plath's 'Insomniac': *Now the pills are worn-out and silly, like classical gods / Their poppy-sleepy colours do him no good*, though frankly I would have killed for a few pills. Finally I decided to get up and read.

And so at three a.m. I ended up in the living room, curled up on the sofa in my dressing gown, yawning my way miserably through Byron's *Childe Harold*. I couldn't take a word in – everything kept irritating me: the tick of the clock, the London traffic outside, the stupid bloody time machine box taking up half the living room. I decided grumpily that I'd definitely sell it on eBay first thing tomorrow.

And then I remembered how soothing I had found it putting the machine together. How I had managed to shut the world out. The thought struck me: *If I try and put the damn thing together again, that is one sure way to get to sleep . . .*

It ought to have been easier the second time, but my head was woolly with tiredness and grief; nor was I aided by Lyra who persisted in trying to sit on the parts. After an hour of hard graft, though, the machine was ready. But nor did I feel tired any more: my mind was alert with a bright, fizzing curiosity. Anthony and Nigel and my unemployed state seemed pleasantly distant.

I got into the machine and typed in a date from the nineteenth century – I'd always fancied giving that era a whirl and hanging out with Byron. Then I typed in the place: London. Then I pressed the green button. Nothing happened. I sighed and gave the machine a sharp, frustrated kick.

Suddenly, the whole contraption seemed to come alive, throbbing as though it was an expensive racing car revving up to do a lap around the track, its sides shaking as though it might spontaneously combust at any moment.

OK, I told myself, you know this thing can't possibly, *possibly* work, but all the same, you cannot go back to the nineteenth century wearing a Hello Kitty nightshirt.

I dashed to my wardrobe, flinging aside old shoe boxes and boots and handbags until I found the musty-smelling carrier bag. Inside was an ivory ballgown which I'd worn to a fancy dress party and always kept just in case. I pulled it on, my hands shaking as I fumbled with the lace in the bodice, then ran back into the sitting room.

I was about to dive into the machine when I thought: *mobile*. I really ought to take it, just to be safe.

I raced into the kitchen, grabbed the phone, then ran back into my bedroom, where I found a white evening bag and shoved the mobile into it.

Back in the living-room, I slid into the machine. It shook so vehemently, I worried that it might collapse. I adjusted the date: 17 April 1813. Not too long after Lord Byron had finished his affair with Lady Caroline Lamb. He would have been twenty-five and at the peak of his fame.

I was about to press the green button once more when an instruction flashed up on the screen: TAKE SPEAKING POTION.

Speaking potion? What on earth . . . ?

Then I noticed a small box poking out from under the seat. Inside were a dozen or so small vials containing green liquid. I uncorked one, sniffing it suspiciously, then, feeling rather like Alice in Wonderland, took a few sips. Well, I didn't seem to be dead yet, nor did I seem to be getting any bigger or smaller. I downed the potion and slammed my fist against the green button before I could chicken out.

There was a long silence. Nothing happened. I glanced around. Yep, my living room was still here. I bit back a smile, feeling absurd, and was picturing myself telling the whole anecdote to Anthony and having a giggle over it when suddenly the machine began to roar . . .

Five minutes later, I found myself lying in the middle of a cobbled street, dawn breaking overhead, with a throbbing ache in my temples.

Chapter Two

Lord Byron (and a brief flirtation with Keats)

It may be profligate – but is it not life – is it not *the thing*?

LORD BYRON, IN DEFENCE OF *DON JUAN*

i) Stranded

I wish I could offer up a glamorous description of time travel. I wish I could tell you that there was a kaleidoscope blur of colour, the wind rushing through my ears at a screaming pitch as I clung to the violently vibrating machine for dear life. But it wasn't like that at all. That was perhaps the most disorientating thing about the whole experience. When I was nine years old, I fell off my bike and suffered concussion. I remember that when I woke up it was as if no time had passed and I had simply been asleep, vaguely aware that I'd lost twelve hours somewhere. Travelling in the machine was the same: complete black-out, and then disbelief, and then *what the fuck . . . ?*

As I came to, I was vaguely aware of something hard and damp curving into my cheek. It was dark. I was lying on a cobbled street. I could hear a babble of voices, a rattling noise, and then a more insistent and more troubling sound that seemed to be getting closer and closer – *clip-clop, clip-clop, clip-clop* . . . I raised my head and—
Screamed. The horse lunged at me. I closed my eyes and curled into a ball, waiting for the hoofs to strike me. I heard the horse whinny; another scream flew from my lips in echo. Then footsteps. I was still too shocked to move. I peered through my shaking fingers and saw the bottom half of a man: a pair of breeches and shiny boots. Then a warm hand touched me on the back and a deep voice said, 'My dear lady! The carriage nearly hit you!'

'Is the fair lady hurt?' another, quieter voice enquired.

I looked up. A large, portly man was staring down at me with shrewd blue eyes. He had the most ridiculous pair of white sideburns you've ever seen; in my hysteria I held back choking laughter. By his side was a thin, rather gangly but also rather dandy young man with big blue eyes and a nervous, twitching face.

Oh my God. It can't be, I shouted inwardly, this can't be.

'Are you injured, my lady?' the man with the sideburns enquired.

No. *No.* The time machine can't have worked, and yet it *has* worked. Unless this is a dream. Yes, it must be a dream. I closed my eyes, feverishly willing myself to wake up. When I opened them again, the two men were still looking down at me.

'My lady, I think you have taken a bad fall,' said the man with the sideburns.

Two pairs of hands reached out and lifted me to my feet.

'Good sir, what year is it?' I cried, then started at my voice – the speaking vial seemed to have gripped my tongue and twisted it into the century's idiom.*

'Eighteen thirteen, of course. I fear the fall has hurt your head. Come into the house and we can give you some brandy.'

'No – no. I need to . . . I need to find . . .' I looked about wildly. Where the hell had the time machine gone? I looked left, I looked right. I looked up. Nothing but street and sky. It had completely vanished.

Shit.

What if it had exploded on the way?

What if I was stuck in 1813 for the rest of my life?

I'd never see Anthony ever again.

The man with the sideburns pressed a hand to my elbow. The pressure seemed slightly threatening, and suddenly I felt a flicker of fear. I recalled one of those BBC TV costume dramas, scenes that had been set in a nineteenth-century madhouse, where women were tied up in filthy strait-jackets and slapped about and fed stale bread. If I carried on like this, they were going to think I'd escaped from an asylum.

'I'm sorry.' I smiled demurely, touching my forehead. 'I was just a little shocked. I, er . . .' I turned, looked at the row of houses. One was lit up, with silhouettes moving around a room. 'I was on my way to a, er, party, and I tripped, so . . .'

'Well, Keats and I are also attending Hobhouse's party,' said the man with the sideburns. 'May we escort you? My name is John Murray; this is my dear friend, John Keats.'

*For the purposes of relating my tale in a more readable manner, I haven't *quite* stuck to the speech patterns of 1813, or other time periods in the book; I felt a little translation into modern English here and there would help.

John Murray! Keats! Oh wow, oh wow. I felt the cold ball of fear in my heart thaw a little. Keats – my favourite poet. Murray – famous, glamorous publisher of Byron, Sir Walter Scott and Jane Austen. Both extremely cool guys. The nineteenth-century equivalent of going to an event sandwiched between David Furnish and Elton John.

I saw John Murray hesitating and realised he was awaiting an introduction.

'I'm Lady Lucy,' I said. 'Lady Lucy, um, Lyon.' Immediately I winced – Lady Lucy Lyon. I sounded like a character in a nursery rhyme.

'It is an honour,' he said, bowing.

I glanced down at my ballgown, fearing it might be torn, but to my relief it was intact, if slightly crumpled and a tad muddy about the hem.

Inside the house, I half expected the doorman, who looked me up and down doubtfully, to say 'Sorry, you're not on the list.' But getting in was fine; it was the bit where a maid came up and asked to take our coats that got a bit icky. John Murray frowned when I said I'd left my coat behind. Then he started asking where my carriage was. Sod the carriage, I thought. What I wanted to know was where my bloody time machine was.

'You must have left your coat in your carriage, or perhaps at home, wherever that is,' Murray said. He had great big bushy grey eyebrows, which clearly had aspirations to become hedgerows. Now they were raised high on his forehead, and I saw a flicker of suspicion in his eyes . . . or was it just my paranoia?

'Murray!' A young woman came up to him, cooing hellos.

I waited for Murray to introduce me but he didn't. Was he ignoring me? Maybe he thought my lack of coat and carriage signalled I was a woman of the night. Or whatever they called them in this century. I felt a dribble of sweat run down my back. If only I'd thought; if only I'd done more research.

I decided I needed a stiff drink. As I wove through the crowds, I suffered another panic attack. Out on the street, the silhouettes at the party had looked like cardboard cut-outs; somehow I hadn't quite believed they were real. But now, as I pushed through them, I could feel the warmth of their breath; skin, cotton and silk brushing by. This was real; it was oh-so-real. I wanted to run away and scream at the sky. I wanted Pringles, I wanted *Big Brother*, I wanted a copy of *Marie Claire*, I wanted a drink . . .

A waiter came past with a tray.

'D'you have any Bacardi Breezers?' I tested him.

He looked blank. I flashed him a quick smile and picked up a goblet of white wine from his tray.

As I sipped my drink, I became horribly aware that people were looking at me. I wondered if they all knew I'd gatecrashed. Then I saw two ladies sweeping their eyes over my dress and sniggering. I looked down, fearing it had a hole or something. Then I twigged.

I hadn't really thought too hard when I'd flung on this ballgown, but it was obviously several decades out of date. It was a lovely ivory colour, but it had a tight waist and a full skirt. The other women's dresses were all lovely flowing things made from silk and muslin, with high waists, low square necks and gossamer shawls. Their hair was pinned up, with little curls teased over their foreheads; a few wore hats with feathers poking out. Whereas my hair – I fingered it self-consciously – was seriously matted and wind-blown. Basically, it was like turning up to a party in 2005 wearing seventies gear, only since retro obviously hadn't been invented in the nineteenth century, I couldn't even pretend to be ironic. I just looked naff.

'Take no notice of them,' a voice behind me said. 'I think you look as beautiful as a nightingale.'

I jumped and turned to see Keats standing behind me, smiling shyly. We stumbled through conversation for a few minutes. I got the feeling he was probably the type who didn't really like parties and ended up talking to the pot plant in the corner.

'Is, um, Byron going to be here?' I broke a long, awkward silence.

'Yes,' said Keats, looking rather sullen. 'I was planning to leave before he arrived.'

I barely registered the barb. I was much too excited by the thought that yes, I was actually going to meet him, one of the most famous men of all time! What would he be like? My mind tumbled joyfully over the possibilities. I couldn't help picturing him as being just like Childe Harold, the brooding, melancholic, world-weary hero of his great poem, though I realised that there was probably a wide gap between Byron and his poetry. For it is the mark of a good author that they write with so much charisma that at the end of the book the reader longs to meet them. Who could tell which of Byron's façades, the various costumes he put on, was real? Tonight, I was determined to try and find out.

ii) Byron

Suddenly there was the sound of breaking glass. The room fell silent. I stood on tiptoe and glimpsed across the sea of heads a boyish-looking woman with a puce, tear-streaked face. She was shrieking, 'I know he's coming tonight and I *insist* on seeing him. I know he wants to see me too!' Still screaming, she was led from the room by two grim-faced footman.

'What's going on?' I whispered to Keats.

'That's Lady Caroline Lamb,' said Keats with a frown. 'Byron's latest. He told Hobhouse not to allow her in.'

'Oh. Oh. Right.'

'He has grown bored with her after only a few months. Mind you, for Byron that is rather a long time.'

Was I picking up just a few bad vibes here? I vaguely remembered reading somewhere that Byron and Keats were never the best of friends. Byron had been rude about Keats, I was sure – but then he was rude about everyone.

But any interest I had in Keats disappeared at that moment, for I realised that Lord Byron was here. I wasn't the only one who sensed his arrival. The chatter hushed and a feeling of anticipation filled the room, like those first ripples of electricity that gently snake through the air before a storm. Women preened themselves and pursed their lips; men puffed themselves up, steeling themselves for the competition.

And then he entered.

The man himself. Mr Mad, Bad and Dangerous to know.

Oh, I thought. He's not *that* amazing. I came back one hundred and ninety-two years for this? He wasn't nearly as tall as I'd imagined. And he definitely had a limp.

He turned to face me, and paused for a moment, drinking in the air as though he could taste it: the sweetness of adoration, the sting of bitter envy. Then, like an actor surveying his audience, his eyes swept over the room. And in that moment, it happened. The magical flash. I felt my knees go weak. I found myself willing him to pin those eyes on me; I came close to behaving like a kid at the back of the class, putting up my hand and shouting, 'Me, me, *ME!*'

He looked away. Then they surged forward: people offering him drinks, handshakes, cheeks to be kissed.

Within a minute he was entirely mobbed by women.

Now I know what my mum meant when she told me how it felt to see the Beatles, I mused.

How the hell was I going to compete against all of them?

Oh dear. I hadn't thought about that. In my idle fantasies I'd envisaged myself just turning up, curling Byron around my little finger, having some fun and then bouncing back to the present day. I hadn't thought I'd have to *work* for him.

'What do you think Byron looks for in a woman?' I asked Keats tentatively.

'The only face Byron can ever love,' said Keats, after much thought, 'is the one he sees in his mirror.'

Ouch. OK. So Keats wasn't going to be much help here.

I tried thinking up chat-up lines. I made a list in my head:

1. What's a poet like you doing in a place like this?
2. D'you come here often (not a cliché, surely, as it's only 1813)
3. What do you think about critics who debate about whether you're really an Augustan or a Romantic poet at heart? (a bit too deep, man)

As I made my way through the crowd, I became horribly aware of Keats following behind me like a shadow. *He's keen on me,* I realised in horror. Great. Just the sort of complication I needed. Keats was sweet, but he was no Byron. When he saw where I was headed, though, he dropped back. I turned and saw his face crease into a vexed expression – almost one of betrayal. I gave him a sheepish apologetic smile and then turned back to Byron.

He was chatting to a woman with peacock feathers poking

ostentatiously out of her hair. Several seconds passed and he failed to acknowledge my presence.

'Ahem,' I coughed blatantly.

Finally he broke off, turned and swept his eyes over me in a languid, lazy manner.

'I am Lady Lucy Lyon,' I said in a slightly shaky voice. 'I'm, um, new in London, and thought I must come to Hobhouse's party because I've heard so much about you and I do love *Don Juan*' – oops, he hadn't written that one yet – 'I mean, um, *Childe Harold*, and so I thought it would be nice to say good evening.' Gulp.

'Good evening,' said Byron.

Silence. The woman next to him put a gloved hand over her mouth to conceal a titter.

Great, Lucy. That was the worst chat-up line in the history of chat-up lines.

Though it wasn't all my fault – he was bloody intimidating, and I could sense him enjoying my distress, which only made me squirm all the more, and I was reminded of Heathcliff saying, '*the more the worms writhe, the more I long to crush their entrails*'.

'You seem to have upset Lady Caroline,' I remarked, a barb of antagonism in my voice.

Byron looked completely unapologetic.

'She sent me a lock of her pubic hair,' he said, relishing the gasp of disapproval from the woman beside him. 'There were even drops of blood on the letter. In return, I cut off a lock of Lady Oxford's hair and sent it to her. Caroline was fooled for quite a while.'

The woman beside him burst into shrieks of laughter, her peacock feathers bobbing madly. I tried to laugh too, but I was rather stunned. Yes, I had known Byron could be mean, but it was disconcerting to come face to face with such nastiness in the flesh.

'Well,' said Byron, yawning loudly, 'I must speak to my other acquaintances.' He ran his eyes over me again. 'Nice dress,' he added lightly, concealing a snigger, then strolled off, leaving his cruel smile hanging in the air like the Cheshire Cat's.

Well. *Well.* I took a big gulp of wine. What a total, total bastard.

Keats came edging up. In my tender state, his cloying sweetness irritated me; I felt an urge to lash out, shove him away, hurt him the way Byron had hurt me. Then I saw the affection in his eyes and I managed a lame smile. We chatted for a short while about poetic scansion, but I could barely make conversation, and Keats, no doubt thinking it was his fault, poor lamb, became more and more shy, curling up inside himself like a snail. I felt so crushed I decided I just wanted to damn well leave the party and sink into a hot bath. I'd look for the time machine in the morning; I didn't much fancy walking around the London streets at this time of night.

So when Keats drifted away and John Murray came over to ask if I was feeling better, I said, 'Actually, I'm still a little faint from my fall.' I touched my forehead, hamming up the damsel-in-distress act. 'Maybe you could call me a carriage . . . ?'

'Of course, my dear lady.' I had a feeling Murray liked playing the role of knight in shining armour.

But then – horror of horrors – he called over to Byron, who turned, his lips curled in an insolent sneer.

'My dear Byron, this beautiful young woman, Lady Lucy Lyon, requires a carriage home. Perhaps your man could take her?'

Byron downed his glass of wine.

'I shall accompany her,' he said. 'I'm utterly bored here. The conversation is all pure *cant*.'

Murray gave him a faintly admonitory but affectionate smile, as though Byron's short attention span was something he'd had to deal with on many an occasion.

He's coming with me? Oh shit! Oh wow. I've got him. I've got him.

'I must just say goodbye to Keats,' I said when we got to the door.

'If you want to waste your time saying goodbye to that pathetic would-be poet, who frigs his imagination in piss-a-bed verse, then you can take another carriage home. I want to leave *now*.'

I smiled prettily and went outside, though I couldn't help feeling slightly upset on Keats' behalf.

As we got into the carriage, I don't think I've ever felt so nervous in my entire life. It was like my first day at school, my first job interview and my first kiss all rolled into one. My body was shaking; my palms were slippery with sweat; my breath was a hot fog. The carriage was dark, lined with a deep purplish silk, and was also incredibly small. Despite my attempts at demureness, I found that my knees touched Byron's as he slid in opposite me.

'My man will drop me off first, then he'll take you,' said Byron.

I nodded shakily, swallowing. I hadn't a place to stay, but hey, I could worry about that later.

The carriage set off. By God, it was rattly; I felt as though I was being shaken up in a beanbag. I'll never complain about the Northern Line again, I thought.

I waited for Byron to seduce me. To gaze at me longingly, to kiss my hand, to compose couplets for me. To my complete and utter outrage, he closed his eyes and, despite the frenetic bumping of the carriage, appeared to fall asleep.

I sat there working myself up into a fuming frenzy. For God's sake, what was the matter with him? I mean, here I was, young and sexy and available. OK, I wasn't Kate Moss, but come on, it wasn't as though Byron was fussy – he slept with his half-sister, for God's sake!

The carriage turned a corner. How far away was Byron's house? What if I never saw him again after tonight; what if this was my one chance? Come on, Lucy, I shouted at myself, *think*. Do something. Something different. Something sexy. Something to make you stand out.

It was then that I realised I was being pathetic. Here I was, smiling at him like some goofy teenage girl, draping myself over him like all the rest. No wonder he was bored. I had to be cool, I had to be tough, I had to be the nineteenth-century equivalent of *Charlie's Angels*.

When inspiration struck, I acted before my nerves could get the better of me. Leaning forward, I slapped him sharply around the face.

Byron woke up in shock.

'Urgh?'

I slapped him again, on the other cheek.

'What in God's name d'you think you're doing?'

'That,' I said, 'was for Caroline Lamb.'

'You're a friend of Caroline's?' Byron rubbed his cheek, his eyes thunderous.

'No,' I said, 'not at all. I'm just slapping you on behalf of women everywhere, for the way you treat them so appallingly.'

I glared at him – I didn't have any trouble feigning anger – and he glared back. For a moment I was terrified that he was going to tip me out of the carriage. Then, to my amazement, he suddenly burst into roars of laughter.

'And who are you again?' he asked.

'Lady Lucy Lyon,' I said.

'I've never heard of you. Where are you from?'

'None of your business,' I retorted.

A slow smile curled on Byron's lips. The carriage continued to rattle. Byron stared at me.

And stared.

And stared.

It was then that I understood the full force of his charisma. It was like being seared by a blowtorch.

I fought the wild sensations in my body and stared back at him. It became like one of those silly games Anthony and I used to play where you compete to see who drops their eyes first.

Then the carriage came to a halt.

'Where are you staying tonight?' he asked.

'At – at an inn,' I improvised. 'I would appreciate your help in finding a suitable dwelling.' *Ask me in*, I begged him silently. *OK, I know I'm not supposed to sleep with a guy on the first date but please just—*

'I suggest you stay at my friend Tom Moore's house,' said Byron, stepping out of the carriage. A blast of freezing night air came in, cooling the sweat on my forehead. 'I shall ask my footman to take you there. Moore will not refuse you.' He paused and then took my hand and slowly pushed up an inch of ivory cloth, planting a kiss in the cup of my palm. It was the most erotic thing I had ever experienced. He looked up at me and saw me shiver, and smiled and said, 'I hope, Lady Lyon, we will meet again soon.'

iii) Courtship

In the morning, I was woken by a beeping noise. A very familiar beeping noise.

I stretched. My hands hit something wooden; I yelped as a

splinter sliced into my thumb. Suddenly disorientation flooded my mind. Where was my alarm clock? Why had my white walls suddenly been replaced with dark ones? I sat up. I was surrounded by a sea of covers. Oh God – Tom Moore's house. I pushed back the covers, swinging my feet on to the floorboards. Then the cold hit me like daggers. I ought to have remembered that there was no central heating in the nineteenth century; I'd once read somewhere that on cold nights people would wake up to find their bedcovers patterned with frost.

I got back into bed and pulled the covers right over my head, burying myself in a warm, safe, white cotton cocoon. Panic gripped my heart in a tight fist. Just what the hell was I doing here? OK, Tom Moore had been a polite and warm host, offering me the best bedroom with the four-poster bed. But this was crazy. I was meant to be getting up and showering, going down to my local newsagent, buying a smoothie and checking the *Guardian* for job ads; I was meant to be sorting out my bills and feeding Lyra—

Oh God! Lyra! She was going to starve, poor thing. I sat up, ignoring the cold. Then I noticed the glow of my mobile phone. I picked it up. I'd got a text message! Well, who would have thought that texts could transcend time and space? The message was from my mother, asking me what I wanted for Christmas – even though it was months away. For all its absurdity I found it supremely comforting. Knowing I could keep in touch with the real world made me feel a lot better.

I lay back, scrolling down through my saved texts. At least three-quarters of them were from Anthony. A wave of longing swept through me and I suddenly missed him so much I felt sick. He hadn't been in touch with me since the *Daily Telegraph* guy date; I was now convinced he was well and truly mad at me.

I decided to text him:

Emergency situation – had to go away. Plse can you feed Lyra for me? R u ok? xxx

A minute later my heart leapt as my mobile beeped again.

Then it screwed into a tight ball of pain when I saw the terse reply:

67

OK.

He was mad at me. I felt tears starting to flow and, hearing a faint knock on the door, hastily wiped my face on the sheets.

'Come in,' I called, quickly hiding my phone under the covers.

A maid entered, a frilly white cap perched on her fair curls. She was carrying a breakfast tray.

The tea looked wonderful. As I sipped at it, I felt a soothing energy and warmth flood my body.

I was draining the cup when I saw that there was something else on the tray. A small white envelope with *Lady Lucy Lyon* written on it in thick, slanting black-inked letters. I put down my cup and tore it open.

Dear Lucy,
    Your company last night was utterly abhorrent. If you
    would like to reprimand me further on the way that I have
    mistreated the female sex, I would be grateful if you would
    join me for an evening of pleasure and absinthe. I will send
    a carriage which will arrive at noon.
    Yours,
    George Byron

I read it through three times. *I will send a carriage.* No asking, just telling me. So presumptuous. And so bloody keen.

Gosh, I thought breathlessly, *I've got him.*

I put down the letter, my heart and mind boomeranging back to Anthony again. One part of me wanted to race back to 2005 and try to repair things, but another part just wanted to curl into a hedgehog ball and hide from my pain, from facing the reality that Anthony and I might never be friends again.

I decided to take solace in Byron.

I thought Byron might play games and turn up late, but his carriage arrived on the dot. When we set off, Byron seemed agitated and excited. Outside the scenery tumbled past, London buildings thinning into countryside.

'Where are we going?' I asked.

'Switzerland,' said Byron casually.

'What? I can't go to Switzerland! I mean, who's going to feed Lyra? I have to look for a job, and I'll miss a whole week of *EastEnders*! And I don't even know where my time machine is!'

In his agitated state, Byron failed to notice my multiple faux pas.

'I'm sick of this country,' he hissed. 'They have reviled me. They dare to question my morals, when they are all swimming in a sea of debauchery themselves, covering it up with smiles and social graces. Well, I shall go, and then they will regret it!'

The journey to Switzerland was not much fun.

We had to go by boat, and boats and I are not the best of friends. The only other time I've had to travel in one was when I was fourteen and we took a day trip to the Isle of Wight. I spent the whole journey hanging over the side of the boat, looking green.

Well, this boat trip though brief, was torture. I spent most of it in the cabin, puking into a silver dish. My immune system was obviously ill-suited to nineteenth-century germs, for my sea-sickness evolved into something more insidious. By the time we had reached Ostend, Belgium, I became delirious, clawed by nightmares; I heard Anthony screaming accusations at me and begged him to forgive me, but he merely stared down at me sternly, shaking his head. In my more rational moments I feared that Byron would grow bored and leave me behind, stranded for ever. To my amazement, however, he was unbelievably considerate and tender. He took away the silver bowls and washed them with his own hands. He had servants bring me broth for my cold fits and ice for my hot. He combed my hair away from my face and planted soft kisses on my forehead and read me verse, some of it his own compositions.

'Listen to this,' he chuckled. '*Coleridge ... Explaining Metaphysics to the nation / I wish he would explain his Explanation.*'

'*Don Juan*,' I said weakly. 'A poem that is quietly facetious upon everything.'

'*Don Juan*! I do like that as a title. Perfect. Lucy, you're not just a pretty face!'

I passed out with a smile on my lips.

As soon as I showed the slightest sign of recovery, Byron sped me off in his coach. It was an exact replica of Napoleon's carriage (which was why he had avoided France). Much of the time I slept with my head on his shoulder. We stopped at another hotel somewhere but I was too weak for even a goodnight kiss. Then we were back in the carriage. When I came round again, it was night. The carriage was speeding at a rollicking pace and through the window I saw shards of countryside spinning past, flashes of grim night sky. I let out a moan. Byron shushed me and touched my burning forehead, whispering that we were close to Geneva now. *Geneva!* I felt panic pulse through my weak body, thumping hotly in my aching head. I felt as though we were in a coach being drawn by the Fates and things were spinning further and further out of control . . . Would I ever get home now, when my vanished time machine – if it was even retrievable – was hundreds of miles away?

I found myself sinking back into the darkness, desperate for oblivion.

I woke up again to the sound of birdsong. I sat up and breathed in deeply. The air tasted pure and sweet. Tentatively I touched my head. Yes, I was feeling better; my feverish head was now cool. But the question was – where the hell was I?

I seemed to be in a castle. I got up and saw a tray by my bed. The tea was still quite hot, and I drank it down and felt revived.

On the bed I noticed a selection of dresses and a note from Lord Byron:

If you're well enough, Lady Lucy, then do put something
on – all are gifts for you. By the way, I was forced to
undress you last night – much against my will, I assure
you – and I was perplexed by the peculiarity of your
underwear.

I let out a giggle. No doubt my strapless white underwired bra from M&S had looked like some sort of alien contraption to him.

I ran my hands over the clothes. They were gorgeous – like something straight out of a Jane Austen costume drama.

Hearing a noise, I ran to the window, peering out through the crisscross of lattice on to a heavenly view: misty mountains staring solemnly over a large lake, where Byron was lolling in a boat. Another couple were rowing on the lake and Byron was calling over to them. At first I thought he was admonishing them, but then he stood up and risked nearly falling out of the boat to shake hands with the man.

It was then that I twigged. Some faint memory stirred of sitting in a dull lecture on the Romantics and my tutor droning on, 'And it was in Geneva that Byron struck up his famous friendship with Percy and Mary Shelley; there, in the Gothic castle, they told ghost stories and ignited the idea for Mary Shelley's *Frankenstein* . . .'

iv) The green goddess

'I've had a rather thrilling idea,' I said, glancing round. 'Why don't we have a competition to see who can tell the best ghost story?'

I expected a tidal wave of enthusiasm, but nobody looked very excited.

'I think I'd rather just smoke some opium,' said Shelley languidly.

'I can think of more interesting things to do,' said Byron, looking up at me from under his lashes.

Only Mary seemed animated, her cheeks flushed, dark eyes narrowed.

'I think it sounds rather fun.'

We were lounging on cushions in the library, having dined on a delicious feast. I had immediately got on well with Mary and Percy Shelley. Shelley was very earnest and a little on the serious side, which made him fun to tease, whilst Mary was lovely – tall, elfin and dark-eyed, with a warm smile and a friendly manner. Even Byron seemed in a top mood – now that he was with friends, he was

71

more at ease, as though he could hang up his *Childe Harolde* cloak and forget about having to live up to his obnoxious reputation.

'I think,' said Shelley, 'that I'd prefer to debate why the upper classes in British society are rejecting atheism.'

We all looked to Byron, the natural leader of our group. He thought hard for a moment and then said, 'Let's tell ghost stories. Since you suggested it, you can go first, Lucy.'

'OK.' Um, now what? I felt all eyes on me, particularly Byron's. And then I thought of a rather cheeky way to entertain them. I remembered an urban myth I'd heard, the one where a couple are travelling along a deserted road at night when they come across a stranger and the man gets out of the car and the woman hears someone thumping on the bonnet (though I adapted it to 'carriage' to avoid bemused looks) . . . 'And as she got out of the carriage, she realised that the thumping noise was her husband's head – on a stick!' I saw Mary's dark eyes widen with fear, and Shelley reached for her hand and squeezed it tightly. Even Byron said in a voice full of bravado, 'That was rather scary, I must admit. Gosh.'

I suddenly suffered a hysterical desire to laugh. It was like telling a knock-knock and being told you're the greatest wit since Oscar Wilde.

But as the evening went on, things genuinely did become more and more creepy. Byron rummaged about in the library and discovered a book of German ghost stories called *The Fantasmagoria*. As the night darkened, we lit candles, the shadows flitting across the walls like spirits, and listened intently to Byron's deep, flowing voice. Halfway through one story an owl hooted outside and I let out a scream. Everyone laughed and Byron patted me on the back. As he carried on reading it struck me that though this was all pretty scary stuff, it was tremendously good fun. Different from parties back home where everyone spent the evening looking around for someone more interesting to talk to. This felt like being a teenager again and having a sleepover with my friends . . .

As Byron read, I watched the shadows flickering in the contours and hollows of his beautiful face and felt myself sigh inside. Every so often he would glance up at me and my stomach would do a funny little dance and I'd think: it's going to happen between us. Tonight. I can feel it. It's going to happen.

At least, I think it is.

Byron even persuaded me to try a little opium, and I found myself sinking back, his mellow voice caressing me, watching the shadows dance and mutate into faces.

As Byron concluded the story, the clock chimed midnight, reverberating throughout the castle.

'I have an idea for a game,' I said, feeling befuddled from the opium. 'Let's play Murder in the Dark.'

They were all intrigued, and after I had explained the rules – the roles of Murderer, Detective and Normal People – and how we would all scatter about the house and wait for someone to be 'murdered' – they looked utterly thrilled.

'My, what a wonderful game,' cried Mary. 'You do have an imagination, Lucy!'

'Your friend is full of surprises,' said Shelley.

Byron smiled proudly, as though he'd invented me.

Byron scribbled the roles on scraps of paper and we each took one. I was the Murderer. Shelley blew out the candles and the castle fell into darkness. I immediately set off after Byron. It was easy, for he had a limp, so he moved slowly and the slightly dragging echo of his footsteps was easy to detect.

He made for the staircase. At the bottom I nimbly slipped off my shoes so that I could creep up on him. The darkness was thick and velvety; the steps were cold and veered with frightening steepness. Suddenly Byron's footsteps stopped. I paused too, my skin prickling. My breath fluttered in my throat and I reminded myself sharply that I was supposed to be the Murderer.

Suddenly a shaft of moonlight slid through one of the slit windows, highlighting a shape behind a velvet curtain. I flicked it aside and held my fingers to Byron's throat in the manner of a knife. He feigned a terrible scream, '*Byron is murdered! Oh woe! Oh woe!*' Then, to my terror, he continued with the sound effects, pinning me to the wall and gasping breathlessly, 'I'm dying . . . oh God save my soul . . .'

Then, just as suddenly, he stopped. I struggled against him, but he held me tight and smiled down at me, licking his lips.

And then it happened again. The ghost of Anthony. My desire flooded away and I was filled with guilt. As Byron leaned in, I lowered my head.

In the distance a voice called out, 'I'm Shelley, the Detective!' and a candle bobbed in the darkness.

'You little flirt!' Byron whispered laughingly. 'I shall get you yet!' He turned back to Shelley. 'I think we ought to have something to drink.'

'The Detective has to question us all . . .' I began, but nobody seemed interested – either that or they hadn't quite got the hang of the game. I noticed that Mary kept looking at me and Byron, her looks curious and slightly concerned. I bit my lip, filled with confusion. I had, after all, come here to escape Anthony and have some fun . . . hadn't I?

Back in the library, I saw Shelley taking out a bottle filled with green liquid, a wicked fairy sketched on its label.

Absinthe.

I watched Byron line up the glasses, clearly revelling in the debauchery. He put a slotted spoon over each glass, with a little sugar cube in the centre, then poured cold water over the spoon; as it hit the absinthe it flared into opalescent clouds that seemed to swirl and take flight in the glasses like little green dragons.

Absinthe. Favoured by all the greats, from Oscar Wilde to Edgar Allen Poe to Ernest Hemingway. Considered by some to be a ticket to the mental asylum – at 68 per cent it was rather stronger than the Bacardi Breezers I drank back home. I felt torn between propriety and debauchery. If I drank it, I'd be pissed within twenty minutes, and how on earth would I be able to keep up my already flimsy nineteenth-century act? But if I held back, I'd just have to sit and watch them get drunk, and how boring would that be? I'd already taken some opium when I didn't even like drugs much; Anthony always claimed it was because I hated losing control. And wasn't the whole point of this journey to forget my boring life back home, to throw off my shackles and go wild?

Byron passed me a glass. He saw the hesitation in my eyes and narrowed his, as though enjoying my struggle between inner angel and inner demon. Then, as I raised my glass, his smirk became a smile.

I took a swaggering gulp and nearly dropped the glass; luckily

Byron's hand steadied my wrist. It felt as though a tiny dragon was hovering at the back of my throat. Then it took flight, spinning down my windpipe in a blur, hitting my stomach in a ball of fire.

'Drink up,' said Byron lightly, pouring himself a second glass.

By the time I'd managed to force down my glass, I already felt drunk. When Byron subsequently suggested we all go skinny-dipping in Lake Geneva, I barely batted an eyelid. Mary was a little reluctant, but Shelley, who was completely gone with opium, yelled that it was a marvellous idea.

Outside, we pulled off our clothes, giggling, and hid them in heaps amongst the reeds. Mary and Shelley jumped in, yelling and shouting at the shock of the cold water. I hid behind a bush, eyeing up Byron, who was standing naked in the moonlight, his body glistening like a unicorn's.

'Come, then,' he challenged me.

'Uh-uh. It looks like ice.'

'If you don't come here, I shall pick you up myself and dash you into the water!'

'OK,' I said, my eyes gleaming. 'Catch me if you can!'

I ran into the forest, Byron chasing after me. I was vaguely aware of my feet curling against brutal brambles and branches, but in my inebriated state I barely felt the pain.

'Come here!' Byron called. 'When I catch you, I shall . . .'

As we ran, my absinthe-addled brain began to slur the scenery. The trees grew gnarled faces, some disapproving, some calling for the police with creaky voices, some serene, their leaves shushing for me to come this way, this way, to keep me safe. Bushes rustled as frightened animals fled; a rabbit wearing a wedding dress and a veil dived into a hole; several birds with brilliant plumage flew up into the trees. Finally I came to a clearing and skidded to a halt, panting. Byron was only seconds behind me. I opened my mouth to ask if we were safe, if anyone could see us; he put a finger to my lips. We stood there, trembling, trying to still our breathing. My hearing seemed dulled one minute, sharp the next; the forest blurred into one vague crackly noise, like an untuned radio, and then suddenly each sound separated and became distinct: birds, rustling, animals, water. A druggy paranoia gripped me.

'I'm frightened,' I whispered.

'Don't be frightened, I'm here,' said Byron.

Moonlight shone down through the trees, painting silvery-blue bars across his bare chest. I blinked and he became a tiger on two legs, covered with beautiful blue fur; the next minute he was Byron again, gently pulling me down into the leaves with a wicked smile on his face; a moment later he was a dangerous nymph, with pointed ears and teeth, tiny red demons dancing in his eyes. I wanted to say to him, *I can't do this, I'm all freaked out, I need to sober up*, but he was leaning forward and then we were kissing. *Oh, this is so beautiful,* I sighed, *the most beautiful, beautiful kiss I've ever had. Mmm, it's so perfect, oh God, I have to stay here for ever and drink absinthe every night and kiss Byron on and on and on . . .*

As he caressed me, I closed my eyes. My body seemed to dissolve into a flowing lake with peaks of lapping pleasure. Then a darkness filled my mind like ink and I was sliding away into some shadowy place where sparks simmered and I felt so, so sleepy, and my body was as heavy as lead and . . .

When I opened my eyes, it seemed as though hours might have passed. Suddenly I was flung back into reality: I was lying on a forest floor with twigs sticking into my back, and Byron was parting my legs and slipping inside me, moaning. Panic erupted inside me. Just what the hell was I doing? The green fairy swirled around my mind, pulling me back into her dreamy ecstasy; I arched my body up to Byron, smiling and aching and sighing his name.

'Am I the best?' he breathed, his eyes satanic. 'Tell me I'm the best lover you've ever had.'

'Oh Byron, you're the best.'

His face became Puckish; moonbeams shimmered around him in a hazy halo and then became fairies, dancing over his head, pulling his hair, winking at me and whooping. A nightingale swooped down, flapping silvery wings. As my moans reached a climax, the bird took each sound and echoed it in a beautiful trill, each note plucking my body like a harp of ecstasy, and I cried and sighed, *oh Byron oh Byron oh Byron . . .*

I woke up the next morning with the *worst* hangover I've ever had in my entire life. An absinthe hangover, I discovered, was not like any normal hangover. My head felt like an exquisite quartz watch that had been filled with sand; my thoughts could barely tick, just struggle thickly. My eyes ached and all noises seemed piercing and shrill.

Mary was the only other one who showed up for breakfast. She seemed distant. She told me that she had barely slept all night, having dreamt of a scientist being chased by a terrible monster he had created in one of his own laboratories. She was so inspired she kept scribbling notes on her hand and soon retreated to write.

I took lunch at noon and Byron still didn't show.

Nor for afternoon tea.

Or dinner.

I felt a wave of uncertainty and loneliness. Finally I plucked up the courage to creep up to his bedroom and knock on the door. After a long pause, he told me to go away.

My head, still weak with hangover, throbbed with hurt. So he was up and hadn't bothered to come and see me. Well, he could damn well see me now. I burst into the room.

Byron was sitting at his desk, writing. His quill hovered in mid-air, dropping splotches of ink on to the page like beauty spots. I saw him flick a glance at me out of the corner of his eye. Then he carried on scribbling.

'Are you well?' I asked tentatively.

No reply.

'What are you writing?'

A long pause.

'A letter. To Lady Oxford. A love letter. I have realised that younger women are not for me; I prefer a more mature woman.'

Bastard. Bastard. Bastard bastard bastard. In my fury, my desperation for attention, I blurted out, 'I came here in a time machine. I came all the way back from 2005. For you! And you treat me like this! You use and abuse me and then discard me after one night!'

That got his attention. He swung round to face me, frowning.

'A time machine? Are you, by any chance, related to Lady Caroline Lamb? Madness runs in her family.'

'Oh yeah? You think I'm mad. Take a look at this!' I thudded my mobile down on his desk. 'It's a portable phone. You don't even know what a phone is, do you? It's a way of communicating. We don't need silly letters any more.'

Byron picked it up and turned it over with a snort. Then, to my chagrin, he started scribbling again.

'So you're just going to sit there and write?' I snarled. I was horribly aware that I was being totally uncool; I was behaving like all the others he had tossed aside, and it was only repelling him further. But I couldn't help it. My heart was bleeding.

'I think,' said Lord Byron, without looking up, 'that you should go.'

And that is how I found myself, several days later, on a boat heading back to Dover. In the ensuing row I had cried that aside from the fact that he'd ruined my reputation, I had no money, and he immediately passed over a wodge of notes. As I stepped into the carriage, he kissed me goodbye with regret in his eyes, muttering apologetically, 'Man is half dust, half deity, alike unfit to sink or swim.' All very profound, but the words did little to soothe my broken heart.

I wasn't sick on the boat this time; I just felt despondent, like a damp dishcloth, watching the grey waves swirl around the boat. I kept telling myself that I had, after all, had my first *ever* one-night stand – after all, the one with Anthony didn't really count, did it? The trouble was, after my so-called one-night stand with Anthony, I'd felt as though I was left washed in a sheen of his loveliness, whereas my night with Byron had left me feeling as though he had scraped a layer off me, leaving me reduced, inadequate, unsatisfied. Perhaps, I thought, one-night stands are just overrated: cool in books and mags and on TV, but in real life draining and bad for the soul.

It was only as we were approaching the white cliffs of Dover that I realised I had left my mobile with Byron. I couldn't even text Anthony; my last link with real life had been severed. How on earth was I going to get back to reality?

v) Keats

I used much of the money Byron had given me to pay for a room in an inn for the night. Fearing men might prey on me, I avoided the raucous-sounding bar and went straight to bed. The next morning I woke up to the sound of birdsong. I thought of Anthony and how I was used to waking up beside him. He liked to sleep on his front and his face would be pressed into the pillow, and he'd feel me staring at me and open his eyes and groan and then kiss me. I felt full of longing and loneliness; my bed felt huge and cold and empty without him.

I wanted to curl up in a ball and hide under the covers but I told myself to jolly well get a grip. I had a bath and it was then, lying in the lukewarm water, that a plan came into my mind. A way to help me get back home *and* wind bloody Byron up. Feeling a bit more cheerful, I dressed quickly and spent the last of my money hiring a carriage.

It took many hours to reach London; finally, around two o'clock, the carriage deposited me at my destination. Luckily the driver had known where to take me, declaring, 'You'll find him at the home of Charles Brown.' Now the door opened and an earthy-looking man with brown hair and a kind face eyed me up and down.

'I think you must be Mr Brown,' I said. 'My name is Lady Lucy Lyon and I am—'

'Oh yes, do come in. Keats has told me all about you. We were about take lunch; perhaps you'd care to join us?'

Keats had told him all about me! How flattering. I was seriously chuffed.

The house was small and poky after the grandeur of Byron's castle, but it was very warm and homely.

Keats was delighted to see me; he spent about five minutes stammering a 'H-h-he-hello,' which was very sweet. He seemed to sense that something was wrong, for as we sat down to eat he said, 'Lucy, you must tell us what the matter is, and if we can help in any way.'

'I'm a lost soul, Keats,' I said miserably. 'I've lost my way. I feel as though I'm in a dream and can't find my way back to the real world.'

I feared my riddles would confuse him, but Keats looked thoughtful.

'Think of Eden,' he said. 'Adam woke from his dream and found it true. If you imagine what you are looking for, perhaps you will find reality. Remember the power of the imagination.'

'Maybe you're right,' I said, pondering. 'Maybe I just need to return to the original place – yes, that might be it – the place where I lost my way . . . where I lost my most precious thing . . .'

Charles Brown listened to all of this in deep confusion.

'If you lost a necklace, Lucy, may I suggest we pay a visit to the local police station this afternoon? Someone may have handed it in.'

After lunch, Keats went into the garden to write. Lost in his poetry, all the tension in his haggard face smoothed out and he looked serene. Charles sighed behind me.

'He's terribly depressed, you know. He wants to earn his living as a poet, but he can't pay his bills . . .'

'Really?' How weird to think his poems were being read in classrooms, and here he was worrying about paying his rent.

'His trouble,' said Charles, frowning, 'is that he's so sensitive. Byron's savage public remarks have hurt him deeply; his health is suffering.'

I recalled how Shelley thought that Keats had died of a burst blood vessel caused by reading a savage attack on *Endymion* in the *Quarterly Review*. I did feel sorry for him. Keats was the ultimate new man. He would have thrived in 2005, but back in 1813 he had to make do with being sneered at by Byron for being in touch with his feelings and his girlie poetry. Byron, I thought sniffily, could learn a lot from him.

I took a walk in the garden. Not wanting to disturb Keats, I wandered through the flowers, sniffing in their delicate scents, but he called me over.

'What are you writing?' I asked.

He blushed and covered his pad with a curved hand, like an embarrassed schoolboy.

'It's just a little something . . . it's called *Ode to a Nightingale* . . . it's not very good . . .'

'No, I'm sure it will be great,' I beamed. Inside, my heart was doing a loop-the-loop. Wow. What a story to dine out on. 'Hey,' I joked lightly, 'why choose a nightingale? I mean, you know, everyone has written about the sweetness of nightingales. Why don't you write about a pigeon? I always feel sorry for them, I feel they're very underrated.'

Now if I'd been teasing Byron, he would have thumped or kissed me by now, then patted me on the bottom and told me to go on my way and leave the genius in peace. But I had forgotten that this was Keats, fragile, sensitive Keats.

'Oh!' He was quite pink. 'Oh!' he mumbled. 'Yes, now I listen to the song of the nightingale, I fear that you are right! The nightingale has been penned to death!'

'Ah – no!' I said hastily. 'I was just kidding, I mean . . .'

To my horror, however, when I looked over his shoulder, he had put a large scrawl through *Nightingale* and instead written *Pigeon*.

He cleared his throat delicately and I realised I was, literally, breathing down his neck.

'I'll leave you to it,' I said quietly, wandering back indoors thinking in horror, shit, what have I done? Still, I thought, look on the bright side. Maybe people will stop tormenting pigeons. Maybe I will come back and find people keeping them as pets. Even so, I felt quite anxious. Who knows how many ripples I might have created? What if the future now fell a different way, like a row of dominoes, wiping out both history and my individual fate? What if I'd never met Anthony? What if I'd never been *born*?

Suddenly a wave of panic swept over me. I had to get back to 2005 before I ruined history for good, not to mention my love life.

I begged Charles to lend me his carriage and I kissed him and Keats a flustered goodbye, promising I would drop by for tea in a week's time. Throughout the journey, I picked nervously at the hem of my ballgown. Oh God, I prayed, please let this work; if this doesn't work, then nothing will. Please, please don't let me be stuck here for ever.

I was dropped off in the very street I had arrived in. It was now busy with horses and carriages, gentlemen and ladies. The gutters steamed with horse shit, and rats wriggled in and out of piles of rubbish. I crossed the road and went to look in the window of a

81

draper's shop, though I was merely gazing at the reflection of the street, forcing myself to remember. There . . . there . . . right in the middle . . . *that* was where the time machine had deposited me.

I waited for the road to clear, for a few carriages to rattle on. Then, my heart thudding, I walked into the middle of the road. Nothing. I couldn't see anything.

Remember, Keats' voice echoed in my mind, *remember the power of the imagination.*

I closed my eyes, my forehead burning in concentration. My heart swelled to bursting as I begged the machine to appear.

I opened my eyes oh-so-slowly, and as I did so, I saw a glint of metal. My eyelids flew open and my heart leapt.

I looked around fearfully, expecting pointing fingers, shocked voices. But everyone just carried on walking and talking. It was as though the time machine had been sitting there all along, in a parallel dimension, waiting for me to shift the angle of my vision and spot it.

Then I heard someone shouting. I turned and saw a carriage heading towards me. The driver was panicking, waving the reins madly and yelling at me to move out of the way.

Now people in the street really did stop and stare.

For a moment I froze. I saw the horses thrashing and kicking up in confusion, hoofs tumbling towards me. Then my body kicked into gear and I dived into the time machine, yanking on my seatbelt.

Now, what date, what date to put in? My mind was blank with panic. Then I spotted the date and time I had left England recorded in green digits on the screen. I typed them in again, and pressed the green GO button. There was a wild *whooshing*, and I hung on tight and said goodbye to 1813.

vi) Home sweet home

As you can imagine, being home was very odd at first. I had left just before dawn and I arrived back just before dawn. Like the children who visit Narnia in *The Lion, the Witch and the Wardrobe*, I found that time was unchanged in the present. But what had seemed familiar was now strange: the sound of cars instead of hoofs, the thrum of an aeroplane passing overhead, a proper toilet instead of a hole in a wooden board. Worse was the feeling of jet-lag. According to my clock, it was 3.46 a.m., but in reality I'd been away for four weeks, two days and five hours. I had treated time like an elastic band, stretching it out of its normal shape and then pinging it back to me. I felt exhausted, my head muzzy and my heart confused. I collapsed into bed, Lyra curled in a purring ball by my head, and slept for fourteen hours straight.

I was woken by my doorbell ringing. Feeling sluggish after so much sleep, I blundered over to the door only to find Anthony standing there.

'Hiya.' His hands were shoved into his pockets in tight balls and stubble crawled in a black forest over his chin. 'You sent me a text saying Lyra needed feeding. Are you planning to go away?' Suddenly he noticed my appearance. 'What *are* you wearing?'

'Uh?' I realised I was still wearing my ballgown. 'Oh, I was just trying this on. I was just about to get into my jeans.' Because time has reverted back to normal, my dress looked exactly as it had when I'd first put it on.

A beat. We looked at each other. The pain of our break-up had subsided to a soft ripple that now rose to the surface, raw and acute.

'Well – I was wondering if we could have a chat,' he said in a tense voice.

'I . . .' I really wasn't in any sort of state for 'A Chat', as it was clearly going to be, but I had a frightened feeling that if I turned Anthony away now, our friendship would be over for good. 'Uh, sure, come in. I'll just change.'

In my bedroom I pulled on my jeans and T-shirt, crumpling up my ballgown and tossing it into the bin. I felt shaky with nerves and hunger. It seemed like forever since I'd eaten.

In the living room, Anthony was pacing up and down so hard it looked as though the carpet might soon disappear.

'Lucy . . .'

'I'll just make some tea,' I procrastinated hastily.

In the kitchen, I removed my favourite shiny pink mugs from the drying rack. I took a box of Earl Grey tea down from the cupboard, rubbing my thumb over the gritty texture of the bag. I watched the

83

boiling kettle puff up happy clouds of steam; I watched as the simmering water hit the tea bag, effusing coils of brown into the water. Milk swirled in, and I added sugars: two for me, half for Anthony. I picked up the mugs and paused to watch an aeroplane slicing through the sky. And for all my tiredness and nerves, a bubble of happiness rose from my stomach and popped, provoking a big smile.

I realised then that although my heart, already bruised by Anthony, had taken another beating from Byron, I felt strangely good. Glad to be back; glad to be alive. All the mundane things in life now seemed thrilling; the ordinary had become extraordinary. My heart dancing, I went into the living room, put down the mugs and impulsively pulled Anthony into a big hug.

He hugged me back just as tightly – at first. And then, to my shock, he pushed me away firmly.

'Anthony . . .'

'I want to know how long you were cheating on me.'

'What? Anthony, I've never cheated on you.'

'Oh really? So that guy who was coming over when I brought that fucking time travel thingummy round – he was just a long-lost brother, was he?'

'No . . .'

'So it *was* a date?'

'Yes . . .'

'Jesus, Lucy, how could you?'

'Anthony, it was just a rebound thing. I literally met him that day – I was so upset about . . . I was just . . . look, we didn't sleep together, nothing happened.' I chewed my lip, thinking of Byron, irrational waves of guilt sweeping over me.

'Really?'

'And what about you?' I cried. 'Were you cheating on me?'

'How can you even *ask*?' His face screwed up in anguish and disbelief. I dropped my eyes in shame; I ought to have known I could always trust his passionate belief in fidelity.

'I'm sorry,' I muttered.

I realised then how much our break-up was killing him. Anthony *never* forgot to shave. His eyes were sunken into his face; he looked as though he hadn't slept a wink. I had managed to escape the pain by fleeing off in the time machine; I had had over four weeks to help heal my heart; Anthony had only had forty-eight hours.

I saw tears in his eyes, and I went over and, very tenderly and very tentatively, gave him a hug. He went limp, his arms dangling by his sides. He was too ashamed of his tears to hug me back; or perhaps it was that he could not forgive me.

'Anthony – I never cheated on you. Not once, I swear,' I said.

'You really swear?'

I looked deep into his eyes and he knew then that I was telling the truth. His arms came up and he hugged me tightly.

Then we sat down and talked it all through again. How we both needed to have space and move on, but how hard it was going to be for both of us. We agreed that it would be unbearable not to stay friends. We discussed the issue of me staying on in the flat; I offered to move out, but Anthony insisted I stay for a while longer. We both cried and hugged some more and used up a hundred-odd tissues and then laughed when we saw the pile.

'I think I need some chocolate,' I said, and Anthony laughed. 'I haven't had chocolate for weeks,' I added, without thinking.

'Oh, you liar,' said Anthony, tickling me, and I laughed with relief; everything was going to be OK between us.

I made some fresh tea and we shared a Kit-Kat, and I had to stop myself from making orgasmic noises at the pleasure of it.

'So this – this rebound guy,' said Anthony. 'You think you'll see him again?' He saw my face and held up his palms. 'Lucy, I'm not jealous. Seriously. I'm not interrogating you. I know I behaved like a jerk, but now I'm just asking.'

'Well, no,' I sighed. 'I don't think I will.'

'Fuck.' He ran his hand through his hair. 'I think I need a rebound relationship. The thing is, Lucy – I'm no good at being alone. I thought in my early twenties that I'd be a lifelong bachelor, end up like Dad. And now here I am, feeling like I need to be with someone.'

So why did you want to break up with me? I thought, slightly puzzled.

'I was even thinking,' he went on, then stopped and flicked me a sidelong glance. 'You won't laugh, will you, Luce?'

'I promise,' I said, my lips already twitching.

Anthony sighed. 'Whenever I say, "Promise you won't laugh, Lucy", you always crack up.'

'I won't, I swear, Anthony,' I cried, on the verge of hysterics already. 'Just tell me.'

'I want to join a dating site, and I want you to help me fill out my application.'

My smile died. 'Anthony, you don't need to use a dating site!' I cried. 'I mean – you're gorgeous, and great and . . .' *And we've only just broken up*, I added silently, aware of my hypocrisy.

Embarrassed by my hurt, I got up, brisk as Mary Poppins.

'Come on then,' I said, 'let's go online right away.'

I switched on my computer, swishing the mouse, then turned and saw Anthony, still slumped on the sofa, staring at me with wounded eyes.

'You want me to be with another girl,' he said, a trace of bitterness in his voice.

There was a brief, taut silence.

Then he grinned quickly, putting down his mug and coming over to the computer. 'That's cool. Let's get online and then I can start finding some weirdo women to torture me.'

We sat side by side and surfed. I soon realised that Anthony didn't really want to sign up with a dating agency. He was playing a game, testing to see if I was jealous. And in turn I was batting the ball back at him, determined not to show just how deep jealousy burned inside me.

'Can't I just sign up with one of those sites where women are looking for other women?' Anthony gave me a teasing look.

'No you can't,' I said primly. 'Come on, leave Google alone and focus! We're going to find you something utterly respectable.' I yawned and stretched as a sudden thought troubled me. 'My favourite poem is *Ode to a Pigeon*.'

'What?' Anthony knocked me gently on the head with his knuckles. 'You mean *Ode to a Nightingale*.' Suddenly he saw the funny side and burst into chuckles. '*Ode to a Pigeon*! I suppose he also wrote *Ode to a Woodlouse*.'

I burst into relieved giggles. Then, glancing down at my hand, I noticed that the splinter cut, which had throbbed painfully ever since my night at Tom Moore's, had healed up, the skin smooth and unscarred. So I hadn't changed the past. I might have temporarily bent events, but with its own divine order, the universe had sprung back into shape and history was as it had always been.

I was so relieved that I hadn't ruined Keats' finest poetic achievement for generations to come that I shrieked with laughter that rapidly became hysterical. Anthony gave me a weird look.

'Lucy, have you been taking drugs?'

'Just a little absinthe.'

'Ha ha. Come on, where's this dating site then? I'm counting on you to sort this one out for me.'

I did my best. We surfed for about an hour and in the end settled on a nice-looking site where you had to pay £20 a month and there were plenty of sane-sounding women. Anthony logged on his details; now he just had to wait for messages to start popping into his box.

'Well, I'm glad that's sorted. So you're not going away, then?' Anthony asked, recalling the panicky text I had sent. 'Lyra doesn't need feeding?'

'Er, no – I was planning to, but now I've realised it's not necessary. Come on, let's have some soup – are you hungry?'

We had supper together, then I began yawning again – I still hadn't quite caught up on my sleep – so Anthony left early. When he went, he gave me a deep, tender hug and we both found ourselves close to tears again. As he walked away, he kept looking back, as though aching for me to call to him and ask him to stay the night. And it took all of my willpower to let him go, knowing it was the best thing for both of us.

I was relieved that Anthony and I were friends, but even so, the next week or so felt strange. It felt odd sleeping in my own bed night after night instead of spending three nights a week in his; my bed seemed huge and hollow without his warm presence. It felt odd sitting down in front of the TV and not fighting over the remote; odd not being woken in the mornings by Anthony bringing me a cup of Earl Grey and a sleepy kiss. We still called each other at least once a day, and each call ended on a jerky, self-conscious note, aware that we were now ringing off with 'goodbye' rather than 'I love you'.

I also felt strange because it took me much longer than I'd expected to recover from my time machine adventures. It was as though I'd spent a week partying without sleep. For three nights I had to go to bed at eight thirty, and I kept having to knock back paracetamols to ease my thumping headaches. I found myself feeling ravenously hungry, as though my body needed fuel to repair itself from the trauma, and I put on at least four pounds.

I started applying for new jobs, but I found it hard to focus.

For one thing, I had no idea what I wanted to do. And besides, every time I skimmed the ads, I found my eyes sliding over the time machine in the corner of the room. I had covered it with an Indian throw, but still it beckoned me, a temple of delights promising love, adventure, beauty, danger. I found myself surfing the internet, looking up articles on time travel, biting back smiles when I read treatises by professors who claimed it was impossible.

There were times, too, when I found myself simply bursting to call Anthony and blurt it all out. Or my mother. Or my sister. I even thought about going to see a counsellor, just so that I could tell *someone*. But I knew that the moment I said a word, they'd be sending the men in white coats over to put me in a straitjacket.

I thought about inviting Anthony to have a go in the machine himself. It could be our secret. We could go back to Roman times, I thought with excitement, and visit Cleopatra – Anthony had always had rather a yen for her. But I felt protective of him; he was in a delicate state as it was, and Cleo might just about finish him off.

A week passed and my memories of 1813 began to blur and become smoky, until I wondered if it had ever really happened, if it had just been a dream.

As my money dwindled, I signed up with an employment agency.

You might be wondering, at this point in my story, why I didn't just get into the machine, whiz forward a week or so and check out some lottery numbers. And before all this happened, if anyone had asked me what I would have done with a time machine, a little lottery cheating would definitely have been high on my list.

But in reality, I felt frightened by the idea. I could change my entire life, yet I found myself clinging to the safety of the present. In the end, I told myself that I would only use the lottery thing if I really really needed it – if my bank account hit its limit, every credit card was full, and nobody would ever employ me.

And just when it was beginning to look as though that might be the case, the agency told me an interview had come up.

The first thing I did was get myself another mobile. As I played about with my new toy, a thought suddenly struck me.

Byron still had my old mobile.

So . . . ?

On a whim, my heart fluttering with excitement, I decided to text him:

Hi, Lucy here. How is life in 1813? By the way, I think you are a total cad. Back in England, I seduced Keats. What do you think of that?

Not entirely true, but never mind.

Later that evening, as I was watching *EastEnders,* my mobile vibrated.

Hello, Byron here – finally got this damned thing to work. How are you? More importantly, how was Keats?

Hmm. So no apology then for his behaviour. No 'How is your broken heart?' But a touch of jealousy – well, good.

I texted back:

Keats was great. More than great. We're in love.

A few moments later there was another beep. Despite myself, my heart fluttered. Perhaps he really was jealous. He might declare he had always loved me and dedicate a poem to me and I'd make the history books after all!

How big was Keats? I want to know the truth, dammit.

Huh. Bloody unbelievable. So all Lord B. cared about was his pathetic masculine pride. With shaky hands and a spurt of triumph, I texted back:

A good eleven inches. Oh, that must be ten more than you, right?

After that, he didn't text me back again.

Chapter Three

Leonardo da Vinci

The art of procreation and the members employed therein are so repulsive, that if it were not for the beauty of faces and the adornments of the actors and the pent-up impulses, nature would lose the human species.

LEONARDO DA VINCI

i) Spring cleaning

'D'you like this picture, Adam?' I asked my nephew.

Adam looked up at Leonardo's famous painting of *The Virgin of the Rocks*. His face screwed up into a serious expression; it was just like the one Anthony used to make when he was taking the piss out of New York critics.

Then he shook his head solemnly and said, 'I think it's crap.'

'*Adam!*' My sister gave him a gentle slap on the back of the head. '*Language!*'

I tried not to laugh, though I saw Sally's lips twitching too.

'Well, my lunch break is nearly up. I suppose I ought to get Adam back to school.' She sighed. 'How are you enjoying the job? I wouldn't have thought that working behind the till at the National Gallery selling postcards was your cup of tea, Lucy.'

Neither would I, but it was all the employment agency had been able to come up with, since I had managed to fail their typing test; my last few years of laziness had slowed my speed down to 45 words per minute, which I had been informed, was just 'not up to scratch'. And I had to get a job doing *something*. I felt a duty now to make sure I paid Anthony every penny of my rent on time, to prove I wasn't taking advantage of our friendship.

'Well, I'm really enjoying it,' I lied stubbornly. 'I think it's educational, I'm learning a lot about art.' I didn't add that I was so bored I had already begun to hate the pictures. It's all very well coming to the National Gallery and staring at *The Virgin of the Rocks* for five awed minutes. But when you've been staring at it for five days in a row it starts to niggle; the serene beauty of the Virgin's face becomes bland.

I could hear a group of schoolchildren screaming like Adam does when he's throwing a tantrum, and as yet another flurry of Japanese tourists began to harangue me, my sister drew Adam away.

'Well, it was nice seeing you, Luce. I'll leave you to it.'

'Yeah – thanks for dropping by,' I called out.

I turned back to the Japanese and explained that they weren't allowed to take photos. They were, after all, meant to be forking out for the postcards in the shop.

'But if we all stood in front of the picture, then nobody could see it in the photo!' the man beamed with a brainwave.

'Er, okay. Sod it, go on then,' I said. 'But be quick, or I'll lose my job.' I wandered back off to the foyer.

The afternoon dragged by. I found a new term to define my boredom – *boremoreboredom* – the boredom of leaving one boring job for another one equally boring.

It was amazing how soon my initial euphoria about my trip back to 1813 had faded, how quickly I had fallen back into the same rhythm. It's just like when you go on holiday and return feeling all fresh with new ambition, and then, in a few days' time find yourself stuck in the same old rut; life is the same as ever. I was beginning to realise that the only reason I'd survived my old office job for so long was because Anthony had always been a backdrop to the day, someone to call or email or merely fantasise over.

Still, we were beginning to adjust to our friendship, wearing it in like a new pair of shoes, and now it felt more softened and creased and comfy. In fact, all morning Anthony had been sending me entertaining texts about the first girl he'd discovered on his dating site jaunt. Her name was Matilda, and he was seeing her tonight.

Back home that evening, I felt slightly at a loss. It was a Thursday night. Traditionally, Thursday nights had always been video nights. Anthony and I had completely different tastes in films. He was very much a fan of the Hollywood blockbuster, whereas I preferred art films. In truth, I didn't mind the odd romantic comedy or weepy or thriller, but I exaggerated my snobbery for the sake of argument. Soon we became quite competitive in our attempts to wind each other up, Anthony choosing the cheesiest films he could think of, while I would hunt down the weirdest ones I could find. Each week we made scathingly sarcastic remarks about each other's choices. It meant we saw a wonderful range of films. It was great fun. How I would miss those days.

But, I reminded myself, *you're young, free and single now, Lucy! You can pick any video you like.* I decided to choose one after I'd cooked supper. Or, rather, found something tasty in a tin. You see, I wasn't exactly the best cook in the world.

The first time I'd tried to cook a romantic meal for Anthony, the entire block of flats had to be evacuated due to the smoke alarms screaming. Anthony felt that was the more positive part of the evening: 'It was the throwing-up-all-night bit I had the real problem with,' he declared. The next time he came over, he politely suggested I try something simple, assuring me that he loved cheese on toast. Every time he took a bite, I asked anxiously, 'Are you *sure* it's OK?' and he said, 'Yes,' and I said, 'Really, you don't have to eat it if you don't want to,' and he said, 'Lucy, I want to eat it, it's wonderful,' and I said, 'What does it taste of then?' and he said, 'To be honest, it tastes like old socks on toast.' I wept for a while and he comforted me. 'Come on, Lucy,' he said, 'you can't be good at *everything*. You are a Renaissance girl, but cooking is not your strong point.'

After that, I let Anthony cook. I was hugely jealous, and hugely delighted, at what a wonderful cook he was.

And no doubt, at this very minute, he was cooking his absolute speciality for Matilda: a simple but delicious roast chicken with glorious crunchy carrots and thick gravy – oh, and his classic crème brulée for desert with that lovely skein of burnt sugar on the top.

As I poured my tin of tomato soup into a pan, I couldn't help thinking wistfully about his roast potatoes. Oh well . . .

I ate my soup whilst watching the news.

I wondered if I ought to phone up one of my girlfriends, Emma or Chloe or Clare. The trouble was, I'd kind of let our friendships slide over the last year. That was the thing about my relationship with Anthony – for all our commitment-phobia, it had been so intense, so all-consuming, I didn't really have anyone in my life except for him.

I put on a video: *2046*. I'd watched it before with Anthony and told him it was my favourite film in the whole world. To be honest,

I was slightly bored by it. Had I only ever enjoyed it to wind him up? After twenty minutes, I found myself switching off.

I had a bath. I dried my hair. It was still only nine p.m. What had happened to time? Clearly its winged chariot was in first gear and the driver was on sedatives.

I trawled back into the living room and stared vaguely at the bookcase on the other side of the room. I loved reading and found it hard to resist walking past a Waterstone's without popping in and buying a book. My tastes were totally diverse; I loved books that entertained me, books that stretched my mind, books that created worlds for my imagination to soar in, books that made me laugh and cry. I'd once sorted the whole case into alphabetical order, but now it was a tip, books stacked up in unsteady piles, competing for space with old magazines, the shelves cobwebbed with dust.

I know! I thought. For once in my life I will deal with all my horrible mess. I'll have a spring-clean!

I kept the TV on, vaguely aware of its gossip in the background, whilst I pulled all the books off the shelves, yanked on my Marigolds and set to work with a sponge and a bucket frothing with Fairy Liquid. After about two minutes, I started to think: God this is boring. *Come on, Lucy, this is fun,* I argued back, *fun, fun spring-cleaning.* Then my eyes dropped to a pile of books. Hey, look, *Perfume.* I hadn't read that in ages. And oh – *Birdsong.* And what was this?

It was a thin volume, entitled *The Idiot's Guide to da Vinci.* It had a jazzy cover and a cartoon of an elderly Leonardo on the front, white hair cascading around his face, still beautiful and graceful even in old age.

I remembered that Sally had bought it for me one Christmas. She wasn't very good with presents, and I had to admit, I thought the book would be naff and superficial. But it was a whole lot better than cleaning. I dipped in. Its style was chirpy and colloquial and it skimmed over things, but it was fun. I flicked through randomly and read:

The word Renaissance means 'rebirth' and it applies to a new age, a golden era when medieval ways were cast aside. It was as though the human spirit was born again. People suddenly woke up and started wanting to know how the world worked. There was a spirit of enquiry in the air as people got into art, science, history and nature.

What a thrilling time it must have been, I thought. Utterly gripped, I flipped on a few more pages:

The Renaissance began in Italy and one of its stars was, of course, Leonardo da Vinci. Leo was a strict vegetarian and loved animals. He was also very charismatic – there is no doubt he would have been a favourite with the ladies.

Suddenly I felt a wave of nostalgia, a desire to leave behind TV for blank canvases, to hear lute players rather than yet another manufactured boy band, to swap my jeans for beautiful silk dresses embroidered with birds and flowers.

Letting out a sigh, I put down the book and carried on cleaning.

That night, I played the going-to-bed game again. My short list came down to:

1. Daniel Day Lewis
2. Gareth Gates
3. Leonardo da Vinci

No prizes for guessing who won . . .

By lunchtime the next day I still hadn't had a text from Anthony. I felt slightly depressed and itchy with intrigue, but whenever I got close to texting him to ask how it had gone, I found myself gulping and shoving my mobile back in my pocket. What if he texted me back saying *I'm in heaven*? How would I feel then?

I didn't feel hungry, so I skipped lunch and escaped the gallery for a little fresh air and a wander. At least I told myself it was only a wander, though I found myself searching down one of the streets

97

behind Leicester Square, looking for a shop I'd passed a few years back. I kept telling myself it had probably closed down and the whole idea was ludicrous, but to my amazement I eventually found it, lodged between a 'specialist' bookshop with red light bulbs adorning its window, and an obscure, dusty art gallery. COSTUMES FOR ALL AGES.

See, a small voice told me, *it's fate. It's meant to be.*

Inside it was cool and shady. It smelt of mustiness, mothballs and cloth. Costume after costume was lined up on racks, bright as the plumage of a cage of tropical birds. As I ran my hand along the length of one rack, my fingers brushed lace, cotton, linen, sequins. My imagination ignited.

'Can I help you?'

A kindly old man with an apple face and spectacles perched on the top of his beaky nose smiled at me.

'I'm looking for a costume,' I said. 'Something sexy. Something a young artist's apprentice would wear in Milan in 1482. Is that too hard?'

'Not at all.' He looked rather offended. 'But if you're going to be an apprentice, I take it you want to be a boy?'

'Ah . . .' Golly, I hadn't thought of that. I guess women in the fifteenth century didn't get to do much except get married and have babies. 'Yes, yes, you're right,' I said. Suddenly ideas exploded in my mind like a heavenly firework display. 'By God, you are right! I have to go as a man! And that means – that means I can go as an apprentice! And that's the way I can hook him . . . and then later I can reveal myself, just like in *Twelfth Night*! Oh my God, you're a genius!' I flung my arms around him.

'Sorry.' I stepped back, seeing his bemused expression. 'I just got a bit excited there.'

'S'allright,' he said. 'We get a lot of cross-dressers in here. I know how exciting those parties can be. Now, how about this tunic and hosiery? You're going to have to do something about your . . . of course . . .'

'My . . . uh?'

'Your . . .' He blushed and cocked his head to one side.

'Oh, right.' I looked down at my chest and flushed and giggled. 'Any ideas?'

'Nothing that a few bandages and some safety pins can't handle . . .'

When I got back to the gallery, I was late and suffered a dressing-down from my supervisor. I hid my costume, tucking *The Idiot's Guide to da Vinci* into the tunic. If I was going to go anywhere, I was going to be better prepared this time. I checked my mobile for a text from Anthony, but there was none.

ii) Meeting Leonardo

I typed the date into the time machine – *19 September 1482* – then stared at it, my finger lingering on the green button. I can't believe I'm doing this again so soon, I thought. At this rate it'll be an addiction, worse than my chocoholism.

Then I thought: Sod it. I've been given a rare and crazy gift. God, most people would die to enjoy this. Stop feeling guilty and just bloody well enjoy it. After all, Anthony's enjoying himself with Matilda, isn't he?

A voice argued back: *But look, I didn't really enjoy 1813 that much. Do I really want to do this again? What if Leonardo turns out to be horrible too and I get my heart broken for a third time in as many weeks?*

I reassured myself. The problem with Byron was that he was only twenty-five, a mere boy. Now, in 1482, Leonardo will be thirty years old. Much more mature. Much more fun.

Oh well, here goes.

I downed a speaking potion, pressed the green button and prepared myself for blackout . . .

I found myself lying on a stone floor in a room filled with sunlight. I sat up, smoothing down my clothes. This time the time machine had been a little kinder. After landing face down in a cobbled street last time, I'd feared I might find myself sitting naked on a stool before a painter. To my relief, I found myself behind a large cream silk screen. It seemed to be doubling up as a sort of artist's cloth, for it was decorated with splotches of paint, random swirls and squiggles, and occasional sketches of beauty – an eye, a face, the outline of a bird.

I listened carefully. I could hear the sounds of a city flowing through an open window. The room seemed empty, and yet I could sense a presence. I crawled to the end of the screen and peered round.

And nearly had a heart attack.

Leonardo was standing in front of a table, making some sort of sculpture. He was wearing a rather beautiful pair of green hose and was naked from the waist up. His body was splashed with paint, and there was a smear of charcoal on his cheek, though this only seemed to highlight the glowing golden beauty of his skin. He was ravishing. A true Adonis. The beams of sunlight shining on his long hair seemed to sparkle even more vividly as though jealous of its dark chestnut hue. His features were exquisite: high cheekbones, full lips, long eyelashes; his face seemed to pulse with energy and intelligence. As though sensing my presence, he looked up. Before I drew back and hid, I saw straight into his eyes. They would have put sapphires to shame.

I sat with my back to the screen, my heart hammering. Thank God he hadn't seen me. And oh God, another thanks for creating such an incredible man. He made Lord Byron look like a dog. Oh boy, I am so glad I decided to come. This beat boring old work *any* day.

I couldn't resist having another peek; I was like a honey bee circling an exquisite orchid. I noticed there was a slightly wicked smile on his face and I wondered what he was up to. At first I thought he was moulding a sculpture of a dragon. Then I realised that it was in fact a real-life lizard on the table. It was sitting very calmly while Leonardo attached a large pair of painted wings to its back, and a pair of horns to its head. How odd. All the same, it was fascinating to watch the enthusiasm dancing in his face, the delicate firmness of his famous artist's fingers.

When he had finished, he stood back and stared. He was obviously happy with the result, because he bunched up his fists and jumped up and down like a little boy. It was so cute, so endearing, that I had to stop myself from rushing out and giving him a big hug.

Suddenly Leonardo froze, and I was terrified he had seen me. Then I realised someone was coming; a door banged, footsteps approached. He quickly turned and ran behind the screen.

I curled up into a petrified ball. At last I plucked up the courage to peer through the gaps in my fingers. Incredibly, he hadn't even noticed me. He was crouched at the other end of the screen, peering out, utterly engrossed in spying on whoever was coming into the room.

I hardly dared breathe. I peered around my end of the screen, wondering what on earth was going on.

A gentleman had entered the room. He looked as though he was in his late thirties and he was plump, with a round face and dishevelled brown hair.

He saw the creature on the table and let out a cry.

'What in God's name . . .' He took a few steps backwards, his hand to his heart. 'Dear God, what creature, what devil's spawn is this – a dragon?' He edged closer, frowning.

Leonardo, unable to help himself, let out a smothered giggle. And without thinking, I did too. Instantly Leonardo's eyes were on me – wide and shocked. I stared back in dismay.

'Who the hell are you?' he whispered.

'Um, I am, er, Signor da Liza,' I whispered back. I shook myself with momentary shock as fifteenth-century Italian fell from my lips, courtesy of the speaking potion. 'I want to be your new apprentice!'

Leonardo looked utterly bewildered, then whispered, 'Wait here.'

As he went from out behind the screen he roared, 'DONATO BRAMANTE, FRIGHTENED OF A LITTLE DRAGON, ARE YOU?'

'Leonardo – so you were hiding there all along! Another one of your practical jokes, you wicked man!'

'My dear Donnino, I know that you love me for them. And look – look at the wing span on my creation. I've been experimenting with designs for wings for humans, wings that will enable us to fly just as the birds do! But . . .' Leonardo lowered his voice and I heard them whispering. I sat up, frowning. I was still confused by how calm Leonardo's reaction to my appearance had been. But maybe Milan was a nice friendly place where people wandered freely in and out of each other's courtyards, unlike today's modern fragmented society where neighbours loathed each other and—

I heard a sudden swishing noise and realised that a sword had been thrust into the screen. It was about six inches away from my ear. I let out a scream.

'Who are you?' Leonardo cried. 'Have you come to steal my ideas? My lute, my canvases, you impudent thief . . .'

'No, no, no,' I cried. I jumped to my feet and came round the other side of the screen. Immediately Bramante, though he was much bigger than either me or Leo, stepped backwards fearfully, but Leonardo continued to brandish his sword, his eyes narrowed. He looked so different from the cute boy I had seen earlier. Now he looked all of his thirty years, and more. I was frightened; I wanted to go home.

'I think your *Virgin of the Rocks* is the greatest painting I have ever seen,' I cried, falling to my knees. 'I'll sweep your floors, I'll wash your clothes, I'll do anything just to work with a genius like you.'

'I see.' Leonardo put the sword down and folded his arms. 'Get up then.'

I stood up shakily, brushing down my tunic, smoothing down my hair. As he looked me over, I lowered my eyes, terrified that some tiny little thing was going to give away my femininity. But Leonardo seemed pleased with what he saw.

'Da Liza. It is a strange name,' he said. 'What province are you from? Not Milan, I presume, with a name like that?'

'I – ah – I come from near Florence,' I said, hoping the mention of Leonardo's birthplace might show him how much we had in common. But he only looked rather suspicious – he probably knew the area well. Damn. 'But my mother was half Finnish, one quarter Italian, and one quarter Spanish and my father half Australian and half German and so my name and roots are very complicated.'

Leonardo and Bramante looked completely confused; I could almost see the cogs whirring in their minds.

'So have I got the job?' I asked brightly.

'I am not really looking for an apprentice,' said Leonardo. 'I am planning to set up a studio, but have only just arrived in Milan. At the moment I am lodging here, in the parish of San Vincenzo; I have no spare rooms for an apprentice.'

'I'll sleep on the floor, I'll—'

'You need not do that,' Leonardo laughed. 'We could put a pallet in this room,' he said thoughtfully, 'and you could sleep in the corner . . . We could draw the screen around you.'

'Leonardo, do you not think that you should ask this young man if he has a prospectus of his talents?' Bramante asked sharply. I frowned, detecting jealousy in his voice.

'*Do* you have a prospectus?' Leonardo addressed me. 'A recommendation, perhaps, from your last master?'

A prospectus? The last time I had a prospectus was when I was applying to go to university.

'Erm, it kind of got lost . . .' I muttered, squirming as Bramante pierced me with a suspicious frown.

But to my surprise, Leonardo said, 'Fair enough. Paint something for us. Here is the easel, here some pencils. Let us see you sketch and paint a little.'

For a moment I panicked. The last time I had really painted anything had been when I was eight years old. I'd done a lovely brown dog and had sent it in to Tony Hart's art programme and my picture had been shown on TV. I remember that I boasted to all my friends until the entire playground hated me.

'Well, I'm a bit rusty, but here goes,' I said, swallowing.

I decided to paint my brown dog again, feeling somehow it was lucky. But I must admit, I was a little out of practice, and in my nervousness my paintbrush shook a good deal. Five minutes later I decided to put down the brush, feeling that the more I went on, the worse it would get.

Now for the verdict.

Bramante stared at it as though I'd just painted a turd. Come to think of it, it did look rather like a turd.

Leonardo's face was inscrutable. He frowned, clucked his tongue, stepped back from the picture and narrowed his eyes, came up close to it and peered at every stroke. My fingers twisted into the hem of my tunic in tension. Oh God, I thought, here goes. I'm going to be thrown out.

Then he turned and looked me up and down as though I was a

103

painting. To my complete shock, he cried, 'Very well, then. You're my new apprentice! Will you accept a wage of two *soldi* a day?'

'Erm, well, yes, that is my usual going rate,' I said.

'That doesn't surprise me,' Bramante muttered. He said his goodbyes and left, shaking his head. I had to curl my hand to stop myself from giving him a V sign. But hey, I'd just been taken on as an apprentice by the world's most famous artist. Ha – I'd always known my brown dog was lucky.

The next few weeks were tremendously hard work, but wonderfully good fun. I didn't want to suffer the pain I had with Byron, so I was determined to get to know Leonardo before embarking on any fling. And being his apprentice was just ideal.

All the same, I had no idea painting was so complex – there were no easy trips down to the local art shop for a set of paints and a few rolls of paper. I was sent to pick the hairs from the tails of ermines and stoats, bind them to quills and then slot them into wooden handles to make brushes; I had to boil wooden panels in water to prevent them from splitting before Leonardo prepared them for painting; I had to grind pigments to make the paints, so that by the end of each day my nails were stained with the colours, the intense blue of lapis lazuli or the deep red of crushed cochineal beetles. There were times when I made awful mistakes, such as when Leonardo asked me to mix him some tempera paints. How was I to know tempera meant egg yolk? Who ever heard of mixing paints with *eggs*? I told Leonardo he ought to get into oils, and he said he was considering it. I'm sure he must have realised I'd faked my CV and had no real experience with a master, but he never berated me; he was always kind and patient.

I fell in love with Leonardo very quickly. It was impossible not to. A great friendship immediately sprang up between us. There were times when he was terrifyingly serious and obsessive about his work, but he also had a deliciously boyish sense of humour and loved playing practical jokes on me. One of his favourites was making wax models of creatures, blowing into them and then setting them off with a series of rude noises.

He was also touchingly determined to turn me into a good

painter, letting me practise with a lead stylus and making me my own trelliswork grid to help me work on my perspective. Many nights we stayed up for hours, painting together. One night we were toiling past midnight and soon my head was drooping and my brush slackened, limp as a dishcloth. A warm hand curled around mine and I looked up to see Leonardo staring down at me.

'Bed,' he said, threading the paintbrush out of my fingers. 'Bed for sleepyhead.'

He'd set up the screen around my bed so that I could change without him having to stop work and leave the room. Despite its shield, I still felt acutely conscious of my nakedness as I took off my clothes; I could feel his consciousness of it too, the electricity in the room. I pulled on my nightclothes and slipped under the covers, then started, hearing a knock. Leonardo was peering around the edge of the screen. He came and tucked me in, planting a kiss on my forehead. As he leaned down, his hair caressed my cheek and my nerve ends burst into flames.

'Are you going to bed now?' I stammered.

His eyes were on my lips. He shook his head, smiling.

'I shall paint,' he said. He looked out through the window at the patch of brilliant night sky. 'The night is only just beginning – and someone has to keep the stars company.'

I was wowed by his stamina. But then I guess Leonardo wouldn't have left behind notebooks and manuscripts totalling over seven thousand pages if he'd spent a third of his time sleeping like the rest of us.

I lay and listened to the small sounds of him working: the swish of his brush against canvas, the creak of his stool, and those lovely little noises he made when he was concentrating, which he was probably hardly aware of himself. There was something comforting about him being there, awake, as I slid into dreams and a shallow sleep.

Some time later I drifted awake. I opened my eyes, aware that the night air was cooler. The night sky above me was now dark, the stars covered by clouds. I became aware that Leonardo had company. I sat up and peered through a slit in the joints of the screen. It was Bramante. Leonardo had clearly finished his painting and now the older man was admiring it. His eyes were like stars; he knew he was on to a good thing.

'I'm glad I dropped by to see how you were doing – this is simply spectacular,' he cried.

'Sssh,' Leonardo whispered. 'Da Liza is sleeping.'

I felt chuffed at the passion, the protective note in his voice.

'And how is da Liza?' Bramante whispered. 'Proving to be a prodigy?' His voice was barbed, teasing and patronising.

Bloody cheek, I thought. I waited for Leonardo to defend me and declare I was the best painter since, well, Leonardo. But he merely let out a long, long sigh and said, 'Oh dear. Oh dear. Oh *dear*. He has the face of an angel. His heart is sweet as honey. But his painting is akin to a donkey's. A blind donkey's.'

I tingled with outrage. OK, so I was never going to be a real Leonardo, but come on, I had been on Tony Hart.

'Well, just keep him on and let him mix your paints if he charms you so,' Bramante said. His tone was paternal now, tender and affectionate with amusement.

'I cannot afford to. I have all these bills to pay, paints to purchase. If I have an apprentice, he must get commissions, it is as simple as that. Unless a miracle happens and it rains money from heaven, I shall have to let him go.'

iii) A patron

The following day was a Big Day. We were going to the court of Duke Ludovico Sforza, whom Leonardo longed to enlist as his main patron.

We spent the morning getting dressed in our most elegant gear. Leonardo was great fun in that respect. He had a genuine love for clothes; being with him was just like going shopping with my sister. He insisted on lending me a new tunic and hose and sent me to change behind the screen, trying on different outfits in mauve, fuchsia and emerald green. The only thing that made me nervous was the bandage wrapped around my breasts. It was beginning to fray, and once I even glanced down to see one had popped out and was swelling beneath my tunic, but luckily Leonardo didn't notice before I dashed behind the screen.

106

Leonardo himself put on his favourite pink tunic, a fur-lined coat and boots made from Cordova leather.

'Now,' he said, 'I must just scent my hands.'

I had learnt by now that this was one of Leonardo's most fastidious habits: he liked to dip his hands in rosewater and then rub lavender oil into them. As I watched him affectionately, I felt my heart screw up into a ball of sadness. I didn't want to be sent home. It wasn't even that I wanted to seduce Leonardo any more, though I was certainly aching for his kisses; I just liked hanging out with him.

As though sharing my thoughts, Leonardo turned and gave me a poignant glance. Then he sighed and said, 'Here, try the blue tunic again. You do look so utterly ravishing in it, my dear boy . . .'

In the early afternoon we set off for Duke Ludovico's. I was carrying a saddlebag containing a notebook and a prospectus. I noticed that Leonardo seemed nervous. He shoved his hands in his pockets, and his step became bouncy to the point of erratic.

'Don't worry,' I reassured him. 'The Duke must know what a wonderful painter you are. I'm sure he'll give you a commission. Perhaps he'll ask you to paint his portrait!'

'It's not a painting that I wish for!' he exclaimed, impatient, almost angry in his nerves. 'I wish to impress the Duke as a manufacturer of tanks, mortars and bombards. In short, I wish to become his chief engineer.'

'You what?' I stammered in disbelief. Yes, in my *Idiot's Guide to da Vinci*, there had been a mention of Leonardo's notebooks, his famous sketches and inventions, so ahead of their time. But the book had suggested they were more of a hobby, like my love for Scrabble, or Anthony's predilection for squash.

'But Leonardo,' I went on, trying to think of a gentle way to tell him he was being an idiot, 'erm – look, you're known as a painter, aren't you?'

'I am not,' said Leonardo stubbornly. 'I left Florence and came to Milan as a musician. On my first entry into court I played the lute. They were impressed, but not that impressed,' he reflected bitterly. 'I will always be a Florentine here, an outsider looking in.'

'But—'

107

'But nothing. I have plans for a magnificent flying machine.' His eyes gleamed with passion. 'The Duke cannot fail to be impressed.'

The Duke's palace was lavish. We were shown into a large hallway where members of the court were drinking and gossiping. Leonardo didn't need to point the Duke out. Aside from the fact that he was sitting on a throne, he exuded an air of power. He was dark-complexioned, with a double chin and a burly physique. A girl was pouring a drink for him and he was flirting with her. As he glanced up at us, I noticed a carnal glint in his bloodshot eyes. I recalled that Leonardo had told me that *sfrozare* meant to force sexually. Clearly the Duke was *Sforza* by name and *sforza* by nature.

'Duke Ludovico Sforza,' one of his henchmen announced, 'this is Leonardo da Vonci . . .'

'Vinci,' Leonardo hissed helpfully.

'. . . da Vinci, and he is here to present his prospectus to you in the hope of acquiring your patronage.'

The court fell silent. Men craned their necks to stare and I overheard several remarks noting Leonardo's beauty. I bit back a smile, inwardly beaming with pride. The girl who had been serving the Duke stared at Leo with wide eyes. The Duke clicked his fingers and she quickly lowered her gaze.

'Well, da Vinci,' said Duke Ludovico, 'artists stream into my court every week asking for commissions. I hear that you impressed the House of the Medici. But our standards are much higher. Tell us what you have to offer.'

I opened the satchel and drew out the prospectus. Leonardo began to read. He spoke quickly, his face flushed, and in his excitement he began to divert from his text.

'. . . I have also designed an architronito, which is a steam-powered cannon made from copper . . .

'. . . We could improve sanitation if we were to build this city on two levels, one for pedestrians, another for the canals, for those dealing in trade and animals, and we *must* build spiral staircases throughout, for people do use the dark corners of square staircases as urinals, which is most unhygienic . . .

'. . . I have an idea for a flying machine, a screwed instrument which will be covered in linen and climb upwards . . .'

I glanced around the court. Several people were whispering and smirking. I looked at the Duke, whose expression had changed from admiring to incredulous.

I tried to nudge Leonardo to indicate that it might be a good time to shut up, but he was totally carried away. His genius had burst into flames and there was no putting it out.

'And an ornithopter, which, using the principles of birds' flight . . .'

'Yes,' the Duke raised a plump hand, 'but—'

'. . . will enable any man to fly as a bird does.'

'Let the Duke speak!' one his advisers interrupted, and Leonardo broke off. I could see that he was shaking slightly.

'You say that you can build a flying machine?' the Duke sneered. 'What, so that we can fly like birds in the sky!' He flapped his arms sarcastically and the court tittered.

'I can prove it. Simply make a wing from paper, mounted on a structure of cane and net twenty *braccia* long—' Leonardo began.

'Leonardo, the only creatures who can fly are the angels. The divine. Those created by God. Do you compare yourself to God?'

Oh shit, I thought. Leonardo wasn't exactly a big fan of the Christian Church. I saw a glint in the Duke's eyes and thought: He knows. He's just baiting him. I turned to Leo, silently pleading with him to be silent, but he shook back his long hair defiantly and said, 'If I can make men fly, and only God can make them fly, then I suppose all that we can conclude is that I am God.'

The silence blazed.

'Only the mad believe they are God. I fear that you do not belong in court but an asylum,' said the Duke curtly. 'You are dismissed.' He waved his hand languidly.

'What?' Leonardo turned pale. 'But . . . but . . .'

Which means I'm fired, I realised, my heart sinking. Leonardo will not be able to afford to keep me. Which means I have to do something. Quick! I gazed at the Duke, who had turned back to his serving girl, and burst out passionately: 'Duke Ludovico, turning down Leonardo will be the greatest mistake you'll ever make! This is a man who, in five hundred years' time, will still be revered as one

109

of the greatest artists who ever lived. Do you want to be remembered in the history books as the man who sacked him?'

Silence. Everyone in the room turned to stare at me. Leonardo looked painfully amused, as though he half wanted to hug me for my bravery and half wanted to slap me for my craziness.

It had been crazy. I was still trembling with anger and nerves. Oh God, why hadn't I thought before I spoke?

'You – you impudent boy! What do you know of Leonardo's future – you're just a snivelling little apprentice! You think that you can predict the future? In five hundred years' time, people will remember me – Duke Ludovico Sforza – as a great ruler, a most compassionate man, a man of wisdom and intellect and imagination.'

As he spoke, four of his guards started to walk towards me. Were they going to throw me out on to the street? Or worse, would I be put in jail? I figured they didn't bother with trials. I also figured that their jails were pretty grim.

Oh God, think of something, Lucy, quick, think.

'As a matter of fact,' I improvised wildly, 'as a matter of fact, I *am* an astrologer!'

Duke Ludovico looked startled. He made a gesture and the guards stopped about a foot away from me.

Of course, if in the twenty-first century you announce that you're an astrologer, people give you weird looks and immediately assume that you're some floaty New Age idiot who believes their horoscope and likes hugging trees.

But in the fifteenth century things were quite different. Astrology was serious stuff. Look at all the references in Shakespeare's plays: the omens in *Macbeth*, the debates in *Julius Caesar*. Many people seriously believed that the macrocosm of the stars influenced the microcosm of men's lives.

'An astrologer, you say?' Duke Ludovico put his head to one side. 'Well, let's see how skilled you really are. Tell me what you know about me, and my future.'

'Well . . . ah . . .'

Nice one, Lucy. Now what do you say?

Leonardo was staring at me with big, scared eyes. The Duke stroked his chin with his forefinger. I trembled, and sweated, and stuttered. The Duke shook his head, let out a '*Pff!*' of frustration, and waved at his guards to take me away. As I backed up, I suddenly felt my *Idiot's Guide to da Vinci*, lodged in my tunic, scrape against my hipbone.

'Wait!' I cried. 'I can tell you your future, in great detail, but first you must allow me to consult my book of magic and . . . er, magery. I have seen portents about you, Duke Ludovico, but now I must consult my sacred text to interpret them.'

The Duke frowned suspiciously, then nodded, with a dubious sneer on his face, as though relishing a few more moments' entertainment before he threw me in the cells.

Ignoring Leonardo's frantic glances, I went over to a corner of the room and surreptitiously pulled out the book. I hastily flicked through the index, found L for Ludovico, and read the entry.

Tucking the book back into my tunic, I walked grandly back to the centre of the room and turned to face the Duke, trying to compose my features into an expression of profundity and mysticism.

'Duke Ludovico,' I said gravely, 'though you are married to Beatrice, you currently have a lover, a girl you see in secret. She is eighteen years old, and her name is Cecilia. She is about to become pregnant with your child. The portents show that you should commission Leonardo to paint her portrait, clutching her pet ermine.'

Though I have no doubt that many people in the court knew of the Duke's goings-on, they feigned cries of outrage and amazement. Leonardo looked even more frantic.

If the Duke hadn't been so shocked, he might well have managed to bluster and cry, 'Who? Me? With an eighteen-year-old girl? Don't be *ridiculous*!' But he was taken aback and he let slip the fatal words, 'How did you *know*?'

The court fell silent, all eyes on him.

'Well,' he blustered, 'I admit there is some truth in your words.' The court rippled with gossipy whispers; all eyes turned back to me, no longer ugly with disdain but shining with awe.

'You are right,' said the Duke. I think he was more keen than ever to throw me into jail, but realised he would be rather unpopular if he did so. With a certain amount of effort, he assumed a graceful smile and said, 'Signor da Liza, I would like to make you my official astrologer. From now on you can do my readings on a daily basis.'

Oh God, no, I thought wildly, you've only a small entry in *The Idiot's Guide to da Vinci*. I'll soon run out of ammunition.

'I cannot,' I said hastily, 'for I am committed to working with Leonardo. I am his apprentice; this is my calling.' Then, seeing the Duke's face, I said quickly, 'But perhaps I could, from time to time, give you a reading, and in the mean time I can see in the stars that it is most important that you give Leonardo a *very* large commission for painting *Lady with an Ermine*.'

Back at the studio, Leonardo and I whooped and hugged and kissed in glee. We had a big celebration and got madly drunk. Leonardo, blushing a little, offered to play his lute. It was beautiful, like listening to some exotic, exquisite bird singing the start of a new morning. I tried to have a go, but I was too blurry with drink and my efforts made Leonardo giggle.

Finally we ended up snuggled up on the pallet, soft and dreamy together, my head lolling sleepily against Leonardo's shoulder.

'Look at the light as it withdraws up the walls and creeps back into the night,' he said softly. 'I'm fascinated by different types of light. I must write it down in my notebook – but I'm too drunk.' He giggled, and then became serious again. 'I like the quality of light when it's constrained and falls through a window, but there is nothing more dazzling than the light out in the countryside, when it is utterly free and only falls through the clouds, those wispy windows in the sky. I like the percussion of light. I think that is the right way to describe it . . . the way it hits an object and then fractures into light and shadow over it. Then there is the light which is spiritual – it illuminates the divine within. You see, I am not so sacrilegious as they all think. It's just that I prefer not to find God in a church but in the beauty of everyday—'

Perhaps it was the drink, but I found tears welling up in my eyes.

'*Mia ragazzo*, are you all right?' he asked tenderly.

'It's just – you reminded me then of someone I once loved.' For some reason I had started thinking about my first night with Anthony and the video he had showed me of the dawn, and I had

112

felt inexplicably moved. 'His name was Anthony ...' I saw something flicker in Leonardo's eyes and added hastily, 'I meant Antonia, of course.' I laughed, drying my eyes. 'I'm drunk.'

'Of course,' Leonardo said, but there was a wry smile in his voice.

My disguise was starting to slip. I just about got away with that faux pas, but a few days later I made an impossible blunder.

iv) The Lady with an Ermine

The following week we went to Duke Ludovico's palace to begin work on *Lady with an Ermine*. We were taken into a large room, the walls adorned with tapestries. There we waited as ten minutes, fifteen minutes, twenty minutes passed. The ermine's claws scuttled in agitation against the cage. Leonardo became impatient and was just muttering that the Duke could go *sfrozare* himself, when Cecilia entered. She was followed by a bored-looking male guard.

The moment I saw her, I cursed myself.

Over and over and over.

She was beautiful. Tall and willowy, with luxuriant brown hair that she wore pinned back from her elegant face. Her skin was so translucent it looked as though it had been laid over her face like finest tissue paper, highlighting an exquisite map of blue veins beneath; her features were so refined they looked as though they had been sculpted by Michelangelo. Her blue eyes were shrewd and she carried about her a calm, resigned air which made her seem much more mature than her eighteen years.

As Leonardo came forward and bowed, she smiled. The guard frowned.

'Erm, this is Benedetto Dei, Ludovico's right-hand man,' she said.

Translation: *I'm young and female and you're young and male, and there's no way the Duke is going to leave us alone together.*

'And I see your apprentice has joined us.' She nodded at me shyly.

113

'Yes,' said Leonardo. 'He'll be sketching you too, and learning from me, if that's all right.'

'Of course.'

Several rather tedious hours passed as Leonardo set up the lighting with his usual fastidiousness, but Cecilia was very patient. The ermine was released from its cage and she seemed pleased to hold it, petting it lovingly. As Leonardo began working, I found myself biting my pencil in agitation. I was convinced that though Leonardo could do nothing with her in the flesh, he was making love to her in his mind; every stroke of his pencil seemed to vibrate across the page like a frustrated caress.

And I'd been *so* close to seducing him. Surreptitiously, I consulted *The Idiot's Guide to da Vinci* and discovered that *The Lady with an Ermine* took two bloody years. Jesus. I couldn't hang around for that long!

I felt black with despair. Maybe this whole time machine thing was a joke. After all, Byron had only ended up hurting me, and now it looked as though I was in a case of unrequited passion. Perhaps these escapades were doing me more harm than good . . .

When the session had ended, Cecilia left, thanking us both, and Leo looked over my sketches.

'I think your sense of perspective needs work,' he remarked. Seeing my sulky face, he chided me. 'Come, come, I studied for years as an apprentice with Verrocchio before I developed my skills.'

I couldn't help it. I burst out: 'She's very attractive, isn't she?'

'Is she?' Leonardo asked. He looked genuinely surprised. 'Beautiful, yes. I had not considered if she was attractive.'

I felt relieved but confused. Was Leonardo being kind or was he just blind?

The week passed. I watched Leonardo intently as he painted Cecilia, but it was impossible to gauge him. I'd always imagined that he would work with hunched-up shoulders and a frown, but he was very relaxed, almost foppish, his pencil spooling easily across the page, brush dabbing lightly. Then I watched Cecilia. After a while I began to realise that the longing in her eyes was one of poignancy, not love. I consulted my book again and read that after giving birth to the Duke's son, she was soon discarded and married off to Count Lodovico Bergamini. After that, I felt a little sorry for her. Women in the fifteenth century were just birds locked in cages. I had made the right decision to come here as a man, I thought, and yet how was I ever going to get Leonardo's attention, his attraction, whilst he thought I was a *ragazzo*? But if he realised I was a woman, would I not instantly be put into a cage myself; would he not immediately view me as a member of the weaker, inferior sex, as all men did in this century; someone to be tamed, caught, seduced, but not respected?

And then Cecilia fell ill with a cold and we could not paint her. Leonardo was restless. He suggested we go down to the market to buy some birds and set them free – one of his favourite pastimes. We went to an alley and let them out and watched them swoop and soar across the sky. Leonardo turned to me breathlessly, his eyes shining, and said, 'I have decided. The time has come. I must paint you. I have been wanting to ask you for so long. I must paint you.'

'You want to paint – me?'

Leonardo took a lock of my hair and curled it around his forefinger, smiling. 'I want to paint you because I want to immortalise your beauty.'

My God, I thought. *My God, my God, my God*. Leonardo da Vinci – the world's greatest painter and all-round genius – fancies me!

Back in his studio, Leonardo set up the lighting and the wooden panel to paint on swiftly. The impatience, the agitation in his gestures – he knocked over several brushes and a paint mix in his hurry – created a deliciously electric frisson in the air. Then, his face flushed, he suggested that I go behind the screen and prepare myself.

'I'm sorry?' I asked.

'Well, I thought . . .' He blushed slightly. 'I felt I could only do justice to the beauty of your form if you were nude, *mia caro ragazzo*.'

'Oh, right,' I blustered, suddenly turning all British in my shock. 'Well. Great. Fab.'

I slipped behind the screen and pulled off my tunic joyfully, shaking with desire. Oh God, this was going to be great. Then I looked down at my chest and let out a cry.

Oh Lucy, how could you have been so stupid? Leo can't paint you nude. Because you have BREASTS, Lucy. They may not be very large ones, but they're still unmistakably female.

I slid down into a heap, locked into a ball of sorrow, my face pressed against my knees. It was hopeless. The best thing to do would be to just go home. This was the very spot where the time machine had deposited me, so all I had to do was will it back and escape right this minute.

Unless . . .

I stopped panicking and started thinking a little more logically. The whole point of my plan had been, after all, to reveal my true identity, for all my doubts about his reaction. Just not *quite* so blatantly: I'd hoped to sidle up to him and confess my femininity rather than revealing my private parts. But didn't Leonardo suspect something anyway? I remembered the glint in his eye when I told him about Anthony. Surely he was playing games too, dropping hints so that I could feel safe about coming out of the closet?

'Are you ready yet, *caro*?' Leonardo called.

'Nearly,' I called back.

Before I could lose my nerve, I decided to take the plunge. I tore off my clothes. I unravelled the bandages, letting my breasts spring gloriously free. I paused, feeling bashful, and pulled my hair over my breasts. Then I muttered a quick prayer and walked out into the room.

Leonardo looked up.

There was a tick-tack-clattering noise as his paintbrush hit the floor.

Finally I summoned the courage to look into his eyes.

Oh dear, I thought, it doesn't seem as if he secretly guessed you were a woman after all. Actually, I'd say he probably didn't have a clue.

In terror, I ran back behind the screen.

'Wait!' Leonardo called. 'Come back!'

'No.'

'Please.'

116

'No.'

'Why not?'

'Because you're quite obviously totally repulsed by me!'

'I admit, it did come as a bit of a surprise, yes.'

'You didn't suspect I was really a woman?'

'No.'

I frowned.

'Not even when I said that I had once loved a man called Anthony?'

Silence.

'Why did you lie to me?' he asked.

'Because it was the only way I could get close to you. Women aren't allowed to do anything in this cen . . . in this place. Look at Cecilia.'

'True,' Leonardo sighed. 'I sometimes wonder whether perhaps women are as intelligent as men and ought to be able to have the same rights as we do.'

'Good theory,' I muttered.

Another silence.

'So, must I leave?'

'You can stay on one condition.'

'Yes?'

'Come out from that screen now. And keep your clothes off.'

I edged out, my hands fluttering over my body, my cheeks burning hotter than ever, my head bowed miserably. Then I slowly dragged my eyes up to his, and I saw the fondness in his gaze and the smile tugging at his lips. In my relief I flew at him, and he gave me a huge hug, and I muttered, 'Sorry,' over and over again. Leonardo rubbed his cheek against mine and sighed that I was forgiven.

'But,' he said, drawing back, 'I'm afraid you can't stay here. I can let you be here another night, but after that . . . it would be . . . Look, when I was in Florence, I suffered something of a scandal. I don't want to talk about it, but I don't want another one here. I came to Milan to make my mark.'

'I guess the Duke wouldn't be too happy if he found out his astrologer was a woman,' I muttered meekly.

Leonardo looked deep into my eyes. 'Knowing the Duke,' he

said, 'he'd probably ask you to examine his stars in great depth in his bedchamber!' and we both laughed.

And then looked at each other.

And then I did something totally brazen. Time was running out, and I craved him so; craved the softness of his hair and skin, longed to feel it against mine. It would be different to Byron, I told myself; Byron's heart was cruel, but Leo's was tender. I leaned up on tiptoe, moved in close. He stared down at me, his expression unreadable. His breath mingled with mine, warm and inviting. I pressed my lips against his. I closed my eyes. His lips were cool and delicious. For a moment I felt him respond, and then—

He pushed me away harshly.

I felt utterly mortified. I was about to dive behind the screen again, but Leonardo grabbed my hand and pulled me down on to the pallet, next to him.

Now what? I stared at his handsome profile, but he looked down at his knees, his face shadowed.

'What's your real name?' he asked.

'Lucy.'

'Lucy,' said Leonardo, rolling my name on his tongue. 'Lucy, I want to tell you a story. When I was twenty-three years old, I was arrested.'

'You were?' I was perplexed; there had definitely been no mention of any arrest in *The Idiot's Guide to da Vinci*.

'What happened was this: an anonymous person put a denunciation into one of the *tamburi* in Florence. *Tamburi* are the holes of truth, as you know. It declared that a seventeen-year-old boy, Jacopo Saltarelli, had been sodomised by four different men. I was named as one of them. It was a terrible scandal; it was one of the reasons I ran from Florence. We all had to attend court, and to my relief it was thrown out. But the fact of the matter is, Lucy, that the charge was true. Jacopo was my lover.'

'Oh my God!' It was sinking in slowly. 'So you're . . . you're . . .'

'*Omosessuale*,' said Leonardo.

'And women don't do anything for you at all?' I cried, my cheeks scarlet with humiliation.

Leonardo ran his eyes over my body and shook his head.

'I'm afraid even your beauty doesn't make me feel I could—'

'You're just being charming!' I cried, jumping to my feet.

'No, Lucy, I'm not!' he replied, jumping up too. 'In fact, I'd still love to paint you.'

'NO!' I cried, folding my arms. I just wanted to yank on my clothes and run away.

'Please – I'd like to have it as a memento of our time together, of everything we've shared. And just because we're not going to make love, it doesn't mean we don't have something special, Lucy! As it happens, I don't think sex is that important anyway,' he added, with a note of disgust in his voice that surprised me. 'Everywhere I go, I see sex poisoning people's minds, blurring their judgement, drawing them from the divine to the debased. Friendship is so much more simple. I've had so many good times with you, Lucy – when we defied the Duke, when we got drunk, when we set those birds free. I feel closer to you than anyone . . .' Leonardo trailed off, his eyes hooded with hurt, hands dangling awkwardly by his sides.

I sighed and smiled shakily.

'You're right,' I said softly. 'Of course you're right.'

'So I can paint you?' Leonardo asked.

'Yes.'

'And I can lend you a dress. I have one, in the back, from another portrait I did . . . Let me go and find it . . .'

It was such a relief to be a woman again, to be free of my sweaty tunic and feel a cool breeze about my legs. The dress was lovely – dark blue and very simple, with flowing sleeves and a matching silk shawl to draw over the top.

As Leonardo sketched me, he kept breaking off from time to time and cocking his head to one side, pursing his lips playfully and chiding me to 'Smile, dear Lucy, try to be happy.' I tried, I did try. But the intensity of his artistic gaze on me, the force of his charisma, only filled me with regret again. The confusion of pleasure and pain in my heart fought over my lips, turning them up and down until I was convinced the tension of comedy and tragedy in my expression would result in a very odd picture.

Several hours had passed and Leonardo had begun to lay down a coat of oils. At last he looked at me and sighed and said, 'It's not finished, but come on, sulky. Come and see how beautiful you look.'

'OK.' Though I dragged myself up to the canvas, I have to admit that I was secretly excited. Hopefully he would have airbrushed out my wrinkles, softened my features with his sfumato technique and added a halo to my head.

And then I saw it.

My jaw dropped. I opened my mouth to say something, but the words never even made it to my throat; instead they pounded inside my heart in shock.

'I know it doesn't look totally like you. I just wanted an impression of you, of what it has felt like to know you. I wanted to capture your sense of mystery. And I've made you slightly androgynous.' He turned to me, nudging me gently, waiting for me to respond. 'You know – to capture the fact that your little game . . .'

'It's incredible,' I said at last. Suddenly I wished Anthony was here. And my parents. And my sister. And the bitch who'd bullied me at school. And anyone I'd ever met.

'Guess what I'm going to call it.'

'What?'

'Well, since your surname is Liza and you have turned out to be a *miss* rather than a mister, I thought *Mona Liza* would be perfect . . .'

I was about to erupt into shocked laughter when Leonardo's eyes widened and he put a hand on my wrist. We heard the sound of approaching footsteps, followed by an excited rapping at the door. Before Leonardo could shout 'Wait!' Bramante had burst in, his face flushed pink with excitement.

'Leonardo, I have amazing news. That old dog Michelangelo has been commissioned to— Oh . . .' He stopped short, eyeing my dress in confusion. Then his unfocused gaze pinpointed my breasts. Instantly my hands flew up, only highlighting their reality. Then Bramante saw the picture. Leonardo leapt in front of it, but it was too late: Bramante had twigged.

He didn't shout or make a scene. He just stood very still, and said in a quiet, intense voice, as though I wasn't there: 'I always knew there was something suspicious about him, Leonardo.'

'*Her*,' I corrected him hotly. 'You mean *her*.'

'In two minutes' time, the Duke's men will be here. They have come to fetch . . .' Bramante waved his hand at me, unable to decide on the correct pronoun, '. . . to take him, or her, back to the Duke's palace to read the Duke's fortune. She . . . he . . . has been promising for days to read it and now the Duke is red-hot with impatience.'

'Let them,' said Leonardo defiantly. He wrapped a protective arm around me.

'But he – she – is a woman.'

'Really?' Leonardo mocked him.

'Women,' Bramante stamped his foot, 'have their place in God's world, and it is not in an artist's studio, or a Duke's palace! She belongs in a kitchen or a nursery! She must leave, Leonardo. Now. For your sake.'

'Leonardo, he's right. I must go back,' I cried. I turned and gave him a tight hug. 'I'm going to miss you.'

As Leonardo hugged me back tightly, I saw the jealousy on Bramante's face, and it was then I understood the true nature of his feelings for Leonardo. I frowned and closed my eyes, shutting him out, lost in the warmth of Leonardo's affectionate embrace.

'I'm going to miss you too,' Leonardo sighed. 'My dear, wonderful Mona Liza.'

'Quick!' Bramante had run to the door and was peering out. 'Hurry – take her out through the back.'

'There is no back door,' Leonardo panicked.

'It's OK,' I cried. 'Bramante – if you can just hold them off for two minutes, I can make my escape.'

'You can?' Leonardo asked.

'D'you remember your beloved flying machine idea? Well, come and take a look at the real thing!' I cried. I grabbed his hand and pulled him behind the screen. He glanced at me in bewilderment, and then at the door.

'Lucy,' he warned me, 'you'd better hurry.'

'OK, OK. Just close your eyes and be with me. Then open them slowly . . .'

I could feel Leonardo's heartbeat pounding into my palm and shivering up my arm, echoing in my heart as I willed the time machine to take me away. I was just opening my eyes when I heard Leonardo gasp and his palm press furiously against mine. Just as I had hoped, he could share my sight and see the machine too. He looked down at me and cried out in wonder, 'Who are you?'

Then we heard the door fly open.

'Leonardo has a woman in here!' Bramante was saying. 'She fooled the Duke. She's behind the screen – arrest her!'

Bramante had betrayed me!

Leonardo didn't care about the guards. His eyes like moons, he was touching the machine with trembling hands. I slid inside and punched in the date. I blew Leonardo one last kiss, and then the machine shimmered and soared and the last thing I saw was Bramante's stunned expression and Leonardo's ecstatic one as he realised his flying machines might work in ways he had never fathomed . . .

v) Anthony again

'Would you like to come to the opera?'

I was on my lunch break, sitting on the steps of the National Gallery, despondently throwing breadcrumbs at pigeons. Anthony had cheered me up with a call that came out of the blue.

'Well, I was planning to give Emma a call,' I said uncertainly.

'Emma?'

'You remember Emma! She was my best friend. I've lost touch with her over the past few months. Mind you . . . I've never been to the opera before.'

'I know you haven't. That's why I'm asking.'

'What opera is it?'

'*Madame Butterfly*.'

'Hang on.' I laughed suspiciously. 'Don't you have that girl from the dating agency to go with?'

'Er, well . . . yes. OK, I was going to take her,' Anthony admitted. 'But she dropped out, and it seems such a waste, and please don't think you're second best or anything, Lucy. In fact, when I tell you about this girl and the date we had, I think you're going to laugh your head off! It was *such* a total disaster.'

'What! Oh God, tell me now,' I begged him.

'Can't – I have a work deadline.'

'*Anthony!*'

'Lucy, I can't. I'll see you tonight, then?'

'Sure, I can see Emma another time.'

'Pick you up at six, OK?'

'OK.' I switched off my mobile and went back into the gallery with a smile on my face.

A minute later, the smile disappeared when I noticed a group of Texans eyeing up Leonardo's *Virgin of the Rocks*.

'Well, it really isn't all that amazing, is it?' said one.

'Nah, I prefer Warhol and those Marilyn pictures.'

'I mean, I just think da Vinci is totally overrated. Take the *Mona Lisa*. She might look mysterious, but there's no denying she's a bit of a dog.'

'*Excuse me*.' I flounced up to them, 'Don't you dare be rude about Leo's picture. He spent years on that, you know, and his apprentice took ages to mix all those charcoals, and I think you're being bloody ungrateful.'

The tourists gave me bewildered looks. My supervisor gave me a very stern look.

'Lucy, a word in my office, please,' she said.

Oh God, I thought, here we go again.

In the end, they didn't fire me, I just got a warning. Though I wouldn't have cared if they had sacked me, to be honest. I was thoroughly fed up. I'd even called up the publishers of *The Idiot's Guide to da Vinci* and demanded to know why they'd failed to mention that Leo was gay. They pointed out that their guide was aimed at kids and they felt sodomy was an unsuitable subject. I threatened to sue them. I think they thought I was insane, but then they hadn't just wasted three weeks in 1482 without so much as a snog.

So all in all, I was glad to be going to the opera. After I'd returned from 1813, I'd found myself appreciating the little things in life. But coming back from the Renaissance to 2005 had left me shell-shocked. The quality of light in Italy had been dazzling, streaming pure and unpolluted from the clouds, caressing the ancient beauty of its buildings, dancing along bridges and leaping over water. In London it seemed as though the sun was a ball of grey, its rays purposefully gloomy, highlighting ugliness everywhere: buildings caked with grime, smeary windows, streets decorated with birdshit. I couldn't enjoy *EastEnders* any more; I longed for the wit and grace of the Milanese court. And so, gradually over the last week, I'd found myself sinking into a vague depression. I remember a friend of mine, who was a great fan of Austen, saying, 'Lucy, I think I was born in the wrong century.' I'd thought her mad at the time, but now I understood. I felt I belonged in 1482.

Most of all, I missed Leonardo. I wished I'd given him instead of bloody Byron my mobile. Every time I saw a replica of the *Mona Lisa* I'd smile a secret smile, and then my heart would twist with longing for my dear friend.

'So, I have to tell you about the girl from the dating site. Her name was Matilda, and she *said* she was thirty-two—' Anthony was saying, but I cut him off. For he'd just led me into an individual box overlooking the sweep of stage, with red velvet-cushioned seats.

'We're in *here*? Our own box?'

'Yup.'

'Oh, Anthony, this is gorgeous.' I frowned and nudged him playfully. 'When we were going out, you never took me anywhere so lavish.'

'I certainly did! I took you to The House,' he joked painfully, and we both winced. 'Anyway – Matilda.'

'OK, Matilda,' I said. 'Tell me everything.'

'Well,' said Anthony, 'the first time we were supposed to meet, she cancelled at the last minute. Anyway, we rearranged and this time we did meet up, at the Häagen-Dazs café in Leicester Square. The moment I saw her, I thought she was really pretty, though she was plastered with make-up.'

'Really?' I asked in a high voice.

'But I thought to myself, she doesn't look thirty-two – more like a twenty-year-old in college. So we go in and she gets me to order her a double choc-brownie sundae and she sits there licking it off the spoon like some sort of Lolita, and then she lets slip that she's in her second year of GCSEs.'

'No!'

'Yes! She was only fourteen! She burst into tears – it turned out she'd been boasting to all her schoolfriends about having an older man and for the first time she was thought of as cool. Anyway, I made sure she got home safely and then made her promise never to visit a dating site again. I mean, imagine if some perve had replied to her.'

'Anthony, you're such a gentleman,' I said, with affection. 'But, you have to keep going. I mean, OK, you've had a disappointment, but there must be loads of other women on the site.'

Anthony snorted. I couldn't help feeling secretly pleased, and then confused, and then selfish: I wanted to have Anthony to myself, and yet at the same time I didn't want to commit to him.

Before I could puzzle any more, the lights dimmed and it was time for me to lose my opera virginity.

It was amazing. I felt as though each voice poured into my heart and swelled it with emotion. Halfway through, I was struggling not to cry when I turned and saw a tear leaking out of Anthony's eye. He brushed it away fiercely, trying to look all manly, and I smiled and took his hand, and he squeezed back tightly. I looked down at the audience, and then at the stage, and then at Anthony again, and suddenly I felt a sense of relief and belonging. I am glad to be here, in 2005, I thought. There is art and beauty, and although we might have to look a little harder for it than people did in 1482, it is here.

Afterwards, we went back to my flat and Anthony told me the story behind *Madame Butterfly* – how it had evolved from a short story penned by a Victorian writer, John Luther Long, to Puccini's masterpiece, and on to our most modern interpretation, *Miss Saigon*. It was silly: just because he worked in computing, I kept forgetting that he did have an artistic side too. As he spoke, the passionate excitement in his voice reminded me of Leonardo.

We ended up talking all night, and drinking hot chocolate and putting the world to rights. It was three a.m. by the time we found ourselves yawning too much to speak, and Anthony retired to nap on the sofa and I collapsed into bed. As I drifted off I felt a new-found happiness fluttering in my heart. I might have lost Leonardo, but I had a firm friend in Anthony.

Chapter Four

Ovid

Et mihi cedet amor.
(Love too shall yield to me.)

OVID

i) On not wanting to have babies

'Isn't it a beautiful day?' Anthony sighed.

It was. Blue skies, the sun splashing about in a joyful fountain, shimmering off trees, sparkling on the water.

My temporary post at the gallery had finished so I was now doing a temping job whilst I searched for a more meaningful occupation, and Anthony had offered to help assuage my boredom by suggesting a picnic during my lunch hour.

We sat down under the cool, spreading shade of an oak tree. We laid out a cloth and napkins and then spread out our feast. I had brought a tub of salad, mixed dips and Anthony's favourite: hummus. He had brought crusty French bread and Brie and – oh! – fresh strawberries with a pot of double cream for dunking! My favourite!

'Anthony, you angel, you angel!' I gave him a mini sideways hug. 'That's fabulous!'

We piled into the food, munching and crunching and tasting and lip-licking with sighs of pleasure.

'Sod it,' said Anthony, patting the slight curve of his stomach. 'Now we really will have to diet. It'll be boot-camp time.' He grinned at me mischievously and I smiled back. Whenever we had decided to go on a diet, Anthony had always been the more enthusiastic. In fact, he had used it as an excuse to playfully torment me. I remembered ghastly mornings when he had literally dragged me out of bed, kicking and screaming, and thrust me out on to the street for a jog. In revenge, I had promised to cook him a healthy meal and served him a plate with a single pea on it. Funny, I thought with a smile, how when we were most in love we were most mean to each other. It was only when things started to go wrong between us that we started resorting to romantic dinners. Candles and napkin rings were a sure sign of trouble.

We finished off our picnic and, happily complaining that our stomachs were bursting, lay down in the grass. It was lovely and peaceful and sleepy lying there, feeling the sun dapple soft rays through the trees, listening to the hum of bees and dragonflies and people laughing and talking and the childhood chime of an ice-cream van. And yet it felt strange too. In the past we had always finished our picnics lying cuddled up. Often we would read a book or a magazine together, my head resting in the crook of his shoulder, sighing impatiently to tease him because I was a faster reader than him. Being together now felt both very intimate and very distant. There was a joy in being together, and yet a sense of nakedness.

'WAAAAHHHHHHHHH!'

I sat bolt upright with a jolt.

A mum had brought a gaggle of her kids over for a picnic under the tree next to us. Seeing my reaction, she sent me an apologetic glance and then turned back to her hysterical three-year-old: 'Hester, will you give Dylan back his soldier!'

'Let's move,' I said, hastily packing up the picnic basket.

'Move? Do we have to? She'll be offended,' Anthony whispered, giving the mother a poignant glance.

'Don't be silly! She'll be used to it with those ... those monsters!'

Anthony looked me and shook his head.

'Monsters? You don't have a maternal bone in your body, do you?' he said, and though his tone was teasing, it was slightly chiding too.

I glared at him and carried on packing up, feeling stung. As we turned to go, one of the kids decided to fling himself down in front of Anthony. Anthony chuckled.

'Hi there, little fellow.' He picked him up and set him back on his feet. While the mother thanked him profusely, I tried not to sulk.

As we walked under the glare of the hot sun, I couldn't help smarting at Anthony's words. He had never once brought up the issue of kids when we were going out; there had been an unspoken pact between us that we just weren't ready.

OK, so I *didn't* have a maternal bone in my body. Or if I did, it was buried rather deep and might well require a huge spade to locate it. So I didn't go all ga-ga over babies, but who could blame me? I knew from Sally what hard work children were. Had the mother back there been sitting there with a bright smile on her face, enjoying the sun? No, she'd been completely harassed. God, the way Anthony had said it, it was as though I was some dried-up, evil, boring career girl who didn't care for children at all. Huh.

'I just need to pop into Waterstone's,' he said as we headed out of the park.

'Sure,' I said, smoothing the sulky edge out of my voice and putting on a smile.

The moment we entered the shop, however, I noticed something rather shifty about him. I could tell he had a book in mind that he wanted to buy. I let him wander off and then tiptoed up behind him.

Anthony jumped.

And blushed.

'Anthony, what is this?' I cried, grabbing for the book. He scrabbled to yank it back, but I tickled him, provoking a hiss of fury; Anthony was the most ticklish person I knew, so it wasn't very fair play. Then I saw the cover. 'Oh my God.' Suddenly everything fell into place. 'You're not really going to spend your hard-earned cash on *Men Are From Mars, Women Are from Venus*?'

I was being mean, I knew, but I was still a little prickly from his earlier comment. Now I had a weapon to wield back at him.

Anthony looked sheepish. Then defiant.

'Well, I know you've always scoffed at this sort of thing, Lucy, but millions of people have been helped by it.'

'You don't need books, Anthony. Just be natural.'

'Well, that's all very well, but I think I do. All this stuff is complicated if you're a bloke. We don't know whether to be a new man and please you, or a real man and act like a dick. The other day I opened a door for a woman and she shot me a furious glance as though I was being a total pig, when I was just trying to be polite. I mean, it was easier in the past, when men were men and women were women. Yes, and before you have a go at me, Lucy, I know women weren't happy back then. But they don't seem that happy now either, and neither do men, so we still haven't got it right yet, you know. Dating guides are a twenty-first-century invention, the ultimate sign that we've made life too complicated.'

'Rubbish,' I said. 'The sexes have always had a tough time, ever since we got booted out of Eden. There were always books about. Come on. I'll show you.'

He raised a suspicious eyebrow but let me lead him over to the poetry section. Here was the book I was looking for! I pulled it out and stared at the cover for a minute. Instantly, memories of Latin classes flooded my mind: the smell of chalk dust, dog-eared textbooks, and the waspish voice of my terrifying teacher repeating: '*Amo, amare, ama*,' in a voice that inspired quite the opposite emotion.

'*Ars Amatoria*,' Anthony said, peering over my shoulder.

'Ovid was a great Roman poet. He wrote this around one BC . . .' I broke off, seeing Anthony give me a funny, affectionate look.

'What?'

'No. It's just you're such a know-it-all, Lucy. Trust you to know when the first ever dating guide was created. Anyway, what tips did Ovid give then?'

'I can't remember – I haven't read it for a good ten years. I remember him saying something like "women are like fish who need to be caught in nets". Oh, and he had some useful tips for what to do if you're at the chariot races and the women are wearing togas. He recommended that blokes should pretend to drop something so they could bend down and get a good look at a woman's ankles.'

'Their *ankles*?'

'Ankles were considered very erotic. I think togas had to come to the floor generally, so it was rather racy to show them off.'

'Well, thanks for that, Luce. I'll remember it when I go to the amphitheatre tonight. Ovid . . .' Anthony savoured his name like a sweet. 'It's very sensual, isn't it? Ovid. Like ovulate . . .'

'Hey, that's interesting,' I said, my imagination hooked. I smiled at him affectionately; I loved the way he had little insights about everything.

'Anyway, Lucy, how about you get *Ars* and I get *Mars* and then in a week's time we swap?'

I sighed and was about to agree when Anthony said quickly, casually, 'You pay for them both and I'll give you the money, OK? I mean, that's quickest.' He checked his watch. 'I have to get back.'

'Oh, really?' I bit back a smile; I knew Anthony too well. He didn't want to look like a girly-wurly buying a book about

132

relationships. Pulling a tenner out of his wallet, he caught me looking at him with a teasing smile and he grinned back with a squirmy one.

I walked up to the till while Anthony drifted over to the door.

And that was when the trouble started.

The guy behind the till was a handsome Australian with curly chestnut hair and laughter-creased eyes. He viewed my choices with interest; now it was my turn to cringe.

'I'm just buying it for a friend,' I said quickly.

He grinned and said, 'Oh, I think it's a good read. It's been useful knowing I'm a rubber band, you know, and that's why I have secret cravings to climb into the filing cabinet.'

A man with a sense of irony and silliness – cool. We started chatting as I passed over the money, and really, we'd only been talking for a few minutes when Anthony called over, 'Lucy?' I felt a prickle of annoyance. It was just the way he said it. The intonation in his voice. It was just like India all over again. Like he was my father, telling me off. The guy behind the till folded his arms, as if to say, 'Oh, so you have a boyfriend, and he's clearly the possessive type.' I felt a flush creep up my face and called over, 'In a minute.'

'I don't have a minute.' Anthony suddenly came stalking up. 'I need my book *now.* I have to get back to work, OK?' He grabbed a book out of the bag and went storming out. I looked in and realised he'd taken the wrong one.

'*Anthony!*' I said an apologetic goodbye to the shop assistant and went dashing out onto the street after him. '*Anthony!*'

He spun round to look at me.

'What the hell is the matter with you? This is just like . . .' *India,* I said silently, but couldn't quite bring myself to say it. The holiday from hell that we had shared a year or so ago, where Anthony had acted like he might clout any man that so much as blinked at me.

'The matter?' Anthony's eyes were flashing with hurt and rage. 'You dump me and then expect me to hang around whilst you flirt with other men? I mean, for God's sake, Lucy, I do have some feelings, you know.'

'But we're not even going out any more. You don't have any right to behave like this!'

Anthony flinched as though each word was hitting his heart like an arrow. Then he blinked very hard and ran his hand through his hair.

'You're right. I'm sorry. I don't.' And he walked off.

I opened my mouth to call after him, but all that emerged from my shocked lips was a faint *Anthony* . . . I watched him until he was swallowed up by the crowds, then I turned and walked off in the opposite direction.

Later that evening, I went out for a drink with my sister and poured out the whole story.

'Well, it's pretty obvious how Anthony feels about you,' Sally said, flicking back her hair and taking a huge gulp of her G&T. I was quite taken aback by her appearance. She looked as though she had aged ten years, her skin pallid with stress. She let out a long sigh and twisted her wedding ring. I sensed something was up and I knew she wanted me to invite her to tell me, to gently unspool it from her. But in my angst I found myself being selfish. I wanted to talk about me.

Trying to sound casual despite the burning in my cheeks, I asked, 'What d'you think is so obvious?'

'Well, he wants you to get back together, doesn't he? If you ask me, you two need a break from each other. You need time to sort out how you really feel.'

Back home, I lay on my bed and opened the curtains. In my hazy-drunk state, the night-time clouds looked like ancient, ethereal gods traversing the sky, following the stars on a long journey. Sally's words burned in my brain: *He wants you to get back together*. Was she right? Perhaps it was obvious – but that's the trouble with love. It's easy to be a bystander and offer wise words, but when you're in the thick of a hurricane of emotion, what ought to be obvious is the last thing you see.

And as for me, what did I want?

I don't know, I thought, racked with confusion. I don't know. I love being with him, but I also love my newfound freedom. And Anthony's behaviour in the street had reminded me of just how possessive and clingy and jealous he could be. I needed some time out to retreat, to be in my own space.

ii) Silent texting

At nine the next morning, I sent Anthony a text:

Hey, Valmont, how r u? Picked up any 14-yr-olds today?

At ten, I tried a different tack:

Work is dull. I think I may end it all by shoving a stapler up my nose.

At eleven, I resorted to pleading:

I miss you. Plse let's talk. This is silly.

At midday, I finally lashed out:

OK, ignore me then. U're obviously too busy with Lolita.

Childish and petty, I know – but I felt mad.

In the whole time that we'd been together, Anthony hadn't ever ignored me.

Until now.

Bugger him, I thought.

I sent him one more text apologising for the last one and there was still no reply. My heart erupted with anger. I felt as though I actually hated him.

My lunch break came. I went and sat in the park, miserably munching on a limp tuna sandwich, on my own in a sea of happy summer couples. Up to now, I realised, Anthony and I hadn't properly broken up. Yes, we'd stopped sleeping together, but we'd carried on texting, talking and sharing. Our friendship had basically been a diluted form of our relationship, an intimacy without sex.

Now, for the first time since our break-up, I suffered the real pain of it: as though the arrow lodged in my heart that day we'd split up had been snapped off, embedding its tip deep in the centre. For the first time in a long time, I suffered loneliness. Huge loneliness, arching over me like the sky above. I felt like a ghost, as though none of these people in the park could even see me, I was so insubstantial.

I checked my mobile for the fiftieth time and felt tears spring into my eyes.

I just wanted to *speak* to him. I just wanted to be able to call him up and tell him all the little things on my mind.

I was making a start on my packet of crisps when, typically, yesterday's mother appeared again, complete with screaming kids.

'Hester, could you please not fill Dylan's nappy with grass—' She broke off, noticing me with a flicker of apologetic recognition.

OK, I thought, this is fine. I can sit here. I can handle this. I can cope with a bit of childish screaming.

And then I felt angry with myself, for my thoughts were wheeling back to Anthony again, seeking his approval, pretending he was here with me.

Sod him, I thought. I picked myself up and walked away, the screaming fading behind me.

As I made my way back to the office, I wondered what he was doing right now.

Probably back at his stupid dating agency, I decided. Looking for some girl who *loved* babies and wanted to have twenty million of them and drown in nappies for the rest of her life. Well, I hoped they would be happy together.

iii) The playboy of the Roman world

I examined my reflection in the mirror and then consulted the book for the hundredth time . . .

In Roman times, the typical dress of a fashionable woman would be a tunic made from linen dyed with madder roots

136

and secured on to the shoulders with stitches and clasps. On top of this would be draped another cloth known as a *palla*.

Well, I thought, even my local fancy dress shop hadn't been able to come up with a decent Roman costume. In a sudden burst of inspiration, I had decided to opt for the sari I had bought during my trip to India with Anthony. It was made of white cotton rather than linen, but using a good number of safety pins, I had converted it from an eastern to a Roman style.

A Roman woman would cleanse herself at the baths. Then she would apply a moisturising cold cream before putting on her make-up.

For foundation, a layer of white paste would be applied – made from lead, chalk or root. Then a layer of rouge, made from red ochre, would be added.

Hmm. I frowned critically at my reflection. Before putting on my make-up, I had applied a fake tan, convinced my lily-white skin would draw suspicion amongst the Romans. Now my body was the colour of a *Baywatch* actor, while my face looked like a clown's. Still, at least my heavy kohl eye make-up looked good. And while I didn't have any eyeshadow made from saffron, my Rimmel offering wasn't bad, and I had replaced 'a lipsalve tinted with alkanet root and ochre' with a pale Boots 17 lipstick, brushed over with a shiny layer of Vaseline.

Lastly, a Roman woman's hair would be dressed with bone pins and a ribbon.

That had been the tricky bit. The woman in the illustration had teased her hair into tiny curls that wafted gracefully around her ribbon. But I had the type of hair that was impossible to do anything with. For work, I just tied it back; for going out, I had to apply about half a bottle of hairspray to tame it into submission.

I had dug out curling irons from the bottom of my wardrobe and produced a head of satisfying ringlets. But by the time I had attempted to pin them up, they had drooped into tired waves. Then the pins kept bloody falling out – every time I moved I heard a *chink*. Still, I just about looked the part.

Once again, I was about to take an adventure in my time machine. This time I was going to visit Ovid.

Not for a love affair.

My row with Anthony had left me feeling sulky and tired of men. I just wanted to *talk* to someone. I needed to sort out the blur in my head, to help me understand what I really felt about him. My feelings for him were so confused, it wasn't even a case of not seeing the wood for the trees; I couldn't even see the trees, just twigs of confusion, woody whorls of doubt and suffering.

I wanted to talk to someone who knew about men and women and why relationships were so complicated. And while I did have some doubts about Ovid's ability to help me, at least he *thought* he knew his stuff. And heck, he was going to be a lot more entertaining than going to some modern-day counsellor. At least Ovid would be witty, and glamorous, and sexy.

Besides which, the thought of those lovely relaxing Roman baths was also deeply appealing. If the worst came to the worst, at least I could have a makeover and come back beaming with good health.

Famous last words . . .

A roar of voices so loud they nearly deafened me. A cocktail of foreign smells. I tried to separate them out: sand, sweat, blood, meat, excitement. I opened my eyes and found that I was sitting on a hard bench, with a soaring view over an arena. My head swam and a wind blew a faint shower of sand into my eyes. My hands flew up to rub them. Then I reminded myself fiercely: *No, Lucy, DO NOT ruin your eye make-up after spending an hour and a half putting it on.*

I blinked the grit away and finally drank in my surroundings. When I realised where I was, my heart leapt with excitement.

I was sitting in an amphitheatre, facing a sandy arena. There were crowds of people, and across the arena the Emperor was sitting on his throne, all white-bearded and fancy-toga-ed. God, it was like something out of *Gladiator*.

I glanced round. The benches were crowded but not packed; I

was sitting alone on mine. Before getting into the time machine, I had examined several pictures of Ovid. Now, however, it was impossible to recognise him, for all the men looked similar, sporting beards and long, flowing hair, wearing sandals beneath their togas. The women, meanwhile, seemed to have all dyed their hair a similar shade of burnished red-gold, curled in ringlets that fell about their shoulders, or pinned up on their heads in tiers of curls. Many were carrying parasols to protect themselves from the burning sun; some waved fans made of peacock feathers. My book hadn't mentioned that touch – damn. Now I was going to roast.

Oh well, I thought, if I can't spot Ovid I may as well just enjoy the games for now.

The arena below was empty and the crowd was hungry for blood. They stamped their feet and took up a refrain.

Anthony had once taken me to a football match. He'd taken a while to adjust to footie after being a big baseball fan back home and he'd decided the team he wanted to support was Manchester United (I suspect because Beckham was the only player the Americans have ever heard of). Now, sitting in the arena, I suffered a sense of déjà vu. It's strange, I thought, for one amused moment, how history never really changes. Yes, the details do but not the fundamentals. Dress everyone in jeans, exchange sand for grass and it could be 2005.

A man came stumbling into the arena. He certainly didn't bear any resemblance to Russell Crowe; he was as scrawny as a sparrow. As a lion came roaring in to fight him, I felt sorry for him. He didn't have a chance.

Nobody else seemed to feel any sympathy, though. Their cries were disturbingly barbaric.

'Excuse me, may I sit here?'

I glanced up, shielding my eyes from the dazzle of the sun.

'Um, yes,' I smiled.

As the man sat down next to me, I felt a jolt of pleasure. I must say, I've never found beards terribly sexy, a phobia which probably originated from reading Roald Dahl's *The Twits* as a child. But this man's beard was dark and sleek and trim and adorned a beautifully chiselled face. His skin was tanned and his eyes were the same colour as Anthony's, dark as olives.

I felt his gaze wander over me and I looked away, blushing. In 2005, such a gesture might have been sleazy, but back here in ancient times it felt rather sexy. For a moment we sat in taut, electric silence.

Then he said, 'Do you know who's racing at the amphitheatre today?'

His stiff manner seemed rather incongruous with his initially relaxed air. And I had no idea what to reply.

'Er . . .' I gazed out into the arena, where the lion was now gobbling up the poor slave. 'I'm not sure. But I feel sorry for them, whoever they are.'

The man smiled. And I knew then, with complete conviction, that he had to be Ovid. I just *knew*. It was destiny that out of all the cities and all the amphitheatres, he had walked into mine and sat down right next to me. I pictured the stars above sighing with pleasure as they looked down on us.

A few more moments passed. He pretended to drop something and rather obviously snuck a look at my legs. My conversation with Anthony floated back: '*Ovid gave useful tips for what to do if you're wearing togas and watching the chariot races. He recommended that blokes should pretend to drop something so they can bend down and pick it up, flashing a glance at a woman's ankles.*' Suddenly I felt cold and silly. How many women had he used that trick on? He obviously thought I was naïve and, worse, easy.

I turned away from him, firmly tucking my ankles back underneath the bench. When he addressed me, I now answered with cool shrugs. Finally he stood up, muttered a rather ungracious goodbye and stormed off.

I watched his progress, smarting. He climbed over a few benches and sat down beside another man. I saw them gossiping, and then the other man looked over at me. Oh – how lovely – now I was being discussed. They were probably calling me frigid. I looked away haughtily.

After that, I could hardly concentrate on the games. One half of me felt proud that I hadn't been sucked in; the other half was still hankering after Ovid in regret. I was also becoming increasingly uncomfortable at the way they were still gossiping so intently. My curiosity aroused, I slid up the bench. Luckily, most people were too interested in watching the lion eat his way through a few more slaves to notice me. Finally I was sitting directly behind them, a few benches back but I could just about catch their conversation.

'. . . That is the way women are, you see,' the other man was saying. 'Women are like boars – they need to be caught in nets.'

'But she did not respond at all to me.' My admirer looked upset, his voice weak with bewilderment.

'But when you are hunting a boar, each boar is a little different. Some will give a long chase and be difficult; some will, when cornered, surrender easily. Some are tough, with long prickly tusks!'

They both snorted with laughter.

'As my apprentice, I will train you so that you have enough nets of dialogue and seduction to trap any boar you please.'

'Ovid, my counsel, my teacher, my guide, please show me the way . . .'

Ovid! Hang on! It wasn't my admirer who was Ovid. So . . .

'I will find her,' Ovid declared, 'and seduce her myself. Demetrius, watch and learn.'

They looked up, no doubt searching for me, and I quickly pretended to be engrossed in the games again.

Noticing that I was right behind them, Demetrius jumped uneasily. But Ovid stared at me steadily. I lowered my eyes to meet his. There was a faint smirk on his face, as though he thought I'd crept up on them because I fancied them and was now trying to play it cool.

Arrogant sod! I thought. And another thing: he wasn't the slightest bit handsome. Whoever had sculptured his busts had been very generous. In real life he was slightly plump, with a wiry beard and a bullish, pitted face. The only pleasant feature was his eyes, which were an intense blue, the colour of the Mediterranean, searing as lasers. But there was a glint of arrogance flashing in those eyes too; his gaze seemed to jeer, 'I can have you whenever I want you.'

No, Ovid was definitely not my type of man. I didn't like men who were bossy or domineering. I liked men who respected women as equals. Men like Anthony . . .

When the games ended, I waited for everyone else to leave first.

141

Finally there was just me and Ovid sitting in the empty amphitheatre, a few benches apart. Ovid looked at me. I ignored him. He let out a sigh and came and sat down next to me.

I stared at him witheringly. He looked at my breasts in a pointed fashion. I coughed. Still he looked.

'For goodness' sake, d'you have to be so obvious? Can't you look somewhere else?' I cried.

'Well, your clothes are rather inviting,' Ovid pointed out.

I looked down and discovered that my tunic was gaping open. Oh dear God, I ought to have applied some Tit-Tape. I hastily rearranged it and flushed, wondering how long it had been like that.

Ovid, meanwhile, rose and with a cheeky 'Bye then!' sauntered off, leaving me with a face like an oven.

Total bastard, crap poet, silly patronising lousy-bearded lunatic! I soon ran out of names, but I felt calmer now. Down below in the arena, men were sweeping sand over the bloodstains – nice. Well, since I didn't seem to have taken to Ovid, perhaps I should go home, I thought.

But it seemed a bit of an anticlimax just to pop home. It was Sunday evening; there was *nothing* on telly except some boring antiques roadshow programme; all I had to look forward to was going to bed alone, ready to wake up for a Monday morning start in the office. I'd actually rather just sit here in the stadium for a while, I thought, enjoying the sun, if nothing else.

I glanced back up the tiers of benches behind me. Ovid had definitely gone. Good. Though I had to admit, I wouldn't have minded a little more sparring with him. It wasn't that I liked him or anything – I just wanted to have the last word.

I stood up. I'll just have a quick wander about, I thought. I might well bump into him again. And in the mean time, I'll get to have a fabulous look around Rome. I felt excitement flutter in my stomach like a ribbon. The last time I had been here had been on a family holiday with my parents when I was about three or four. It would be amazing to compare the two eras.

In many ways, Rome wasn't all that different. There was no frenetic traffic, no tooting horns, no Vespas zooming about at top speed. But it was still a hot, noisy, dusty cauldron of energy and Italian spirit. I spotted the Forum, the place where people shopped and traded and where speakers loved to come and test their skills; a distant voice pounded out Latin phrases with verve and punch. School was clearly over for the day, for children were playing in the streets. I watched girls playing with rag dolls or jumping through hoops that rang with little bells on them. I watched boys clashing wooden swords and walking on stilts. One group played tic-tac-toe; another was playing Troy, a game I remembered reading about in Latin. One boy stood opposite a whole line of friends and screamed and struggled as they surged around him, trying to pull him over a line.

It was fascinating watching this whirlpool of human energy. It struck me that though fashions might have mutated a thousand times since 1 BC, people hadn't. I saw a woman, walking with her husband, giving another man a lingering glance; I saw a young boy swooning about with a book of poetry in his hands; I saw two men arguing furiously in the street. Love, jealousy, hatred, friendship, rivalry: every feeling was being painted here in every colour. At this very moment in time, I thought, both here and in 2005, the wheel of life is turning. Right now, at this very moment, someone is making love, someone is giving birth, someone is getting married, someone is saying a final goodbye to life.

I felt very small and my life so short, just a wingbeat of time.

And I suddenly wished Anthony was here so I could talk to him about all these feelings. But he wasn't, and so I walked on.

I began to grow tired. Worse, I started to notice that my fake tan was melting in the heat, rimming my tunic with a brown hue. Perhaps it was time to go home.

I also began to fear that I was lost. Was that the baths I had seen earlier, or another one? How far back had that shop been? I turned left into an empty alley, glad to be away from the crowds. I paused for breath, momentarily distracted by the graffiti painted across the stone. I recognised the word *furcifer,* which meant – shock horror – *scoundrel.* I laughed – well, that was certainly more imaginative than the 'f' word. I wish I'd known that earlier; I could have used it on Ovid in the amphitheatre.

Suddenly I became aware of a shadow falling on the wall.

Someone had crept up behind me.

I let out a gasp and spun round.

Ovid.

143

He planted both hands on the wall on either side of me, trapping me, his piercing gaze pinned on me. Despite myself, I was amazed to find an electric frisson ripple up my spine. I gazed at his lips and then looked down, appalled.

'You thought you'd lost me, didn't you?'

'I'd hoped so,' I sighed.

'Well, now I know your secret,' he said.

What on earth did he mean? I wondered shakily. He couldn't have seen the time machine; and even if he had, nobody in Roman times would have been able to conceive of what it was . . .

'What secret?' I pretended to sound confident, looking him boldly in the eye.

Ovid took a lock of my hair and gently breathed in its scent. It was almost romantic – if it hadn't been for the arrogant look on his face. Incensed, I tried to push him away and he laughed.

'The scent of your hair – the scent of you – it isn't Roman. Your skin is too pale. You're not from around here. You don't even know your way around Rome. You're an escaped slave, aren't you?'

I was so astonished, all I could do was stare at him open-mouthed. Then I pushed him aside and started to walk away. He came after me, taking my arm. I stopped, meeting his gaze again.

'Don't you realise the trouble you're in? I could easily tell the Emperor and have you passed over to the lions.'

God, what a *bully*. For a moment I considered slapping him and making a run for it. But he was extremely muscly and his grip around my wrist was painfully strong. Then inspiration struck: I would play the helpless female.

I pretended to cry. It wasn't hard; I just thought of Anthony and our row and I was surprised at how easily the tears welled up.

As I'd hoped, Ovid suddenly became manly and gentle.

'I promise to keep your secret safe,' he said. 'But on one condition.'

'What?' I asked nervously.

'You become *my* slave.'

Well, I didn't have much choice, did I? All the same, as he walked me to his house, I felt tickled with excitement.

144

Ovid's home clearly confirmed his status as a patrician – an upper-class Roman – as opposed to a lower-class plebeian.

We passed the pleb dwellings along the way. They lived in wooden flats, where entire families were crowded into one room. Ovid's house, by contrast, was a lavish red affair with a tiled roof, the rooms arranged around a central courtyard. Inside, our feet clicked on the beautiful mosaics that wound across the floors like snakes.

We passed a beautiful slave girl with dark hair. She was pregnant – in fact she looked as though she was ready to give birth at any minute.

'Tiryns!' Ovid stopped her. 'Have you seen Adrasteia?'

Who? Then I realised. His wife. Of course, I should have known. Why did I feel such a sharp stab of disappointment in my heart?

'She's just back from the baths,' Tiryns said. I noticed that she was so intimidated by her employer that she could barely look him in the eye.

'Ovid!' A voice rang out and Adrasteia appeared in a doorway.

Ovid's wife was tall, voluptuous and rather intimidating; her face was stern, with sharp black eyes beneath swooping brows.

'I've, ah, got us a new slave girl,' Ovid said. I stood there feeling like a lemon, as she swept those black eyes over me. Automatically I found myself tightening up my shoulders as though on the parade ground.

'Ovid,' she said. Just one word was all that was needed to convey her annoyance. 'Who is she and how much did she cost?'

'Ah – what did you say your name was?' Ovid asked me.

'You don't even know her name!' his wife exclaimed, laughing cruelly.

'I'm . . . ah . . .' What? Lucius? Or was that a boy's name? All I could think of was those poems by Catullus, the weepy ones about the sparrow and his beloved . . . 'Lesbia,' I said. 'I'm Lesbia.'

'Well, Lesbia,' said his wife archly, 'Ovid would be grateful if you would wait outside in the corridor while we discuss matters in our bedroom.'

The door closed on me and I waited, trying to pretend not to notice when their voices began to rise.

'Where've you been all day? So I'm left to run the house while you go off hunting down pretty slave girls?'

'Your place is in the home,' said Ovid, but he sounded slightly nervous.

Well, fancy that! I thought, a smile breaking over my face. Old chauvinist-piggy Ovid is a hen-pecked husband! I'd thought wives were meant to be under male thumbs in Roman times. I'd read, for example, that they weren't allowed to drink; if a husband smelt even a whiff on his wife's breath, she would be beaten. But perhaps that was just for public show; after all, social conventions can dampen or distort human nature, but it always springs back to its true state in the end; and Adrasteia was clearly never going to be the sort of woman who was seen and not heard, however hard he tried.

Suddenly I saw the other slave girl, Tiryns, approaching. I flushed, waiting for her to reprimand me. But to my surprise, she stopped and listened too, whispering, 'They're such a pair, aren't they?'

I giggled and then stopped short as she put a finger to my lips. We both stood there, enjoying the row.

'I suppose you've been off writing your silly poetry again?'

Oh God. I nearly stuffed my fingers into my mouth.

'I will write some this evening – I'm working on *Metamorphoses*.'

'*Metamorphoses*? Oh, sure. I expect it's more of your *smut*. Well, I hope you can manage to keep your verse under control after *Ars Amatoria*. I hear the rumours daily now at how displeased the Emperor is.'

'The poem is a celebration of love. It was inspired by my wife!'

'Oh, spare me, please.'

The bedroom door suddenly flew open.

'Lesbia,' said Adrasteia, looking weary, and for a moment, I felt quite sorry for her. 'You may work here as a slave. You will begin tomorrow in the kitchens preparing breakfast. Then Tiryns will bring you to my chamber to dress me. Thank you.'

Behind his wife, I saw Ovid gaze across and give me a challenging stare. I looked away, though for the rest of the night that stare seemed to echo in my retinas, twinkling and fizzing and whispering excitement.

146

iv) The games

But I didn't want to have an affair.

The idea held no excitement or glamour for me. I had seen my father's affair destroy my mother, ageing her by ten years overnight. I had seen the damage Anthony's parents had done with their infidelities. Ovid didn't have any children, mind you, and Adrasteia was hardly a dream wife, but even so, I wasn't prepared to inflict that pain on her.

And yet. Ovid flirted with me outrageously; and I didn't go back to the time machine.

Had it been 2005, he would definitely have ended up in one of those sexual harassment cases worth millions splashed across the papers. But this was 1 B.C. and he regularly brushed against me when I passed him in the corridor, or ran his eyes over me as though undressing me. At first I was huffy with him, convinced he was a sleaze who tried it on with any slave that came his way. But then I saw how coolly he acted around Tiryns; he would barely utter a monosyllable for her. And I felt a little flush of happiness inside: I was special to him.

The work was horribly hard. I realised I was never, *ever* going to complain again about shit office jobs. Office jobs involved comfy chairs and tea breaks and internet-surfing. They didn't involve the endless dawn-to-dusk washing of togas, cooking of meals on the smoking fire in the kitchens, sewing, cleaning, gardening. And worse, *we had to cut up food for Ovid and his wife using a spoon.* There were no knives and forks about, so they ate with their fingers. And Adrasteia took as much advantage as she could of me.

'Lesbia, I need my food to be cut into bite-sized pieces. Take this back to the kitchen.'

'Oh, Lesbia, now you've brought it back, it seems a bit cold. Cook something else, will you?'

'Lesbia, I need a cloth.'

Tiryns warned me that when Adrasteia was in a particularly cruel mood, she would wipe her greasy fingers in her slave's hair.

'God, if she ever tries that with me, she'll be in trouble!' I cried.

Tiryns gave me a curious warning look and I quickly laughed, pretending it was a joke. I was beginning to feel sympathy for the immigrants who come to England with PhDs and end up cleaning toilets in stations. I kept wanting to turn around to someone and just yell, 'I have a degree, you know, and I've read the works of Chaucer *and* Shakespeare, so please wipe that patronising look off your face.'

I struck up a lukewarm friendship with Tiryns. She confided in me that the father of her baby was Servius, one of the other slaves, but I noticed that he seemed a reluctant father, barely interested in even conversing with her. Tiryns was obviously hurt by his behaviour and her moods swung rapidly, honey-sweet one minute, stinging the next.

The job I enjoyed most was cleaning out Ovid's study, because it meant I got a chance to look at his poetry. As I leafed through his papers and parchments, I winced at the red blisters that were forming on my hands and thought longingly of home and the tub of hand cream sitting in my bathroom.

Then I noticed the poem I was holding and I felt a shiver scuttle over me. My God. This was *Metamorphoses*, Ovid's finest poetic achievement. And it looked as though he had only just begun it.

And time without all end,
(If poets as by prophecy about the truth may aim)
My life shall everlastingly be lengthened still by fame.

So he had begun at the end. For these were the final lines of Book XV; I remembered reading them at school. It had seemed such an arrogant ending to me, but the verse was covered with nervous scribbles and crossings-out. Between the lines, I sensed a frightened sense of his own mortality. Without even thinking, I picked up his stylus and wrote a reassuring postscript:

You will be remembered for thousands of years to come; your verse will make you immortal.

I suffered butterflies for the rest of the day. My moment of inspiration now seemed like a moment of madness. What if he sacked me for cheek? Or had me beaten? Or . . .

148

I saw him in the corridor and hardly dared look him in the eye, but he seemed preoccupied and distant.

That evening, Adrasteia called me to her room to help arrange her hair.

'I am taking my other slaves with me tonight. I am going to Fronia's house to celebrate Bona Dea.'

'What?' I asked in bewilderment.

'The Festival of the Good Goddess.' She frowned and rolled her eyes, as though to say: *The slaves you get these days.*

'Oh, right. Is Ovid going?'

'Very amusing, Lesbia. Of course Ovid would be welcome at a festival for women only. Now, you can stay behind and attend to my husband. I shall leave Tiryns here too,' she added, wincing slightly.

The house seemed eerily quiet without Adrasteia and her screeching. But it was a deadly type of quiet – like the pause of a snake before it strikes.

Evening came and I felt a little irked with Tiryns. I had confessed to her early on that I was a dangerously bad cook, so I normally got the easy tasks like chopping vegetables. She knew that I really needed a hand preparing supper, but there was no sign of her anywhere. I was terrified that I was going to produce something so bad Ovid would take one mouthful and send me off to the amphitheatre.

Finally I cobbled together some sort of meal of bread, vegetables and chicken. In Roman times a fish-based sauce called *garum* was all the rage, so I doused that liberally over everything in the hope that it would blot out all the other flavours. Not to mention the, ah, burnt bits.

Ovid normally ate in the atrium with his wife. But as he was alone, he asked for his food to be brought into the dining room. There I found him lounging on a couch.

I put down the food and turned to go.

'Wait,' he said. 'I don't think I want to eat this.'

Was my cooking really *that* bad? Then I saw a lazy smile creep across his face.

'I'm not hungry.'

Oh, how hilarious, Ovid, I thought sullenly, to make me prepare your dinner when you don't even want it.

'I think I'd like to take a walk.' He stretched like a cat. 'And I'd like you to join me.'

'I'm feeling tired,' I said.

'You forget I'm your master,' said Ovid. 'I'm not asking you – I'm telling you.'

It was a beautiful night. Balmy, a celestial blue twilight. I could hear the sounds of the city in the distance, alive and alight with decadence. Scents wafted from the flowerbeds, heavy and heady, like the love flowers I imagined in *A Midsummer Night's Dream*. The garden, pretty but somewhat mediocre in the daytime, now looked mysterious and shadowy. The Romans had a fondness for topiary, and we passed shrubs that had been cut into the shapes of birds and lions that looked as though they might pounce at any moment. As we strolled past statues of the gods, it felt as though they were watching us.

I am not going to sleep with him, I kept repeating over and over like a mantra. For one thing, he's bound to be useless in bed. It would be just typical for someone who writes guides on love to be a lousy lover himself. Plus, he's so arrogant. He'll only think of himself.

Ovid paused by a statue of Venus. He reached out to stroke her face.

'Venus, Goddess of Love,' I said, stating the obvious in my nerves.

'*For young Love's guide has Venus chosen me.*' Ovid quoted his own poem boldly. '*And Love,*' he concluded, '*shall yield to me.*'

'Well, you're very confident,' I said cheekily. 'Surely the whole point of love is that we lose ourselves in it. We surrender to something bigger than ourselves. Like Virgil . . .' A flash of Latin A level came back to me. '*We too must yield to love.* I mean, that's why we say that we *fall* in love. We fall. We let go . . .' I frowned, thinking briefly of Anthony, of how I'd always been afraid of taking that jump. Then I looked back at Ovid, and his eyes flickered with arrogant amusement.

He stepped closer. I moved backwards against the statue, Venus' stomach pressing against me, her head serene and protective above. He was so close that our bodies were nearly touching; his eyes held my gaze and I felt his breath on my lips.

'I'm a hunter and Rome is a forest. There are boars teeming about all over the place and I can have any one I want. It is simply a case of finding the right net.'

He gazed at my lips. I was ready to slap him. But to my relief and frustration he stepped backwards. I breathed out and my breath caught with a flicker of desire. I saw Ovid quickly hide a smile.

'Come,' he said, offering his hand to draw me deeper into the garden.

I ignored his hand and strolled on ahead, holding my chin up high. The path became deeper and darker as we entered an avenue of cypress trees.

'So once you've caught a boar in a net and enjoyed the tussle – then what, hmm?'

'I boil it up, feast on it and throw away the bones.' I glared at him, and he added softly, 'I mock you, Lesbia. Women deserve love, of course they do. They deserve to be treated like goddesses.'

'Oh.' Now I felt mollified, and in turn even more irritated because I didn't have an excuse to hate him. So I took a cheap shot. 'Well, your wife seems to enjoy playing at being the hunter.'

I hadn't meant my jibe to cut so deep. I saw the pain on Ovid's face before he quickly concealed it.

'Yes, I am a cuckold.' He laughed bitterly. 'Ovid – Cupid's revenge. He has maimed me, in the end, with an arrow of poison.'

Now I understood where Ovid's inspiration came from. He wanted to counsel others so that they could experience the amorous perfection he had failed at.

Then I thought of my father; and of Anthony's parents; and my sister; and all the couples I knew that seemed to be falling apart.

'Why is it so hard for people to be faithful to each other?' I suddenly cried.

Ovid turned and touched my cheek, and I recoiled from him, my desire stamped out by my anger.

'Right now, my wife is not at Bona Dea. She is risking her life by joining my friend Calchus in bed.' He paused and looked at me with eyes full of sadness. Then, as though his masculine pride repulsed at such a show of vulnerability, he turned away, plucking a violet. I thought he was going to give it to me, or thread it through my hair. Instead he shredded it slowly, tearing off the petals, fixing his predatory eyes on me.

The last petal fluttered to the ground like a teardrop.

'Take off your tunic,' he ordered me suddenly. 'Undress for me.'

My eyes widened in outraged shock.

'No,' I said, yet once again I felt desire snaking up inside me. For a moment I was lost in surprise and self-analysis. I couldn't understand it. He was the opposite of Anthony. He was everything I loathed in a man. He wanted to crush me and dominate me. And yet I was turned on.

'You forget I'm your master. I alone can grant you manumission. Your life is in my hands.'

He caught my gasp with his lips, then pushed me back against a tree and lifted my arms up behind me so that the bark bit into my skin. I kissed him back just as roughly, giving up all my pretence at resistance. He reacted by softening his kisses, pulling back, teasing me.

'Venus rose from the ocean on a scallop, entirely naked. I want to picture you as Venus. Now, take off your clothes and lie down on the floor.'

I was about to obey, when suddenly I heard a scream in the distance. It sounded human.

'What's that noise?' I cried.

'It's nothing, I'm sure—' Ovid began, then broke off as the screaming grew louder.

I hurried through the trees. The screams led me to a small summerhouse. I burst in to find Tiryns lying on the floor, gasping for air, her face a violent, sticky shade of red.

'Ovid – please, please . . .'

'Oh my God, her waters have broken,' I cried. 'We have to get a doctor.'

'That won't be possible,' said Ovid. His face was white; he stepped backward, away from Tiryns. 'You deal with this, Lesbia.'

'*What?*'

And Ovid, literally, ran off.

'Tell him to call the midwife!' Tiryns screamed. 'Tell him to send a messenger to Hilara!'

'OVID, BRING HILARA!' I yelled after him, and I thought I heard a faint cry of acquiescence before he fled towards the house.

I knelt down beside Tiryns, stroking hair back from her face.

'He's gone,' she puffed tearfully. 'Oh God, it's his child, and he's so ashamed . . .'

'What! You're pregnant with Ovid's child!' I cried. In the space of thirty seconds, my opinion of him did a sharp U-turn. And to think I had just nearly . . .

'He tried to make me give my baby up.' She stared at me, her eyes filling with tears as she hissed for breath. 'But I couldn't – I just couldn't. Oh God, help me.'

'But why didn't you use contraception?'

'We used a pig's bladder, like everyone else.'

'*A pig's bladder?*' I was aghast. The next time someone said 'Just what have the Romans done for us?' I knew that contraception wouldn't be high on the list.

'My baby is coming,' Tiryns cried, 'and you can only talk of bladders. Oh help me, Lesbia, please be my midwife!'

Ah. I had no idea how to deliver a baby. I had a vague idea that I needed towels . . . and hot water . . . and . . . er . . .

'Push,' I cried, leaping on the word hastily. 'You've got to push – that's it – push!'

The next few hours were horrible. As each contraction bit sharper teeth into her body, Tiryns kept groaning and wailing and writhing and lacerating my palms with her nails. I had a vague idea that I ought to check to see if she was dilated to a certain width, but when I stuck my head between her thighs, I was utterly foxed. Wasn't it ten inches, something like that? How much was an inch? The top digit of my thumb? So, how many thumb-lengths fitted against her—

'What the hell are you doing?' Tiryns screamed. 'Is it coming?'

'Push!' I cried helplessly. 'Keep going.'

Tiryns, as though possessed by a beast, arched her back and howled like a banshee.

Fuck, I thought, sweat cascading down my face, *I am never, ever going to have children.*

And then we heard the sound of footsteps. Oh, thank God! A

middle-aged woman appeared, carrying a strange-looking stool and a bag of equipment. Hilara. I stepped backwards, more than happy to let her take over.

'Here,' said Hilara sharply. 'Get her to take this.' She passed me a bottle and I knelt down beside Tiryns, gently trickling its contents into her mouth. She gulped it down in fits of panting breath.

'Drink up, child, it's water with goose's semen,' Hilara said, frowning as I nearly dropped the bottle. 'Yes, I know powdered sow's dung would have been better, but I could not find any in such a hurry.'

Goose semen? I wondered. *Fuck, this was even worse than their idea of contraception.* But it got even more bizarre. Next Hilara tied a snake's slough to Tiryn's thigh and gave her a stick from which a frog had been shaken from a snake to clutch. After assessing her cervix, Hilara then forced poor Tiryns to get up and sit on the weird stool.

'Are you sure she shouldn't be lying down?' I asked, feeling this was all getting a bit much. But as Hilara turned her fierce blue eyes on me, I shut up and quickly muttered an apology.

'Stand behind the stool and give her support then!' Hilara cried, shaking her head impatiently. I darted behind it, allowing Tiryns to lean back into me as she clutched the arm-rests of the chair. Hilara knelt before her; there was a crescent-shaped hole for the baby to emerge through. I noted that Hilara had wrapped her hands in thin papyrus, though whether this was to help her grasp the slippery baby with ease, or for luck, I couldn't say.

I soon became exhausted from supporting Tiryns. My body was covered in sweat and my back groaned from holding her up. As she bucked and wailed against me, I felt as though her pain arrowed from her shoulders, up her arms and into my heart. But just when I felt I couldn't last out any longer, it happened. I heard the faint sound of crying. A bawling face, a head, shoulders . . . slowly but surely, a sticky lump of flesh emerged and fell into Hilara's hands. Tiryns immediately collapsed like a burst balloon and I helped her to lie down again.

'Hold it while I cut the cord,' Hilara instructed.

'Oh – no – I couldn't possibly.' I shied away, but Hilara thrust the baby into my hands.

'Ooh, it's a boy,' I cried, frowning and then checking again that he really did have a willy and it wasn't just the umbilical cord.

He was sticky and covered with blood and his screams were blasting my face. But he was beautiful. My heart stopped. I could hear Tiryns whimpering and reaching out, but for one dazed moment I couldn't let go; I wished with all my soul that he belonged to me.

Then I passed him over and she clutched him, crying and laughing and cooing over him. Dazed, I muttered that I needed some fresh air.

Outside, the night wrapped its arms around me in a cool caress.

It was bizarre. I had spent all of my twenties being petrified of getting pregnant. Whenever I'd had sex with Anthony, I had surreptitiously waited for him to go to the loo afterwards and then carefully checked the condom for minute holes where one naughty sperm might have wriggled out shouting, '*Escape, escape!*' Once or twice we had got tired of them and taken a chance, which had then always put me into a state of panic. Luckily I'd never suffered a disaster, though my period only had to be a few days late for me to start feeling jumpy and irritable and paranoid.

And yet when I had held Tiryns' baby, all I felt was love. Simple as that. I couldn't analyse it or explain it or be intellectual: it was a purely emotional gut response, and it was one of glorious euphoria.

I went back into the summerhouse to find that the baby was now quiet in his mother's arms. But Tiryns was weeping; her tears fell and splashed on the baby's face and he blinked in innocent curiosity.

'Tiryns, are you OK?' I put my arm around her.

'Let her be,' said Hilara, guiding me away. 'You know how hard it is for a slave to give birth. Of course, if that boy really had been Servius' baby, he would have become a family pet and Ovid might have loved him as his own son until he grew up and became a slave. The trouble is,' she lowered her voice, clearly enjoying the gossip,

'Adrasteia knows the baby is Ovid's, so they say. They say she might send the child away, or else make sure he becomes a gladiator and goes to an early death!'

'But that's terrible,' I cried fiercely. 'Look, I'll speak to Ovid. He has to be strong about this. No, don't laugh, Hilara, I will. I swear I'll help Tiryns out.'

Over the next few days, Ovid – how convenient – found himself called away on urgent business.

Adrasteia had allowed Tiryns to keep her baby for the present, but had had her moved to the most distant room in the house. Every time she heard so much as a tiny whimper, she would look deeply pained.

As for poor Tiryns – well, the Romans didn't seem to have any concept of maternity leave. She had to combine cooking with nappy-changing and washing with breast-feeding. I did my best to help her out with her chores – and from time to time she let me help with the baby too.

'Here, take him, but be careful with him.' She passed him over, her expression fearful. 'Oh God, what if he ends up in the gladiator's ring? I already love him so much; I cannot bear to lose him.'

I gripped the baby, feeling close to tears myself. As I gazed down at his chubby face, I made a promise that I wouldn't go back home until I had done all I could to help Tiryns and ensure her baby would be safe.

v) The fight

It was meant to be the highlight of the amphitheatre calendar. It was the Emperor's birthday, which meant weeks of games galore. In Roman terms, this was like England vs. Germany in the World Cup final. The benches were packed; the air shook with bloodthirsty roars. Ovid had just returned from his business, and much to my surprise, he had chosen me to accompany him and his wife to the games. I was sitting next to Ovid; Adrasteia sat on his other side. Ovid waited until Adrasteia was engrossed in the games and then turned to me with a glint in his eye.

'I've missed you,' he whispered.

I looked into his eyes, trying to search his soul. I could hardly believe his cheek.

'Oh really?' I whispered into his ear. 'And did you miss Tiryns too? And her baby? I know you're the father.'

'We'll talk about this later,' said Ovid, dropping his eyes.

'We won't,' I hissed. 'I want you to promise that you will treat her son as though he's yours, and look after him and care for him and prevent him from being a slave.'

'Impossible,' he whispered back fiercely. 'You have no right to tell me what I should do! I am your master.'

'I don't care. You should take responsibility, and you'd bloody better, or . . . or . . .' I searched wildly for a threat and came up with something pretty lame: 'I'll write that he's your son all over the walls of Rome.'

A wave of hysteria swept the crowd; they jumped up, cheering on their favourite gladiator. For a moment Ovid and I remained seated, locked in our private circle of shock. Then, carried by the crowd, we stood up too, cheering weakly.

We didn't say anything at all for the next twenty minutes. I stared down into the amphitheatre unseeingly as two gladiators locked swords with ferocious clangs.

It suddenly struck me that I was in exactly the right place to summon back the time machine.

You could go back now, I reminded myself. *You've done your best for Tiryns . . .*

I saw it then, in an instant: a hover of gold, like the sweep of a bird's wing.

Then it was gone, and there was just sand and air again.

Stay a little longer, my conscience begged me. *Just try and see if you can win Ovid round. Your threat was foolish; see if you can charm him, be diplomatic . . .*

I became aware that the crowd was dispersing. It was break time: no doubt they wanted to sweep up the bodies. Ovid turned to me before I could speak.

'I have been invited to visit the Emperor's box. Please accompany me and my wife as our slave.'

There was steel in his eyes and his words. I felt uneasy, but I nodded. Once we had seen the Emperor, I would try to speak to Ovid again, and this time I would use my feminine wiles on him.

The Emperor Augustus was seated on a throne. He smiled at Ovid with his mouth, but not his eyes. Ovid bowed slightly, nervous, eager to please. I suddenly felt a flash of sympathy for him. In a year's time the Emperor would exile him to the island of Tomis. Ovid blamed the exile on a 'poem and an error'; whilst everyone knew that the poem was *Ars Amatoria*, nobody was sure of the fault.

'Are you enjoying the games?' the Emperor asked.

'Oh yes.'

'Almost the best we've ever been to.'

'Not almost, Ovid. You mean the *best*.'

Ovid and his wife competed with each other in the effusiveness of their praise. The Emperor Augustus smiled thinly, enjoying their bumbling more than their words. For a moment it was like a twenty-first-century cocktail party, with a balding middle-aged man and his wife trying to please the boss in the hope of a good Christmas bonus.

'And this is your new slave girl?'

I jumped, for I thought I had remained unnoticed. But suddenly the Emperor's eyes were on me.

'Yes,' said Ovid. 'And no.'

'Yes and no?' said the Emperor. 'Ovid, you are a man of poetics, I am a man of politics. Pray, give me an answer that is black and white.'

'I found her on the street and she begged me for work, so I took pity on her and hired her as my slave. I have since discovered, however, that she ran away from Athens, for in the last house she worked she stole all their jewellery and money.'

I let out a shocked gasp. Adrasteia shook her head uncertainly.

'And so, Great Augustus, my wife and I would be honoured if you could accept this girl as our gift – if she might participate in your games.'

I shook my head wildly, as though trying to shake some words of protest from my numb mouth. Though I doubted words would have made any difference anyway. As far as the Emperor was concerned, I was just a slave and a liar. Augustus gazed at me, and for a minute I thought there was hope, thought I saw pity in his eyes. I made the mistake of gazing back at him with a pleading look; his hard heart was repelled and he looked away without interest.

'Well,' he concluded, 'why not? She'll certainly liven things up. Thank you, Ovid, for your generosity.' His voice was laced with sarcasm.

The next thing I knew, several guards were by my side, grabbing my arms.

'Ovid!' I cried. 'Ovid – you're lying. This all wrong – you know I'm—' I broke off, remembering his wife, wanting to spare her such a public humiliation. Yet I couldn't believe his cruelty. If only I had been selfish and gone on my way, I could have been back home by now, happy, in bed, safe. '*Ovid!*'

My voice cracked, and unable to help himself, he looked over at me. I saw tenderness in his eyes, tenderness and appalled shame. But not enough to change his mind.

Then I was being hauled down into a small, dark chamber. They handed me some armour, a helmet, a shield and a sword. I found myself laughing slightly hysterically. I felt as though I was rehearsing for a play; the sword felt chunky in my hand and I barely had the strength to swing it. I tried a few practice swipes, picturing the lion I would face – but all I could imagine was a cartoon creature. On my third swing I dropped the sword with a clumsy clang. The guard gave me a pitying look.

I heard a huge roar rise up in the amphitheatre. I realised it was for *me*. Dear God. I closed my eyes and prayed: *Oh God, help me. I know the rules of the time machine, I know that I have to get back to my original place, but I can't, God, I can't get back into those stands, I'm stuck here. Dear God, please change the rules, please defy time and space. Please can I open my eyes and see the time machine right here, right now, in this cell with me.*

I heard a rumbling noise. My eyes flew open. Brilliant sunshine flooded into the chamber as the gate was lifted. I looked about for the machine. But my cell was empty; just pools of light and dark corners.

I edged uneasily to the end of the cell. From up above the arena had looked small. But at ground level it stretched out before me like a vast, shimmering desert. I could see faint marks in the sand, and I realised they were the bloodstains from past gladiators.

The crowd's roars deepened. They were baying for blood, animal in their thirst.

'Go on then.' The guards had noticed my reluctance to leave the cell.

I let out a yelp as they pushed me out, so forcibly that I tripped and landed face down on the sand. I heard the sound of the gate closing behind me. I coughed, sand thick in my mouth.

I had barely staggered to my feet when I heard the sound of the gate at the far end of the arena rising up. A creature bounded in, hovering like a tawny mirage on the horizon.

Uh-oh.

I swayed. For the first time, the panic truly hit me, screaming through me like a banshee, howling round my body, turning my limbs to jelly. I felt my knees shake and I half swooned. The crowd jeered.

I turned to face them. I wanted to pick out Ovid's face, I wanted him to see what he had done, but it was impossible: there was just a sea of faces. My fear crystallised into anger. For God's sake – how could he be such a coward? He could have just passed me on to another household. But no. He was going to feed me to the lions. I gripped my sword tightly and stood upright. If I could just plunge the weapon into the animal's side, then I might have a chance. Then I might go free.

Whenever I'd watched fights in films, they always unfolded in relatively slow motion. In reality, the lion was as fast as lightning. One minute it was heading towards me, a thing of terrifying beauty, body arched, muscles rippling beneath its golden coat, jaws bared. The next I was lying on the floor, dizzy. I gazed up as the lion soared over me then loped back up the arena, circling: it had obviously been trained to prolong the torture as long as it could.

The sun and the crowds seemed far off, and I suddenly became aware of pain. I looked down and saw blood gushing from my left arm.

I staggered to my feet. I picked up my sword. Right, I thought. No more Ms Nice Guy.

The lion was pacing about, ready for strike two. I shut out the crowd, narrowing my concentration into one line of intense focus. Just me and the lion. Silence except for the thump in my heart and the warning growl of the beast.

And then it came, bounding across the arena, spraying up small fountains of sand with its paws. I gripped my sword tightly, my heart in my throat. Closer, closer, closer – *now!* I reached out and stabbed wildly, my eyes squeezed shut. Then it was galloping away, and in my shock I stumbled, only just keeping my balance. I saw blood glinting on my sword, silver-red in the sun. I gazed at the lion. By God, I'd struck it! I turned to the crowd, listening to their roar. But despite their cheers, I only felt empty. The lion paused in the distance, staring at me with cruel yellow eyes; I could sense its rage, saw it quivering in the swirl of its tail. I thought: what I have done except harm a poor beast? What is the point of this? They call this entertainment?

When the lion came at me this time, my resolve crumbled. There was no room for weakness in this game, and the animal struck me on the arm, leaving three gashes, like red stripes on a uniform. This time, though, it was my right arm. I could barely hold my sword; any movement of my fingers sent ripples of pain shooting down to my elbow.

The lion stood in the distance, silhouetted against the sun. Perhaps it was just my wooziness, but there seemed to be an aura of sadness about it now. It seemed to be saying: *I should kill you before you kill me, but it's such a pointless waste.* I felt rage burn inside me. I couldn't win. I'd wanted to defy Ovid and save Tiryns and her child. But it was no good.

I made my decision there and then. I threw down my sword and ran across the arena, spraying up sand. At the end was a stone wall, and I closed my eyes and mustered up every last drop of energy to vault over it, crying out as the pain tore through my arms.

The crowd were so stunned that they didn't even try to stop me at first. In ancient Rome it was better to die a noble death than run and risk loss of honour; I was behaving with a brazen cowardice that was beyond comprehension. I ran up the steps, breathless. And then they came at me. Rising from their benches, shouting and pushing and reaching out to get me. I stopped, my heart screaming, and willed the time machine to come. It appeared and I dived into it, wrenching myself away from a grabbing arm. I punched in the date, blood splashing everywhere, and collapsed into the seat, my eyes closed.

And then I was back in my living room, and I rolled out of the machine and lay on the carpet, breathless.

vi) Pineapple Lyon-Brown

A few days after I had returned home, I went to have lunch in the park again. It seemed as though the world had changed; it seemed as though it was a very different place.

I had hardly noticed them before, unless forced. Now they were everywhere I looked. Mothers and babies. Mothers struggling with buggies on buses; mothers fighting with their children over sweets at supermarket checkouts; mothers in the park, giving them ice cream and wiping their sticky mouths and planting kisses on their heads. In the park, I sat on my bench and, in the manner of some broody thirty-something ready to run to the nearest sperm bank, I watched them. I felt bewildered by my emotions, by the strength of them; at one point a kid fell down on the gravel and his mother scooped him up, and the sound of his tears made me feel like crying myself.

But then the tears ebbed away. I realised that I was suffering less a sense of grief for Tiryns' situation and more a sense of longing. Something had opened up inside me that had previously been in bud. It surprised me how strong the emotion was – both a personal ache and also a universal one. I had a desire to protect every child being born right now; it was a love for humanity, an instinctive, universal, motherly love.

*

Oh God, what shall I say? How shall I say it? Just a casual 'Hi, how are you?' Should I mention the fight? Apologise?

And all the while the phone was ringing, and then suddenly he had picked up.

'Hello, Anthony here.'

'Anthony, it's Lucy.' I could feel my breath in the receiver, reverberating hotly on my cheek. 'I was wondering if – if you might like to come over to dinner.'

A silence.

'I presume you mean would I like to come over and cook us both some dinner?'

'Uh – well . . .' I blustered, and then I realised that he was laughing, and that the row was over and I was forgiven.

In the early phase of my relationship with Anthony, I loved to watch him cook. He was the type of man who couldn't do anything half-heartedly. He always narrowed all of his energies into one intense, passionate beam of concentration. Now I stood in the kitchen, leaning against the fridge, taking slow sips from a glass of wine, my eyes soft on him. I watched him pluck herbs like a magician weaving a spell; I watched him lift a spoon and close his eyes intently as he took a taste; I watched him wrinkle his nose ponderingly. I felt a flood of appreciation and affection for him.

There were times, you see, in our relationship, when Anthony had been cooking for me, or shopping for me, or massaging my tired feet, and a tiny voice in me had actually objected. It had looked at Anthony and whispered, *All this new man stuff is very sweet – but is it really very sexy?*

Now I knew better. Ovid *had* ended up teaching me a valuable lesson, and it was simply this: that a man who is considerate and kind should be treasured. It was folly, I realised, to hanker after men like Ovid who, for all their charisma and swank and manly arrogance would, inevitably, only end up treating me like shit. I frowned for a minute, wondering why I felt any attraction for these types at all.

Oh God, I prayed, watching Anthony's shoulder blades move beneath his shirt as he stirred and salted, *please can our friendship be properly repaired. Just seeing him now reminds me of how much I've missed him. Please can it all work out.*

I swallowed and walked up to his side.

'This smells *so* yummy,' I cried, breathing in the succulent scent of warm chicken bubbling in oil, and the sweet red fragrance of carrots roasting. I rubbed his shoulder. 'You deserve your own TV show.'

He turned to face me, a lock of dark hair flopping over one eye, and grinned.

'Well, you need some proper food. I mean, Lucy, I spotted a Pot Noodle in your cupboard. Beyond belief!' He rapped my knuckles with a wooden spoon. 'Obviously I threw it away. Good Lord. You're a disgrace.'

We sat down to eat. We kept asking each other how our day had been, how we were. There was a sense of cheerful strain in the way the conversation ping-ponged back and forth, but it was a nice strain. We were both eager to be ultra-considerate, to heal wounds.

Then the issue of my sister came up. I confessed how worried she was; how she seemed tired of her husband and even of her son.

'Well, kids do take up masses of energy,' said Anthony, which I knew was a veiled apology for his comments in the park.

And yet I couldn't quite swallow it.

'Well, I wouldn't know much about that. I mean, I don't have a maternal bone in my body.' I'd meant to say it lightly, but I was aware of the barb, the hurt in my voice, and I blushed, looking down at my napkin.

Oh God. I shouldn't have said that.

'Hey, I was just kidding,' said Anthony, pouring some wine. He bit his lip. 'I'm sure you'd be a great mother, Lucy. Really.'

I pulled a face: half gratified, half pretending to be revolted.

'I just thought you didn't really want to get into that commitment-marriage-kids thing.'

'Oh, I don't,' I said quickly, taking a sip of wine. 'But . . .'

But what?

'Well, what would you call kids if you had them?'

'Anthony, don't tease me. Really. I'm not broody.' I just wanted to get off the subject; it hurt too much.

But Anthony, of course, had no idea.

164

'No, really,' he insisted. 'I'm not teasing you, I'm not bullying you.' He waved his glass carelessly. 'I'm talking about a purely theoretical situation, OK? I'm just curious.'

I paused. God, this was strange. We'd never had this conversation when we were going out. I don't think we'd ever dared, for fear of where it might end.

Then I looked up and saw Anthony looking at me with curiosity and tenderness. I felt moved. I felt soothed. I *could* talk about this with him; in fact, I wanted to. I couldn't tell him exactly what had happened to me with Ovid. But to talk just a little about the subject would help me feel better.

'So,' said Anthony again. 'What would you call them?'

'Well,' I said, blushing slightly, 'I think something unusual is good.'

'Oh God.' Anthony put down his knife and fork theatrically. 'You're going to name your child after a piece of fruit, aren't you? You're going to have a girl, or worse – yes, worse – a boy, and call him Pineapple!'

'You read my mind!' I joked. 'I was thinking about Pineapple for a girl and Passionfruit for a boy. No – seriously – I didn't really mean weirdo-celebrity-unusual. I meant something unusual like a Shakespearean name. Like Ophelia. Or Perdita. Or Lysander. Now I like that. Lysander Lyon.'

'Of course, he'd have your husband's surname.'

'Oh, I'm not taking my husband's surname. I like my name very much, thank you.'

Anthony grinned.

'You could always go double-barrelled.'

I found myself automatically thinking: Lysander Lyon-Brown. Gosh, that sounded deliciously grand. Then I quickly wiped the thought from my mind.

'What about you?' I asked.

'I like Claire or Chloe for a girl, Joshua for a boy.'

A brief silence.

'Anyway, I always thought you didn't want kids,' I retorted, though the funny thing was, I'd always felt he did.

'Of course I want kids,' said Anthony hotly. 'Life without kids would just be lame. I mean, it's OK now, but to get to forty and spend your Christmases alone, without family – well, that would be pretty sad, I think. Anyway, I want to do it because I think I'd be good at it. There are so many rubbish parents out there. I was on the Tube the other day and this kid was running all over the carriage and his dad was just swearing away at him. Maybe it's easy to be arrogant and say, I can do better. But I reckon I can.' He gave a slightly self-conscious laugh and a sheepish shrug.

I stared at him, wide-eyed. It really sounded as though he had been putting a lot of thought into this.

'Of course, if we're going to have kids—' said Anthony. Then he realised his faux pas and blushed furiously. 'So how is work?'

'Um, fine, fine, bit busy but fine,' I said, my ears burning. 'Um, work is fine. How about you?'

The baby subject was closed and we didn't return to it again that evening.

Many hours later, after we had watched a video and sipped hot chocolate and hugged goodbye, I put the dirty plates into the sink, idly squirting in Fairy Liquid, sloshing pans with water to soak. Anthony's presence still lingered in the flat: his laughter, his voice, his sweet teasing. I paused and stared into the reflection in the window, picturing a fantasy scene. A few years on, I'd be in the kitchen, preparing an amazing meal, and Anthony would come in from work. Our kids (two: one boy, one girl) would run out, shrieking, 'Daddy!' He'd scoop them up in his arms and shower them with loving paternal kisses. He'd ask them about their schoolwork; Perdita would, of course, be a genius, whilst Lysander would be a musical prodigy. And then he'd come over and give me a big kiss and say, 'God, Luce, that smells delicious, what's for dinner?'

And I'd say, um, burnt chicken, burnt peas, burnt gravy . . .

My fantasy scratched to a halt. I was a lousy cook. Besides, I was hardly the staying-at-home housewifey sort, was I? I'd be bored out of my skull without intellectual fodder for my hungry brain. So we'd have to get a nanny. I had another vision of Anthony and me in a car in the rush hour, snarling at commuters as we raced to get to a crèche to pick up our screaming, neglected offspring before it closed. I thought of all those offputting articles about working mothers getting only three hours' sleep a week and having to go to the office like walking zombies in a haze of exhaustion before coming home to begin their second job of feeding and changing nappies all night.

But then I pictured Anthony and me lying in bed, our little baby between us, and the look of soft joy on Anthony's face, and I went all gooey again. That was the trouble: my emotions kept on conjuring up images that my fierce intellect wanted to bat out of the way. It was a true battle between my head and my heart.

It's not really a battle at all, though, I told myself as I changed into my pyjamas. Because you're not together. You're not even going out any more.

I decided to stop this mental nonsense by watching some TV. But there was nothing on but boring celebrity TV shows, so instead I curled up in bed with a mug of warm milk, and Lyra as my hot-water bottle, and my old, lovingly dog-eared copy of *Wuthering Heights*. An hour passed and I grew pleasantly sleepy. *See*, I told myself, *if you had a baby, you wouldn't be able to loll about like this in your spare time. You'd have to break off in mid-Heathcliff-swoon and attend to screams or a dirty nappy.*

It was moments like this that made me feel uncertain, that reminded me of how self-sufficient I was, of how I loved my own company, my peace, my privacy. After all, children were handcuffs that signalled the end of freedom. I remembered a wistful remark my mother had made a few weeks ago when she had been lecturing about Anthony. 'In our day,' she said, 'marriage and children were life. Even if you didn't like your husband very much you stuck by him. It's different now. People won't settle for second best. People want to get more out of life.' She'd said it as though my generation were terribly selfish. Well, maybe we *were*, but wasn't that better, to squeeze the best juices out of life? Wasn't that the spirit of this age, wasn't that why there were so many articles yelling 'TEN PLACES TO GO BEFORE YOU DIE'? Wasn't 2005 about seizing the day?

And I wasn't really all that convinced by Anthony's broody streak either. He was far too work-obsessed. I reckoned he just liked the fantasy of it all.

As I turned out the light, I decided: no relationship, no Anthony, no babies.

My head had won.

A few days later, delayed shock suddenly hit me. It was my lunch break; I stepped out into the road and a taxi came hurtling past, missing me by inches. I stumbled back, my heart pounding. Images swam before me: sand, teeth, the lion roaring towards me. I sank down on to the kerb, holding my head in my hands, provoking passers-by to ask if they needed to call 999.

Back in the office, my hands were shaking so much I couldn't even use my computer keyboard. I ended up having to take the afternoon off.

If luck or God or fate hadn't been on my side, I told myself, stroking the cat, if I hadn't run from that lion just in the nick of time, then Lyra would have now been without an owner. And how long would it be before trips in the time machine did kill me? Every era was fraught with danger. It was like playing Russian roulette.

And that was when I made a promise to myself never, ever to risk using the time machine again.

Chapter Five

Al Capone

You can get a lot more done with a kind word and a gun, than with a kind word alone.

AL CAPONE

i) Dressing up

I was late meeting Anthony. As I raced up the escalator at Oxford Street Tube station, I spotted him with grimly folded arms, curses pinched into the corners of his lips.

Anthony was extremely punctual. He tended to get worse when he was working very hard – it became a sort of angry nervous tic.

'Anthony!' I panted. 'No . . .' I had to stop him from telling me off. 'I really do have a good excuse. Oh God, Anthony, Sally wants a divorce! And my mum's totally freaked out and it's a big family crisis and everything's a total MESS.'

'Shit!' Anthony looked appalled. 'Oh Luce, I'm so sorry. Here.' He pulled me in for a tender hug. 'Come on, let's go get you a good strong mug of tea.'

We weren't meant to be stopping for tea. On Saturday morning we would be setting off for Suffolk; Anthony's father was celebrating his sixtieth birthday with a 1920s theme. But our costumes were forgotten as we sat down over two steaming mugs and I poured out the whole story. Of course, I'd seen the divorce coming; the signs had been there. Sally's tiredness. Her boredom. Her restlessness. But still, it was a shock. My sister had always been rather smug about her supposedly fantastic marriage, and though it had irked me, I had secretly admired her for it.

'And what about Adam, will he live with Sally?' Anthony asked.

'I don't know. I guess. For now he's with Mum. Sally says she needs some space to think.' I saw a flicker of hurt on Anthony's face and bit my lip; given his own history, his protectiveness towards Adam was understandable.

'But look, he has two parents who love him like mad, he'll be fine,' I said quickly, before sinking into grey glumness again. 'It's just depressing, that's all. I mean – they've only been together seven years. And I thought they were different. That's naïve, I know. I mean, I bumped into a friend from uni the other day, and

171

she's only thirty and she's already been married *and* divorced *and* remarried.'

'Yeah,' said Anthony, his idealistic streak burning bright, 'some people damn well need a car sticker that says, "Marriage is for life, not just for Christmas".'

He looked relieved when I laughed.

'Have you cheered up enough to come and do some shopping?' he asked tentatively. 'I mean, are you still OK to come this weekend? Maybe you'd rather . . .'

'God, no,' I said. 'I really need to escape. I'm OK. Well, just about.'

I forced a smile and found it wasn't so hard after all. Anthony really was the best person to be around in a crisis, because he was so kind and reliable. I could tell that he felt anxious about me, and just the fact that someone cared – really cared – made me feel cocooned and cheered.

It wasn't too hard finding a snappy suit for Anthony. In the first shop we went into we found a gorgeous black gangster suit, as well as a pearl velour hat with a black brim.

'I hate dressing up. Will Al Capone be there?' I grumbled as Anthony changed in the cubicle.

'Well, I think we sent him an invite,' Anthony called through the door, 'but he might be a bit on the maggoty side, Luce. Anyway, I thought you were into Byron. Is Capone more or less sexy than Byron, then?'

'More,' I asserted, for Byron was definitely no longer in my going-to-bed list; he wouldn't even make the top one hundred.

'Oh, more?' Anthony popped his head over the door, looking surprised and impressed. 'So what's Capone got then?'

'Well, I'm not wild about him – but he's an icon, isn't he?'

'Go on. Tell me. I'm interested.'

'Well, he's dangerous. And exciting. I mean, he was a rogue but I guess the reason we like rogues is because they're so unbounded. They don't play by the rules of society like the rest of us do; they have the will and the strength to do their own thing.'

'Like torturing and shooting innocent people?'

172

I grinned.

'OK, OK. I don't know how to describe it. It's just that he's so . . . I don't know . . . so tough. He seems like a real man. Not a trace of boy in him, you know.'

'So?' Anthony emerged from the cubicle and flipped his fingers into the lapels of his jacket. 'Am I a match for Capone?' He put on a deep, gravelly voice.

I stared at him, about to jest back. But then I found myself absorbed in making a genuine comparison. The suit did make him look good. Taller, broader. Anthony had been a little on the skinny side when we'd first met, and I liked to run my hands teasingly over his rib cage, but in the past two years he'd filled out, and regular trips to the gym had added to his beef. And yes, he did look hot in the suit, hat cocked. But he was disappointingly unsexy. He just didn't have that mean-guy attitude. I couldn't get away from the reality: he was Anthony Brown, head of a computer firm, who spent his days shuffling paper.

Anthony frowned, sensing my doubt without being able to quite understand it.

'You don't think it looks any good, do you?' he cried.

'No, really, it's fine. You look absolutely gorgeous and fantastic and all the girls will be all over you,' I gabbled quickly.

Anthony grinned, called me a flatterer and went back to change. I frowned, feeling confused.

Finally, Anthony and I had got our friendship back on track. We'd had a frank discussion and laid down some ground rules, declaring that we weren't allowed to interfere in each other's love lives. Now things had settled down again into something warm, comfortable and easy. We called each other a few times a day; we texted at least twenty. If anything, we were getting on better now than we ever had as a couple. It was all rather ironic. Now that we expected less of each other, we seemed to give more; now that the pressure was off, we seemed to enjoy deeper affections.

And yet.

It was still slightly messy separating the yolk of friendship from the white of a relationship. Sometimes I looked at him and some of

173

the little things he did – the curve of his smile, a protective arm on my waist – reminded me of just why I had fallen in love with him all those months ago and my heart tumbled as though ready to take the fall twice. And then other times I looked at him and it was gone, my desire in ashes, burnt by my urge to find a man who was . . . who was . . . well, I wasn't sure *quite* what, but something more, something special . . . *something* . . .

Still, at least he had stopped being jealous. These days I felt I could flirt with anyone right under his nose and he wouldn't blink. In fact I was beginning to think that he had stopped fancying me altogether.

Which I guess made our friendship a whole lot simpler.

The search for my outfit proved more complicated. We discovered many glorious dresses, but none of them were remotely 1920s. Nor could we give up and leave it for another day, since we had left it right until the last minute as it was.

I began to weary and lose concentration; black worries about Sally began to surface again. I suggested we stop for a break.

And that was when the trouble started.

We took a detour down an oh-so-familiar side street. Suddenly Anthony broke off in mid-conversation and cried, 'Lucy, look! A costume hire shop.'

'Oh – oh, no . . . I really really really have a deep urge for some Belgian chocolate,' I gabbled, but Anthony ignored my protest and dragged me towards the shop.

'Really, Anthony, I don't want to hire something, I need to buy something.'

'But we haven't got much time; you'll never get anything.'

He pushed me, struggling, through the door.

Into the very costume shop I had ventured into that time I'd hired a costume to visit Leonardo da Vinci.

Oh well, I prayed hopefully, *they must have many staff here. I mean, I'm sure it won't be the same man who served me before, and besides, even if it is, he won't remember me—*

'Lucy!' he cried, pushing through the racks of clothes. 'How lovely to see you again! How did your Milanese male-apprentice outfit go down? I'm sorry I missed you when you brought it back, I was dealing with another customer. Do tell all, my dear!'

Anthony shot me a look of pure amazement.

'Oh – well, it was great . . . Now I need—'

'Don't tell me,' the assistant cut in, raising a playful eyebrow. 'More cross-dressing parties to attend?'

'Uh . . .' I blushed so brightly that the man suddenly realised his faux pas and muttered a quick apology. Anthony, meanwhile, looked rather stunned.

'I want a twenties dress, something glamorous,' I said.

'Of course, of course,' the assistant said hurriedly, keen to clear up his mistake. 'I have just the thing. Why don't you try it on here; with a dress like this, you'll want to be sure it fits.'

Anthony, who had now recovered, nudged me and whispered into my ear, 'I'll have to hear about these parties later, Lucy – what have you been up to?'

I dived into the changing room. *Shit, how the hell am I going to explain that to Anthony?* Then all my nerves were forgotten as I pulled on the dress and gaped at my reflection. It was a classic 1920s flapper dress, the colour of a pale blue winter's sky, covered in glittering teardrop beads. I actually looked . . . OK! In fact, I looked good. It was impossible *not* to look good in a dress as shimmery and skin-kissing as this. I pulled on the accompanying feather boa and the whole thing looked just perfect.

Out in the shop, I whirled around in excitement, waiting for Anthony to tell me I looked beautiful. After all, that was the whole point of taking a man shopping with you, wasn't it?

And Anthony was so good at making me feel good about myself. When we'd first started dating, I'd insisted we make love with all the lights off. I'd even make Anthony laugh by twitching the curtains firmly shut so that a sliver of street-lamp couldn't sidle in and pounce on my small breasts, or the cellulite on my thighs, or the funny knobbly shape of my feet. A year later, I was happy to make love with all the lights blazing. Because Anthony had slowly given me confidence. He'd told me that I was perfect because I wasn't perfect. Whenever we'd gone shopping in the past, he would make me come and twirl in front of him and declare I looked wonderful, and then to prove he wasn't just saying it, he'd come up with some thoughtful detail, like 'It shows off your legs' or 'It makes you look more curvy.' In that respect, he had been a dream boyfriend.

Now, however, he had taken a work call on his mobile. He swung round, looked me up and down, broke off and said vaguely, 'Very nice . . .'

'Oh, thanks,' I said, but he had turned away.

The shopkeeper said hastily, 'You look absolutely terrific, my dear.' I nodded and held my head high, but back in the changing room I couldn't help smarting. Obviously Anthony really didn't fancy me any more. Maybe I was putting on weight. Maybe I was too *old*. But I didn't really fancy Anthony either, so surely my hurt was just sheer vanity? I was reminded of a quote from Coleridge: *The desire of a man is for a woman; a woman desires the desire of a man.* There was some truth in that, I thought, suddenly feeling horribly egotistical.

All the same. *Very nice.* That's the sort of compliment your granny pays when you give her a tea-cosy. *Very nice,* indeed.

As I paid for the outfit, I flirted outrageously with the shopkeeper, but Anthony barely seemed to notice. The shopkeeper, who was about seventy, looked deeply confused.

Then I took my *very nice* outfit home, feeling strangely despondent.

ii) Anthony and the time machine

Well, at least I had a nice dress. I had a party in Suffolk to go to. There'd be food, music, glorious dancing. I could get insanely drunk and blot out all my family misery. Plus, I would be away from the time machine so I could avoid that temptation.

I just had Friday to get through.

And boy, did it drag. The hands on the clock shivered forward, minute by minute, like those of a teasing lover. Finally 4.55 came and I ran out five minutes early, resisting the urge to dance down the pavement and scream, 'IT'S THE WEEKEND!'

And then, on the way home, I got a text from Anthony:

In yr flat. Got a surprise for you.

My heart quickened. My walk became skippity as I happily pondered all the possibilities.

I let myself into the flat.

'In here,' Anthony called from the living room.

I danced in. I stopped. I dropped my handbag in shock.

'Uh . . . uh . . . what the hell are you *doing*?'

Anthony looked up. Ironically, he'd never looked more sexy. His hair was dishevelled and he'd taken off his shirt and there was a smudge of grease licking across his naked torso. He was holding a screwdriver between his teeth which he now removed.

'Well, you said that having this stupid time machine thingy in the corner of your room was a pain in the neck. So I thought I'd save you the time and trouble and take it apart. That way it's much easier to get it to the dump.'

'Oh shit!'

I ran over, examining the damage. The time machine looked like a building which had suffered the wrath of a storm; chunks and hunks were scattered like windblown blocks around the carpet. But he had been working from the outside in, so the central section was intact: the seat and more importantly, the time pod. All he had really attacked was the outer shell.

'Oh thank God!' I cried. 'We can still save it.'

'But – but . . .' Anthony faltered, looking disappointed. 'Luce, you've been moaning about how this thing is a waste of time and space and—'

'I didn't ask you to take it apart, though!' I wailed. 'I mean, you could have asked me!'

'So you're saying you want me to put it all back together?' Anthony asked incredulously.

'Yes!' I cried. I breathed out. 'Yes. Please do.'

'But . . . but . . . why?' Anthony stared at me with a deep frown. 'You said it was useless junk!'

'It's – it's got sentimental value,' I said, avoiding his eyes. 'I've grown fond of it.'

177

'Fond of it? It's a heap of metal! You'll be proposing to your washing machine next.' Anthony's voice was high and sarcastic, but underneath his jokes I could see he felt hurt and sheepish at having done the wrong thing.

'Look – can you please just put it back together while I go and make some tea?' I said and went off to the kitchen.

As I made the tea, a queasy feeling started in my stomach. I knew that I was going to tell him the truth; I'd been wanting to for so long, and my mouth was pregnant with words aching to be released. The logical, rational part of me kept screeching at me to stop and think but I knew that I was going to ignore it. I had to tell him the truth. It was now or never.

Of course, he didn't really believe me.

At first he thought I was just joking about. He kept nodding at me solemnly and quipping, 'Well, I can imagine it's very handy, Luce, for nipping forwards in time and going to check on the lottery.' I didn't dare tell him about Byron and Leonardo and Ovid so I tried to keep my explanation as neutral and logical as possible. He went all quiet and funny and started staring into his coffee cup. So then I tried to explain the science behind it again, which wasn't much help either. Anthony had barely even heard of quantum physics. He was a businessman; his idea of physics harked back to his school days, to solid experiments that could be scrawled into books with neat conclusions.

'Look,' I said, 'remember that years and years ago people thought it was utterly shocking to imagine that the earth was round or that it wasn't the centre of the universe? Well, logically, there are things that exist right now that we don't believe in simply because we've been brought up not to. Our boundaries are shaped by society and newspapers and parents, so when quantum physics comes along and tells us that there's a unified field and we can defy time, then yes, it's hard to swallow. But it doesn't mean to say it isn't true.'

'OK! Let's try it then. If it really does work, we can go anywhere in time.' He managed to keep a straight face – just.

'Well, what period would you like to visit?'

'Erm – the Crusades might be fun. All that blood and fighting – cool!'

'Well, we don't have the right costumes. I mean, we can't just turn up in jeans when everyone else is in chainmail.'

Anthony erupted into incredulous laughter.

'Oh, you mean you don't have a facility on your machine for automatically changing your outfit? God, I think you need a better model, Lucy.'

'Well I'm hoping to bid for one on eBay,' I quipped, though inwardly my heart was thudding. Oh my God, I kept thinking, how on earth is he going to react when . . . 'I know – hang on. We can use those clothes we got for . . .' I ran off into the bedroom. After our shopping trip we had dumped the carriers for both our outfits in my wardrobe so we could easily shove them in his boot when he picked me up. Then I stopped short. *Are you sure about this, Lucy?* I asked myself. I searched my heart and it kept circling back to the same answer: yes. I realised that most of all I just wanted to share this experience with Anthony. It didn't feel right to keep anything from him. Using the time machine myself had been fun, but I was bored of silly love affairs. I wanted to share an adventure with my best friend.

I ran back into the living room.

'Come on then!' I cried. 'We can go into the nineteen twenties if we put these on!'

'Hey – cool, we can meet Al Capone,' said Anthony.

'First things first,' I said. 'Before we go anywhere, we have to fix the machine.'

It took us a good hour to put it all back together. At the end we found ourselves with a leftover part, an L-shaped piece of beige plastic, and couldn't for the life of us work out where the hell it ought to go.

It was fun dressing up. We played about a bit with some make-up. I painted my lips into a scarlet rosebud and pencilled a silly moustache on Anthony's upper lip. Finally we were ready.

'Maybe we should get something to eat,' Anthony said, suddenly nervous.

179

'Oh come on, don't tell me you're going to chicken out!' I cried.

'No, no, I'm not saying that . . .' Anthony puffed up with male bravado. 'I just know it's not going to work. Come on, I'll bet you a hundred pounds it doesn't.'

'OK, sure,' I said.

Now he really did look nervous. Especially when I forced him to take a speaking potion, which he declared tasted like cat's piss.

'Lucy, I think this potion thing is taking the joke too far. I mean, you *are* just bluffing me, aren't you? OK, OK, let's try it then. But you're going to owe me a hundred quid. OK, what buttons do we press? Right, I'll let you do it . . . OK, then we press this green one, do we? Lucy, you are so going to owe me— Shit, Lucy, what's happening, what's all this darkness and . . . *Lucyyyyyyyyyyyyyyyy* . . .'

iii) Coffee for two

The time machine deposited us, rather unceremoniously, in the middle of a basement bar. Nor did it have the grace to land us neatly on some chairs; we found ourselves lying face down on the floor. My nose wrinkled as I ingested a cocktail of debauched scents: woodgrain, alcohol, layer upon layer of cigarette smoke so thick it seemed to hover above the floor like a miniature yellow smog.

Anthony and I looked up, gazing around in shock. A man came out of the gents, did up his flies, and stepped over us to get to his seat, looking down at us with a snort. No doubt he thought we were drunkards. Jazz music played in the background and people sat behind tables sipping from fat white coffee cups.

'Lucy, where are we?' Anthony hissed.

I tried to get up – I felt we might be able to handle this better if we were upright – but like a frightened child clinging to his mother, Anthony grabbed my hand and pulled me back down.

'Lucy, Lucy,' he whispered frantically. 'It worked, didn't it . . .' He swallowed and whispered in shock, 'I owe you a hundred pounds.'

I clutched his hand, and stroked his hair, suddenly feeling very motherly and protective.

'It's OK, we're safe,' I said gently. I leaned over and gave him a light kiss on the cheek. 'Trust me.'

'But the machine . . .' He kept looking about with frightened moon eyes. 'It's gone, it's gone!'

'We can get it back,' I reassured him. 'Now let's stand up before we get into trouble.'

We stood up. It must be said that we were dressed much too smartly for this place. They were all wearing everyday clothes, the men in suits, the women in coats and cloche hats. The clock on the wall said 5.30 p.m.

We tried to ignore the suspicious glances we were getting and took a seat in one of the booths. Was it my paranoia or had everyone gone quiet around us? All except for an old man sitting in the next booth. He was tall, with a bald head, wrinkled as a walnut, and a face like a pixie. He was sitting alone but talking out loud, telling an anecdote in part to the passing waitress and in part to anyone else who might be listening, his Irish accent flowing out in a colourful rasp . . .

'And I said to him, I said, if you're going to play the piano, you've got to get it right . . .'

I couldn't help noticing that the waitresses gave us a wide berth. Finally we were approached by a large woman. I had thought the flapper fashion was a rebellion for young women below the age of thirty, but despite the fact that she looked as though she was heading for sixty, she was wearing a gorgeous black beaded dress frothing with ecru lace, her face caked with make-up.

'Hello,' she said. Was it my imagination or was her tone just a tad unfriendly? 'What can I get you?'

'I'd like a Guinness,' said Anthony authoritatively. 'And Lucy would like a Baileys.'

The woman froze, tapping her pencil hard against her pad.

'I'm afraid we don't serve drinks here. Ever heard of a little something called Prohibition?'

Anthony and I exchanged uneasy glances. Of course we had heard of Prohibition. It was the banning of alcohol in the US in the 1920s, pushed into place by fervent Christian groups. Unsurprisingly, turning alcohol into a forbidden fruit only made more people hungry for a bite, and alcohol had never been so popular.

'Oh, come on, haven't *you* ever heard of a speakeasy? That's a place where you serve us alcohol while we all wink and pretend to be drinking coffee,' said Anthony, colouring.

I groaned silently, but Anthony's jaw strengthened and he said firmly, 'OK, we won't bother drinking if you won't serve us what we want. We'll sit here and talk.'

'You can have coffee, if you like. That's what everyone else is drinking. Take it or leave it, but if you're not drinking, you can leave,' she said smartly.

'I . . .' said Anthony.

'We'll have two coffees,' I said hastily.

She gave us suspicious looks and waddled off. I leant towards Anthony and hissed, 'I think she's suspicious of us.'

'What d'you mean?'

'Well – I think this *is* a speakeasy, but we've freaked her out. I think everyone thinks we're Prohibition agents or something. Look at the way people are leaving.'

Anthony looked around and saw that I was right: everyone was downing their drinks hastily and saying their goodbyes. Then I saw that our hostess hadn't gone to get us drinks at all. She was now talking to a rather burly-looking bouncer and pointing at us.

'. . . because the piano, I mean, the piano's like a girl, you only have to look at the curves on the thing . . .' the old Irishman wittered on, his voice slurring.

The bouncer came strolling up to us and said pleasantly, 'Excuse me – I don't remember seeing you earlier. Can you remind me of the password again?'

'Erm . . . is it . . . ?' Anthony paused, wincing, feigning amnesia. 'Er . . .'

Suddenly there was a gunshot.

It seemed to come out of nowhere. It hit one of the mirrors on the wall, which shattered and tinkled on to the floor. People screamed and either fled for the door or cowered under seats. The jazz music came to a halt.

Only the Irishman seemed oblivious. He wandered over towards the gents, fiddling with his zip, staggering as though drunk.

Tap, tap, tap, footsteps clicked down a series of steps. A man appeared. He was wearing a velour hat and his face was sharp with anger. His gun was slack by his side. He grabbed one of the coffee cups from the table and then took a swig.

'Lovely stuff,' he said. 'Yep, I can see this place serves the finest coffee in town. Can I ask if the proprietor could please step forward? Because I'm afraid you're under arrest.'

The bouncer standing by us backed up quickly. There was a scream in the background and to our amazement the Irishman reappeared. He was now looking distinctly sober and he was ushering the large woman in front of him. He snapped a cuff around her wrist and shook hands with the man with the gun.

'Nice work, Inspector Tessaro. Good one.'

'McClough, good on you. Now,' Tessaro raised his voice, 'nobody here *move*. And you, Mrs Torrio – you're under arrest,' he told the woman.

'I was only selling coffee,' Mrs Torrio wailed.

'Oh sure you were,' said McClough. 'And I'm sure your *coffee* was in line with the Eighteenth Amendment and only contains half of one per cent alcohol, is that right?'

'Shit!' Anthony whispered to me. 'Can we get arrested just for being here?'

'I don't know,' I hissed back, shrugging. 'Maybe!'

I was about to suggest it was high time to will the time machine back when Anthony suddenly got up and strolled right over to McClough.

Anthony, I cried silently, watching in bewilderment as he shook McClough's hand firmly. What the hell was he doing? I got up hastily and sidled over to him.

'Hi, I'm Anthony Brown. I'm here with my sister Lucy. I'd like to say congratulations. We're working for Eliot Ness and we were about to close in on Torrio here when you beat us to it.'

'You're working for Ness?' McClough's expression warmed up at once. 'Good on you. I'm sorry – I had no idea he'd sent you.'

'Oh, well, normally we work in New York, but we're here for a few days,' Anthony rambled on. I gave him a sharp nudge in the ribs that warned him, *We're not going to get away with this.*

*

183

But to my amazement, we *did* get away with it.

Having dispatched Mrs Torrio to a cell, Tessaro and McClough invited us back for some real coffee at a Chicago police station. I kept quiet, feeling rather intimidated by it all, but Anthony did some fine smooth-talking. For Anthony, back in 2005, was a good businessman; he could play the chameleon, shape his words to please other people. Now he switched on his charm at full blast. I couldn't help glowing with admiration for him. He improvised carefully, telling stories – without too many details – of speakeasies and dirty saloons we had invaded. He commiserated with McClough on how badly Prohibition agents were paid – 'Can you believe we earn even less than garbage collectors?' McClough cried, and ranted on for a good while about how it was no wonder most of the agents were so corrupt and secretly protecting Capone.

'Speaking of Capone,' Anthony said. 'We're making good progress in closing in on him. You see, we've got a secret weapon. And she's sitting right beside me.'

The officers glanced at me and I grinned uneasily. Now what was Anthony playing at?

'Lucy here has managed to get *very* close to Capone,' said Anthony knowingly. 'And I think she could get a lot of information about where he's sourcing his goods. In fact, it's kind of frustrating. We've run out of expenses and we're due to return to New York tomorrow, just when we're close to a breakthrough . . .'

An hour later, Anthony and I found ourselves in the Atlantic Hotel on Clark Street. Anthony had managed to persuade McClough to put us up for one night; in return we would meet him tomorrow evening with information on Capone.

Up in the hotel, Anthony and I gazed around the room in a state of disorientated awe. It was really rather plush and the view from the window was thrilling: a street filled with 1920s hooded cars, the sparkle of city lights. I made for the bathroom, but Anthony caught my wrist.

'Lucy, you're not going anywhere before you tell me everything. I mean – what the fuck happened back there?' The shock, which he had managed to hold at bay during our time at the police station, now seemed to hit him in a tidal wave. 'I mean, one minute we were in your living room – and then – and then – and now – and—'

'I'll tell you everything,' I said, laughing a little. 'But let's get ready for bed first. I'm completely knackered. I find the time machine does that – it's a sort of jet-lag thing.'

We took it in turns to use the bathroom, draping our clothes carefully over the sofa, since they were the only ones we had. We had no pyjamas, so we made do with fluffy dressing gowns, and our fingers had to serve as substitute toothbrushes.

'I can sleep on the sofa,' Anthony volunteered.

I was about to agree when I saw how exhausted he looked.

'Well, we can put a bolster in the bed,' I said, blushing. My voice took on the prim tightness of a Victorian governess. 'We can use some pillows, and those cushions on the sofa.'

We made a squashy line down the centre of the bed and then got in and switched off the lamp. We lay for a while in the grainy darkness, listening to the traffic outside. Then Anthony rolled over to face me, nestling his face in the pillow.

'Now,' he said. 'tell me everything.'

So I told him everything. I told him how upset I had felt when we'd broken up, and how I had gone to visit Byron. I told him how I had ended up in 1813.

'Jesus!' Anthony cried. 'Shit – I mean – that's just unbelievable. I mean – what was it like?'

'Just like 1813,' I said, laughing. 'Ballgowns, carriages, that sort of thing. That's why I've been using that costume shop, you see.'

'Aha, now that makes sense. And you really seriously met Lord Byron.'

'Yes . . .'

'Lucy, you didn't . . . ?' Anthony asked.

I bit my lip, fretting he might be jealous, but he let out a whoop of laughter.

We both laughed then, but I stopped before him and began to pleat the covers nervously, watching him wipe hysterical tears from his eyes.

'God – I want to go back and have love affairs with Cleopatra. And Marilyn Monroe. And Sylvia Plath.'

'Sylvia Plath was mad,' I pointed out.

'I'd make her sane,' Anthony said with a dash of irony, and we both giggled again.

'And who else – Greta Garbo. And Katharine Hepburn—'

'Well you can't,' I interrupted petulantly. 'Because the time machine – it causes trouble.'

'What? Lucy, it doesn't cause trouble, it causes adventure. I mean – fuck – it's like – it's better than the best computer game in the world. People would *die* to have something like this.'

'But Anthony, we have to be careful. I mean, look, when I went back to Roman times, I suffered a near-death experience . . .' And I told him all about Tiryns and her baby, and my fight in the gladiator ring.

'Good God, Lucy!' Anthony shoved the top pillow out of the way and held me tightly. 'You could have been killed!'

'Exactly,' I said emphatically. 'That's why I think we should just leave tomorrow, before we get into any trouble. All we have to do is go back to the exact spot that we landed in, and the time machine will reappear. I'm not sure if I know the way back to the speakeasy, but we can ask the police, make up some story about something we need to investigate there.'

'I guess.' Anthony's hand paused on my hair. 'But . . .'

'But?'

'I don't know, Lucy. I mean, I know what happened to you was terrible, and I never want anything like that to happen to you again,' he said, kissing my forehead. 'But I mean – fuck – this whole thing – I can hardly believe it's happening, and I'm totally freaked out, but I just think that if this is the last time we're going to use it – and I agree it should be the last – then couldn't we just stay one more day? I mean, don't you want to even *meet* Al Capone? C'mon, Lucy! Al Capone!'

'He might not live up to our expectations.'

'Lucy – just one more day. Please. Then we'll go. We'll go before the big bust-up happens. And we'll stick together – that way we can protect each other.'

I pulled a face. My intuition was telling me that this was a bad idea, that the danger was too great. But then I looked at Anthony's face. I hadn't seen him like this in a long time; he looked like a little boy who had just been promised he could meet Santa. And

I had to admit that meeting Capone *was* an interesting prospect . . .

'OK,' I relented, and Anthony pulled me into a big hug of gratitude.

We both agreed then that we seriously needed some sleep. Anthony mended the bolster and we lay there, the room gradually becoming cloudier with darkness.

'This really is so weird, isn't it?' I said out loud, but when I turned to face him, I saw he was asleep. I smiled and snuggled up under the covers, and it struck me, as I sank peacefully into sleep, that tonight I felt closer to Anthony than I had done in months.

iv) The Green Mill Cocktail Lounge

The following evening, Anthony and I found ourselves at the Green Mill Cocktail Lounge, a regular haunt of Capone's. I felt fraught with nerves. My mission was clear: to seduce Al Capone. For the first time in my life, I was meant to play a *femme fatale*.

And let's face it, I was hardly Marilyn Monroe. I kept secretly imagining horror scenarios. Like Capone looking me up and down and declaring that I looked 'very nice', but hey, I really wasn't his type.

Or me and Capone lying in bed and his face dropping in dismay when I took off my dress and he saw my lack of curves. Capone wasn't Anthony. He was undoubtedly the type of man who judged women purely on their looks.

The Green Mill Cocktail Lounge was in uptown Chicago, and was owned by Jack 'Machine Gun' McGurn, one of Capone's favourite henchmen. As we entered, we were greeted by a rich blast of Chicago jazz from the band.

I was convinced that everyone was going to look up from their booths and point at us in deep suspicion. But to my relief, nobody even blinked at us. The jazz rolled over my tense body, helping me to relax a little, my foot automatically tapping along to the aggressive tempo. I glanced around, thinking that it was all rather snazzy. The bar was decorated in art deco and everything was bathed in a green glow from the neon 'Green Mill' in cursive script that blazed above the band. On the walls there were long, ornately wooden-framed murals of mountains and seashore landscapes, and behind the bar was a bronze Schlitz statue and a sign above it proclaiming, *Niema Schlitza, niema piwa*.

This time we knew what to ask for.

'We'll have two coffees, please,' said Anthony. 'There he is,' he added quietly, nodding.

I looked. Capone was sitting in a booth to the right of the bar, with three other guys. He was tucking into a large meal of meat and veg, shovelling in great mouthfuls in a bestial manner. He was wearing a white hat with a black brim and his face looked slightly more puffy than I had imagined. But his features were certainly striking, and his face was dominated by a pair of huge glowering black brows that arched over narrow, cunning grey eyes.

Suddenly, Capone looked up. I jumped. He eyed me up and down – then looked away without interest.

Bastard, I thought.

'Anthony,' I said, taking a sip of my 'coffee', 'I'm just not sure if I can pull this off.'

'Well, to be honest, you should be careful,' said Anthony. 'He has syphilis, for one thing.'

'No he doesn't!' I cried.

'He does, Lucy. I don't know much about this period but I remember seeing on a TV documentary that when he went to prison he had a hard time. He got dementia, because the syphilis, which he'd had since he was a teenager, went untreated.'

'Oh,' I said, my fantasy bubble bursting. 'Oh.'

'Look,' said Anthony, 'let me go over and ask if we can join in with one of Capone's card games. The other thing the documentary said was that he always put on a charming and friendly front.'

'You're going to go right up to him?' I asked, gulping. 'I'm not sure if that's a good idea ... I mean, TV doesn't always get it right ...' I trailed off, for Anthony had already gone.

Once again, to my complete amazement, Anthony pulled it off.

I was expecting Capone to sock him in the face, but the gangster nodded and shook hands, his face stretched into a charming smile, then gestured for us to follow him upstairs.

There we found a group of about six or seven men seated around a table. There was one spare chair, and Anthony ushered me forward, gesturing that he'd pull up another. I was about to sit down when a weaselly man placed his palm on the seat.

'That seat's saved for your friend,' he said, nodding at Anthony.

I stepped back, flushing in indignant confusion. For the first time that evening, Capone looked directly at me. There was a slightly mocking glint in his eyes.

Anthony sat down, frowning.

'You play poker?' Capone asked. I was still amazed by how friendly and jovial his manner was; he didn't seem at all threatened by the presence of a complete stranger.

'Sure.'

Capone dealt the cards in a deft blur of colour and symbols.

'You new in town?' he asked.

'I'm Anthony – and this is my sister, Lucy. We're so glad to have met you, Mr Capone,' Anthony said meaningfully. 'We were hoping to find some employment.'

I froze. Anthony was being far too obvious and forward. But to my surprise, Capone smiled warmly, reached into his jacket and said, 'Sure – here's my card.'

I leaned over Anthony's shoulder, examining it. I only just swallowed my laughter.

AL CAPONE

SECOND-HAND FURNITURE DEALER

2220 SOUTH WABASH AVENUE

'Hey, thanks,' said Anthony, managing to keep a straight face and slotting the card into his jacket.

'I'm sure we can find something for you,' said Capone, patting him on the back.

Then the game began.

Without me.

I stood there feeling like a total lemon. Then a platinum blonde sashayed in and went behind the bar, pouring some drinks. She beckoned me over.

'Hey, I'm Dolores, I'm dating Ralph Capone,' she said, nodding at the weaselly guy. 'I'm afraid we girls don't get to play,' she said in a conspiratorial whisper.

'Why ever not?' I whispered back furiously.

She looked surprised. 'You know what these boys are like. They're all devils, but they want women who are angels. In fact, the more devilish they are, the more they seem to like purity. Now, Angel, take this drink over to Mr Capone. It's a Kemmerer Moon – his favourite,' she added with a wink.

When I set it down in front of him, Capone merely grunted. But as I turned away, I felt his hand gently brush my backside before it returned to his cards.

'Well, Capone seems interested in *you*,' Dolores said with a wink.

'And you're dating his brother?' I asked, blushing.

'Yup. We're getting married tomorrow,' she said.

'You're kidding, congratulations.'

Dolores turned to me and smiled.

'Thanks,' she said warmly. 'You and Anthony are welcome to come.' She let out a sigh and lowered her voice. 'My only worry is – you know – Capone is going to use the wedding as a cover.'

'What d'you mean?' I quickly smoothed the excitement out of my voice, though inside I was tingling. This could be just the breakthrough we were looking for.

'Ralph said Al is going to smuggle some drugs in inside the cake. And I said to him– how does that make *me* feel, using our wedding day to do his dirty business?' She broke off quickly, noticing that her fiancé was giving her a long look. She blew him a kiss and then bit her lip uneasily.

The next time I took a drink over to Capone, he startled me by pulling me on to his lap. I smiled and smoothed down his collar, feeling rather self-conscious.

As the next round of cards proceeded, I felt Capone gently rubbing my knee with his palm. Every so often his fingers trickled up my thigh and then – thank goodness – returned to my knee again. And then he would reach up and nibble my ear lobe and

190

whisper, '*Lucy!*' in my ear. Which might have been nice, but I couldn't help noticing he had rather bad breath, tinged with cigar smoke and too much booze.

I can't say that I was turned on. Maybe it was partly embarrassment that this was all happening in front of Anthony, or maybe it was just the bad breath thing, but I had to steel myself not to jump up and run back down the stairs. I was quite relieved when the game finished and the men packed up, leaving me and Anthony behind at the table with Capone.

'You!' Capone suddenly barked, nearly bursting my ear drums. It turned out he was addressing Anthony. 'I don't trust you. I don't know why. There's something about you.'

And then, to my horror, he took out a gun and laid it casually on the table.

Oh God, I thought, Anthony is just not cut out for this. This is the man who likes to slump in front of the TV at night in stripy M&S slippers. Give him a PC with a problem and he'll fix it, but stick a gun in front of him and he'll go to pieces.

But to my astonishment, Anthony kept his cool.

'I can understand that,' he said, shrugging. 'But I assure you, I want in.'

'Well, how about a little test,' said Capone. He hailed one of his men, who came over and laid out a white line of powder on the table.

'This,' said Capone, 'is a little present. Now, it could be the real thing. Or it could be some sort of flour, or even rat poison, in which case those guys in Cuba are trying to pull a fast one on me. Try it for me, Ant-to-nee.' He drew his name out softly.

I froze. I wanted to catch Anthony's eye and signal it was time to leave. To let him know he didn't have to do this, that things had gone far enough.

'Sure,' said Anthony, shrugging again. 'I'll give it a go.'

What? Anthony hated drugs; he got offended if he was standing at a bus stop and someone so much as lit up a cigarette.

I felt my whole body coil up inside as Anthony lent down and snorted. Then he sat back, wiping his nose, a zing on his face.

'It seems to be the real thing,' he said with a smile.

Capone clapped his hands.

'I like you,' he said. 'I like this guy.' And then he picked up his gun and fired.

Straight at Anthony.

I let out a scream.

Capone laughed.

'Don't worry,' he said, waving his hand. 'There were no bullets in it!' He glanced at Anthony, who was still clutching his chest in shock, and grinned. I think the stupid bastard was rather proud to have succeeded in penetrating Anthony's cool.

'Speak to Ralph and he'll sort you out with a little job we're doing tomorrow. Now – I think it's time to take Lucy for a spin.'

He tipped me off his lap, stood up, grabbed my arm and led me from the table. I kept glancing back in shock, wishing I could shove Capone away and run to Anthony. He looked horrified that I was going off on my own. We'd sworn that we wouldn't separate, and now it was impossible not to.

I knew this whole thing was a mistake, I thought. Oh God – we're already in so deep – how are we going to get out?

Capone's car was impressive. It was black and shiny as patent leather. He opened a door and I slid in. The smell inside was very distinctive. Cigar smoke. Cloth. Expensive leather. And danger. I had to admit it – I liked fast cars.

Capone got in on the other side. He put his hand on my knee, and I felt a flicker pulse through me – more fear than desire. Capone was rather like a black panther – entertaining to observe from a distance, but terrifying to be put into a cage with. I had no idea where we were going, but I had some idea of what he wanted from me, and I felt queasy and panicky at the thought.

Capone fired up the engine and we set off. The streets were relatively empty and Capone put his foot down. I watched the accelerator needle creep up to forty. He put his hand back on my knee.

'This speed OK for you, darlin'? I'm not scaring you, am I?'

I feigned a nervy-damsel look and he grinned.

'We'll see if she can go a little faster.'

I had to turn away to bite back my laughter. Probably 1920s cars would explode if they hit sixty – cars in this age were still a novelty. Perhaps in the year 3000, I mused, they'll all be driving at 200 m.p.h. and will laugh at us for our limits.

As we pulled up at some lights, I noticed a black car behind us – it had been on our tail all the way. I wondered if we were being followed. If I was a gangster, I mused, I wouldn't last five minutes. I'd be constantly worried people were out to kill me. But Capone was completely relaxed, absorbed in his toy. I had thought he was a cool guy; now I realised that he simply lacked the heart and morals of a normal human being.

Unlike Anthony. Anthony had morals, I thought, but he could also be cool. I still couldn't get over how brilliant he had been back in the saloon.

The speedometer hit fifty. I feigned excitement – anything to avoid stopping.

Unfortunately, Capone had other ideas. He brought the car to a halt. The view – downtown Chicago – was hardly picturesque, but then, I thought with a weary sigh, this was Sin City, not the Lake District.

'Lucy,' Capone crooned thickly, leaning in, 'the moment I saw you in the saloon in that dress, I knew I had to have you.'

Have you. As though I was a possession, a car he wanted to own.

I tried to duck my head, but he caught my chin between a fleshy thumb and forefinger. Before I could protest, his mouth was on mine. I kept my eyes open and stared at his face, at his scars and chubby cheeks; he was so close I could see the pores in his skin, and I felt a shudder of revulsion. He mistook it for desire and gripped my hair tightly, pulling me in, his tongue forcing its way between my lips like a writhing eel.

I tried to pretend he was Anthony. It worked for about thirty seconds. Anthony would *never* try to shove his hand up my skirt in such a hamfisted manner.

I began to panic. I had a feeling that the usual sort of excuses weren't going to save me; that he would force me anyway. My eyes wandered around the car. I wondered if there was a gun in the glove compartment.

Oh God, I thought, what am I going to do?

Suddenly we were interrupted by a sharp rap on the windscreen.

A police officer. Oh, thank God.

'For fuck's sake,' Capone moaned. 'What the hell does he want?'

He wound down the window. The officer informed him that he wanted us both to step out of the vehicle.

It is the stuff of legend that Capone, despite killing and torturing dozens of people, was only ever prosecuted for the utterly mundane crime of tax evasion. I wondered, with a vindictive thrill, if I was temporarily about to warp history and give Capone a little taste of life behind bars.

'You, ma'am.' The police officer addressed me. 'What's your name?'

'I'm Lucy Brown,' I said, close to kissing him for being my knight in shining armour.

'I'm afraid you're under arrest. I can see who you are – you're a charity girl, aren't you?'

'*What!*'

'I'm afraid I'm going to have to ask you to put your hands up.'

'Well, Officer,' said Capone in a cool, charming voice, quickly slithering back into his car, 'I do apologise for this misunderstanding. I think I'd better leave you to it. I'm sure you'll understand that I'm a busy man.'

The officer glanced over at him. Then I saw it: the flicker of fear dancing across his face like lightning. That, I realised, was it. That was why it took so long for Capone to be arrested. People were simply terrified of him.

'You have to stop him!' I jabbered. 'Tomorrow there's this wedding, and he's planning a big job, and I'm actually *meant* to be seducing him—'

I broke off in despair as Capone revved up his car and then drove off in a spit of gravel.

'Yes, ma'am, we'll discuss this at the station. Now, please step into the car.'

'I just don't get what this is all about,' I cried, as we drove off. 'I mean – like you say, I'm a charity girl.' Surely that meant I did good things to help other people, right? Perhaps it was code for my work in helping the police.

'You were reported by your brother Anthony.'

'Oh, right,' I said in relief. 'I get it! Oh, thank God for Anthony.'

He would have told the police everything, I realised, and they would have known I had failed and stepped in to rescue me.

The police officer gave me a steely glance in the mirror.

'I hope this is a signal to you to change the error of your ways,' he said, in a rather Bible-bashing tone.

'Oh, very funny,' I laughed, playing along with the joke. 'Sure, I'm going to give up my wicked charity work and stop helping you guys.'

v) Charity girl

When we got to the police station, however, I was more than a little alarmed when the officer didn't remove my handcuffs. Even more worrying, there was no sign of Anthony. When I questioned the officer, he told me that Anthony could bail me out in the morning.

'But – but I thought you said I was a charity girl,' I cried as I was walked down a grey corridor.

'Exactly, ma'am,' said the police officer in a tone of disgust. 'And I'm afraid that prostitution is against the law.'

'What? You think I'm a . . . oh, oh shit. I think we've had a misunderstanding.' *Charity girl.* It was 1920s slang, no doubt. 'Look, Capone was about to rape me, and so Anthony made it up about me being a . . . a prostitute! I'm actually meant to be helping you – you see, I'm working undercover.'

'I'm sure you are, ma'am,' the policeman said drily, looking my rumpled dress up and down. He unlocked a door in a large cage.

Hang on, I thought in panic, I can't share a cell with – what? – six other women! They were all slouching about like wild cats, and now that I had entered, they sized me up with brutal eyes.

'Er – can't I have my own cell?' I asked the officer.

'What d'you think this is, a hotel?' one of the women sneered, and the officer laughed.

'Step in, ma'am, and we'll bring you some fresh towels and a pot of tea,' he said sarcastically.

I stood in the cell, hands dangling by my sides, squirming with self-consciousness. I listened to the steps of the officer slowly fade away. Still, I thought, he'll be back soon, won't he? Won't he?

'So, what are you in here for?' The woman who had sneered at me addressed me again.

'They think I'm a prostitute,' I said sullenly. 'And I'm not, of course. I mean, it's just crazy, and completely unfair.'

'Yeah – I guess a girl like you is way too good to be a prostitute,' the woman spat out. The other women sniggered and jeered in support.

I quivered at my faux pas.

'I didn't mean . . . I mean – really, being a prostitute is obviously a great job if that's your calling in life. I'm sure it brings great job satisfaction and real, um, prospects . . .' I trailed off and stared around at the circle of sullen faces. One of the women was about six foot tall and looked more man than woman. Except for her nails, which she clattered ominously against the bars, as though sharpening them up for attack.

'I – I . . .'

Anthony, this is all your fault, I shouted at him inwardly. *You put me here, and now I'm about to get beaten up by a gang of ladies of the night.*

'Yes?' the woman drawled, giving me one last chance at survival.

'Actually, I'm here because I'm Al Capone's girlfriend,' I cried.

I cringed, waiting for them all to scream and spit at me.

But to my amazement, the atmosphere in the cell immediately changed . . .

'So what's he like in bed? I bet he's a real tiger, isn't he?'

'Is it true he sleeps with a gun under his pillow?'

'And it is true that it's a really, really *big* gun?' one of them asked, and the others burst into laughter, punching her on the shoulder.

'Well, in terms of guns, I'd say it was a rifle,' I said, chuckling. They looked faintly confused, so I said quickly, 'I mean – it's very long.'

'Oh wow.'

'Oo, what a man.'

Several hours had passed and I was now the most popular girl in the cell. They wanted to know every single juicy detail of my relationship with Al. Of course, I'd had to set my imagination to work and start sketching in my own details of our sex life. But they were all utterly riveted. I could hardly believe the kudos; it was the equivalent of being back in 2005 and announcing Brad Pitt was my new man.

'And does he—'

She broke off as footsteps approached the cell. The officer was back and McClough was by his side. My heart leapt.

'I'm sorry, ma'am, it appears there has been a mistake,' the officer said, looking very hot under the collar.

Oh, thank God.

But now how the hell was I supposed to find Anthony?

I realised that McClough was my best hope. I told him all about Dolores' wedding to Ralph and how she suspected that Capone was going to smuggle drugs into the cake. McClough did a little research and discovered that they were going to be married in St Christopher's chapel the next morning at ten o'clock.

McClough suggested I should turn up without him, declaring that his presence might make Capone suspicious. So I went back to the hotel for a few hours, though I was much too worried about Anthony to sleep a wink. I lay in the cold bed, hugging the pillows that had divided us yesterday, watching the pale dawn light streak the room. What if Capone, having left me to get arrested, had gone straight back and shot Anthony?

But he wouldn't do that, I kept telling myself. Anthony hasn't caused him any trouble. He thinks Anthony wants to help him. He trusts us. Doesn't he?

The next morning, I pulled on my flapper dress with shaking hands. I noticed that, due to my various adventures, some of the beads had fallen off. I was swept with a deep longing to be back home with Anthony, trying on our outfits and having a giggle, safe and domestic.

I hailed a taxi to get to St Christopher's. As we pulled up, I had a sneaky feeling that the place looked familiar. Then it clicked: it was right next to the very speakeasy we'd arrived in.

Suddenly I felt a wave of buoyancy. It was a good omen, I was sure. As soon as the wedding was over, I would insist that Anthony go back home with me.

I joined the throng entering the church, spotting Anthony at once. He looked tired and pale and rather fraught, but when I slid into the pew next to him, his face lit up in relief.

'What the hell were you doing getting me arrested? I can't believe you let your jealousy interfere at a time like this,' I hissed.

I was rudely interrupted by the organ echoing tinnily in the high ceilings of the church. The doors swung open and Dolores entered, looking pretty in swirls of white lace and satin. Her father, grey-haired and grim-faced, clutched on to her tightly, as though reluctant to let her go into the arms of such a big, bad man.

'Anthony,' I carried on whispering hotly, 'we're meant to be a team. We're meant to be working together!'

Several people in the pews in front frowned in annoyance. Anthony tried to shush me with a finger on my lips. I shoved it away. He reached down and slipped his hand into mine and hung on tightly.

'Lucy,' he whispered, staring down at me with such a tender expression, it felt impossible to stay angry with him, 'I didn't do it because I was jealous. I just wanted to protect you.'

I let out a deep breath.

'I know,' I said at last. 'I know. I was just so worried I was going to lose you.' And I squeezed his hand back just as tightly.

I shut up then, realising that the vicar was about to start the ceremony. I listened to his quavering voice and felt my heart unclench like a fist. I had found Anthony. In half an hour we'd back home. Everything was OK now.

And then I saw her. I felt someone's eyes on me and found myself instinctively glancing backwards. A woman was staring at me with narrowed eyes. She looked familiar. Then it clicked, and I quickly turned away.

Mrs Torrio! The woman who had been arrested for running a speakeasy! What the hell was she doing here?

She must have got bail, I realised. And if she'd been invited to this wedding, she must be in with Capone.

What if she knows we're working for Capone now? What if she knows we're double-crossing him? What if she's already told him?

I found myself beginning to break out in a sweat. The church walls seemed to close in on me; the voices declaring their vows blurred. We have to get out of here, I kept telling myself. But if we made a run for it now, we would only attract attention and suspicion.

The vows over, the happy couple kissed and glided back down the aisle. They had just made it to the door when I spotted Capone. He was staring straight at me and Anthony with deadly eyes. Then he turned and spoke to a man in a grey overcoat, pointing us out.

'Anthony,' I said feverishly, 'we have to get out of here. Fast.'

'No,' Anthony hissed. 'We have to stay. Lucy – I know what Capone's about to do. He's using the wedding cake—'

Bang!

I didn't quite understand at first. I realised the guy in the overcoat had fired, and I was aware of Anthony crumpling beside me, but I still couldn't quite believe it.

Dolores, who was just leaving the church, turned back. Her mouth tightened.

'Ralph!' she screamed, hitting him with her bouquet. 'I can't believe you let them gun someone down *at my very own wedding!*'

'Lucy,' Anthony moaned, collapsing on to the floor. Guests began to cry out in shock and panic.

'Get everyone else outside.' Capone and his henchmen began ushering people out quickly. 'Time for wedding photographs! Hurry!'

I stared down at Anthony in shock. *This can't be happening*, I thought, as a river of blood oozed from his body.

I didn't clutch his hand and weep over him like something out of a movie. In a situation of such extreme shock, it seemed impossible to feel anything except blankness. It was as though the wave of grief that filled me was so strong my mind clamped down a flood barrier; later it would burst and emotions would pour in. As I ran to his side, I felt oddly detached, as though I was watching myself from above. I cradled his head in my cupped palms; it suddenly seemed so fragile, I feared it would break like an eggshell. He stared up at me through woozy eyes, then reached out, clawing air. In the manner of a child feeling for his mother, he grabbed a fistful of my dress, clinging on tight, a smile breaking the pain on his face. Then he sank back with a groan, eyes closed. His face was pasty with sweat, so pale you could see the rivers of green veins; all the muscles in his neck were thick and contorted with pain and his body kept twitching with spasms.

It was when I looked down and saw the blood seeping on to my dress that it hit me.

'We have to do something!' I screamed. 'We need a doctor!'

I stared up. Capone's men stood in a circle, at a cautious distance, all looking faintly embarrassed.

I saw Al pull out his cigar case from his jacket pocket and flip it open. His hands shook ever so slightly. He pulled out a fat cigar. Then he started in shock as I reached up and knocked the case across the aisle with a clang, his cigars rolling all over the floor. His face screwed up in anger and for a moment I thought he was about to hit me; then he let out a deep sigh.

'We need a priest,' he said. 'Get the vicar back here now. The guy deserves to have his last rites.'

'A priest? We don't need a priest, we need a DOCTOR!' I heard myself shouting, my voice echoing around the church. How I hated them; I wanted to grab them by the lapels and shriek into their white, indifferent faces.

'Lucy!' a voice called. 'Are you OK?'

McClough ran into the church. He stopped short when he saw Anthony.

'My God,' he said. He turned to Capone, white-faced and trembling. 'Don't think you're going to get away with this.'

'Help me,' I begged him. 'You have to help me get Anthony next door, and we have to do it now.'

'What? I'll call Tessaro. Capone and his men are going nowhere.'

'No, listen to me – I don't even want a doctor, I just want to get Anthony next door into the speakeasy. Do you understand me? I can't carry him by myself.'

'But—'

'You have to help me,' I screamed. 'You have to help me!'

'OK, OK.' McClough took hold of Anthony's shoulders and together we carried him out of the church. Guests turned to look and point; I sliced my way through them, hardly aware of Dolores by my side, weeping and begging me to forgive her.

We took Anthony down the staircase that led to the basement speakeasy. The bouncer was back.

'Password?' he said.

'For God's sake, let us through!' McClough shouted. 'Can't you see this man's dying!'

Inside, McClough tried to carry Anthony to a booth, but I shoved him away. He stumbled back in confusion; I didn't care. I willed the time machine to appear with blurry eyes, my heart choking with relief when it came.

I dragged Anthony inside. His body collapsed against me, his head lolling on the seat. I checked his pulse: barely a flicker. I opened one of his eyes. It stared back at me. As a flash of life sparked in that eye and then faded, leaving nothing but a blank pupil reflecting my face. I let out a ragged gasp and bent down and showered his face with kisses, whispering, 'Don't leave me, Anthony, don't leave me, don't leave me.' I kept talking to him as I typed in the date. When I got to the time, I made it ten minutes before we had got into the machine. That way, Anthony would never know that it had worked; that way he would never be tempted to use it again and risk his life. I pressed the green button and then time spun past and I clutched him tightly, pressing my cheek against his pale one, desperately praying to God to bring him back to me . . .

'Lucy, this can't really work, can it?'

Where were we?

Back in my living room. On the rug. Traffic outside. Oh, thank God. And Anthony – Anthony was alive!

He was just walking over to the time machine and examining the controls. For a moment I couldn't say a word. I just wanted to watch him. I stood there, tears hot in my eyes, drinking in his body, his expression, his beauty. I walked up close to him, my eyes fixed on his Adam's apple, on the leap of life pulsing in his throat.

'Hey, we should try it! I just know this thing will work,' he said.

He doesn't remember, I realised with relief. I've wound back time, and wiped out his memory. I felt puzzled. How come I remembered our adventures when Anthony couldn't?

Perhaps the shock had been so great that when he was shot he had blotted out all the events.

'I mean, I've always been cynical about these things, but I just know it's going to work. Don't ask me how I know, Lucy, but I know.'

He was about to get into the machine. I heard a howl emerge from my lips. With a force that surprised me, I leapt on him, yanking him back.

Anthony laughed in surprise.

'Oh, you want to go first, do you? Honestly, Lucy! How about learning some manners, young lady!' He fought me off, heading for the machine again.

'*NO!*' I leapt on to his back, grabbing him. Still thinking this was all a game, he let out a howl of laughter, spinning me round and round until he dislodged me and I slid on to the floor. I collapsed in a heap and he laughed and dug his fingers in my rib cage, tickling me fiercely. I burst into shrieks of laughter; then my laughter shattered into tears.

'Lucy!' Anthony cried in surprise.

'Don't get into that machine,' I begged him in a choked voice. All the grief that had been locked in my shocked heart now poured out in a waterfall. I sat up, but couldn't quite make it to standing, so I clung to his leg, burying my face in his black trousers. 'Please stay, please stay.'

'Lucy, are you OK?' Anthony reached down awkwardly, half caressing my hair, half trying to gently prise me away from his leg.

He lifted me up and peered into my face. I tried to smile and appear normal, but it was impossible. He pulled me into his arms and gave me a hug, stroking my hair and shushing me as though I was a little girl. I clung to him tightly, crushing his rib cage against mine, revelling in the feel of his heartbeat. He waited patiently for the sobs to retreat from my body and my breathing to soften, then he pulled back a few inches. I stared at him through blurry, bloodshot eyes. It's all right, I told myself, over and over. It's all right. We're here, in the present, and he's safe. He's alive.

I stared into his eyes and pulled him into another hug. Anthony hugged me back, then pulled me down on to the sofa next to him.

'Lucy, you're scaring me,' he said in an intense voice. 'What on earth is going on?'

'It's just . . . just . . .' For a moment I was gripped by an urge to tell him the truth, to relive everything we'd shared. But if I told him, the desire, the temptation for him to use the machine again would be irresistible. It wouldn't make any difference if I told him he had died; he would still ache to try it out. I knew the pull it exerted over me. I looked up into his eyes. He gently stroked a strand of hair back from my face. A beat passed between us. Suddenly I became acutely conscious of his body: the curve of his lips, the strength of his jaw. The air around us seemed to gather like invisible thunderclouds before a storm. My tears were dry now, my stomach hollow, but I felt flushed with the desire to make love to him, to cancel out his death with the ultimate life-affirming act, and then to fall asleep nestled naked in his arms, his skin warm against mine.

He leaned in closer; I stared at his lips. I saw them move . . .

'Lucy? *Lucy?*' He snapped his fingers in front of my face.

'It's just – it's just PMT,' I concluded with an embarrassed laugh.

'But you never get PMT,' said Anthony, looking unconvinced, stroking my hair again. He knew that I didn't cry that often, and bursting into tears for no reason just wasn't my style.

'I'm fine,' I said, patting his knee. 'That's the main thing.'

I got up to go and he pushed me back down.

'Lucy, don't shut me out,' he said with a flash of anger. 'Something's up. OK, you don't have to tell me what it is, but don't fob me off. I'm your best friend, for God's sake.'

'I'm sorry – I'm really sorry . . .' I felt tears prick my eyes again, and then he put his arm around me, pulling me in close, and sighed. 'Sorry, I've set you off again. I didn't mean to snap.'

I finally managed to gain control of myself, packing a lid down on my grief and sealing it back in my heart.

'Really – I'm fine. You're right – something happened, but I can't talk about it.'

'You're sure?'

I nodded, staring at my knees.

'Well, remember, you can call me any time, OK?'

I actually wanted him to go at this point. I wanted to be alone; I wanted to have a hot bath and just cry and cry and cry until my body was dry and withered and waterless. But he insisted on staying, cooking me some tomato soup and then making me watch a comedy video with him to cheer me up. I remained quiet the whole time; I had to, to stop myself breaking down again. I kept wanting him to stop being so unbearably kind, because the more wonderful he was, the more I realised what I might have lost.

I couldn't sleep that night.

I couldn't even play the going-to-bed game. It seemed too trivial.

I thought of all the people out there who had lost someone they loved. I felt a wave of compassion and found myself praying to God for all their souls.

I was just dropping off to sleep when some dark-edged fragment of childhood memory, of a movie I'd once seen, rose to the surface. I blinked awake, my heart throbbing.

It was one of those silly horror movies in which a man had escaped Death. He'd been meant to get on a plane and had missed it at the last minute; the plane had crashed, killing fifty people. But the man, having slipped out of the noose, found that Death kept trying to lasso him again and again. It had been comic in places, for Death appeared as a figure in a grey cloak, wielding an axe, green eyes flickering with vengeance, following his poor unknowing victim about, scattering accidents like confetti. But the point was this: if it's your time to die, it's your time. You might escape it once, but not for long . . .

I closed my eyes, telling myself not to be silly. It was just a film. Besides, I had dragged Anthony back in time to a situation which had caused his death. In the present he was meant to live. Right?

An hour passed and I found myself still awake, thinking through possibilities, until I couldn't bear it any longer. I grabbed the phone and called him.

'Lucy, it's one o'clock.' His voice was thick with sleep.

'I know, I know. I just wanted to check you were OK. Because, um, you left your green umbrella behind.' Actually, he'd left it a few weeks ago, but I hung on to the excuse with both hands.

'Oh, well, gosh, I'm just lying here, rain *thundering* on to my bed, desperately wishing I had an umbrella. Are you *insane*? Lucy, I have to sleep, OK? Night.'

'Hang on, hang on – before you go, have you locked your front door properly? Because London is full of weirdos, you know.'

'Sure I have. Lucy, are you OK? D'you want me to come over?'

My heart leapt. Oh yes, I want to handcuff myself to your side and walk about with you everywhere.

'Because we have a long drive up to Suffolk tomorrow . . .'

I shook myself.

'I'm sorry,' I said. 'Go back to sleep. I'm fine. And please do lock the windows. And the door. Good night.'

'Night, Lucy.'

Oh God, please protect him, please look after him always . . .

vi) Suffolk

All the way to Suffolk, I infuriated Anthony by telling him to slow down.

'*Lucy*, I'm only doing forty miles an hour now. I'm the slowest person on the road. If I slow down any more, we won't get there until some time next September. Now just stop *fussing*, OK?' He leaned over and ruffled my hair.

I looked sheepish, biting my lip, trying to squeeze paranoid images of car crashes out of my brain.

We arrived at Badingham just after lunch. It was a lovely Georgian house, set deep in the Suffolk countryside. As we entered the building, I insisted on grabbing Anthony's arm – hard – in case he tripped and dashed his head on the stone floor. He gave me a look that said he was nearing breaking point. Realising I was driving him insane, I hurried off to my room, where I sat on the bed and said a quick thanks to God that we had arrived safely. Letting out a deep breath, I told myself to get a grip. It was going to be OK. It was going to be OK.

My room was a lovely quaint affair. The sloping roof gave it a cottagey feel. There were sheepskin rugs on the bare boards, a sink with bent taps and a rather musty-smelling Narnian wardrobe. I decided to take a bath.

As I lay in the warm water, I listened to the sounds from the main entrance below: cars coming in, the crunch of gravel, people calling hellos. I pictured the evening ahead. I couldn't really get interested in Anthony's father, or which guests might come. I just kept picturing myself sitting next to Anthony. Sharing jokes, pouring each other wine, getting drunk together.

Oh God, I was in love with him. Maybe I had never fallen out; maybe the love had always been there, wrapped in a chrysalis. And now something was emerging under the sunlight of our friendship, fluttering its wings and breathing in the scents of . . .

The only trouble was – did I love him because of what had happened back in 1925? What if in a few weeks' time the illusion slipped away again? And besides, I thought miserably, immersing myself under water, holding my breath, more to the point – does he care for me any more? Yes, he'd had feelings for me in Chicago. But time had twisted back now. Back to me buying a dress and his only response being, *'Very nice.'*

I burst up out of the water, gulping in air. *Very nice.* Bloody hell! Right, I thought. I'll show him. I'll make him fancy me again.

I spent the next two hours making a huge effort with my appearance. I shaved and brushed and blushered and lipsticked, and was just slipping on my white satin shoes when Anthony knocked and burst in.

He was wearing his gangster suit. An image of him bleeding in my arms left me jolted and breathless. Then I came back into the present and saw the anger on his face.

'Anthony, what is it?'

'Dad has invited Mum. He's invited *Mum*. Can you believe it?'

'Oh.' I bit my lip as Anthony walked about in tight little circles, lightly kicking the bedpost.

This was touchy indeed. Whilst Anthony idolised his father, he had problems with his mum. She had left him when he was ten years old. Later, she'd tried to get in touch, and during his teenage years they'd exchanged letters. But reaching his early twenties, Anthony had decided he couldn't forgive her behaviour and decided to cut her off. Privately I sometimes felt he ought to make amends and forgive her. After all, I loathed my father for what he had done to my family, but I still called him and sent him birthday presents and played the dutiful daughter. I didn't love him; I was angry with him; but family was family and blood ties ran deep. Then again, maybe it would have been different if my dad had walked out when I was ten rather than twenty. I had to respect Anthony's feelings.

Anthony sat down on the bed. He looked utterly haggard.

'Anyway,' he said, pulling himself together, 'can you tie my bow tie for me?'

As I fiddled with it, my fingers went all buttery. I tried not to get distracted by Anthony's cheek and lips so close to mine. He kept his eyes firmly fixed on the bedpost behind me, a faint blush on his cheeks.

'It's done,' I said softly. His eyes flickered to mine and we gazed at each other. Then I stepped backwards and the moment passed.

'How do I look?' I couldn't help asking. After all, two hours of intense effort ought to produce some sort of response.

'Very nice,' Anthony mumbled. 'Now shall we go down?'

Down below, the dining hall had come alive.

There was a band at the front, all decked out in white suits, a guy crooning in a brilliant impersonation of Ray Charles, a saxophone duetting sexily with his melted-chocolate voice. The male guests were all wearing suits and sharp hats; the women were glittering in flapper dresses. Outside, the rain hammered in fierce diagonals against the glass, making the candlelit room seem all the more warm and cosy.

'Dad!' Anthony went over and gave him a jubilant hug. 'Happy birthday!'

'Anthony! And lovely Lucy!' He gave me a kiss on each cheek. I smiled affectionately. Anthony's father had obviously been wildly attractive during his youth, and he possessed the confident, suave air of a man who was used to being a hit with the ladies.

We took our places for dinner.

Anthony looked murderous to discover he was seated next to his mother.

I was next to a tedious man called Eliot French who delighted me with his tales of life as a derivatives lawyer. Thankfully, he preferred talking to listening so I didn't have to do much beyond nodding and feigning interest. Every so often a flash of lightning would interrupt us, illuminating the room with an eerie blue glow.

After dinner, Anthony stood up and made a beautiful speech about his father. I found my heart bursting with pride at the depth of his love. At the same time I found my eyes flicking curiously to his mother. She was listening intently; Anthony didn't mention her once during his speech.

I couldn't help feeling sorry for her. She looked haggard, much older than her fifty years. There was an air of brittle vulnerability about her, as though all she wanted to do was make amends, give Anthony a big hug and weep on his shoulder, but was too proud to show it.

Dinner over, the dancing began. I found myself searching for Anthony. And then I found that he was looking for me too.

Suddenly it felt as though time had unwound, spun backwards. As though we were meeting for the first time, drinking each other in with thirsty curiosity.

We stood opposite each other, swaying gently. Our pupils burned on each other. Anthony moved in and I thought he was going to pull me close, but then at the last minute he merely clasped his hands around my shoulders, like a gauche teenager. I blushed in confusion: perhaps this electricity only existed in my imagination and he literally wanted to keep me at arm's length.

'D'you want to dance then?' Anthony asked softly.

I looked up into his eyes.

'I don't want to dance with any man except you,' I blurted out in a whisper.

Anthony froze; his hands tightened. A moment of raw agony. I wanted to pull my words back down my throat. Now he'd make an excuse about needing another drink and hurry off . . .

Anthony whispered back, 'The moment I saw you in that dress, I wanted to dance with you. Every man who's talked to you tonight has made me feel jealous, I admit it.'

'But you . . .' I trailed off. 'In the shop, you said I looked . . .'

Anthony looked confused; then he twigged.

'I thought you were so gorgeous, it was terrifying. I was scared that if I complimented you it would show and you'd . . .' He trailed off too.

We stared at each other, too nervous to confess any further. A slow exhilaration was tingling over me as my paranoia slipped away. Anthony liked me. He thought my dress was beautiful. He wanted me.

A smile of absolute joy suddenly burst out on my face. He grinned too, his eyes sparkling, and we both laughed breathlessly.

Anthony stepped forward . . .

. . . and then the lights went out and the music died.

Blackness, laughter, cries. A blue lightning flash outside, illuminating a sea of confused faces. Then a voice, calm and confident, undoubtedly Anthony's father.

'It seems the storm has finally got the better of us! Don't worry, we'll sort it all out as soon as possible; now, if everyone could just stay still and calm . . .'

Someone brushed past me in a panic. I stumbled against Anthony's body and felt him take hold of me. And catch his breath.

He reached out, feeling me, murmuring, 'Where are you?' and I laughed lightly again. His fingertips tingled on my face and brushed the outline of my lips. Then his hands cupped my cheeks. My whole body felt as though it was one beating heart of yearning. I leaned in; his breath came down warm on my cheek, and we kissed gently.

'Leave the lights off – this is so romantic,' someone cried in the distance, and Anthony laughed softly and pulled me in tight.

Then we just held each other. Ribs crushed tight. Relieved to have found each other again.

Memories flooded back. This was how I had held him just before he – and I felt tears begin to swirl about my eyes, brimming over no matter how hard I tried to force them back.

At the front of hall there were glimmers of light as candles were lit.

'Shall we escape?' Anthony whispered.

'Yes,' I whispered. 'Yes please.'

How glad I was of the dark, for the tears kept coming. Anthony guided me to the front, his hand tight and urgent in mine. He took a candle – 'Just going off to see if we can help,' he told his mother distractedly – and led me out of the hallway, up some stairs, guiding me carefully. A moth, attracted by the light, whirred across our faces. As Anthony flicked it aside, he saw the glint of my tears.

'Lucy?' he asked in astonishment. 'Are you OK? Are you – come on, let's get you upstairs, my darling.'

My darling. The tenderness in his voice only provoked a fresh gush of tears. I sobbed harder and then laughed a little, just to let him know I was OK really.

We stumbled into the bedroom. Anthony set the candle down in the sink, then came over and sat down beside me, passing me a tissue. I blew my nose noisily. We both laughed. I looked at him shyly, biting my lip.

'Lucy . . . what is it?' His eyes were wide and worried. He took my hand firmly in his, caressing little circles in my palm; the circles seemed to expand into ripples that spread and diffused through my body. More tears came. I felt him stroke my hair; I heard him shushing me. His voice reminded me of being a little girl and listening to the wind in the trees as I lay awake on summer nights.

'Look,' said Anthony with fierce gentleness, 'last time you cried, I let you get away with it. Not this time. You're not leaving this room until you explain what on earth the matter is, so if we're to stay here all night, so be it.'

I smiled, feeling a little silly.

'I'm just afraid of dying,' I said in a choked voice.

At which point the lights came back on.

We blinked, confused, the spell broken somehow. Anthony put out the main light and then switched on a little lamp; that was better.

'Lucy,' he said, coming back to my side, 'I don't understand. You've got me worried. Is something wrong with you? Are you ill?'

'No – no,' I laughed, increasing his confusion. I worried a tissue between my fingers and he stroked back my hair so I couldn't hide my face. 'But I've just realised that life is unpredictable, and anything can happen at any time. We could walk out of this hotel and be hit by a car tomorrow, or shot by gangsters.' I swallowed.

'Lucy, you're worrying too much. I don't understand . . .' He trailed off. 'You were crying yesterday, and now today . . .'

'I think I'm in love with you,' I blurted out.

'I love you too,' he said sharply. 'Is that what this is all about?'

'Yes . . .' Well, it was close enough. 'I just feel . . . I just feel I've been such an idiot in the way I've treated you and . . .'

'Sssh,' said Anthony, smiling. 'Ssh.'

I smiled wearily. My tears had faded now and I simply felt tired and fragile, as though a layer of skin had been rubbed away, leaving my heart red and raw. Perhaps this was why my skin tingled so as he stroked my cheek with his thumb. As he knelt down in front of me, I closed my eyes and felt his lips sweet against my eyelids, and then soft on my cheeks and then firm against my lips. His kisses were slow and soothing. They were dreamy. They seemed to whisper: *I want to make you feel better.* And: *We've got all the time in the world.* And: *Why did we ever stop doing this?*

He pushed me back on to the bed and undressed me with love in his eyes and his hands. Then he lay back and with shaking fingers I undid the buttons on his shirt, smoothing my palms across his chest, the curved muscles of his arms. He leaned up to kiss me but I darted my head away, playing our old game, and he let out a faint groan and pulled me in tight, my breasts pressed against his chest, his skin luxuriously warm against mine. I felt his body shudder and a thrill rippled through me in wonder at the effect I was having on him, at how much he wanted me and I wanted him. Then he took my face in his hands and kissed me voluptuously, hungrily. He ran kisses all over my nervous body, breaking off to whisper how beautiful I was, how wonderful; with any other man it would have sounded clichéd, but because it was Anthony, I knew that he meant it. I caressed him in the ways I knew he loved; everything felt familiar but fresh, and profoundly right, as though all the nights we had made love like this were there looking over our shoulders, reminding us of how much we ought to be together.

When he entered me, I felt a sharp shock of heat suffuse my body and a momentary pain. He stopped, still inside me, searching my face. His expression was so tender that I felt my heart uncurl and open up to him; I felt a wild urge to bite him and draw him beneath my skin, to become utterly one with him. Then I smiled up at him and gently reached up to kiss him, and he smiled in relief and happiness. We made love staring deep into each others' eyes,

211

and as he came, he buried his face in my shoulder, his stubble deliciously prickly, and lightly bit my skin.

We lay in each other's arms, trembling, sharing sweat, and he rubbed his cheek against my head and let out a long sigh of contentment. After a while I became uncomfortable and wriggled away a little, but he didn't want to let me go. I whispered that I was hot and he blew cool circles on my face. Then we lay and stared at each other, exchanging the odd peaceful kiss, and there was no need for talk, for asking what the other might be thinking, for worry or analysis; we lay in the pure contentment of the present, listening to the noises of guests going to their rooms, our eyes travelling sleepily around the golden light making shadows on the ceiling, the speckle of stars outside, and then inevitably back to each other's faces, and each time, like excited teenage lovers, we experienced a jolt of love and exchanged smiles so ecstatic we had to bite them back before they turned into whoops of joy.

Then I felt my eyes closing, and I fell slack in the crook of his arm. The last thing I heard before I drifted into dreams was Anthony telling me he loved me and had always loved me and would always love me . . .

When I woke up the next morning, initially I felt a sense of peace. I was aware of Anthony's warm arms wrapped around me, his soft breath buffeting the back of my neck, the lilt of birdsong outside. I pulled away slightly from his embrace, rolled over and smiled at him dreamily, recalling and savouring every detail of our lovemaking. I closed my eyes, enjoying a warm feeling of expectation. Anthony would wake up soon, and then we'd make love again, and perhaps go for a walk together, and then have lunch in a little pub somewhere . . . It was going to be heaven.

I became conscious of how heavy his arm felt on my rib cage. It hurt to breathe. I wriggled upwards so it rested on my stomach. I stared at his face, willing him to wake up. Minutes passed. I tried to close my eyes and go back to sleep, but they kept popping open.

I began to feel oddly itchy and uncomfortable. I had never really liked sleeping with Anthony; I often found myself tossing and turning, easily woken by his snores. I remembered how Sally had told me that being able to sleep with someone was the ultimate test of a relationship; a good deep sleep was a sign that you felt truly relaxed in their company.

Suddenly Anthony woke with a jolt. Seeing me, he broke into a smile of such spontaneous warmth that I felt joy and relief suffuse my body. He leaned in and I responded instinctively, sharing a long, warm, loving kiss. Then he drew back, staring at my face, stroking my cheek gently with the back of his hand.

'Move in with me,' he said.

'What?' I whispered. I let out an awkward laugh. 'I think you're still hungover from last night.'

'No, I'm not. Move in with me.'

I lowered my eyes.

'Lucy?'

'Well – it *is* a bit sudden. I mean, it's a bit early in the morning for this.'

'Oh? So there's a recognised time of day for asking someone to move in with you? I ought to wait until lunchtime, then?'

'No, I just meant . . .'

He stared at me fiercely; I kept my eyes on his chest, on the fine layer of dark hair that tapered to a V at his belly-button.

He suddenly rolled over and lay back in bed with a big, frustrated sigh. My cheek felt cool where his warm hand had been.

'Well don't get mad at me!' I cried. 'I'm sorry – I'm just . . . I mean, it's not every day you wake up next to someone and they ask you to move in with them.'

'No, I should think not.' Anthony turned back to face me with a smile of warmth and pain. He began to circle his arms around me again, but I pulled away. I saw his face flicker and I smiled apologetically, lowering my eyes.

Now that Anthony's embrace had slipped away like a shawl, I suddenly realised how cold the room was. Goose pimples began to wake up and dance over my skin.

'The thing is,' Anthony said, and I knew he was trying to keep his voice steady, but it trembled with just the faintest intonation of anger, 'this is silly, Lucy. I mean, it all seems so simple to me. We're meant to be together. It's obvious . . . isn't it? I just feel that over the last few weeks . . . it's as though we've never really broken up. Don't you?'

213

I remained silent.

'I mean,' Anthony went on, 'it's not as though we've even *tried* to really go out with anyone else. I've had a couple of dating agency fiascos, and you've been like Mother Teresa.'

I looked down, blushing. Then, suddenly, I felt an irrational surge of anger. A minute ago I had been lying in a bubble of bliss, eager to savour the day with Anthony. Why did he have to *rush* everything? Why did he always have to press the fast-forward button? What was wrong with just taking things slowly?

'So . . .' Anthony trailed off. 'What about it? Why not move in together?'

'Well . . . I . . . I mean . . .' I raised my eyes. 'Couldn't we . . . just . . . date each other like we did before?'

Anthony's eyes flashed with intensity, with love, with exasperation. 'Lucy – I just feel it's taking a step back. It's . . . *stagnant*. Look, things can't stay the same; the nature of life is change. Things either progress, or they die. And I think we have to move on, you know, grow up, grow together.'

Grow up. The words made me flinch. Did I really have a Peter Pan complex? Or was I just a woman who wanted her independence?

'But . . .' I began.

Then his mobile rang.

'Fuck.'

'You should get it.'

'I'll ignore it.'

'No, get it.'

Anthony rolled over and took it. It was work. He tried saying he was busy, but the person on the line just kept jabbering. Judging from Anthony's expletives, it sounded like a crisis of earthquake proportions.

I slid out of bed and quickly pulled on my clothes. I felt better. Being naked made me feel vulnerable; clothes made me stronger, a fortress around me.

Only I couldn't find my knickers. I searched about desperately, but – nothing. Suddenly I felt almost panicky. I can't be here, I kept thinking, I can't have this discussion. I'm an independent young woman, I don't have to move in with him, I can do what I like. It

214

was as though my independence was a candle that Anthony wanted to blow out. I couldn't quite understand why or think it through or analyse it, I was just desperate to cup my palms around it and keep it burning.

'Sorry about that – God, to call at a time like this.' Anthony turned. 'Oh. You're dressed.'

'I am. I – I have to go, actually. I just got a text,' I lied frantically, 'from my sister. She needs me.' I waved my mobile meaningfully. 'I can order a taxi. I'll do it right now.'

In the end, Anthony insisted on giving me a lift to the station. He drove me there in the most deafening silence I have ever suffered. Outside, the sun gently warmed the fields and birds twittered sweetly in the trees.

Anthony pulled up at the station just as we heard the sound of an approaching train.

'Oh, brilliant, I think that's mine,' I said hastily.

'Lucy, can't we just—' Anthony broke off in exasperation. 'OK. Go get your train.'

I leaned over to give him a kiss goodbye, but he turned away, hurt, and the kiss landed on his jaw.

Suddenly I didn't want to go. I felt a wave of confusion. *Stay with him,* a voice said. *Don't do this, Lucy. Remember how it felt when he was shot. Remember how it felt when he made love to you.*

But my train was now standing at the station; and I found myself leaping out of the car and running on to the platform, leaping aboard in the nick of time.

Later that evening, I heard the phone ring.

I was sitting eating baked beans on toast – only with my culinary skills they had come out more like squashed turds on black cardboard – forcing it down even though I wasn't really hungry.

The answerphone clicked on.

Then, Anthony's voice: 'Lucy, will you please just pick up the phone. I'm not chasing you, OK? I just want to *talk*.'

It was the third message he'd left that evening.

I took another mouthful, trying to drown the butterflies of panic in my stomach.

vii) Regret

Why did you do that, Lucy? Why, why, why?

I had escaped my flat and the terrifying ring of the phone. Now I was sitting in Regent's Park, in the twilight. For a moment the beauty of my surroundings pulled me above my misery and gave me a moment's detachment. A moment later my confusion had sucked me back in and I was lost again.

I felt like slapping myself. The crazy thing was, I *did* love Anthony, I was in no doubt about that. But the moving-in request had completely thrown me. I couldn't understand why, now that I had got him back, I wanted to run once more. I felt exasperated with the tango my emotions seemed to play – when I didn't have Anthony, I wanted him; when I had him, I pushed him away.

The last embers of the day were dying; I got up and made my way home. *You can't keep doing this, Lucy,* a quiet voice told me off. *It's just not fair on Anthony. You're destroying him with your behaviour, and if you carry on like this you won't even be friends. You've got to make your mind up. If you love him, why can't this just be simple? What do you find so terrifying about moving in with him?*

Back home, I stared at the phone in panic. There was a fresh winking light on the answerphone. A headache pulsed beneath my forehead. Oh God, I thought. If only I could undo time; if I could just go back to that night when I dumped Anthony and stop myself from making that mistake . . .

Suddenly everything became clear. That was it! It would be much easier to go back to the time when I was with Anthony, rather than undoing the knot and trying to tie it again. I could go back, and this time I'd appreciate him. That would sort everything out.

Wouldn't it?

But, a small voice inside me pointed out, *what if I find myself wanting to run again? I'll still be me, remember?*

I pushed the voice away. I was convinced it was my best shot.

I heated up some milk, figuring I would need the energy for my journey. I took sips in between yawns. I was about to head for the time machine, when I caught sight of my reflection in the window:

216

ghastly and ghostly. I felt exhausted, wrung dry with emotional turmoil. I decided to go back to bed and get some sleep first, prepare for my new journey. Just before I left, I split some milk on the table, but mopped it up easily.

Chapter Six

Peter

Established in Being, perform action.

LORD KRISHNA

i) Attempts to undo things

I had keyed the date into the time machine – the day before Anthony and I had broken up. I shuffled about a bit, adjusting my seat. Now all I had to do was press the green button and I was away.

I paused, trying to still my shaking breath. In thirty seconds this would all be over. I had even put on the exact clothes I'd been wearing that day – my jeans and a white cashmere rollneck. This had meant removing the rollneck from the washing basket, which was a tad smelly, but never mind.

Throughout the night, worries had been flickering through my mind, and now they resurfaced. Could it really be that easy? What if I went back and unravelled everything? What if I found that I had lost the wisdom of hindsight, that I was just as naïve and foolish? I jumped out of the machine, ran to my bookcase and pulled down T. S. Eliot, flipping frantically to the *Four Quartets*.

Time present and time past
Are both perhaps present in time future,
And time future contained in time past.

'There, you see,' I told a bemused Lyra. 'There will be a thread of wisdom still with me. Anthony and I will go to the restaurant and I'll sit there and think of dumping him, but some big, deep instinct in my tummy will tell me I mustn't. And so I won't.'

Right. I settled myself back in the machine and put my finger on the green button. Here goes . . .

My doorbell suddenly shrilled and I jumped violently.

Ignore it, I told myself. It won't be important. Come on, just press—

The bell rang again, more urgently. And then I remembered: I had promised Sally I'd babysit Adam. For the entire day. I

221

swallowed. I looked at the date; I looked at the door. I found myself getting up.

'LUCY!' Sally was extremely red-faced. I looked down to see that my white doorbell was now brown; clearly Adam had had Marmite for breakfast. 'What the hell are you playing at?'

'I'm sorry,' I said. 'I just – are you OK?'

'I am, actually,' she said, much to my surprise.

'So you're getting back together with Richard?' I cried.

'God, no, I just feel better having had a whole week to myself without him!' She laughed with an odd mixture of bitterness and freedom. Then she looked down and saw her son's face and gave him a tight hug, ruffling his hair. 'You'll be all right with Auntie Lucy for the day, won't you, darling? Mummy won't be long.' She passed me a bag filled with videos and toys and then started reeling off a list of instructions, even though I'd babysat a thousand times before.

After she'd gone, I offered to put on *Postman Pat,* which was normally his favourite.

'Boring, boring, boring.' He seemed a bit despondent.

I chewed my lip.

'How about a drink?' I asked, waiting for his usual demand for Coke.

Instead, he replied with a sarcasm that shocked me: 'Can I have nice healthy good-for-my-teeth orange juice?'

I laughed faintly; he looked sullen.

'Hey,' he said, suddenly brightening, 'what's that in the corner? That looks cool.'

Oh God. Now he would think the time machine was some sort of elaborate playpen.

'That is . . . a death machine,' I improvised. 'If you so much as touch it, you get an electric shock. And if you get into it, it will eat you, I'm afraid, so I think you'd better stick to *Postman Pat.*' I worried I had gone too far, but Adam just widened his eyes and said, 'Wow.'

I nudged him firmly away from the machine and in front of *Postman Pat.* As I went into the kitchen to get him some juice, I looked back at him gazing at the TV with a slack, innocent face and felt a wave of affection. It was funny – normally I loathed babysitting, and had only agreed to it in the past because I felt I ought to. After all, I was his aunt. But I'd always found him utterly exhausting. Just one hour of his hyperactive cheekiness and I felt ready to collapse into bed for a week from exhaustion. At the end of the day I'd always passed him back eagerly, secretly thinking: How on earth do parents survive?

But today I felt different. My experiences with Tiryns' baby and my love for Anthony had changed something inside me. I could see beyond Adam's playfulness. I could see the seed of adult potential in him, the man he might become. I could see how much his parents' troubles were hurting him and how he was trying to make sense of it all on his own. Maybe, I thought, I ought to have a word with Sally. Only she'd probably feel I was patronising her. Maybe there was nothing I could do but give him a little bit of love . . .

And what about the time machine?

That would have to wait until later.

I suddenly became aware of a thrumming noise. I put down the cup with a thump, orange juice spilling over the surface. I heard Adam shriek and dashed into the living room. He was sitting in the time machine, his eyes wide.

'Lucy, the machine's eating me!'

I rushed over.

'It's not going to eat you, it's just . . .'

'Turn it off, turn it off!' he sobbed tearfully. 'Turn it off!' He jabbed buttons randomly; the date blinked out and then reappeared. Then, as though in slow motion, I saw his finger heading for the green button. I yelled, '*NO!*' and dived into the machine to stop him. But it was too late. Blackness swirled and glittered with beads of green and red light. Then our world turned upside down and we found ourselves in another time, another place.

We were in India. There was no mistaking it. We were staring at the Taj Mahal. I'd only visited India once before, with Anthony, eighteen months back and we'd taken a brief trip there.

I noticed with great relief that the tourists milling about were wearing modern dress. It seemed that we had kept the same time, just sidestepped the place. Which was just as well, given that neither of us had taken speaking potions.

It was clearly midsummer. The heat lay thickly in the air, prickling my pores, and beads of sweat welled up all over my face and body. But the intensity hardly seemed to matter when we were standing in front of one of the most glorious wonders of the world. In the midday sun, the dome and minarets shimmered and gleamed a radiant white. I thought of those famous words by the Bengali poet Rabindranath Tagore: *The Taj Mahal is a teardrop on the cheek of time.* I felt the building was achingly sad, every curve of perfection echoing the desperation of Shah Jahan in trying to capture the lost beauty of his dead wife.

I looked down at Adam, who was staring round with big eyes. I grabbed his hand.

'Don't worry, Adam. We can go back right now. Only not a word to your mum, OK? I'll give you five pounds,' I added.

But Adam didn't seem to have heard me.

'This place looks cool,' he said, and ran off.

'*Adam!*' I pounded after him.

I suddenly became aware of a tall, dark-haired man in his early thirties, who was watching me with an amused look in his eyes. His English dress and pale skin suggested he was a tourist. I slowed down slightly, giving him a raised-eyebrow 'Kids, hey?' expression. He winked at me. I blushed, surreptitiously wiping sweat from my cheeks. Then I realised that in my distraction I'd lost sight of Adam.

'He's over there,' the man directed me helpfully.

'Thanks,' I cried breathlessly. I ran over towards Adam, but he spotted me and dodged away. I changed direction and lunged at him, but the little bugger jumped aside at the last minute, and I found myself grabbing at air. And then my legs were flying up and the Taj Mahal's reflection came up to meet me and shattered into a thousand pieces.

As I emerged, spluttering, from the ornamental lake, a military policeman came running up.

'It's not my fault!' I gasped, wiping water from my eyes.

'Oops.' Adam had stopped his games and was now eyeing me sheepishly, trying to hide his laughter. Then he erupted. 'Oh, Auntie Lucy, you look like a drowned rat!'

To cap it all, a couple of American tourists passing by stopped to take photographs.

The policeman waved his arms and shouted at me to get out of the water.

'Stop yelling at her and help the poor woman out.' It was the dark-haired tourist who came to my rescue. He extended a hand and I grabbed it tightly as he hauled me out. A small puddle formed around my feet. He drew out a handkerchief and gently mopped my face before passing it to me.

'Thanks,' I said, touched by his kindness. I grabbed Adam's hand and gave him a look that clearly said, 'Be quiet and behave.'

'Are you OK?' the stranger asked. 'Where's your hotel?'

'Um . . . our hotel . . . yes, well, it's not really been my day,' I confessed. I could feel the sun arrowing down on to me, drying my wet clothes. 'We woke up this morning and found that our passports, money and luggage had been stolen! We think it must have been, um, this dodgy guy who'd been hanging about the hotel. When we complained to the manager, he just booted us out without any sympathy. So we're stuck in the middle of nowhere!'

'That's terrible. Did you contact the police?'

'Well . . . we . . .'

'They're useless, aren't they? I expect you ended up in a queue for ten hours. You poor thing – we need to contact the British Embassy. In the mean time, I'll lend you some money so you have a place to stay for the night.'

'God, that's so kind of you – thanks so much.' My heart swelled at his warmth.

'No trouble at all. Now, let *me* pick a hotel for you this time.'

'Can we stay in your hotel?'

'Ah, no,' he replied, slightly jumpily. 'I'm actually renting my own place – I'm living here at the moment. Come on, I'll take you to a hotel now.'

He hailed a rickshaw and we all squeezed in. I had forgotten how wonderfully crazy it was to travel in India. Traffic lights were exuberantly ignored; instead the traffic system seemed to be dictated by who could beep their horn the hardest. Our rickshaw competed crazily with trucks, cars, taxis, and the occasional cow wandering across the road. It was rather like being on a rollercoaster, only with more dust.

The hotel was indeed plush – very different from some of the guesthouses I'd stayed in when I'd visited India on my travels. There was a pleasant, clean bedroom with a double bed, a fan that actually sliced the air rather than just shuffling it around, and an ensuite bathroom.

'Thanks,' I kept repeating, in a terribly British way. 'Thank you so much.'

'Really, it's fine. I know how scary it is to be a foreigner in a country you don't know.' He headed back to the door and opened it. 'Well, I guess I should leave you to it.'

'Well – yes.' I looked down at Adam and caught him smirking. I flashed him a cross look. Was it that obvious? I fretted. That I was desperate to see this man again, that somehow there was a connection between us? And I know this sounds clichéd and corny, but I really did feel as though I'd known him for much longer than the last twenty minutes.

I paused in the doorway and he just stood there with an awkward smile balanced on his lips. I realised I was behaving like a lemon, so I smiled and closed the door.

'Auntie Lucy, are we staying?' Adam cried out eagerly, bouncing up and down on the bed.

'No! *No!* We're having a very quick break and then we have to go back this afternoon—' I broke off, for there was a knock at the door. I ran to it, yanked it open and stood there breathlessly.

My dark-haired stranger was still standing in the corridor.

'Um – I was wondering if we could meet tomorrow? I could help you sort out new passports.'

'Yes, yes, please, yes—' I broke off, realising that I sounded as though I was practising my orgasms again. 'Um – yes.'

'Great.' When he smiled, it was so shy-making: his eyes crinkled up and two white sparkles danced in the centre of his pupils. He turned to go and then turned back. 'I've just realised that I don't even know your name.'

'Lucy,' I said. 'And you're . . . ?'

'Peter,' he said. 'Well, bye, Lucy.' He spoke my name as though it was a blessing.

226

I closed the door. Adam gave a whoop of excitement, declaring how much fun it was to be on holiday. I grinned too, his childish abandon rubbing off on me.

But as we lay in bed together that night, I found myself with a deep feeling of unease. Now that my initial euphoria had faded, I started fretting that I ought to take Adam back; imagine if anything happened to him . . .

Still, I told myself, this wasn't a dangerous place, not like going back to the 1920s to meet Al Capone . . . Like Adam said, we were just on holiday. And God, I needed a holiday, some time to be away from Anthony, to reflect on how I felt about him. Surely we couldn't run into any harm . . .

ii) A memory of Anthony

Perhaps one reason why I felt so uneasy was because India held bad memories for me. Someone only had to mention the place and I'd feel my heart throbbing as though full of splinters. I'd always sworn that I would never return, for India was the place where Anthony and I suffered our first Major Row.

It was just after our fifty-first one-night stand. Anthony and I had reached that awkward point in a relationship. It was the end of the Honeymoon Period; the ushering in of the Compatibility Era. That strange, transitional time where we were popping bubbles of bliss, getting to know each other's faults and weaknesses, gracefully allowing each other to climb down from our pedestals. Anthony had discovered I was an awful cook; I had discovered he liked cutting his toenails in front of the TV. I'd discovered he owned the world's worst pair of pyjamas, a horrific tartan-checkered pair; he'd discovered I turned into a banshee if I didn't get my beauty sleep. He'd also discovered I could, if provoked, be a bit of a flirt.

I say a *bit* of a flirt because that is the truth. I never meant any harm by it. I didn't walk around wearing tops cut to my navel, giving blokes come-hither smiles and fluttering heavily mascaraed eyelashes. It was more that I loved being friendly; I loved meeting new people; I loved slashing past superficial chit-chat and slicing to the heart of them. And I suppose in my fascination for this I sometimes became what Anthony called 'flirty'.

Anthony *never* flirted. If we went anywhere, he had no interest in anyone else at all. We existed in a cocoon. Literally. We could go out to dinner and be served by the world's sexiest waitress and he wouldn't even give her a second glance, let alone a first; in fact, he'd just stare at the menu, giving orders, utterly determined to show his disinterest. It made me feel loved and cherished and beautiful because I knew no other woman in the room mattered to him but me.

But sometimes, when we were travelling, I grew a little tired of his desire for us to always be a twosome, doing our own private thing. Though he had been brought up in America, sometimes he could be terribly British: this is your space, this is ours. And sometimes, when I chatted to people, I noticed little tell-tale signs of his annoyance: a flicker in his jaw, in his eyes. But I never worried much.

Until India.

Our first few weeks in India were utterly euphoric. Everyone had warned me that I would suffer from culture shock when I hit India, but I immediately fell in love with the country and felt completely at home. I fell in love with its messiness and its chaos. I fell in love with the people; when they weren't trying to scam us for an extra rupee, I was amazed by their warmth and generosity. On the train from Delhi to Agra, Anthony and I shared a compartment with some Indians who shared their nuts and bananas with us and, at the end of the journey, embraced us, declaring we were family. It was certainly a big change from the coldness of London commuting. I loved the temples, too. One day we stumbled on a *yagya* taking place and surreptitiously watched Brahmin priests performing sacred offerings to the devas to erase a person's bad karma and bring them good fortune. The sound of their chanting reverberated in my heart all day.

I noticed that Anthony was a little tense on the odd occasion. But for much of the time we were dreamy and happy and hazily in love. We drifted through temples, took siestas in the afternoon, came down for meals and then spent giddy nights walking by the Yamuna river, watching the full moon on the dark water. We could see the Taj Mahal from behind, and while it burned a bright white during the day, under the glow of the moon it turned golden and seemed to float above the river like a heavenly palace in a fairy tale.

One night we stopped by the river, gazing down. The moon hovered and the water swirled and cut different expressions across her face, but the main one seemed to me to be one of serenity. The light shone down on us like a hot embrace, sealing our love; the air was tinted with the scent of sandalwood Anthony had dabbed on his skin; in the distance a saringi tingled sweetly. This was India at its most beautiful; this was a perfect moment. I turned to Anthony and it was as though our hearts trembled in recognition of the same feeling; we stared at each other like two children who had just discovered the existence of love. As he held me, my heart swooped with ecstasy and peace and pride. All my life, I'd suffered failed love affairs, love that seemed more hate than love, affairs that had left my heart scratched or shrunken. I was beginning to worry that I would never find love, that I was unlovable. And now I had found it. It made me feel grown-up in the most fulfilled way. This, I thought, as we kissed, this sweetness is all there is in life.

That night, as we lay in bed together, whispering and kissing and giggling, I felt truly cherished, wrapped up in love. For being in love softens the heart, cushions and confirms your sense of identity: the knowledge that for all your faults and neuroses and dysfunctional upbringing, someone aches to be with you. At the same time, there was a feeling of astonished fear. A sense that this couldn't possibly last – that it was so good I didn't quite deserve it.

I lay there, watching him sleeping, terrified he was going to wake and, like one of those fairy tale heroes released from a spell, wonder what he was doing with me, an Ugly Sister, and go off to find a proper princess.

That is the trouble with fear. It's as though the universe listens

229

to those little whispers of worry that scuttle about in our minds and decides to make them come true.

Then came the dinner that changed everything.

We were sitting in a restaurant in our hotel. We had just ordered food, giggling meekly on how lame we were for not being able to handle the strong curries. We sipped lassis and yawned between sentences; we hadn't been able to sleep properly in the heat and our tiredness was catching up with us.

I suddenly became aware that the guy sitting at the next table was listening in on our conversation.

He looked quite nice. Classic backpacker material: tanned, Hawaiian shirt, dyed blond dreads worming down his back, a weather-beaten face, slanting blue eyes. He also seemed lonely.

When I glanced over, he quickly looked away, embarrassed to have been caught out. I gave him a reassuring smile.

'Hi,' I said. I was vaguely aware of Anthony giving me a dirty look, but I ignored it. I just wanted to be friendly. 'You out here on your own?'

'Yeah,' he said. He was Australian. 'Hiya.' He leaned across and proffered a hand to shake. 'I'm Dom.'

Anthony and I immediately looked at each other, remembering the wonderful Dominic on that first fateful plane trip who had brought us together. We repressed giggles.

'Don't worry, private joke,' Anthony said to Dom.

Dom looked a little hurt; I felt like pinching Anthony for his lack of tact.

'Well, I should leave you guys to it,' said Dom.

'No, no, it's fine,' I said. 'Look, come and join us if you like. Come on. There's room at the table.'

'Are you sure . . .?' Dom asked.

'Sure!' I said, ignoring Anthony's 'what-the-fuck-are-you-doing?' glances.

Dom sat down and we all started to chat. Well, Dom and I started to chat. Anthony fell decidedly silent. I felt exasperated with him – couldn't he just join in, be friendly for once? And Dom, as it turned out, was buzzing with interesting stories. He'd been travelling for the past year. He'd experienced all kinds of adventures, from meditating in the Himalayas, to getting robbed in Kerala and suffering dysentery in Delhi.

'Wow, that's so interesting, isn't it?' I turned to Anthony and grinned. He looked back at me stonily and declared he needed the loo. I noticed then he'd barely touched his food.

Suddenly I felt sheepish. Dom, who was now telling a story about just how bad his dysentery had been in terms of toilet-flushes per minute, was beginning to grate a bit on my nerves. And I had spoilt our romantic dinner; maybe I wasn't being very fair on Anthony.

Anthony returned from the toilet. He picked up his jacket which had been slung over the chair.

'Well, I'm off,' he announced, staring at me with livid eyes. 'Hope you two have a nice dinner together. I'll leave you to it.'

'*Anthony!*' I cried.

For a moment I sat there in shock, watching his retreating back. I thought: *this has to be a joke.* If I followed him, I knew he'd turn around and shriek with laughter and say, 'Got you, Lucy! I had you going there for a minute, didn't I?'

But he didn't come back.

Dom winked and said, 'Well, I guess that leaves room for you and me to gel, babe.'

'What!' I leapt to my feet. 'Anthony is my boyfriend!'

'Well, we could always try a threesome . . .' Dom's voice faded away.

I set off across the restaurant. The stupid buggering lift was broken, so I went clattering up the long staircase, bursting into the hotel room in a sweat. Anthony was sitting on the bed with his back to me, staring out of the window.

'Anthony! What the hell was all that about?'

When he turned back, I was shocked by the rage and pain in his eyes.

'I'm sorry I got angry,' he said, sounding a lot more angry than sorry, 'but you clearly didn't want to be with me down there. I mean, everywhere we go, you flirt like mad, but this is the last straw – I mean, for God's sake!' His voice rose. 'Why go out with me if you're going to chase after other men?'

'What? Anthony! What are you talking about? I mean, that guy down there – he was obviously lonely!'

'Well, why don't you go back down there and comfort him then?' Anthony snarled sarcastically.

'Comfort? Anthony, I don't fancy him – I want you – and – and – what's all this about me flirting everywhere we go?' I demanded, trying to keep up.

'You know what I mean. I don't have to spell it out and cite all the times . . .'

'*All* the times? Anthony, please do cite *all* the times.' I put my hands on my hips, my heart hammering. I felt all shaky at having to assert myself; I simply wasn't used to being attacked by Anthony. 'Really, I'd like to know.'

'Okay, d'you want me to give you a list?'

'Yes – please do give me a list.'

'Okay – one – there was that time that we went to the pub in Islington and you went over to the guy who was filling up the condom machine and asked for a freebie.'

'I was being cheeky – it was just a laugh! And come on, Ant, we did end up using those condoms that very night!' I winced at the memory; they had been mint flavoured and just the scent of them had made me feel as though I was cleaning my teeth, which hadn't been very sexy really.

'We had to throw them away. And the next evening you said you wanted to go back to the pub—'

'Because I liked it! I thought it had a nice atmosphere, and that log fire was lovely—'

'Oh yeah, right, I knew you wanted to see him, and then he wasn't there, and you went all quiet for the rest of the evening.'

'Was I? I don't remember that. I mean, maybe I was tired . . .'

'Okay – number two –' God, he was relentless '– that guy we met in Berlin. The musician we met in that bar. You said to his face that you thought he was nice-looking.'

'Well.' I felt as though I was being whiplashed here. Suddenly I understood why Anthony was such a good businessman. I'd once overheard one of his secretaries saying he was tough and I'd secretly laughed; but now I was seeing a glimpse of his ruthless side. 'Okay – I admit it.' It seemed easier to. 'I was flirting with him but—'

'You said you thought he was nice-looking—'

'No—'

'Oh, so you're lying now . . .'

'I . . .' I opened and closed my mouth.

'Three,' Anthony pushed on. 'You smiled at that hot black guy.'

'Who? I – what – I smiled at someone?'

'You know who I mean. That guy. The one in Covent Garden.'

'*Who?*'

'That day we went Christmas shopping. He was standing watching—'

'Anthony, I have no idea who you're talking about! This is crazy. Really crazy. I can't even remember who that guy was but,' my voice rose in frustration, 'I do remember that I was so happy that night at being with you that I was smiling non-stop.'

No answer.

'Don't you believe me?' I cried.

Silence. Anthony swallowed. He broke off to slap a bloodsucker which had just landed on his arm, muttering, 'These fucking mosquitoes!'

I stood very still, still shaking. I kept thinking: is this the real Anthony? Is this the Anthony I know and love?

And did he really mean all those comments? One look at his face showed me that yes, he did. I felt as though a long shadow had been cast over our relationship. So: all those times when I'd thought we were having a nice evening out in an Islington pub or shopping together, or having picnics, Anthony had been silently simmering, scoring points. I rewound events scene by scene, rewriting the past from his viewpoint. And yet I couldn't really understand it. I am in the right, I thought, I'm not just being a contrary Lucy at this point, I am in the right. He's crazy. My stomach churned. So this was the real Anthony. The real, raw Anthony, with all his layers of niceness peeled away. He's one of those nightmare boyfriends who want to put you in a box or on a leash. He'll have me wearing a burka next. Or handcuffing me to an Aga, declaring women shouldn't work.

Oh God.

'Oh God,' said Anthony. He suddenly got up, his face contorted with pain. He ran into the bathroom and threw up.

Immediately our row was forgotten. I ran in to his side, touching

233

his face. He stared at me with bloodshot eyes. I saw the mistrust in them and revulsed, I pulled my hand away. Then I felt my stomach churning like a cement mixer. I thought: that meal hasn't gone down very well. Then I realised.

'Anthony, I think we're in trouble . . .'

'I knew we shouldn't have had meat,' Anthony groaned, clutching his stomach. 'Oh God . . .'

We spent the next five days in bed, taking it in turns to use the bathroom. Being in that room was pure hell; when I remember it I can still hear the monotonous whirr of the fan offsetting the more insidious whisper of mosquitoes and the cacophony of traffic outside, all coalescing into one big pounding noise that thumped against my brain like a hammer.

After our row, such close physical proximity was both wonderful and awful. There were times when I turned back to him, our row circling over and over in my mind, and a terrible sadness swept over me. It was a sense of failure. When we'd started this trip, I'd been convinced that for the first time in my life I'd got it right, that the books and movies and magazines weren't lying after all: that if you just waited patiently The One would come along and everything would fall into place. Now I felt my vision of our relationship melting like a mirage in the desert. I had no doubt that when we got back to England our relationship would be over. Yet again, I'd suffered another flop; I felt depressed with the repetition of my love life. Would I ever get it right or was I going to spend the rest of my life stuck in a cycle of bad relationships? And, a small voice whispered beneath my confusion, *Is it really him or is it actually* me?

And then there were times when Anthony would hold me tight and we lay, shivering and sweating, kissing feverishly, kissing away our misery, trying to heal each other. And then, one night, he apologised.

'I know I was being a jerk before,' he said. It was dark and I couldn't see his expression, just stripes of shadow moving over his face as the fan slashed the moonlight. 'I've told you about my mum and what happened . . . about how she went off with another guy . . . but at the same time I know it's really lame just to come up

234

with some Freudian mumbo-jumbo. It's just that – this is the very place we all came to.'

'What do you mean?' I asked, reaching for his hand and gripping it tightly, our palms slick with sweat.

'This is the place,' he licked his dry lips, his voice weakening, 'this is the place my parents came to just before they split up. I remember Mum screaming at Dad, and he just got fed up and brought a girl home, probably to wind her up, and then she got up the next day and left.'

'Oh, Anthony, I'm so sorry,' I whispered. 'If I'd have known . . .' Now that I thought about it, our trip had been a toss-up between two places; I'd pushed for India despite Anthony's reluctance. 'We should have gone back to Paris.'

'We definitely should have gone back to Paris,' he echoed and we both smiled weakly.

Back in England, things just weren't the same.

We didn't call or text for a few days. Then we organised a dinner out. Anthony took me to an expensive restaurant, but I couldn't relax. Every time I glanced around the room I was paranoid Anthony was watching me and thinking, *Lucy's sizing that guy up.* By the end of the meal I felt sulky and fed-up. Conversation turned into long silences. Back at my flat, we tried to make love but my heart felt too scrunched up with resentment; I couldn't open up to him. So I told him I had a headache and we both lay in bed, pretending to be asleep. The moonlight slid in sad silver beams across the ceiling; the room felt blue and cold. Even though he was right next to me, I felt so alone. As though he was a stranger. I thought sadly: *this is it. It's over.*

Finally, I asked my sister for advice.

'He's being awful, isn't he?' I said.

'Absolutely,' she said thoughtfully, sipping her Martini.

'I'm going to have to break up with him,' I said sadly.

'Absolutely not!' she cried.

'Why? What d'you mean?'

'Lucy, you always come to me for advice and you always decide whoever you're going out with is dreadful and then decide to dump them. But look, nobody is perfect. You're always going to have something wrong in a relationship. So he has a jealousy problem – well, it sucks, but it's not as though he's an axe murderer. You just have to talk to him about it and sort it out.'

'Yeah, maybe—'

'You're always reading all those books and expecting to find a Mr Darcy or a Heathcliff—'

'I am not,' I replied indignantly. That's the trouble with family, they always remember you as a teenager and forget you've grown up since then.

'You know, I think you just need to grow up, Lucy. You've got to see relationships through. You've got to work at them. You can't expect it all to be roses and candles. Talk to him and see if it gets better. If not, then think about dumping him. But don't give up at the first hurdle.'

'I guess,' I said, feeling chastised and slightly irked. Her advice had hit me straight in the heart because there was truth in it. Sally was such a know-it-all. I *did* tend to give up on relationships the moment something went wrong. It always seemed easier just to walk away rather than work at things.

So Anthony and I went for another dinner. This time, we opened up and talked things through. When we made love that night, we stared deep into each other's eyes, every caress a confirmation of our love for each other. As I lay in his warm arms, our noses nuzzling in an Eskimo kiss, I felt so relieved I had decided to give things a second chance. *How annoying,* I thought, as I drifted off, *that Sally's turned out to be right once again . . .*

But, inevitably, after the honeymoon there were more problems. And more honeymoons. And then more problems.

Our relationship improved and didn't improve. It followed a cycle: times when the tide was flowing out and we were surfing it, deep in love, and times when Anthony suddenly went back to being jealous and possessive and I went back to being flighty and indecisive and our love ebbed right back on to the shore.

236

During those times, I felt uncertain. Is Anthony really right for me? I would wonder. Is my sister wrong to say I'm being idealistic? What if there *is* a guy out there who wouldn't ever get jealous and who I wouldn't ever row with, who is The One for me? What if he exists?

iii) Shopping

Peter turned up promptly the next morning. My first surprise was that he had brought his son along. That meant there was a Mrs Peter lurking about somewhere. Unless he was a single father, I thought hopefully. As he patted his son's head, I glanced at his left hand. No rings.

'This is Tony,' he said. 'Tony, this is Lucy.'

Tony was a few years older than Adam. But whilst Adam, for all his bravado, tended to be shy and hide behind people's legs, Tony was very confident. He stared up at me with cold black eyes, sparky with suspicion and fear.

'Well, how lovely,' I said. 'Adam, here's a friend for you to play with.'

'Uh, yeah.' Adam smiled at Tony. Tony didn't smile back. Something subtle passed between them: a silent exchange in a language that only children could understand. I realised that if they had been alone in a playground right now, Tony would have been taunting Adam into a fight. I felt uneasy and made a promise to myself not to let Adam out of my sight.

Perhaps this whole trip was a mistake, I thought. I couldn't let any harm come to my dear nephew.

Then I looked up at Peter. He smiled, a lovely, slow, sexy smile. It was a very reassuring smile too. It seemed to sweep away all doubts and clouds and promise that everything would work out just fine.

'Come on then,' he said. 'Let's go!'

We had a wonderful morning together. Well – wonderful and strange.

237

We never did sort out the passports, for we were too wrapped up in having fun. Peter insisted, with amazing warmth and generosity, that I needed some new clothes and swept us along in two rickshaws to a local market. On the way we passed elephants strolling alongside the road, their sides painted with colourful designs, and barbers cutting hair under the shade of trees. We browsed through stalls proffering saris and beautiful cloths and shawls and spices and neon-coloured notebooks with Ganesh smiling across their covers, and kept Tony and Adam happy by buying some *petha*, a speciality of Agra that was made from sugar and cucumber and was deliciously cool and sweet.

As we explored, we chatted a lot. I was curious about my handsome stranger and kept meaning to ask him more about himself. But somehow he always shifted the conversation back to me. Like all great charmers, he was a good listener, interrogating me as though I was the most fascinating woman ever to have been born, bathing me in flattery like warm milk.

Answering his questions, however, involved a certain amount of verbal tango-ing. He asked me what I was doing in India, and I told him I was on holiday. When I told him about my job and career ambitions, he looked really surprised. I felt quite confused by his reaction. Then he covered it up quickly, smiling, his face bright again.

Our shopping done, I realised with a pang that it was probably time to go back.

'You must come and see this local temple,' Peter said. 'It's dedicated to Lord Shiva and the silence inside is quite profound.'

As we entered the temple, I stumbled slightly on the step and he quickly put his hand on the small of my back. I felt a burst of lightning tear up my spine. We exchanged hot glances. And then looked away.

Inside, the temple was cool and incredibly serene after the bustle of the market. We sat down, incense swirling sweetly around us, while Adam and Tony explored. They both looked faintly intimidated and walked about whispering and poking each other, daring each other to touch something. I noticed a woman shuffling in wearing a white sari, her face etched with grief. She knelt down before Lord Shiva and began to weep softly.

'You know, when I first came here, I felt pretty cynical about India and all this enlightenment mumbo-jumbo,' Peter said. 'But when you look at the way Indians live life, it's inspiring. In the West we put money first and religion last. Whereas in the East they do it the other way round.'

'What about all the scams?' I said. Then I felt churlish. 'I mean – I can't blame them, I guess, with the difference in our incomes. What *is* enlightenment exactly?' I asked, feeling a little stupid for having to ask. But he didn't do that male thing of patronising me with his superior knowledge; he just responded sincerely.

'I think the best way to look at it is through that story which is the centre of the *Bhagavad Gita*, the story of Arjuna. Arjuna is an impossible situation. It's his dharma – his sacred duty – to fight in battle, but he finds himself in a war where he will have to fight his own friends and family in order to defeat evil. And so he turns to Lord Krishna for help. Krishna tells Arjuna, "*Yogasta kurukarmani*", which translates as, "Established in Being, perform action." By being established in Being, Arjuna can act perfectly, freed from karma.'

'Karma – it's such a naff term, though,' I laughed. Then I saw his face and bit my lip.

'I kind of like it,' he said. 'I mean, it's the same if you're a Christian – *What ye sow, so shall ye reap.*'

I've discussed this all with Anthony when we'd visited India, and I brought up the same point now that I'd made then.

'I guess the idea of karma just makes me feel uncomfortable. I mean, I know that atheists sneer and say religion is the opium of the people, but actually I think atheism is the ultimate form of hedonism. It's so much easier to enjoy life, doing whatever you like, if you don't believe in heaven, or the possibility of hell, or a God who might send you there. There's no sense of responsibility, because if you hurt someone else it will never reverberate back to you. But karma – karma makes me feel nervous. It's like, whatever I do will have all these tiny little actions and reactions all rebounding off people and the stars and the sun and the moon and finding their way back to me wherever I am. It makes me scared to bloody do anything at all!'

Peter smiled. 'Tell me about it. Though it also says in the *Gita* that

239

karma is unfathomable, so I wouldn't go worrying about it, we just have to be natural. The point about karma, though, is that until we're enlightened, we're caught up in it. When we act, we create latent impressions, which give rise to more desires, which give rise to more actions, which in turn bind us. It means we're never satisfied.'

'Hmm . . .' I chewed my lip. 'I guess that's true. I have all these fantasies, and when I play them out I find they never quite fulfil me. I mean – you know – you fantasise about, I don't know, changing your job, or your house, or your boyfriend, and then you go through all the hassle of it and you get there and sometimes it's like, "Oh, nothing's really changed. I still feel the same inside." And there's this feeling of anticlimax . . .' I frowned, suddenly full to the brim with self-questioning. Because despite the fact that Byron had been a bastard, Leo gay, Ovid a chauvinist, and Al Capone a lousy lover, I was still bouncing about in my time machine, still searching for the butterfly of happiness that always fluttered slightly of reach.

'It all seems so horribly pointless,' I said in a doleful voice. 'I mean, if we're just doomed to repeat our mistakes over and over, stuck in this karmic trap, doesn't it make life ultimately meaningless?'

'I think the idea is that we all have lessons to learn. So we find ourselves in the same situation until we work out how to deal with it and get it right.'

'A bit like *Groundhog Day*?' I said, grinning.

'A bit like *Groundhog Day*,' he echoed, but a sigh escaped from his lips.

I came out of my own worries, realising he needed sympathy too.

'Do you feel you're stuck in some karmic trap, then?' I asked.

'Oh yes,' he replied heavily, rubbing his stubbled chin.

'Care to talk about it?'

We were interrupted by Adam's cries – Tony was trying to set fire to him with an incense stick.

'I think we'd better go,' said Peter.

Outside, I noticed that the woman in white who had been in the temple was lying on a makeshift wooden pyre.

'Daddy, what's she doing?' Tony asked.

'We have to get out of here,' said Peter quickly, but it was too late. The pyre had already gone up in flames.

Peter tried to shield my face, but I wrenched away with a horrible curiosity to confirm what I had dreaded. I couldn't see *her*, for the pyre was now surrounded by women in white, their screams hitting the sky like daggers. *Sati:* the ancient Indian practice whereby a woman who loses her husband takes her own life in devotion. The flames roared up in jets of cerulean blue and saffron yellow, incongruously beautiful. The smoke carried the scents of flesh and death; I choked on it, coughing.

The crowd had made no move to stop her. They watched with pale, sober, stupid faces. I stumbled forward, ready to push through them, to do something, anything. I was vaguely aware of Peter rounding up Adam and Tony, ordering them not to look. He caught me, cradling me in his arms, crying that it was no use, it wasn't our place to interfere. I collapsed against him, lost in his embrace. Everything became blurry; smoke billowed around us, bitter in the back of my throat. I looked up at him and through my tears I saw his face in its true expression, with all the charm stripped away. His eyes were heavy with anguish; not just the pain evoked by today's tragedy, but something lodged deep in his heart that he had been carrying for years. We leaned together, desperate to cling and console. We ached to kiss, to find, in the black death swirling about us, a memory of love, of life.

'DADDY!' Tony suddenly screamed, bursting into tears.

Peter scooped his son up in his arms, holding him tight. Adam, bewildered and unable to digest what was happening, copied Tony and began to cry too. I held him tightly, and we all hurried away. When I looked back, the fire was still licking tall tongues against the sky, smoke blistering the clouds.

'I'm so sorry,' Peter kept apologising as he dropped us off, as though the whole tragedy had been his fault.

'It's OK. I'm fine . . . well, a bit shaken . . .' I broke off, still choked with emotion.

'Perhaps – perhaps you could have dinner with us tonight, at our house. With me and . . . my wife,' he said awkwardly.

I lowered my eyes.

'I'd love to,' I said quietly. 'Thank you very much.'

Back in the hotel room, I hugged Adam tight and fell into a deep, nightmare-filled sleep.

iv) The dinner

I was woken by a violent banging on the door. A taxi driver had come to collect us and take us to Peter's house. I hastily put on the new sari I'd bought in the market, fumbling with a thousand safety-pins to keep it in place.

As we hurried downstairs to the taxi, however, Adam suddenly got cold feet.

'I don't want to go, Auntie Lucy,' he moaned. 'I want to watch *Postman Pat*. I want some orange juice.'

This was a first.

'Oh Adam . . .' I stroked his hair. 'Look – just one dinner and that's it. I promise.'

'But I'll have to play with horrible Tony.'

'Well – look – when we get back home, I'll buy you a new *Postman Pat* video, OK?'

'And a Power Rangers video?' Adam bartered. 'Two Power Rangers.'

Finally, we compromised on one of each.

The taxi journey was rather fraught. The wind breezed through the windows, cruelly flapping open the various bits of my sari which hadn't been pinned, and I kept having to slap them down in embarrassment. I was convinced that only one pin had to drop out and the entire thing would unravel. Hence, when I stepped out of the taxi, I walked at the speed of a snail, ignoring Adam's impatient cries.

The house was like an enormous white birthday cake, surrounded by a profusion of plants. The door was open and we were just entering when a portly, middle-aged man with a jolly red face and sideburns came out.

'Thanks, Peter,' he said, shaking his hand. 'I'll be in touch.' He smiled and nodded at me before walking off.

'That was just Roger, my business partner,' said Peter. 'Now, Lucy, don't you look fabulous.'

He shook hands and I smiled. Behind him a woman stared at me coolly.

She was beautiful. She had long dark hair like a mermaid and was dressed in that sort of seventies retro look that is so fashionable now: a tiered white hippy skirt with a flowing flowery shirt. Then I became aware of something small and dark and faintly threatening lurking by the door. The next thing I knew, water was flying over me and I was completely drenched. Adam only just ducked away in time.

'Tony!' Peter roared with laughter.

'Tony!' the woman cried. 'Oh, Lucy – you are Lucy, aren't you? – I am sorry. Tony, what on earth do you think you were doing?'

'It's the Holi festival!' he said sulkily.

'Tony, Holi is months away, and anyway, they throw coloured powder over each other.'

Tony shrugged apologetically.

'Sorry, wrong date,' he said to me. Then he turned to look at Adam, and smirked, sensing Adam's repressed fear. 'Hello.'

'Hello,' Adam said warily.

Peter introduced his wife as Marie, and she took me upstairs to her bedroom to change. It was a pretty room with a marble floor, patterned grey as though rain had fallen and dried in swirls. Everywhere were draped cloths blazing with colour, hovering over wardrobes and couches like enormous butterflies, quivering in the faint balmy breeze that wafted in through the window. My eyes fell on the bed. Only one side was slept in. She caught me looking and I quickly glanced away.

'I rather think you need a lesson in how to put on a sari,' she said, smiling.

'Maybe you could teach me,' I said, eager to be friends.

'Well, I'm quite busy now, being a wife and a mother,' she said, her warmth disappearing behind a cloud of mistrust. 'Here, change into this.' She passed me a hippy skirt and a droopy blouse.

As she left, I wanted to shout after her, 'Look, I'm not having an affair with your husband, OK, and I'm not even sure why he invited me here!' But I swallowed my words back like an aspirin.

Dinner was a rather tense affair. The servant, a stooping, elderly man called Jagabhandu, brought in a delicious meal of lemon rice and dahl. The conversation was decidedly stilted, and for once I felt quite thankful for Tony, who kept interrupting the silence with demands and tantrums.

I noticed that the servant poured wine for everyone except Marie.

'My wife is pregnant,' Peter said, with a touch of pride.

'Oh, wow.' I quickly concealed my shock. 'Well – congratulations!' I raised my wine glass and chinked it against Peter's, but somehow the gesture seemed inadvertently conspiratorial and mocking.

'So, do you run a business here?' I attempted to keep the conversation chugging along.

'Peter does,' Marie said acidly.

'You saw Roger, my business partner, back there,' said Peter.

'He's a very capable man,' said Marie, in a tone that implied the exact opposite.

'Marie is a great fan of Roger,' said Peter. 'She feels the slight loss in profits we made last year is his fault.'

The use of the third person was starting to make me feel uncomfortably like a marriage guidance counsellor. I could hardly wait for the meal to end. I snuck a glance at Adam, who, in Tony's presence, had become quieter than I had ever seen him before.

After dinner, Peter insisted that I stay for coffee. To my relief, Marie took Tony off to bed and I tried to cheer Adam up by suggesting he could help Jagabhandu make the coffees in the kitchen.

Peter disappeared to go to the toilet and I examined the stash of English newspapers on the coffee table – I remembered Peter saying that they had them specially delivered to make them feel more at home. I picked up a copy of *The Times*. That's strange, I thought. The logo's changed, and they've gone from tabloid size back to big serious broadsheet. How fickle. Then I saw the headline:

THATCHER DEFIANT OF IRA. My eyes flicked to the date: *13 October 1984*. My stomach lurched, and that feeling of unease returned.

Peter returned, along with Jagabhandu, who was carrying a tray. Adam followed behind, proudly bearing a little silver sugar bowl as though it was the Shiva Lingum.

Then Marie came back downstairs. I noticed her red eyes but pretended not to. I was keen to escape, but I felt compelled to ask the question that was nagging away at me.

'Um, what's your surname, by the way? You never mentioned it to me.'

'Brown. I'm Marie Brown.' She grimaced. 'I was Marie DeLillo before I married.'

Oh God. It couldn't be a coincidence. It couldn't.

'And your son is Tony Brown. Anthony Brown,' I said. 'What's his middle name?' She gave me a weird look and I blundered, 'Sorry – I just – I have this thing about names and their meanings. I mean, take Anthony. Did you know it means "worthy of praise"? I, ah, just happened to know that.'

'His name is Anthony Lewis Brown. Now there's a funny story.' She finally managed a smile. 'Peter and I had a bit of a fight over his name. Peter wanted Lewis, I wanted Anthony. In the end we tossed a coin.'

She paused, frowning at me when I didn't laugh. I quickly feigned amusement, trying to conceal my stunned shock.

A second later there was a scream from upstairs, and Marie hurried off. Adam, meanwhile, retreated to the kitchen with Jagabhandu as though keen to take cover.

'Lucy,' I heard Peter saying in the background, 'I know you'll be leaving India any day now and I just want to say . . . I just want to say I'm going to miss you when you're gone.'

I couldn't quite hear him. My head was spinning. So that *brat* – that boy who had chucked water over me and was now upstairs throwing a tantrum – was the man who in 2005 cooked me beautiful meals and massaged my feet before bedtime.

'Oh, Lucy.' Suddenly I became aware that Peter was sitting right next to me, his eyes full of longing. I realised I was in a very dangerous situation. The father of my ex-boyfriend was making advances towards me nineteen years before I would even meet the said boyfriend, something that would surely cement their divorce and ruin their lives for ever.

'Lucy . . .'

'Well, he's settled down,' Marie said, entering the room. She took one look at us – at the way Peter was leaning in on me, at the sweep of his arm around the back of my chair – and went white. 'Lucy,' she said, through clenched teeth, 'I think it's time for you to go home.'

I stood up quickly, my face flaming.

'Sure. Adam,' I called weakly. 'Adam, it's time to go.'

'Marie!' Peter suddenly said sharply. 'Just what do you think you're doing, throwing our guest out at this time of night?'

'What do you think *you're* doing, flirting with her right under my nose?'

'I don't know what you're talking about.'

I quickly sidled out, grabbing Adam's hand and making a run for it before I could cause any more trouble.

A few streets away, I found myself stopping short. A rickshaw driver spotted us and waved eagerly, but I shook my head.

'Auntie Lucy, what is it?' Adam asked.

'Maybe I should go back and explain,' I said, my mind spinning hotly. 'I mean – she's going to walk out any day now. Anthony told me she left when he was ten. What if I've put the final nail in their coffin? I mean, surely that's why we ended up here? It can't be an accident – I've got to do something.'

Adam looked utterly bewildered. I opened my mouth to explain, and then closed it. I felt he had enough to deal with right now without knowing we were back in 1984, which was actually a good fifteen years before he'd even been born.

Suddenly I wheeled round and turned back to the house.

'Where're we going?' Adam cried.

I ignored him, tugging him after me. He kicked up a fuss, and I put a finger to his lips and said, 'Look, we've got to pretend to be spies, OK? You're James Bond, and I'm – I'm, um, Lara Croft with a slightly flatter chest, and we have to creep up *very* quietly now.'

246

Adam immediately stopped grumbling and looked thrilled. We walked slowly, my footsteps dragging in my uncertainty as to what I should do. Maybe I should just ask to speak to Marie alone and explain everything . . .

I heard Marie's voice outside and quickly crouched down behind the bushes in a fit of cowardice, pulling Adam down with me. She laughed and I shivered in surprise at the softness, the happiness in her voice. Maybe she and Peter had made up – thank God. I parted the leaves, forming a jagged peep-hole to spy through, Adam's cheek pressing against mine in impatient curiosity.

And then I saw them. Marie and Roger. No wonder they had been so rude about each other. They weren't kissing or holding each other – they were just standing side by side – but there was no mistaking the intimacy between them. Then I saw Roger reach out and with a proprietorial hand gently caress the bump in her stomach.

'Come on, Adam,' I whispered. 'We're going home.'

v) Tony

The next day, I persuaded Adam that we should go back to the house one last time. My desire to see Anthony once more was a craving too strong to deny. So when he came out of the house and flung a small red ball which hit me on the forehead, I blinked away my tears of pain and said gaily, 'Anthony! How lovely to see you!'

'I'm not Anthony, I'm called Tony,' he replied sullenly.

'Is your dad in?'

'He's out. So's Mum. You can wait.' He shrugged and turned away.

I sidled into the kitchen, clutching Adam's hand tightly. And then I saw the letter, lying on the kitchen table. The moment I saw the word *Tony* in swirly letters, I knew exactly what it was. Anthony's angry words floated back to me: *She went without even leaving a note . . .*

Oh God. Today was the day. Marie had gone, walked out. And this letter was all Anthony had.

I knew it was wrong, but I found myself opening the note and skimming it, just to check. After only a few sentences, I felt tears fill my eyes and slotted it back into the envelope. Bewilderment overcame me – why the hell hadn't Anthony ever received this?

Peter, I realised.

In about ten minutes' time Peter would return home, see the letter and feel destroyed. And in turn he would feel so bitter, he would, I presumed, tear it up. Then he would call Anthony and tell him they were going to live in America.

'She didn't get in touch with me for years,' I remembered Anthony saying. But maybe she did try to, I thought feverishly; maybe when they moved to the States she had no idea where they were. By the time she did track them down, it was too late: Anthony had hardened his heart against her and refused to let her back in.

In the meantime, Anthony would live with his father in California. Peter would get a job as a film producer and date a series of younger, pretty women who all tried to mother Anthony, hoping that in time this would encourage Peter to put a ring on their fingers. But due to his failed marriage, Peter would never really trust a woman again. And Anthony, in turn, would grow up copying his father, eating his way through women until perhaps, one day he woke up and decided he was sick of such a shallow lifestyle, that history was repeating itself. Perhaps that was the moment he decided to come to England, where he would meet a girl called Lucy and flip over to the other extreme – a desperate desire for a traditional relationship.

Suddenly I felt a flood of sympathy for Anthony's behaviour. In truth, though I had tried to understand why he could be so jealous at times, I'd never really got my head or my heart around it. Now, finally, it all fell into place. I suddenly felt full of longing for Anthony to materialise here and now so that I could give him a huge hug and say sorry.

Suddenly I heard footsteps in the distance and Jagabhandu's lilting hum. Quickly I grabbed the letter.

'You can't take it Auntie Lucy, it's not yours,' Adam hissed in protest.

'Adam, you're never going to make it into MI5 with that attitude,' I hissed back. 'Now come on!'

I ran out into the garden and grabbed Anthony. I knelt down in front of him and shoved the letter into his hands.

'I want you to take this letter and hide it. It's very important.'

Anthony, taken aback by the intensity of my voice, nodded obediently for once.

'And then you wait for a time when your daddy's gone out and you take this letter out and read it. It's very important, see? It's got secrets in that only you are allowed to know.'

'OK,' said Anthony, looking dumbfounded. 'OK.'

I will never forget how it felt to walk out of that garden and glance back at Anthony, standing under the hot sun, his face screwed up in frightened confusion, the letter wilting in his hands. It was a letter that would change his life for ever, that would drag him, at the age of ten, into an early adulthood.

I knew that I couldn't change time. Back in the machine, time would spin forwards and my good deed would be undone.

And yet, a part of me hoped – however naïvely – that somehow a little of that letter would linger in Anthony's subconscious, that somehow he would grow up with some intuitive knowledge of the truth.

We had just slipped into the time machine when Adam, with the typical contrariness of a child, magically forgot how tired he was and demanded that we go somewhere else.

'Adam, we have to go back and see *Postman Pat* and have some nice orange juice, remember?'

'Oh Auntie Lucy!' he begged. 'Please, please, *please* times one hundred.'

'OK, OK,' I snapped. 'But we're not going somewhere where it might be dangerous. We'll take a tiny, tiny little trip to 1813, OK?' For I had to admit that I had been pondering over the last few weeks as to how Byron was doing.

The time machine whirred and landed, with a jerky thump, on the exact grey cobbled street that I had visited before. Only this time it was a wintry London day and the streets were bustling with carriages and people. I grabbed hold of Adam so that he couldn't jump out, insisting he peer through the window. Over the top of his head I suddenly noticed a doorway I recognised.

249

Suddenly Hobhouse's door flew open and out stepped an unmistakable figure.

'Byron!' I cried.

What was even stranger was that Byron *seemed to notice me*. I was certain he couldn't see the machine – but he was staring right at me.

'We have to go!' I said hastily, tapping in numbers, ignoring Adam's squeals of protest. I saw Byron running towards us, his mouth moving frantically as though calling out my name – and then time folded in on itself like a paper rose and twirled and danced and then opened up again.

Well. Thank God for that. Back in my living room, Adam, whacked by jet-lag, was fast asleep. I opened the door of the time machine and it came off in my hand. Great. My machine clearly needed an MOT.

In a brief moment of panic, I checked the clock. But it was still 9.36 a.m. Time in the present had remained still, which was just as well, or Sally would have been freaking out as to where her darling son was.

'Come on, sleepyhead.' I picked Adam up and laid him on the sofa, where he slept soundly until Sally came at five to pick him up. Much to my relief, he didn't seem to remember anything of the trip.

'So, Adam, what did you do all day with Auntie Lucy?' Sally asked.

'Nothing!' Adam replied sulkily. 'We didn't even see *Postman Pat*! It was the most boring day ever!'

After Adam had gone, the house seemed very quiet. I got a roll of masking tape from the cupboard and succeeded in sticking the door back on the machine – it would have to do for now.

I was feeling knackered and ready to go to bed, but too many emotions, stirred up by seeing Anthony, were swirling about inside me. The niggling thought came into my mind: *Why not finish off what you intended to do? Just go back and wipe out what happened. Let Anthony take you out to dinner and . . .*

Dump me, I finished silently. That was the one big flaw in my plan. I'd been so emotionally fraught, I hadn't thought it through properly this morning. Even if I did go back, Anthony would still take me out to Burger King and tell me it was all over, and it would be worse this time, like a knife stabbing through my heart.

I couldn't go back in time and smooth our relationship out, like a kink in a knot. Our problems had to be dealt with here and now, in reality, in the present, between us.

I jumped up, suddenly alive with determination. I grabbed my handbag, put on some lipstick and brushed my hair in a wind of static. Then I left the flat and hurried outside to find him . . .

vi) A row

Anthony wasn't at home, nor did he answer his mobile when I called. But it wasn't hard to guess where he was: I knew exactly the place he went when he was upset and needed to go into hedgehog mode.

There were only a few lights on in the block on Bedford Road. I counted the floors up and then the rooms along. Yes, Anthony's office was lit up.

Inside, the porter made me sign the visitors' book and then directed me to the lift. How quiet, almost eerie, the offices sounded without the usual buzz of daily activity.

The moment I entered Anthony's office, I could see at once just how much I had hurt him. Whenever he was upset, he threw himself into his work. At various times in the past when he'd had spats with his mother, he had been known to work for seventy-two hours straight, though I would frequently march in with takeaways and demands for him to come home. Tonight he looked absolutely exhausted, his eyes lost in a sea of purple, the veins in his forehead pulsating with strained concentration. There was something guarded in his eyes too, something mistrustful. I felt my heart twist. I wanted to jump on him and engulf him in a tight hug. But I knew it wasn't as easy as that. I had to explain.

But how to begin? All the way to his office, I had been trying to assemble my emotions like a jigsaw, to create a clear picture to present to him. I'd imagined myself making a messy sort of speech, like a heroine in a movie, and Anthony, like the perfect hero, smiling at me, his heart softening, forgiving me. The scene would end with a kiss, and then on a more practical note we would go out for dinner and talk late into the night and finally, once and for all, find a happy ending to the History of Lucy and Anthony's Love Life.

But now that I was standing here, I felt foolish and awkward and I didn't know where to begin, and Anthony really didn't look like a romantic hero.

'So,' he said, swinging back in his chair and tapping his pen impatiently. 'What can I do for you?'

'*What can I do for you?* Anthony, I'm not one of your clients,' I said, wounded.

'Well, I'm busy,' he said tersely, stinging me with the sharpness of his tone. 'This really isn't a good time. I'm snowed under, I have a pile of paperwork and—'

'I just wanted to talk,' I said quickly. 'Look – maybe when you've finished we can go out for a meal. I'll treat you. We'll get Chinese . . .'

Anthony shook his head solemnly, his glazed eyes returning to his computer screen, fingers tapping on the keys.

'I don't expect to be finished until three a.m.,' he said. Then he glanced at me. I hated, *hated* it when I called him up and heard the clatter of keys; I would refuse to speak to him, in fact. And now he was doing it right in front of me.

'Sorry,' he said, dropping his hands and flexing them. 'It's just not a great time, and look . . .' He broke off, taking a sip of coffee from his Bart Simpson mug, then wincing. 'Shit, that's cold. Anyway – Lucy, I think . . . I think we need some time apart. OK?'

'No,' I said, taken aback. 'Anthony – look, I know I hurt you, I know I shouldn't have run away from you in Suffolk, but I've come here – well, I've come here to say sorry. I've come to say I really think it can work between us.'

'Do you?' Anthony said, in such a soulless voice that I quailed inside. 'I'm not so sure.'

Then he started tapping away at the keyboard again.

'Anthony!' I cried. 'For God's sake, can't it wait one minute? I'm trying to talk to you!'

'No, it can't wait!' Anthony suddenly exploded. 'Lucy, for God's sake, we've had plenty of time to *talk*. Fuck, we've spent weeks having *talks* about whether we should be friends, or not be friends, or date other people, and we never get anywhere. We just end up back at square one all over again. I mean – I just – I don't know . . .' He trailed off miserably. 'It seems that however hard we try to move up a ladder, we just fall back down a snake. I give up, Lucy. I've given up on talks, I've given up on us.'

I stared at him in shock. It wasn't so much the truth in his words as the way he delivered them in such a matter-of-fact, businesslike tone. As though his subconscious had been grinding through it all and already reached a conclusion.

Oh God, I thought, I've blown it. I've pushed him too far. I've been too selfish. And now I've well and truly blown it.

'Anthony, I know I've hurt you . . .' I managed.

'It's not that,' Anthony snapped. 'Yes – you've hurt me. But it's me really. I've put myself up for it. I've kept coming back after you, I've kept trying to patch things up, and it's all just a pointless waste of time.'

'It's not a waste of time, Anthony. I really think we can do this. I just . . . I just needed to think and I've . . . I've realised it can work . . .'

'Lucy, you're just . . .' Anthony trailed off, chewing his lip.

'Just *what*?'

'I don't think that, emotionally, you're quite mature enough for a big relationship.'

'*What!*' I cried.

'That came out . . . I didn't mean . . . look, don't take it the wrong way. I'm not having a go at you, Lucy—'

'Oh, so you think I'm immature.'

'I just think I'm ready for something that you're not.'

'Well, what d'you think I'm ready for? Come on, say it!'

'Lucy, this is not what I intended . . .'

'No, come on, I want to hear it. We're both being honest, right? We're both laying all our cards on the table. So tell me.'

'Lucy, I kind of think you have this fantasy guy in your head, someone who's a bit of Lord Byron, and a bit of Al Capone, and a bit of that poet whatever-his-name-is, and you're somehow

253

secretly reaching for him, waiting for him to come along on a white horse. And Lucy, I'm not that guy, and frankly all I want is—' He broke off. 'I want a relationship that's *real*. That's here and now.'

'I . . . I . . .' I was lost for words. 'I mean – I guess . . . I see what you're saying, but . . . I think . . . Look, I just feel . . . OK, maybe you're right,' I admitted. 'I know what you're saying, Anthony, but I just feel . . . I understand you a lot better now, after—' I broke off. 'Um, I feel . . . I feel . . .'

Anthony stared at me, his eyes big and open, as though he wanted to believe me. And yet I could feel, in my heart, that he wasn't quite convinced.

He dropped his eyes.

'I think a break would be good,' he muttered. 'I think I need some time apart from you to think about it all.'

'Well, I guess I should go then.'

Anthony smiled – a tight, pinched smile – and then turned swiftly back to his computer. I felt like punching him. Here he was, having a go at *me* for having a rich fantasy life, and now he was burying himself in his work, hiding from the world in just the same fashion.

'Anthony,' I burst out in desperation, 'I know about your mother.'

'What? What are you talking about?'

'I just – I think you need to know this.'

'What . . .'

'Look, she didn't just walk out on you. Yes, she was having an affair – but so was your dad. She just felt she'd had enough. I think the reason she had an affair at all was as retaliation against him. And she didn't want to leave you, but she was pregnant with another man's baby, so—'

'What! Have you been speaking to my mum behind my back?' Anthony suddenly snapped. 'LUCY, WHY THE HELL ARE YOU DOING THIS?'

'BECAUSE,' I screamed back, 'YOU'RE A REALLY LOVELY GUY BUT YOU'RE ALSO FUCKED UP BY IT AND YOU NEED TO SORT IT OUT!'

I broke off. Our screams hovered in the air like invisible barbs.

The sound of traffic outside suddenly seemed extraordinarily loud and intrusive.

'Lucy, I really don't need this right now,' said Anthony. 'Look – can you just go? Please? I have to do this work.'

Some masochistic desire kept me rooted to the spot. I knew I'd ruined it now; perhaps our friendship would never be repaired again, and so I figured that I might as well just throw everything at him.

'Anthony, I think you should stop blaming her for everything and just go out and find out what really happened. I know you've said—'

'You just don't get it, do you?'

'I do get it, Anthony. You've never really listened to her. I mean – what about the fact that she was pregnant? What happened?'

'I . . . I . . .' Anthony broke off, overwhelmed. 'Lucy, who the hell have you been talking to?'

I was close to tears of exasperation – how on earth could I explain?

'I just want you to leave.' Anthony stared at the screen, the swirling screensaver casting patterns on his stony face. He had shut down; he felt more absent than present. 'Just go, OK?'

'OK,' I said quietly, and I left.

Well, I thought back home, that went well.

I lay down on the sofa, sobbing, berating myself for making such a mess of things. Hours seemed to pass, and tears kept coming over me in waves. I flew through a rainbow of emotions, one minute hating Anthony, the next minute loving him, the next minute hating myself.

In the corner of the room, a ray of moonlight slanted through the curtain and rested on the machine, making it glisten like some rare, exotic beast ready to take flight. I jumped up, wiping my eyes, breathing in a snotty breath. Right, I thought in desperate misery, I'm going to go and damn well get into that machine. I'm going to go away for months and months. I'm going to meet men who are a million times more sexy and wonderful and funny than him. Sod him, I thought, sod him sod him sod him. I hate him hate him hate him.

I ran over to the machine, slipping into the seat. It was well worn now from my adventures; there were several splits in the leather cover where stuffing was wriggling out like yellow worms. For one surreal moment I almost felt the machine sigh, as though it was tired itself from so much turbulence and just wanted a rest.

I told myself not to be silly. Now, where did I want to go? And more importantly, who did I want to meet?

My mind was a blank. All I could see was Anthony's face as we'd parted. All I wanted to do was set the machine for his bedroom. For a moment I sat dreamily and pictured myself surprising him. He'd be lying in bed now in his pyjamas, reading; and I'd just appear, glide across the carpet and kiss him on and on and on . . .

Concentrate, Lucy. For God's sake. Just pick someone. Pick a great lover. The greatest of lovers. Casanova!

Casanova. Perfect. The one man who would extinguish Anthony for good. The only trouble was I didn't know what date to type in, and I couldn't even bring myself to get out of the machine and look it up.

Eventually I did get out and stumbled back to the sofa. Tears began to pour down my face and I felt exhaustion weighing me down like grey tar.

It took a while to sink in, for the shock to hit me. I didn't want to use the machine. I had no wish to go back in time and dally with anyone, even Casanova.

So now what?

Up until now, the time machine had always been there, an open door, a way out, a chance to run away, to escape the boredom of my job, my fear of commitment. But now all I could think was: What's the point? I could see it all now. I'd end up in whatever century. I'd see Casanova. I'd woo him, or he'd woo me. Even if he did succeed in making me fall for him, I'd always have to come back, in the end. And no matter how hard I tried to picture Casanova, how hard I tried to envisage a beautiful face, or winsome eyes, or a gravelly, seductive voice, all I saw was a cartoon, a caricature. I didn't want perfection: I wanted Anthony. I wanted Anthony with the little scar on his cheek and his slippers and his frightful pyjamas. If I was going to play the going-to-bed game now, all I could come up with was:

256

vii) The email

In the morning I woke up feeling like death. I ate a few mouthfuls of cornflakes for breakfast and left the rest to form a soggy mountain in a sea of milk. I turned on the TV and stared at the screen with glazed eyes. I checked my emails. As I typed in my password, I thought about telephoning the temping agency and saying that I was ill.

And then I saw it.

An email from Athony!

Suddenly I was awake and alert, my cells singing and twitching with excitement and hope. My hand shook on the mouse as I clicked on it. I drummed my fingers, cursing at the snail's pace of my connection speed, ready to shout at the screen.

I gulped. I didn't know whether to laugh or cry. I was thankful that he was still speaking to me. I noticed he hadn't mentioned his mother once, so I guessed he had just buried that hurt deep and decided not to bring it up. But it was such a *frustrating* email. I read it several times, taking apart each sentence, zooming in on each word. *I think we both know we're not meant to be together . . .* and *I'm sure you'll be glad to hear that I'm going for a date . . .*

He wasn't trying to wind me up. I was struck by the straightforward honesty of his tone. He genuinely hadn't believed a word of what I'd said last night. He'd assumed it was just another one of my whims, to be forgotten in the morning.

Oh God – how was I ever going to make him see that this time it was different – that this time I was serious?

Chapter Seven

Anthony Brown and Lord Byron

Lovers may be – and indeed generally are – enemies, but they can never be friends, because there must always be a spice of jealousy and a something of Self in all their speculations.

LORD BYRON

i) A plan to win back Anthony

What is the best way to say sorry to someone you love?

A gift, I decided. Gifts were glorious gestures that epitomised all the great affairs. Antony, for example, had given Cleopatra the land of Syria as proof of his passion. Napoleon had given Josephine an exquisite golden medallion on their wedding night inscribed with the words *To destiny*. A gift, if properly thought out, could be treasured in a lover's possession and memory until death.

The only problem was, I couldn't really afford something like Syria. So I had considered and rejected gloves, a Pink Floyd CD, and a new set of golf clubs. The trouble with Anthony was that, like all men, he was simply impossible to buy presents for. At Christmas I always nagged him endlessly and he would always come up with socks. When I gave him dagger glances, he would shrug sheepishly and say, 'Well, they *are* useful, Lucy.' I mean, Guinevere hardly gave Lancelot socks for the battlefield, did she? And Juliet didn't die with Romeo's sock clutched in her hand. And yet I found myself in a shop dallying with the second worst option after socks.

Ties were dull. They represented work and repression. They always looked better in the shop, in their rows of blazing colour, like a shoal of tropical fish. Alone, back home, their glitter faded.

I felt my heart wilt. Perhaps I'll just have to send him an amazing email, I thought in despair. Or phone. But . . . oh come on, there must be *something* . . .

Then, just as I was to leave, my eye caught something.

Yes, I thought, my heart skipping. That's Anthony.

Five minutes later, I walked out, swinging a fancy little cardboard carrier, full of hope.

A week had passed since Anthony's email had arrived and I had read it so many times that by now I knew it by heart.

I'd been very good. I hadn't called or emailed him once, despite having to sit on my hands to stop myself. In fact, a week apart *had* been the best thing for both of us. I'd taken time to sift through my emotions, to poke and prod my heart. And I was certain: I was ready to commit to Anthony. When I looked back on myself, on the Lucy who had broken up with him that night, she seemed terribly selfish and immature and naïve, with her head in clouds that were so thick she couldn't see reality, and a severe grass-is-greener syndrome.

But I knew that I had hurt Anthony. It seemed as though we were standing on opposite ends of a sheet of ice and I sensed that it would crack unless I trod oh-so-softly. A present was a gentle apology; a present was a good first step.

Humming Vivaldi, I let myself into my flat. And then I stopped. And frowned. That's strange, I thought. Without fail, every single time I opened my front door, Lyra would come running up and roll over, exposing her fluffy tummy for a tickle, followed by a sharp *miaow* that said, yes, since she was so very cute, surely a plate of tuna was in order?

But – no Lyra.

And – God – what was that?

My eyes fell on a large muddy footprint on my beige carpet. And another. And another. A whole line of them leading to my kitchen. Then I heard a clinking noise. It sounded like someone was playing with my knives. I felt my heart explode in panic, adrenalin rollercoastering through my bloodstream.

OK, I told myself. Keep calm. Just step back very quietly into the hallway and call 999.

I backed up slowly. Foot-sole by foot-sole. My heart tore at the muscles. I kept thinking: This can't be happening, this is like the movies, this can't be real life. Finally – the door. My hand on the latch. Open it slowly, make sure it doesn't squeak. Inch by inch, I twisted the knob. *Squeak!* Footsteps creaking, from the living room. A tall, dark, shabby figure – coming towards me!

I screamed, and grabbed an umbrella from the coat-hook. I slashed about wildly with it. *Get out, get out!* I yelled at myself. *You'll never win this fight, just run.* But to my surprise, he didn't seem to be putting up much of a fight. He bellowed and sank to the floor, shielding his face with his arms.

Suddenly I realised that the heap lying at my feet looked very familiar. And smelled strange. And was wearing clothes that clearly belonged in the nineteenth century. Good Lord – it couldn't be . . .

'Byron!' I gaped down at him.

'Lucy!' He smiled up at me. 'Well. Help me up, then.'

I helped him up, wondering if I was hallucinating.

'But . . . but . . . have you got a time machine too?' I cried in bewilderment.

Byron roared with laughter, then turned and strolled into the living room. He pointed to the TV and my remote control, whose plastic case had been ripped open, coloured wires poking out like worms.

'What the hell is *this*?' he asked. 'Your age simply isn't as I envisaged; the machines all appear to be utterly pointless.'

'Byron, can you please just tell me how on earth you got here?'

Byron flopped down on the sofa with an elegant sigh, twiddling his cravat.

'I'm rather tired from my journey and I could do with a little tea and opium, but yes, I shall tell you. You paid 1813 a visit yesterday, I believe, with a small boy. I spotted your metal carriage and ran along behind you, yelling, but I don't believe you heard me. I leapt after it, and much to my surprise I found myself passing through metal and in the back of your time carriage.'

'But . . . but that's so weird,' I mused. 'I mean, you must have slipped in just as the machine was suspended between past and present. Perhaps in that transitional state the metal became malleable.'

'And then,' Byron went on, looking terribly pleased with himself, 'I hid in the back of the carriage and waited until you'd retired to your chamber. I spent the night on your chaise-longue –' he pointed to the sofa '– which, I must say, Lucy, needs some serious embroidery if you want anyone to think you have any style. In the morning, I hid behind it as you performed your morning toilette.'

I froze, recalling how I had run through the sitting room in my blouse, trying to pull on my panties and brush my hair at the same time.

'Great,' I yelped. 'So you saw me . . .'

'I saw a beautiful forest which bewitched me with its dark

263

density,' Byron said in a very naughty tone, his smile curling into a seductive smirk.

Too seductive. I felt something pull in my stomach, then turned away, resisting his amorous magic. My head was spinning. I just kept thinking: I can't handle this. I wanted to wash my hands of the time machine once and for all, and now *this*. Things were out of control. I couldn't have Lord Byron, of all people, hanging about my flat. I had to deal with Anthony, and work, and – and whatever would the neighbours say?

'I can see why Sir Anthony has fallen for you,' Byron murmured. 'It seems I was wrong to let you go, Lucy. I do hope you can forgive—'

'What?' I cried, spinning round. 'What did you say? What did you mean by that? Has Anthony been round?' Oh God, no, please no.

'He, er, sent a verbal letter through your . . . your . . .' Byron nodded in confusion at my phone. 'That *thing*. He wrote that he wanted to see you.'

'A verbal letter,' I giggled. Euphoria rippled through me. Anthony had called, he had called, he had called.

'I told him not to bother,' Lord Byron added. 'I told him that you were far too busy making love to me.'

'You said what!' I screamed. 'We're not having sex!'

'Not yet we're not!' Lord Byron said, with a glint in his eye.

ii) Not having sex with Lord Byron

After I informed Lord Byron, very firmly, that we were not having sex, he threw a terrible sulk.

He slumped on the sofa, borrowed a biro and my phone notepad and scribbled lines of poetry. I asked if he wanted a cup of tea and he ignored me; then, when I made him a mug and put it by him, he took a few sulky sips, as though he was doing me a massive favour by drinking it at all, and then muttered about it tasting like 'cant'. I felt prickles of irritation in my stomach. He was behaving like a five-year-old in a twenty-five-year-old's body, and I began to wonder what I had ever seen in him. It seemed strange to think that this man, who had written poetry that had survived for several hundred years, dissected and adored and torn apart by some of the greatest minds in our country at some of the highest institutions, could behave like such an imbecile. But just because people produce great art it doesn't make them great people, I realised.

I suddenly thought of the end of *Middlemarch*: *For the growing good of the world is partly dependent on unhistoric acts; and that things are not so ill with you and me as they might have been, is half owing to the number who lived faithfully a hidden life, and rest in unvisited tombs.* Then I thought of Anthony, doing his mundane computer business, but still making his contribution to the world in the sweetness and generosity and thoughtfulness of his personality. Anthony who thought I was shagging another guy, too busy to even phone him back. I felt tears burn behind my eyes. Oh God, what timing.

'I need to make a phone call,' I said.

'But what *is* this?' Lord Byron seemed to have realised my patience had run out and was now gesturing at the television, waving about the ruined remote control.

'You've broken it now,' I said tartly, snatching it back. 'Oh here, I'll switch it on.' I flicked on the button by hand; at least it would keep him quiet.

Byron looked puzzled.

'What is this?'

'Entertainment,' I said wryly.

'But it's just a screen of coloured dots,' he said, frowning. 'What a strange way to entertain yourselves. You have replaced poetry and opera and fine art – with *this*?'

I suddenly remembered reading an article which described an experiment where jungle tribes were shown TVs and, like Byron, could not see a picture. Their minds took some time to make the leap and connect the dots together; at first sight a TV was such an extraordinary thing to them, they couldn't quite compute.

Byron's imagination had been set alight. He started picking up all the mechanical and electrical objects in my house, demanding explanations. As I showed him how a blender worked, and what the fridge did, and the crucial difference between a fridge and a freezer, I felt like a bloody saleswoman at Currys. Besides which, the moment I turned my back, he kept breaking things – or worse, forgetting how they worked. After he failed to put the lid on the blender, my ceiling rapidly became covered in strawberry and banana splat. Then he discovered a packet of condoms in a drawer.

'What are these?' he asked, curiously stretching one into a milky-coloured balloon.

'If you really want to know, you put them on during sex,' I said, feeling horribly like a biology teacher. 'You can get different flavours and sizes. Now – *please*,' I went on, ushering him back into the living room and sitting him in front of the TV like an irate babysitter. 'Just behave, OK! Please, can you just look at the dots. I desperately have to make a call, all right?'

Over the next hour, I tried and failed to get hold of Anthony. His personal line was permanently engaged and on voicemail, and I definitely wanted to avoid dealing with his evil secretary. In the mean time, Lord Byron sniffed, prowled and shifted his way through my twenty-first-century home. I began to curse him silently, then caught myself. How crazy it seemed that just a few weeks ago I thought I was in love with him. All his flaws had seemed so endearing; now they were just infuriating. How strange that such a deep passion could become such a deep indifference. Was love just a fantasy bubble, waiting to be burst? Would I ever feel this indifference for Anthony?

I tested my love, prodding and poking it once again. No, I thought, what I felt for Anthony wasn't just passion. It was so much deeper than that. My love for Lord Byron was just a butterfly; after a long cocoon of fantasy, the reality only flitted about for a day. My love for Anthony, however, had been putting down roots, slowly but surely, and was now ready to grow . . .

When I emerged from my bedroom, I discovered that Lord B. was now in the process of exploring my hoover by taking it to bits.

'Byron!' I cried, close to tears, ready to snap. 'Look, you just have to stop this! I'm really broke, OK.'

'I haven't laid a finger on you,' Byron shot back.

'No – I mean broke as in poor. It's a twentieth-century expression. It means I am in a lot of debt and I don't have much money and I can't afford to have a mad poet mucking up my hoover because I don't have another hundred-odd quid to buy another one.'

'The English language, 'tis a whore,' Byron mused mistily. 'I thought a second Great Vowel Shift might have taken place, since you speak so strangely.'

'Oh no, the vowels have stayed put.'

'It seems the English language has been cruelly raped by modern man. Raped and left for dead.' He shuddered.

'Hmm, well . . .' I looked down at my hoover, the disembowelled bag spewing yellow dust. Byron's imagination, however, was caught by the subject. He asked me to tell him more modern words.

'Oh, I don't know,' I said tiredly. 'Fuck. Um, bootylicious. That means gorgeous, sexy.'

'Ah.'

'Or coolio. That means cool. When we say cool, we don't mean cold. We mean things are good, y'know, hip. Hip, by the way, is quite similar to cool. In 1813, you would have defined hip.'

'Oh.'

'A lot of words have come from rap music. Like the word blinging. It means flashy jewellery, kind of gangster gear, very over the top.' At least, I thought it did.

'Blinging,' said Byron thoughtfully, rolling the word round in his mouth like a sweet. 'I see. *Bu-ling-ing*. Blinging.'

'OK, here's another modern expression for you. Girl power. It was invented by the Spice Girls.'

'The Spice Girls?'

'They were a group of very cool girls who wore sexy clothes and were idolised all over the world. They all had names which were based on various spices.'

'What, like cardamom, and ginger?'

'No, no! Well, there was a Ginger. But they weren't trying to promote cookery classes, if that's what you're thinking. Anyway, they were feminists, of a kind, and they invented girl power.' I paused wickedly, unable to resist getting him back after my Anthony disaster. 'And life mirrored art. The politicians took note. Girl power is now law – the law of the land. Men have to do *everything* that women tell them. Men are our slaves! And if a man defies a woman, he can be arrested and thrown in jail.' I improvised wildly.

'Basically, we rule the world now. Which means you have to behave yourself and do whatever I say.'

Byron went quite white. He breathed out deeply.

'You mock me.'

'I do not.' I picked up a ruler and waved it at him. Unfortunately, he rose to the challenge and picked up a kitchen knife.

'A duel we shall fight!' he cried. 'I shall represent my sex, you the feebler.'

Oops, I thought. My experience at fencing was clashing knives at the table with Adam. Byron's father, meanwhile, was infamous for killing a poor innocent man in a pub brawl, and I had a feeling Byron could definitely follow in the family tradition. And I had plastic, whilst he had steel. Before I could cry that this was most unfair, he lunged at me and I squealed, jumping behind the sofa.

'How have women come to rule the world when men clearly have the greater physical strength?' He lunged again and the knife plunged into the sofa: yet more damage to my possessions.

'You brute!' I cried, waving my ruler back. 'All right, men may have the physical advantage . . . but hey, actually, maybe not. The gap between male and female runners, for example, is closing – scientists are even predicting that in a few years' time women will be able to run faster than men. We'll break every one of your records. You see, women have always been as strong as men, but we've just never had a chance to show our potential. Now, finally, it's emerging.' I slashed forward and rapped Byron on the wrist; he flushed purple with shame.

'You lie! This is poppycock! For one thing, how can a woman race in a ballgown!'

'We no longer wear bloody ballgowns. Bloody doesn't mean bloody, by the way – it means "damned". Anyway,' I held my ruler erect again, 'in this century, women wear the trousers – literally. One of the greatest prime ministers of the last century was a woman called Margaret Thatcher.'

'A woman! Running the country! I've never heard such cant in all my life!' Byron broke off from our swordplay to howl with laughter. 'You must be jesting, you – you blinging vixen.'

'I jest not! Girls now get better results than boys in school exams! Year in, year out!'

Byron, incensed, watched me jump on to the dining-room table. I had been hoping for a height advantage but, in a most ungentlemanly fashion, he followed me. We stood at opposite ends of the table, buffered by a box of Kleenex and a small pile of *Vogue*. Lyra, who was sitting on the window ledge, looked at us as though we were completely bonkers.

'It was a gradual victory,' I told him sweetly. 'It began during the war. The men went off to be stupid and get themselves killed. The women, when they weren't bandaging the men up, did useful, sensible things, like driving buses and building bridges. So in a funny sort of way, the Second World War—'

'There was a *world* war?' Byron cried.

'Don't try to change the subject. Basically, things came to a head in the seventies when Germaine Greer published *The Female Eunuch*. It was an amazing book that empowered women. It made the point that women can be proactive about sex, that we can take control, we can have balls, we can go out and get it whenever we want it—'

'Well, I can't disagree with that,' said Byron.

'And when we've finished with them, we can damn well tell men where to go,' I continued, relishing the collapse of Byron's smile. 'Germaine Greer is my idol!' I kissed my ruler and pointed it at him. 'I fight for her legacy!'

'This Germaine Greer,' Byron cried, 'is my sworn enemy! Once I have killed you, I shall challenge her, and then we'll see how well she manages, hmm!'

And with that, he threw himself at me. I let out a scream and half jumped, half fell off the table. I staggered backwards; the backs of my knees collided with the sofa, and I sank on to it and lay prone, irritatingly enough in the manner of a damsel in distress.

Byron climbed on to the sofa and caught my waist between his knees, perusing me through narrowed eyes. I scrabbled about a bit and – oh, the shame – he easily reduced me to a heap again by digging his tickly fingers in my ribs. I giggled hatefully. Then I felt the cold curve of the knife flat against my cheek. I gulped. Surely Lord B. hadn't really been serious when he said he was going to kill me?

'I shall kill you now,' Lord B. murmured, 'and you shall suffer *un petit mort*.'

'More like un petit suicide,' I said tartly.

Then I heard the shrill of the phone ringing and I tried to shove Byron away.

'No!' I cried. 'No, no, no, NO!'

'A woman says no when she means yes,' Byron crooned, his lips still warm in my neck.

I tried to push him off, desperate now, but he pinned me down, and then the phone stopped.

'Look,' I said desperately, 'in this century, if a man uses force on a woman, he gets his balls chopped off, OK?'

He let me go pretty quickly after that.

Rising to his feet, he slumped sulkily on to the sofa and muttered, 'This Germaine has a lot to answer for.'

I ran over to the phone, pressing 1471 with shaking fingers. The bloody BT woman informed me that they did not have the caller's number to return the call. I was convinced it had to be Anthony. But when I called him back it went back to voicemail. I nearly screamed with frustration.

Right, I thought. If I can't speak to him, I'll go and see him. Right now.

I looked over at Lord Byron, who was now examining my PC with a dangerous look in his eyes. Shit, I thought, I can't leave him here on his own. Unless . . .

'Byron, I've thought of something that I think you'll find very interesting. It's called the internet . . .'

Byron was indeed very intrigued and impressed, his eyes shining with wonder. By the time I left, Lyra had jumped on to his lap in a furry white ball and he was stroking her absent-mindedly whilst surfing with glee. Having discovered Google, he cried, 'Before you go, Lucy, you have to hear about this – I've got 1,070,000 sites all devoted to me!'

Arriving at Anthony's office, I could hardly believe how nervous I was: butterflies frantic in my stomach, throat misty, words jumbly, brain electric-shocked. I'd decided it was best simply not to bring up our row. We'd only get back on to the subject of his mother, and that was best avoided. I'd just act like everything was hunky-dory.

Anthony's smug secretary smiled a smug smile at me.

'Hello, can I help you?'

She always did this, even when we were dating – acting like I was a complete stranger she'd never seen before in her life.

'Hi.' I was horrified that she might see my nerves. 'Um, is Anthony in?'

She looked me up and down and then looked at her nails.

'I think he's busy.'

'He's in a meeting?' I gulped. 'I can wait.'

'He's not in a meeting, he's just incredibly busy.'

'Well – could you ask him if he's so incredibly busy he can't see me for five minutes?'

'OK. Take a seat.'

I took a seat. The smug secretary shuffled some papers about. Well, wasn't she going to even call him, or did she work by telepathy? I bit my tongue, my nerves at breaking point. I thought: when did I last feel like this, approaching Anthony? The answer came quickly: the night of our second one-night stand.

We'd arranged to meet at Charing Cross tube station. I was fifteen minutes early and when I arrived he was already waiting for me. He was wearing a suit with a silk tie that kept flapping in the breeze; his hair had caught a drizzle of rain and sparkled beautifully. He kissed my cheek and we walked awkwardly down the road, my arms crossed, his hands in his pockets. He said, 'Would you like to see my new office? It's just round the corner.' I said yes. It wasn't very exciting – lots of furniture still in bubble wrap and smelling of new carpets – what *was* exciting was the proud thrill on his face. He drew me into his private office and confessed he got a kick out of picking up the phone and saying, 'Anthony Brown speaking.' I thought this was so cute and so honest, I kissed him. A few seconds later, we were pulling down the blinds and making love on the carpet.

As I remembered all of this, a flush came to my cheeks and my nerves mounted and mounted. Hurry up, hurry up, I willed the smug secretary. Because if Anthony doesn't emerge in the next fifteen minutes I shall spontaneously combust and he'll come out to find nothing but a bit of my leg and a pile of ash.

I cleared my throat and was about to launch into an attack when Anthony came out.

'Lucy – it's good to see you!' His face lit up and he spread open his arms. I flew into them and hugged him tightly. I breathed in the smell of his aftershave and sheer Anthonyness.

In his office, I sat on a chair and spun round giddily, all girlish with excitement.

'You look different! You've had your hair cut!'

'Yes.' He smoothed his hand over his dark head. 'D'you like it?'

'Awful!' I teased him. I had to be mean, because otherwise I'd end up saying something about how utterly gorgeous he looked and how the cut set off the shape of his cheekbones and the fullness of his mouth.

'Thanks!' He pulled a face and punched me playfully.

'Look, I want to explain something about when you called earlier.'

'Oh God, yes. Who was that bloke, Lucy? I hope you're not following in my footsteps and picking up psychos on dating sites!'

'Of course I'm not,' I cried, stung that he could even conceive that I might be interested in anyone but him; oh God, I had such a long way to go to convince him.

Anthony smiled, and I swallowed hotly.

'So, my darling Lucy, why are you honouring me with a visit at this time of day?'

I reached towards my bag, but nerves caught me again. Suddenly the time and place seemed wrong. And what if the smug secretary waltzed in right in the middle?

'Er – would you like to come over to my place for dinner tonight? I just thought we could, ah, talk—' I broke off, wincing and smiling awkwardly, realising it wasn't his favourite word right now.

Anthony frowned. 'Well, I kind of have a date . . .'

'A date?' My throat went dry. Suddenly I felt as though I was standing on a sheet of ice that was starting to snap and crackle and break. 'Oh, another one of your nutters from the dating site. Can't you cancel?'

'Oh, but listen to this, Lucy! You won't believe what happened. You know I said I was going to meet a girl called Kerry? Well, she turned out to be Kerry Prendeghast!'

'Who?'

'Kerry – you remember – my ex. I told you all about her. I was with her just before I moved over here from New York. It's just so bizarre. I mean – can you believe this – she came over to London for three weeks to research internet dating for an article she's writing. And then who's the very *first* person she has a date with – me!'

'Well . . . Well . . .' My words hung in the air; my tongue seemed to go on strike. Anthony was looking at me very strangely. 'Well – I, by coincidence, have a date too, so why don't you come round and we can have a foursome? I mean, it'd be so great to meet her!' And I can poison the risotto while I'm at it.

'Well . . .' Anthony looked uncertain. 'I mean, she was expecting dinner out . . . but why not? I've been telling her all about you and she can't wait to meet you. Oh, Luce, I just know you're going to love her.'

'Oh, I'm sure I will.'

'So is your date with the psycho?' Anthony asked curiously.

'Um, yes,' I said, flushing. 'He . . . he's not really so bad when you get to know him . . . So, anyway. A foursome would be lovely. Can't wait to see you!'

'And we'll order some food in, right?' Anthony asked, a teasing note in his voice.

'Of course not. I'm going to cook,' I cried defiantly.

'Oh,' said Anthony, playfully flipping the pages of his diary, 'I don't think I can make it tonight after all, actually. I think I might be washing my hair . . .'

'Anthony!' I cried hotly. 'I know you think I'm a rubbish cook but I've been practising. I'm really good now, so there.'

'OK, OK. I'm sorry if I offended you,' he said, more gently. 'Are you all right, Lucy?'

'Oh, I'm fine,' I said, wearing a smile on my face like a label on a bottle. 'I . . . I . . . actually . . .' I paused, fingering the bag with the present again. I was dying to give it to him. 'I was just going to add,' I said, swallowing back a lump in my throat, 'that I've got a present for you. A surprise.'

Anthony looked wide-eyed.

'But you can't have it until tonight,' I added firmly.

'I can't wait,' said Anthony, smiling thoughtfully. He frowned slightly, then smiled again. I couldn't quite decipher what that frown might mean. Suddenly I felt so churned up I couldn't bear to be in his company any more.

'Well . . . see you tonight then!'

We hugged, and then smug secretary called with an important call to put through, so we hugged again and I left the building and managed not to cry all the way down eight floors and not to cry in the reception area, and I only broke down when I was halfway home, weeping and weeping all the way back.

Outside my flat, I paused and dug another tissue out of my pocket, blowing my nose miserably. I didn't want Byron to see me crying; I didn't want to suffer his sneers. I drew in a deep breath and squeezed my eyes shut, contracting my heart as though trying to prevent any more tears from leaking out.

Face it, Lucy, I told myself, as I'd told myself over and over on my masochistic journey home: you blew it. You had a relationship with Anthony and you dumped him. You had a chance to get back together with him and you ran away. And now you've blown it. You've lost him.

That much was obvious. Today, in his office, he had been completely confident, his emotions intact, his heart closed against me. He had moved on.

I opened the front door. No doubt Byron had discovered internet porn by now, I thought. But as I was wriggling my coat off, my heart stopped. I heard voices. Uh-oh. Now what? Had he borrowed the time machine and gone back and picked up Shelley et al? That was great, just great. My house would be full of Romantic poets ready to rave.

Then I heard laughter. There was *no* mistaking that laugh; I'd been brought up with it; I'd inherited a diluted form of it.

I ran into the living room.

Lord Byron was sitting on the sofa between my mum and my sister. I panicked.

'Um, sorry about this . . . he's, um, a neighbour and he's, um, about to go, aren't you?'

Sally and my mum stared at me in shock.

'What on earth d'you mean?' my mum asked.

'Byron's not going anywhere,' said Sally.

'You are being rude, Lucy,' said Mum. 'We just dropped by to see you as you haven't been in touch for ages, and then we met your nice friend Byron. I think he needs some more tea,' she said pointedly.

Uh?

I looked at Byron and he gave me a sly sneer; then, seeing my sister looking at him, he composed his face into a sensitive expression. It seemed that Byron's knack for putting a spell on women hadn't been lost in his passage through time.

This is insane, I thought. This is out of control. Lord Byron is entertaining my family and I've lost Anthony and I need space; I need an empty flat and a hot bath and I can't deal with this.

I stormed into the kitchen, filling the kettle with water, banging cups about, tears pricking my eyes again. My mum followed and took me by the shoulders.

'Are you OK?' She sensed, with her maternal bond, that I wasn't.

'Not really,' I sniffed, staring down at a packet of tea. 'I nearly got back together with Anthony, but now he's gone off with another girl.'

'Oh, Lucy.' She gracefully pretended not to notice me crying whilst surreptitiously pressing a piece of kitchen roll into my hand. 'But still – Byron out there is so lovely, can't you go out with him? You said you wanted someone artistic.'

'But he thinks he's *Lord* Byron and he's not! He's obviously totally delusional,' I said hastily, fearing he might have spilled the time-travel beans.

'No, he says he's a *reincarnation* of Lord Byron,' said my mum. 'I used to think that sort of stuff was hocus-pocus, but the way he described it has made me understand that he's a very spiritual person, Lucy.'

I was quite confounded, until, as I was pouring the tea, I noticed a copy of *Cosmo* lying open on the surface, with the article, 'Have you been born again?' face up. Very clever, Byron, I thought. You've done your homework. You're adapting to 2005 fast. You've already sussed out that rhyming couplets aren't a good chat-up line around here and you've moved on.

'Look,' I said to Mum, 'I really need to be alone and have a bath, and Anthony's coming over later. Maybe you could chat with Byron a bit longer and then let yourselves out. I'm not being rude, I just . . .'

My mum gave me a hug and said of course.

As I made my way over to the bathroom, I saw Sally looking at Byron with big eyes, her knees brushing his, her hand curled in her hair as she said, 'God, that's just *so* manly of you to practise fencing as a hobby. I mean, I know new men are all the rage, but it's kind of refreshing to know a *real* man . . .'

iii) The dreaded dinner

This has to be temporary, I told myself. I mean, it's not too horrible of me to break them up now. After all, they've only just *met*.

Well, except for the fact that they dated two and a half years ago in New York. But that was a lifetime ago.

I sat down on my sofa and ran down the corridors of my memory, flinging open doors frantically, desperate to recall every single minute detail.

I remembered the night that Anthony had told me about Kerry. We'd been lying in bed together, sharing a postcoital chat about our exes. We were still fascinated by each other's histories then, by finding pieces of each other's pasts and slotting them together to make full pictures. I remember teasing Anthony about his wild time in New York and then asking if there had been anyone special. He'd sighed. I remembered that sigh now. It had left me feeling cold, and acid with jealousy. And then he'd told me about Kerry, his only serious relationship, his mermaid in a sea of one-night stands. The brevity of detail had only made it worse: I'd felt there was something he was trying to hide. Eventually he'd confessed: 'OK, I did love her. I admit it. I couldn't even admit it to myself at the time, let alone to her. I feel bad about the way I hurt her. I mean, she proposed to me, can you believe that?' No, I said, I couldn't. Anthony had explained then that his commitment phobia had made him break up with her coldly and callously; it had been, in part, the reason he'd jumped at the chance to come to London. But that had been the behaviour of the old Anthony, the Anthony who had been young and flighty and nervy. Now he had softened and matured and learnt to trust and love a lot more.

Shit, I thought. Shit times a trillion. Tonight I'm going to have to be amazing. Byron is going to have to be amazing. The dinner is going to have to be amazing.

And then I remembered that I couldn't even cook.

Byron wasn't much help. Whilst I scurried off to Waitrose and M&S for ingredients, he flipped through *The Guardian* and discovered our present-day Poet Laureate. When I came back, laying out the ingredients on my worktop and desperately scouring Nigella and about six other cookery books, he kept making sarky remarks about Andrew Motion's poetry. I detected a hint of jealousy in his comments, but the main thing was that I couldn't care less about his testosterone-fuelled rants.

'Byron,' I said, trying to be strong and firm, 'you have to help me cook. If you don't, I'm sending you back in that time machine.'

'Only if you sleep with me,' he said idly.

'You're serious, aren't you?' My jaw dropped. 'Even after all I've told you about Germaine?'

Byron shrugged, a smile flickering at his lips.

'OK, thanks so much.' I stormed into the kitchen, banging pots and sieves and plates. Then I stormed back into the living room. 'And by the way, you have to behave tonight. You have to pretend to be my boyfriend, which means I can't introduce you as Lord Byron, OK?'

'Why not? Your mother's invited me to a WI meeting to make broccoli jam. She thinks I'm going to be a real hit with the ladies if I tell them my name.'

'There is *nobody* to hit on tonight. It's just going to be a nice dinner with Anthony and Kerry, his new girlfriend,' I said pointedly, trying to stem the acid jealousy flowing into my stomach. 'So I can't introduce you as Lord Byron.'

'Why not?'

'Because they'll think I'm mad.'

'But you *are* mad; surely, if they're your friends, they've already worked this out.'

Keep calm, I told myself, don't let him know he's getting to you or he'll never stop.

'I'm just going to say you're George, all right? Look, just keep saying this rhyme in your head.' I improvised wildly: '*I'm not a famous poet, I don't like lovemaking / My name is George and I work in computing*.'

'I don't think I'd care to remember such a frightful piece of poetry. The scansion doesn't work at all.' Byron's eyebrows knitted together in an elegant, faintly disdainful frown. 'Perhaps you ought to be dating Andrew Motion, not me.'

'Well, since he's a much better poet than you are, that might be a good idea,' I replied, throwing the dishcloth at him.

Byron simmered.

In my despair, I couldn't even face the kitchen. I decided to get ready first and then think about food. As a last resort, I figured that I could always order a takeaway, but pride was holding me back. I knew that Anthony would know, and then he'd probably tell Kerry later, in some giggly postcoital chat, and then he'd probably tell her all about me being a crap cook, and damn it, I wanted to prove I could compete.

I spent two hours getting ready, and everything I tried on was assessed in comparison to how I imagined Kerry would look. My picture of her began to escalate in my mind until I felt she could be no less beautiful than Aphrodite rising out of the ocean: hair aflame, face an oval of perfection, body a sea of curves. Suddenly all my faults glared out horribly: tiny breasts, massive hips, thunder thighs. By the time I had finally decided on my little black dress, I was nearly hysterical with nerves. Twice I picked up my mobile and nearly called Anthony to pretend I was sick and wanted to call it all off.

I decided that a shot of Archers might help before tackling the cooking.

As I stalked back into the kitchen, dress flaring, silver earrings jingling, Lord Byron looked up from *Now* magazine and let out

278

a piercing wolf whistle. I jumped and glared, but felt faintly cheered.

I opened up the cookery book. *French onion soup is a simple recipe,* I read. The word 'simple' was always a dangerous one in recipes. For me, anyway.

I looked at Byron and thought: what the heck. Promise now and barter later.

'Byron,' I said, fluttering my lashes, 'I've been thinking about your, um, proposal, and I was thinking it was a good one. If you help me cook for you, I'll, uh, you know . . .'

Byron grinned widely, threw the magazine aside and leapt to his feet, pulling me to his chest.

'Later,' I said. 'We've only got an hour.'

Byron, to his credit, was a great help. I can't imagine that he'd done a lot of cooking back in 1813 when all that was considered woman's work, but as time went on, he actually got his teeth into it. I think it was rather a novelty for him to shut down the much-used cerebral part of his brain and channel his imagination into something earthy and practical. When a little French onion soup splashed on to his cravat, he even ended up borrowing my apron with rubber ducks on. It made me feel strange. That was the apron Anthony wore when he'd cooked for me.

Byron made the stock for the soup whilst I took care of the onion-chopping; then he helped me to locate a roasting tin at the back of my cupboard, covered with dust; we washed it and set the chicken pieces in it – and to my surprise I found I could be a reasonable cook. I realised that the reason I was lousy was because cooking bored me and I tended to start wandering off and checking my emails until I was disturbed by the smell of burning. A little focus made the world of difference. Soon the stove was bubbling and frothing with Brussels sprouts and broccoli, the chicken pieces were sizzling away nicely and a tiramisu was sitting in the fridge (OK, I'd cheated and bought that straight from M&S, but I figured I was allowed a little leeway). Now all I had to do was the gravy.

As I started to crumble the Oxo cube, Byron came up behind me. He took my hair and twisted it into a tight coil and pinned it up with his fingers, leaning in until I felt his breath on my skin.

The doorbell rang.

'Don't answer it,' he said, turning me round and kissing me.

'I have to.'

'Leave them out in the rain.'

'*Byron!*'

'What the hell have you been doing?' Anthony grumbled five minutes later as I finally opened the door. He was soaked, rivulets trickling over his face. 'We must have rung that bloody doorbell thirty times, Luce!'

'Sorry – things were just a bit . . . crazy,' I said, gazing at Kerry.

'Hi, Lucy,' she said. Her accent – a hybrid of Aussie and US – was as odd as Anthony had promised. I held out my hand for her to shake, but she leaned in and gave me a hug. It was so warm and confident that I felt endeared despite myself.

'Come up,' I said. Relief soothed the anxious grinding of my stomach muscles. She was pretty, but not *that* pretty. She had short hair, for a start – an autumnal haze of highlights – and Anthony had confided in me that he hated short hair on women. She was tall and slender, and a very snappy dresser. Her black suit made her look as though she ought to be shouting commands behind the editorial desk of a women's magazine.

'Wow, this is such a lovely flat,' she said, as we went up the stairs. 'It's so nice of Anthony to rent it you, hey?'

I whipped round, suspecting sarcasm and jealousy, but once again she was smiling warmly.

'Um, yes,' I said.

I looked at Anthony and he was gazing at me, eyes questioning, seeking approval, a verdict. What I really wanted to say, of course, was *Chuck her this instant!* But I gave him a little nod and he broke into a relieved smile. I smiled back, feeling my facial muscles quiver. I had no doubt that by the end of the evening my face would be aching from all the lies I was going to superimpose on it.

I realised that Anthony and Kerry were looking at me expectantly.

Oh God.

Now for Lord Byron.

Dear God, I prayed, as I led them into the living room, *please, please can he behave.*

Unfortunately, God was off duty, for Byron did nothing of the sort.

It didn't start off too badly, which was unfortunate, for I was lulled into a false sense of security.

We found him sitting by the table, holding up a knife and examining his teeth.

'Good evening,' he said, rising. For one moment, as he puffed up his chest and his chin, I saw the vulnerability beneath his arrogance. Then I saw him eyeing up Kerry, quite openly. Something flickered in his eyes, rather as one might imagine a wolf would look when spotting an innocent rabbit.

'Hi,' Kerry said, preening slightly, enjoying his attention – as any woman would, I supposed grudgingly. 'Great to meet you!'

'I'm Byron,' he purred softly, ignoring the frantic look I gave him.

'Oh, Brian – oh cool. I once knew a Brian and he was great,' she enthused.

Thank God for Kerry.

'I'm Kerry,' she said. She held out her hand to shake, but Byron picked it up and kissed it. She blushed and gave a little laugh. I saw Anthony give me a faintly pained look, as though to say, *Well, we seem to have a bit of a smooth operator here.*

Then Anthony saw the dinner table.

'So you really did cook.' He checked his watch. 'Ah. Must dash.' He winked at me affectionately, but I didn't wink back.

'We're having French onion soup to start, then roast chicken and then tiramisu for dessert,' I said icily. 'So please do sit down and Byron . . . I mean Brian . . . can pour the wine.'

'Sounds lovely,' said Kerry, giving me another warm smile that melted another layer of my frost. *Be nice, Lucy,* I kept telling myself. *Remember that this is hard for her too.*

But I didn't want to be nice to her. I wanted Anthony back.

In the kitchen, I ladled out the soup. Out of the corner of my eye, I watched Anthony and Kerry together. It was the little gestures that got to me. They possessed the familiar, fond intimacy of a newly married couple. Anthony pulled out her chair for her; Kerry laid his napkin on his lap; he lifted a strand of hair from her face and brushed it behind her ear. I wanted to throw a tantrum like a little girl, shout that life was unfair, that he was mine. But I was an adult, and being an adult, was all about putting on a show, about hiding your feelings under layers of social decorum. So I walked pleasantly into the living room and set down the bowls, and Kerry helped me pass them round.

I saw Anthony lift his spoon and bring it to his lips. He paused, staring at it dubiously, and Kerry laughed and gave him a little nudge to tell him off for being rude. I felt an urge to slap him. Then he sipped at the soup and glanced over with such a beautiful smile that I wanted to kiss him.

'Lucy, this is great. Well done.'

'Well, thanks,' I said lightly.

'What do you think, Brian?' Kerry asked. I whipped round to look at her, but there didn't *seem* to be any malice in her face.

'Delicious.' Byron smacked his lips, looking at her breasts.

'It's great.' Anthony rubbed my arm and I knew he was saying sorry. I bit my lip, telling myself to calm down, not be uptight.

'So, Kerry,' I said. 'What do you do?'

'Oh, I work for a magazine you might have heard of. It's called *Time*. It's pretty big in the States . . .'

'Oh. Oh wow.' So, high-powered stuff then.

We spent most of the first course playing Q and A. Kerry was an only child. Kerry had studied English at Harvard. Kerry had only come to England to write an article on dating agencies over here. And – *yes!* – she was going back to the US in two weeks' time.

Then I felt a flicker of guilt. *Put yourself in her shoes*, I told myself sternly, *and remember she's only human too*.

'So what do you do for a living, Brian?' Anthony asked.

'He's a—' I began to say, but Anthony interrupted, smiling gently.

'I think Brian can answer by himself, Luce.'

'Uh-huh,' Kerry echoed under her breath, and I had to force myself not to give her an utterly monstrous look.

'I'm a poet,' said Byron importantly. At which point, normally about a hundred women would have collapsed at his feet. But this was the twenty-first century, and if you announced at a dinner party that you were a poet, people would react with polite distress.

'Well,' said Anthony, 'good for you. But it must be tough trying to get recognition, right? I mean, I had a friend at uni who decided to become a poet and he spent years scraping by, sending things out to magazines and radio stations and never getting anywhere. By the time he finally managed to get something accepted by Bloodaxe, the bailiffs had taken away half his flat.'

By now Byron was nearly purple.

'He has had stuff published,' I said quickly. 'And it's been well received.'

'Oh wow, what about?' said Anthony, pointedly addressing the question to Lord B.

'He likes writing about nature,' I cut in. 'About birds and trees and that sort of thing.'

'Sounds very Wordsworthian,' said Kerry, and I saw Byron's fingers tighten around his knife as though he wanted to plunge it into her chest.

'I can assure you that Wordsworth has never been an influence on my work,' said Byron acidly. 'Blake – a fellow Romantic – once blamed a lifelong bowel complaint on reading Wordsworth's poetry,' and we all laughed.

'So what about you, Lucy?' Kerry asked. 'What do *you* do?'

'Well, I was working for a scientist, but that job finished. So I'm kind of between jobs. I've been temping,' I added lamely.

I saw Kerry look at Anthony and raise an eyebrow, and just a flicker of something less than kind passed across her face for the first time that evening. But then she smiled warmly and said, 'Hey, I could help you out. I know a friend who runs a secretarial temping agency. Anthony said you used to be a PA.'

'Yes, but Lucy's much too intelligent for that,' Anthony said.

My heart soared. Beside me, Byron snorted. I poked my fork into his thigh. That shut him up.

'I mean,' Anthony went on, 'I remember last Christmas, we went over to Dad's and we all sat down to play Trivial Pursuit. Now nobody, *nobody*, can beat Dad at Trivial Pursuit.'

283

'Oh, Anthony, don't tell them this!' I blushed.

'No, go on,' said Kerry. 'Tell us.'

'Lucy thrashed him,' Anthony said. 'She even nailed him on Geography, which is his forte. She scored the winning point by somehow managing to know the capital of Belarus. Remember that, Luce?'

'I do,' I said. 'It's Minsk.'

For a moment it was as though we were sharing our own private dinner and nobody else was about.

'That's fascinating,' Kerry cut in. 'I have a friend, James. Nobody could beat him at Trivial Pursuit either – I mean, not even Lucy could. In fact, I'm going to introduce Anthony to him when we go to the US at the end of the month.'

Hang on!

What!

Anthony was going to the US with Kerry?

Suddenly I felt as though the sheet of ice had cracked beneath me and I was drowning in icy water.

'Really?' I said, getting up to fetch dessert and hide my face. I passed round the tiramisu, ignoring Byron's whispered objection: 'What on earth is *this*?' My hands were visibly trembling. 'How lovely.'

'Yes, well, I can't go for too long,' said Anthony. 'Work.'

'He's such a workaholic,' I said to Kerry, and for one moment we smiled in a moment of unexpected bonding.

'Well, I've persuaded him to take a week or two off,' said Kerry. 'Then he'll have plenty of time to meet my parents.'

'Oh, right. Wow. How lovely.' I felt as though my tiramisu was about to start rushing back up my throat. 'So – is it serious between you two? I mean, obviously, it must be.' I laughed.

'Well, it . . . it is, yes, I . . .' Anthony said, and Kerry touched his wrist lovingly.

I swallowed. 'I know how scary it is, the whole introducing-your-man-to-your-parents, I mean. I introduced Brian to my mum and sister this morning, and boy, was it scary.'

'Really?' Anthony's spoon froze in mid-air. 'So you two are serious too?'

Under the table, I held my fork near to Byron's balls. He smiled and sloped his arm around me, declaring:

284

She walks in beauty, like the night
Of cloudless climes and starry skies;
And all that's best of dark and bright
Meet in her aspect and her eyes . . .

'Wow,' said Kerry. 'How *romantic*. A guy who writes poetry. I mean, years back I once tried to write a poem for Anthony and I rhymed *love* with *dove*.' Seeing Byron wince, she said quickly, 'Well, Brian, maybe I could call upon you to help next time.'

'I should be delighted to educate you in the finer merits of the iambic pentameter,' said Byron. I saw Anthony's jaw clench. 'But Lucy is my only pupil right now and I must pay her due attention.' Then, revelling in his role, he leaned over and nuzzled my cheek and neck, until I turned my face and was forced to suffer a kiss. I fought the urge to slap him, before wrenching away, flushing.

'Anyone for coffee?' I muttered.

Anthony was very quiet after that. I felt myself float in euphoria for a while – the look on his face must indicate jealousy, surely? But as we sipped coffee, I had to admit it was probably just shock. After all, I was the world's worst commitment-phobic and now I had a new bloke out of nowhere and I was introducing him to my mother. Oh God. My head throbbed. Everything was just getting more and more messy; every minute, every word, seemed to be driving Anthony further and further away from me.

'Hey, Lucy,' Anthony suddenly piped up, 'you said you had a present for me.'

'Oh?' Kerry sat up.

'So I did.' I laughed uneasily. Once again, the moment felt all wrong, but I was backed into a corner now; the more I protested, the more suspicious I might appear. Trying to still my shaking hands, I went into the bedroom and brought it out.

Anthony unwrapped it. Kerry watched intently.

'A cravat!' Byron exclaimed. 'Of course, I changed the whole fashion of cravats in 1815, when I suggested they should be worn with an open collar . . .' He trailed off, realising nobody was listening.

Anthony slid the silk through his fingers. I felt happiness and hope blossom in my heart for the first time that evening. It was just the sort of artistic, romantic present I would never have bought him when we were going out. And I could tell he was both surprised and pleased.

'It's so lovely, Lucy,' he sighed, leaning over and hugging me. 'What have I done to deserve this?'

'Oh, it's just a friendship thing,' I said, laughing quickly. It was then that I made the fatal mistake and gave the game away. I glanced at Kerry, and she saw, in a flash, before I could cover it up, the naked longing in my expression. I saw the glint in her eyes that registered: *I have competition.*

What made it all the more painful was that Anthony hadn't got it at all. He was just smiling with cheerful innocence, thanking me over and over. Then the conversation ran out and the coffee cups were empty.

'Fancy a game of Trivial Pursuit?' I asked hastily, desperate to prolong the evening.

'Yes . . .' Anthony began.

'Actually,' said Kerry firmly, 'we have to get going, don't we, Anthony? We're going down to the coast tomorrow, so we'll have an early start. Maybe another time.' And she smiled at me again, only this time, any flicker of warmth had gone.

We waved them goodbye, and I stood on the doorstep, watching them walk down the street. Anthony drew off his coat and put it around Kerry's shoulders, and I felt as though someone had stabbed an icicle into my heart.

Just look back, I willed him. *Just look back at me and show you care.*

Byron put his arm around my shoulders and whispered into my ear, 'Now, my darling Lucy, you owe me a favour . . .'

I ignored him, my eyes fixed intently on Anthony.

Just look back. Just once . . .

But they rounded the corner and the darkness swallowed them up.

I turned back to Byron, feeling sick with misery. I barged past him, stormed into the kitchen and downed nearly half a bottle of wine. He watched in astonishment.

'OK,' I said, slamming the bottle down. 'I give up. I've lost, haven't I . . . I've lost . . .'

I went into the living room and curled in a miserable ball on the sofa. A short while later, Byron marched into the room, naked except for a huge erection and a raggedly angled condom.

'You've broken it,' I said, rolling my eyes. 'See, there's a hole in the top.'

'Well, that's because my cock is so huge,' he cried. 'Keats would need an extra-small variety.'

'Look, I'm really sorry, but I'm not going to have sex with you,' I sobbed. 'I just can't . . .'

'Even if I put the condom on properly?'

'*No.*'

Byron, to my amazement, didn't throw a sulk. For once, his more gallant side came into play. He chucked away the condom, got dressed and made me some hot chocolate. We snuggled up on the sofa in pyjamas (I lent him an old pair of Anthony's), sighing and mulling over why on earth we bothered with love at all when it brought us so much suffering.

'Still,' said Byron, 'you're lucky love has hit you so young. Like the measles, it is most dangerous when caught late in life. You'll get over him, and the next time the disease hits you, you'll be a little more immune.'

'Maybe,' I said, pursing my lips. I already felt immune, for I simply couldn't imagine falling in love with anyone but Anthony.

iv) Byronmania

What happened next was totally unexpected.

I kept meaning to tell Byron that it was time for him to get back into the time machine and return to 1813. I didn't want him to get into any more nerve-racking encounters with my family, or, worse, Anthony. I was also worried for him – if he became too much of a modern man, how was he going to remember how to behave when he finally did make it back home? He might start rapping instead of scanning and telling Lady Caroline Lamb she was a crazy fan who looked like a man.

The sad thing was, I was so heartbroken after Anthony, I desperately needed company. Sally, for some reason, wasn't returning my calls, and whenever I rang my mum she kept asking whether I'd got it together with that nice Byron. I think she was already hearing wedding bells. And though Byron was obnoxious, domineering and full-on, he did cheer me up. He even cooked the odd lunch, quoting lines of poetry as he sprinkled and stirred.

I kept waiting for a call from Anthony. Just something along the lines of 'Thanks for the dinner' and a verdict on Byron. But it never came. I felt raw with hurt. After we'd broken up, he had put so much emphasis on wanting to be friends, and now he couldn't even be bothered to get in touch. At one point I went into my bedroom, locked the door, squeezed my eyes shut and desperately *willed* him to call. Sure enough, the phone shrilled, and my heart leapt. I picked up – and it was Barclaycard, asking me why I hadn't made my minimum repayment and if I was in difficulty.

I knew that with my debts piling up, I ought to be looking for a job, but I felt too listless. Thoughts of lottery numbers surfaced again. It was very tempting, but a strong gut feeling held me back. I'd seen too many TV programmes where lottery winners had complained how all those millions had only made them more glum. I felt I'd caused enough trouble as it was with that machine; there was no doubt it was more of a curse than a gift.

So I tended to sit around reading a lot, burying myself in fantasy worlds in order to hide from the pain of reality. This was why Byron was such good company – we'd curl up at opposite ends of the sofa, sharing a packet of chocolate digestives – happy to be silent together.

Then, a week after Byron had arrived in 2005, he started moaning about Andrew Motion again.

'Well,' I said sarcastically, 'if you think you're so much better a poet, why don't you challenge him to a duel?'

'There's an idea,' said Byron. 'I could write the challenge in verse.'

I frowned as he leapt across the room and snatched up my

phone. Then, hearing him ask for the literary editor of *The Guardian*, I thought: Oh God. They're going to think he's insane. The reincarnation line might work on my mother, but not on *The Guardian*.

I think they did think he was insane, but he managed to switch on the charm, and the poem he sent across was so outstanding, they had no choice but to publish it. A gay photographer was sent to snap him and had orgasms over Byron's cleft chin and forehead-kissing curls. The article came out the following Monday and caused an absolute furore. By that I mean that everyone hastily jumped on the bandwagon, desperate to get themselves into print and have a point of view. The critics called his poem everything from 'sick' to 'hilarious' to 'inspired'. Then an It girl started selling T-shirts in her boutique saying SUPPORT BYRON and SUPPORT MOTION. The literary establishment got very sniffy about it, which resulted in another round of intellectuals expressing their points of view. But secretly I sensed they were rather excited by the T-shirts. After all, how long had it been since society was remotely interested in poetry? Society had, for so long, been aching for an upswing from dumbing-down and finally it had come. Suddenly poetry was cool; it was sexy; Byron and Motion's poetry collections were reissued and went storming up the book charts as though they were new albums released by Oasis and Coldplay.

What happened next was inevitable. History repeated itself. Byron had created Byronmania back in the nineteenth century, and his thirst for fame recreated it in the twenty-first. Within a few days he was being invited to every celebrity party going. He offered to take me with him but I had no wish to be snapped hanging off his arm like some piece of fluff, and besides, I felt too listless and depressed. Soon he was photographed coming out of Chinawhite. This cemented his fame, and he was splashed over every tabloid in town.

Frankly, I was quite glad when he moved out. I didn't want photographers sniffing about, snapping me in the morning taking out the rubbish and looking like shit.

But I had to admit I missed him. Now that he was gone, I was left all alone with nothing but my aching for Anthony. I went out with some girlfriends for a drink and managed to forget my pain for a few hours. But when a group of handsome guys began to chat us up, I simply couldn't raise any enthusiasm. I knew I ought to move on, but every other man seemed a limp pastel compared to the bright colours of Anthony.

A few nights later, I was curled up in front of the TV, channel-hopping despondently. I settled on *Celebrity Big Brother,* figuring it might be a good laugh.

Then my jaw dropped.

There was Lord Byron – trust him to get on there! And he was lying on a sofa, alongside, of all people, Germaine Greer. The camera zoomed in on them. Germaine's normally stern face was flushed with a youthful bloom that could only have come from one thing.

'Since arriving in London,' Byron whispered, 'I've slept with many a pretty face. But you, Germaine, are the first woman I have met who has *brains*.'

v) Kerry offers consolation

I found myself bursting into an ocean of tears. I kept reminding myself that I hardly cared about Lord B, but it didn't stop them. I think it was just the blow to my self-esteem. Byron with Germaine; Anthony with Kerry. The whole world seemed to be pairing off into happy couples while I was left out in the cold because I couldn't make up my stupid mind at the right time.

In despair – or perhaps because I felt I had nothing to lose – I called Anthony.

'Hello?'

A female voice. *Kerry.*

I was about to put the phone down when I heard a noise in the background.

'Um – hi, is Anthony there?' Trying to disguise my voice.

'Who is this?' Territorial now.

'It's Lucy,' I admitted, swallowing my tears quickly.

'Oh, Lucy! *Lucy!* Great to hear from you!' As though we were the best of friends. 'Look, I'm really sorry, but Anthony's not here right now.'

'Oh. Will he be in later tonight?' I was desperate, close to begging. 'I could try his mobile.'

'Please don't. He's got it switched off. He's got this crucial power meeting which isn't going to finish until really late. But look . . . I'm here, all alone, totally bored, and I was just watching *Celebrity Big Brother,* and my heart went out to you. I mean, dumped by your boyfriend on TV!'

'He's not my boyfriend.'

'Well, I'd still be upset. I was thinking anyway that we didn't really get a chance to meet properly over dinner, did we? I mean, we didn't have a girlie chat. Why don't you come over? We'll let down our hair and have some wine and chocolate.'

I was half suspicious and half sucked in. Finally, a masochistic desire to find out everything I could about her and Anthony prompted me to say yes.

I wished I'd dolled myself up before going over. In my fraught state, I barely gave a second thought to my jogging bottoms and T-shirt, an old navy one with a picture of Dougal, and *WOOF* in kitsch letters over the top. When I arrived at Anthony's flat, however, Kerry greeted me wearing a flared white skirt, kitten heels and a slinky sleeveless silk top. Immediately I felt small and ugly and I wanted to turn back and go home. How could I have imagined I'd find comfort here?

My comfort zone shrank even further when I saw the effect she'd had on Anthony's flat. Whenever I'd stayed over at Anthony's, we always joked about how I managed to turn his spotless pad into a tip within one night, leaving his floor scattered with clothes and his bathroom a wreck. But Kerry had kept the place spick and span, and added all sorts of feminine touches: a bowl of flowers on the mantelpiece, embroidered cushions on the sofa.

To my surprise, however, as I stepped in, she pulled me to her for a tight hug. And then she passed me a box of Maltesers and a glass of wine.

'Wow.'

'Don't look so surprised.' She nudged me. 'Don't worry, Lucy, I'm a girl's girl.'

Oh God. People are always the opposite of how they seem, and I knew from experience that women professing to be girl's girls were normally nothing of the sort and usually had a tremendous penchant for competitiveness and cattiness.

Then I noticed that the TV was on, the volume turned down low. Lord B. was asking Germaine, if she could pick any men in the world to go to bed with, who her top three would be.

Pretending not to have noticed it, I collapsed on to the sofa, downing my glass of wine and cramming as many Maltesers as I could into my mouth.

'I've just been panicking like mad.' Kerry paused to eat a Malteser. She had a ladylike approach to them: she nibbled off the chocolate and then slowly crunched the honeycomb centre bit by bit. The whole process took about five minutes. 'You see, Anthony and I are off to the US tomorrow.'

'You are?' A Malteser melted in my mouth into a gooey mess. Anthony hadn't even called to say he was going, to say goodbye. I felt tears prick my eyes and shouted at myself fiercely: *Don't cry, Lucy, don't cry, not in front of her.* But I couldn't help it. The tears came flowing out; I hiccuped a sob.

'Oh my God.' Kerry panicked for a bit, as though I was having an asthma attack, and finally, after flapping about, passed me a tissue box. 'Oh God, I'm sorry, I know this is so hard for you, what with Anthony dumping you, and now Brian.'

'No, it's not that – it's my sister,' I cut in, determined to put on a tough show. 'My sister's having family problems.' I blew my nose.

'Well, that's not so bad. I was so worried you might not be taking me and Anthony well. I mean, I know he only recently broke it—'

'Excuse me, but I broke it off with him,' I said stoutly. She didn't look too surprised. 'Really, it's fine. How's it going between you two anyway?'

'Good.' Kerry began on another Malteser.

Silence.

'D'you think we really go together?' she suddenly blurted out.

I looked at her and saw the anxiety in her eyes. She had changed tack: we were no longer rivals, batting back and forth balls of conversation. I felt a flash of sympathy for her.

'Well, I don't really know you well enough,' I admitted. 'But Anthony does seem happy. But then, I haven't spoken to him since the dinner.'

'Really? I've been telling him to get in touch, I've been telling him I'm happy for you to be friends, but he keeps saying he can't, he's afraid he'll hurt me.'

I felt another wave of misery, tempered this time by wisdom. For the first time a small voice of resignation said: *You're going to have to let him go, Lucy. You're going to have to wave the white flag.*

'I mean, sometimes I just don't know if it's going to work,' said Kerry.

'Well,' I said curiously, rolling a Malteser between my fingers, 'why don't you tell me all the good stuff and all the bad stuff?'

Her face lit up: she seemed to like the idea of the game.

'Well, the good stuff is – well, he's obviously got lots of money, and I love the way he's so hard-working. I mean, I love a guy who just wants to go out there and make it happen, y'know?'

Funny, I thought. That isn't the good stuff I would have picked up on.

'And the bad?' I tried not to sound too eager. After all, if she was making him happy, I ought to try to help them.

'Well – he has terrible pyjamas,' she said, smiling when I laughed in agreement. 'And he has this lousy sense of humour. I mean, he's always trying to be funny, and he's just, like, *not*.'

'Oh.'

'And . . .' She paused, pondering, and then crunched full into a Malteser. 'Sometimes . . . sometimes I feel he's not totally what I want in bed,' she blurted out. Then, immediately realising that this was a case of too much information, she clapped a hand over her mouth. 'Forget I said that.'

'Don't worry,' I said, bemused. I instantly had a flashback: of lying in bed together, and Anthony pulling me hard against him, and I felt a flash of heat curl in my belly and a shiver ripple down my spine. 'Everyone has different sexual tastes, right? I mean, let's be frank.'

'Yeah – well, you know – Anthony's a good kisser and all that, but I . . .' She giggled. 'I kind of like guys who are a bit, you know, animalistic. My ex-boyfriend said that maybe it was because I like to be in control all the time in real life, so when it comes to the bedroom I like having someone in control of me.'

I quickly hid my surprise and my smile. Here was Kerry, sitting with her beautifully polished nails and demure little smile, and she wanted a *beast*.

'One good way to really figure out if you fancy someone is to play the going-to-bed game,' I said without thinking.

'What's that?' she cried.

'Well – it's silly, but you have to work out that if you could go to bed with anyone, I mean anyone, but only one person in the world, who would it be?' I laughed, and Kerry squealed with laughter too, and we both grinned, aware that just when we'd given up on each other, we were bonding.

Kerry seemed quite excited. 'Oh God.' She clapped her hands to her mouth. 'If you were to ask me this question and I was to give an honest, honest answer, I'd choose Casanova. I studied him at uni. I even wrote a thesis on him. He was just totally untamed.'

I smiled. 'Obviously. You can have a top three list, by the way.'

'Well, my second choice would be Jon Bon Jovi. Or Ozzy Osbourne. I mean, they're both so *wild*.' She looked worried. 'So Anthony's only third. What does that mean?'

Suddenly the front door banged and I jumped. Kerry blinked. I knew at once that it was him – I could tell instantly by the telltale jangle of his keys hitting the table. How many times had I heard that sound? In the early days, the moment his key was scraping the lock I would jump up and dash to the door and he'd play Tarzan and pick me up like a ragdoll and spin me round, or else make me scream by hauling me over his shoulder in a fireman's lift. Towards the tail-end of our relationship, I had tended to sit watching TV when he came in and would pretend not to notice him, and he'd come up behind me and lift up my hair and kiss the back of my neck. Then his kisses would trail over to my cheek, and if I was in a good mood I'd twist my head and give him a proper kiss; if I was in a bad one, I'd shake him off irritably. I tensed miserably at the thought, wondering how I could ever have pushed him away, ever denied him a kiss.

But kisses aside, the point was that Anthony was meant to be in some watertight mega-important late-night meeting. I looked at Kerry in suspicious confusion, and she looked back at me with a slightly shifty expression.

'I thought you said . . .' I began.

'Oh, darling, you're back!'

She jumped up and flung her arms around him. Anthony didn't swing her around. He looked surprised, and then even more surprised when he saw me.

'Lucy!'

I pulled my T-shirt down self-consciously, horribly aware that I was looking like an unwashed tramp. And yet for all my embarrassment, it was wonderful to see him. Liquid sunshine poured through my body, sparkling in my cells. I noticed that he was wearing my cravat; it was tucked almost surreptitiously under his collar, but a little bit peeked out.

'I just thought it would be nice to invite Lucy over for a girlie evening,' said Kerry.

'Oh, wow, this is perfect timing,' Anthony cried. 'Have you given her the tickets?'

'No, not yet – I mean, I kind of forgot,' said Kerry, looking shifty again.

What on earth were they talking about? Anthony looked at me, and then at her.

'You haven't told her yet, have you?'

'What?' I cried. 'What's up?' I laughed in bewilderment.

Anthony removed an envelope from the mantelpiece. A funny look came over his face.

'First of all, we've got a present for you,' he began, but Kerry cut in, taking the envelope from him.

'Lucy, we'd like you to have this.'

She passed it over. Frowning, I opened it up. It was an airline ticket. Heathrow to JFK. I looked up in a daze.

'We thought it would be a nice treat for you,' said Anthony.

'I mean, we know you need cheering up after what happened with Brian,' Kerry added.

'Thanks.' I was stunned. My confusion thickened to a fog. I had clearly missed a crucial element in the script here, turned over two pages without realising. Why on earth were they paying for me to go and gatecrash their lovers' trip in the US? Why? Did they want to generate some sort of love triangle?

Then I looked up. Kerry was standing beside Anthony and they were clutching hands tightly, exchanging nervous smiles.

'There's a reason why we'd like you to come to the States,' said Kerry.

Surely not?

I stared at the silent TV, unable to cope with reality, with the present. I watched Byron waltzing Germaine across a sofa.

'Lucy . . .'

I raised my eyes unwillingly.

'We're engaged!'

'The wedding's in the US next month . . .'

'So we'd love you to come!'

'In fact,' said Kerry, coming over and putting her arm around me, 'I want you to be my maid of honour!'

Chapter Eight

Kerry

I am to be married, and am of course in all the misery of a man in pursuit of happiness.

LORD BYRON

i) To America

> *Mr and Mrs Prendeghast*
> *cordially invite you to*
> *the wedding of their daughter*
> *Kerry*
>
> *&*
>
> *Anthony Brown*
> *St Sebastian's Church*
> *on*
> *17 November 2005*

The invitation sat on the mantelpiece, beneath the curling petals of a vase of roses. I did my best to ignore it, but its cordial italics seemed to keep leaping out and crying 'Look, look!' every time I strolled past it, or sat down to watch TV, or read, or lifted my purring cat on to my lap, until it felt as though the card was no longer nine inches but thirty feet, crowding out everything else in the room, impossible to evade.

Two weeks later, I found myself on a plane to New York, my head still spinning in shock.

Engaged, I kept thinking. *Engaged.* En-gaged.

To be honest, if I really pushed aside my jealousy, if I really stepped back in detachment, I didn't know what to make of Kerry. My mind wanted to be black and white, to decide either way, to throw her into a box marked 'good' or 'bad' or 'nice girl' or 'bitch'. But in truth she was an odd mix. One minute she'd seemed so wonderfully warm, the next incredibly manipulative.

That night, the night Kerry and Anthony had announced their engagement, kept spinning round and round in a repetitive loop. The more I analysed it, the more I felt confused. If Anthony hadn't come back, would Kerry ever have told me about those tickets? Or would she have lied to him, claimed I'd rejected them, or refused to come round? Would I still be sitting here now, trying to scrape the fare together? There was no doubt in my mind that Kerry might be nice, but honesty wasn't her strong point. She was manipulative and she had a tendency to play games; it made me wonder what other webs she might spinning, what else she had told Anthony about me.

And then there had been our conversation about what Kerry liked in bed. The animalistic variety. She ached for Casanova. So was she really happy to be engaged to Anthony? Still, the whole going-to-bed game was fantastical rather than revelatory, I thought glumly. Maybe Kerry was way ahead of me: wise enough to know that in reality you couldn't marry perfection, or all of your fantasises rolled into one ball; that you had to settle for sensible second-best.

And what about Anthony? Did he really like her? I couldn't help wondering if he really felt she was all that amazing, or if he was just so keen to get married that he'd jumped on the first suitable girl who had said 'I do'. Which unnerved me, because I'd always thought he was more intelligent than that. Funny, I mused, you can think you know someone inside out, every riddle and fault, and then they can still turn around and surprise you.

What made me even sadder was that Anthony and I barely felt like friends any more. Over the last fortnight we'd only exchanged one breathless call, and Anthony had rung off quickly because Kerry kept interrupting and crying, 'Anthony, we're going to be *late* for the Theodores and you haven't even put your *bow tie* on yet!' I hadn't had time to tell him I was moving out of his flat. I didn't feel comfortable staying there any longer and it was obvious he would throw me out soon anyway. For the time being, I had moved into the spare room in my sister's house, which was hellish.

She and her husband had suddenly surprised us all by getting back together and were now as disgustingly gooey as newly-weds. Poor Lyra was currently being fed by my rather overenthusiastic nephew.

The only vaguely entertaining thing had been seeing Lord Byron again. After the tabloids had reported that he had participated in a wild cocaine-fuelled orgy, the police had arrested him for possession. Sick of celebrities getting off lightly for drug offences, they had decided to make an example of him and come down heavily on him. I had saved him from life in prison by packing him back off to 1813, chaperoning him in the time machine and then swiftly winging back to 2005 alone.

I looked out of the window and sighed. I was used to time-machine travel, to centuries whizzing past in a merry-go-round of wormholes. I wasn't even nervous of flying any more, I realised. How slowly planes go, I mused, as the clouds inched past, how slowly . . .

At JFK I had to pay an absolute fortune in excess baggage. I had two cases, one full of clothes and the other so huge and heavy I could barely heave it off the conveyor belt.

'I expect you've got about three hundred outfits in there, haven't you?' the man behind the desk teased me patronisingly.

I smiled along with him. But as it happened, I wasn't the type of girl who needed to take three hundred outfits for a single trip. The heavy case contained something far more interesting.

Neither Kerry nor Anthony was there to meet me. Instead there was a taxi driver holding up a sign with LUCY LYON FROM ENGLAND on it.

It was my first time in New York in over two years, and I'd forgotten how I loved its fizzing air of manic energy. My hotel was very, very plush. In fact, I don't think I've stayed anywhere more impressive. But every time I drank in the luxury, the taste was bittersweet. Anthony and Kerry had insisted on paying my hotel bill, and it only drove the daggers deeper. *Look at us, Lucy,* their gift sang, *aren't we so rich and happy and wonderful, while you're poor and useless and single . . .*

On my bed, there was a scrawled note from Kerry:

Dear Lucy,
  SO sorry not to be there to meet you but things manic with wedding preps. See you tomorrow for bridesmaid's fittings and later dinner with my parents – can't wait! Will give you a ring. Have a good sleep and get rid of all that jet-lag.
    Kerry x

There was no note from Anthony.

As for the dinner tomorrow night, I was already dreading it. I had a feeling it was going to be horrible, and that Kerry's parents were going to hate me, and besides, what the hell was I supposed to wear?

I jumped up and went over to my case. Not the case that was full of clothes, but the heavy one. There, inside, were all the various pieces of the time machine, each lovingly cocooned in bubble wrap.

I knew I was being completely crazy and obsessed bringing it over. I also knew it was also a serious sign of addiction. The time machine was becoming my drugs, my alcohol, my way of escaping from reality.

But, I promised myself, I'm only going to use it in case of absolute emergency. Only if things become completely unbearable. And hopefully it will all be fine. I'll go to the dinner tomorrow, I'll attend the wedding, and then I'll be back home. I can survive that without needing to put on a corset and go gallivanting back a few hundred years, can't I?

Can't I?

ii) Dresses and dinner

The next morning, I met up with Kerry for my bridesmaid's fitting. I must say, she was incredibly warm and friendly to me.

302

'Oh God, Lucy, it's just so *fantastic* to see you!' she cried, and then didn't stop talking for about five minutes. 'Manic preparations . . . dress taken up . . . taken in . . . taken out . . . napkin rings . . . mother mad . . . vegetarian sausage rolls . . . ceremony . . . hen night . . . oh, and I'm going to have male strippers. Tons of them.'

'Animalistic ones?' I said, and then mentally slapped myself: I'd only just got here and I was already being sulky.

Kerry gave me a sidelong glance, and then suddenly laughed, tossing back her hair.

'Maybe a few,' she admitted. 'After all, it'll be my last chance to have a bit of fun before boring married life.'

I felt shocked, and then told myself she couldn't be serious. Could she?

Kerry tried on her dress first. When she stepped out of the fitting room, I literally gasped. She looked amazing. Her dress was made of ivory silk, a soft sheath that clung to and caressed her body like a devoted suitor, as though it knew just which curves to conceal or congratulate. Soft flower bracelets hung around her wrists and ankles; ivory rosebuds studded her hair like kisses. She looked like a goddess of spring.

'Here's yours,' Kerry said, bursting my bubble.

'Oh. Oh wow,' I said. I tried it on. It was worse than I'd thought.

'Oh wow, you look *fabulous*,' said Kerry.

'It's, um, very different from your dress,' I said.

'So it is. But I want all the bridesmaids in purple. There'll also be my god-daughter, Jeannie, she's only six, so she'll look really cute . . .'

Purple, I thought, was a very optimistic word. Plum, more like. I looked a big fat overripe frilly plum.

I turned to Kerry and saw the glint in her eye. Well done, I thought. One up to you. A significant victory in the battle for Anthony Brown. Well, great. I *so* cannot wait to walk down the aisle wearing this . . .

I would have liked to have spent some time on my own, but Kerry insisted on pretending we were the best of friends, looping her arm through mine and dragging me round shop after shop.

Finally she dropped me off at the hotel with an hour to get ready for dinner, giving me the address of the restaurant so that I could take a taxi there.

'Just put something casual on,' she said airily before she left.

After hours of trying on everything in my suitcase, of throwing inner tantrums – *why did I leave my best red velvet top behind in Sally's wardrobe?* – and so on, I had decided to dress up. Yes, Kerry had said to wear something casual, but I had a sneaking feeling I shouldn't trust her. I could just see myself in tatty jeans walking into a restaurant of people draped in Gucci and Dior. So out came my favourite little black dress.

I kept getting serious attacks of butterflies. It wasn't so much the thought of meeting Kerry's family, but the fact that, after two whole weeks, I was going to see Anthony again. Hear his voice. Breathe in his scent. Feel his smile on me. *Oh!*

The moment I entered the restaurant, I felt self-consciousness crawling over my skin like bugs. Anthony had told me that Kerry's parents were well off, but this place was seriously glitzy. The men all had power faces and suits, their sculptured dentures flashing as they sipped wine; the women were glossy and blonde, with perfect plasticine noses and breasts cupped in dresses like ice cream scoops. The atmosphere was charged with glamour and money and competition. As the waiter showed me to the table, I pulled down the hem of my little black dress and thanked God I had ignored Kerry's advice. In a moment of paranoia I was convinced that everyone was looking at me, but then I realised they were too busy looking over their shoulders at neighbouring tables, fearing other people might be having more interesting conversations than they were.

The table was set for seven people. It was empty except for a young man with a brilliant tan and glossy hair who, despite the low lighting, was wearing shades. He smiled and stood up to shake my hand.

'I'm Morrison – and you must be Lucy.'

'Um – yes.' I paused, wondering if I was on the right table. 'Nice to meet you.'

'I'm Kerry's ex.' When I looked surprised, he frowned and added, 'We're still great buddies.'

I smiled quickly, but inside I was quite shocked. What on earth was Kerry doing, inviting her ex to her special dinner? Didn't she know how jealous Anthony could be, that she was needling his most sensitive spot?

Thankfully, we were saved from awkward chit-chat by the arrival of everyone else, who surged in all together.

They were led by Kerry's parents, Mr and Mrs Prendeghast. Mr Prendeghast was tall and very handsome, in an elegant, silvery sort of way; Mrs Prendeghast had very coiffeured bronze hair and looked as though her handbag alone cost a million pounds, not to mention her nose.

'You must be Lucy!' she cried, looking me up and down. Despite the smile on her face, she somehow made me feel as though I wasn't quite up to scratch. 'Oh, heavenly to meet you.'

'Hi,' I said, shaking her hand, her rings cool and hard against my palm.

Then I saw him.

He and Kerry were holding hands, winding through the tables. He looked so handsome, so very, very handsome. Better than Byron and Leonardo and Capone all rolled into one.

I noticed Kerry looking my dress up and down with a disappointed frown, but I couldn't be bothered to play along with her game. All my attention was spotlighted on Anthony. I waited for him to come up and throw his arms around me in his usual way.

Instead, he gave me a faintly cool smile and a nod.

'Hi, Lucy, good to see you,' he said.

We all sat down to eat.

I stared at the menu, my face burning. *Hi, Lucy, good to see you.* As though I was his fucking accountant or something. I glanced up and saw that Anthony and Mr Prendeghast were exchanging jolly pleasantries, discussing a game of golf they'd played a week ago. So. Anthony was well in with the family, then. I couldn't help noticing that his accent had reverted to a distinctly American tinge; all English traces were fading fast.

'Can you read this menu, my dear? I'm afraid my eyes are not what they used to be.'

I jumped, suddenly realising there was an old lady sitting next to me. Then I dimly remembered that she had been introduced as Grandma Rose; in my excitement over Anthony, I had barely taken her in.

'I'd be happy to help,' I said.

As I read through the specials, she looked at me with such a shrewd, hostile gaze, I felt as though I was taking an exam.

A waiter came and took our orders, and then poured some wine, and still Anthony barely seemed to notice me. I took a big fat miserable sip of wine, trying to reassure myself. Maybe he was just trying to placate Kerry. Maybe he would warm up as the meal went on.

'I'd love to know,' said Grandma Rose, interrupting the flow of chit-chat, 'just how Anthony proposed to my granddaughter.'

'Hey, that'd be a great tale,' Morrison agreed, winking at Kerry.

'I'd love to hear too,' I chimed in, with burning curiosity.

The table fell silent; all eyes were on Anthony. He blushed, fingering his collar.

'Well . . .' He smiled across at Kerry lovingly. 'We'd, ah, gone away for the weekend. To Paris. We were in a chocolate shop and I just felt I had to propose. And . . .' His eyes travelled around the table, flickering over me and then sliding away, fixing on a large Italian pepper pot in the centre of the table. 'She said yes.' He shrugged bashfully and took a sip of wine.

'Oh, now, hang on a minute!' Mrs Prendeghast cried. 'Hang on one minute! Kerry told me all about this and it is *so* much more romantic than Anthony is letting on. He didn't take her to just *any* chocolate shop!' She spread out her hands, bracelets tinkling against each other. 'He took her to Patisserie Marie, the finest chocolate shop in the world! And there he spent *hundreds* on her, buying her the best chocolate ever made. And *then* he proposed! And no wonder she said yes!'

'No wonder,' Mr Prendeghast echoed. 'Chocolate is clearly the answer to all the world's problems. No doubt a little more chocolate passed around the UN would have averted the war in Iraq.'

'That is such a sweet story,' said Grandma Rose, cocking her head to one side and nearly trailing her pink hair in her gravy.

I didn't think it was a sweet story. My hand was stiff around my fork; the piece of spinach in my mouth seemed to grow thick and swell and double in size. I closed my eyes for a moment. I recalled the day Anthony had taken *me* to Paris. The sweet scents of the chocolate shop, our nerves, our laughter, the anxious look on his face as he passed a truffle over for me to taste. I'd always treasured that memory in my heart like a flower, and from time to time I would lean in and breathe in its scent, glowing with happiness. It was the most romantic thing that had ever happened to me.

But no. It was Anthony's standard parlour trick. I wondered how many girls he had used it on before me. And now Kerry.

I felt my flower wilt, petals drooping, its sweet scent turning to rot.

'Yes,' Kerry went on. 'It really was some chocolate.'

I let out a breath, opening my eyes and looking straight at Anthony. Challenging him. His eyes touched on the table, the ceiling, the guests, the waiter, Kerry – anywhere but me. I felt like shaking his lapels and yelling, 'Look at me!'

And then suddenly he did. I saw panic in his eyes; panic and apology. He half opened his mouth, as though about to say something. I glared furiously, showing that I wasn't going to forgive this.

Anthony shifted uncomfortably. Kerry, noticing the glance we had shared, flicked me a look, then quickly turned her attention back to Anthony.

'I was terrified she was going to say no,' said Anthony. He managed to sound confident, but I could sense the nerves underneath; he began to gabble slightly. 'But she did, she said yes – so I guess she loved the chocolate.' He laughed nervously.

'That is *so* romantic,' Mrs Prendeghast sighed. 'D'you remember the day you proposed to me, darling?'

'Yes,' said her husband. 'If I remember rightly, you said no.'

'I said yes in the end.'

'After I'd asked you ten times.'

'Well now, a girl has to make a man work for her.' Mrs Prendeghast laughed. 'That's what my dear mother taught me. Speaking of mothers, Anthony, I'm so sorry yours couldn't make dinner tonight, so horrible to come down with flu and then pass it

307

on to your father – all from a quick afternoon tea. I so hope they'll be well soon. Is she definitely coming to the wedding?'

'She is indeed,' said Anthony.

For a moment I was overcome with amazement and blurted out: 'That's a surprise.' When the Prendeghasts gave me a weird look, I added quickly, 'I mean, I thought Anthony didn't get on with his mother.'

'Oh, he didn't,' said Kerry, 'but I got them to make up. Now they're the best of friends.'

Well, I thought hotly, he obviously listens to her. My head was spinning with all these revelations – I couldn't believe how quickly things seemed to have changed.

'So,' Morrison said, 'when you were in Paris, did you get to see any of the art?'

'After Anthony proposed, we spent most of the time in our hotel room, didn't we, darling?' Kerry blushed smugly, nudging him. She flicked me a momentary glance. I could almost see her painting an invisible 'one' in the air.

Anthony looked down, his jaw flickering, embarrassed. Discussing his sex life in public just wasn't his cup of Earl Grey. He could be very prudish and reticent about that sort of thing.

'We visited the Louvre,' he said, straightening his tie and smoothing down his shirt. 'It was fascinating.'

'Did you get to see the *Mona Lisa*?' Morrison asked.

'Oh, that's me!' I blurted out without thinking. 'Leo painted that of me! I *am* the *Mona Lisa*.'

Oh God. Six pairs of astonished eyes fixed on me. Kerry blinked and then exchanged a look with Anthony that clearly said, 'Are all your exes this loopy?' I felt my cheeks grow hot.

'What I mean is . . . I mean . . . some people say we look a bit alike,' I said, frowning and staring down at my plate.

'The resemblance is astonishing,' Mr Prendeghast said, and I cringed, for while I loved his dry wit, it wasn't much fun being on the receiving end of it. 'I've been sitting here all night thinking, "My God, who does this British girl look like?" and now I know.'

I winced, still staring at my plate.

'Well I can't see it,' said Morrison slowly. 'I mean, maybe her eyelashes are a bit similar . . .'

'I admit I can't either,' said Mrs Prendeghast. 'But you know, so many people think I look like Barbra Streisand.'

I let out a breath, thankful for her egotism. Then I took a sip of water, aware of Mr Prendeghast's eyes on me. When I looked at him, however, he gave me a light wink and I smiled in relief. I looked at Kerry, who was watching us, and she quickly shot me a sunny smile, as though patting me on the back for my mistake.

'I think you look like Kate Winslet,' said Grandma Rose beside me, 'She's quite lovely.'

I looked into her eyes and realised that though she hadn't got the gist of the conversation, she was no fool; she sensed my feelings, she saw the undercurrents flashing beneath the words like lightning. I smiled at her, feeling a warmth between us.

'Thank you,' I said gratefully.

The conversation swept on, but I still felt stung and embarrassed by my faux pas and I had lost the confidence to shine. I think that was why I did what I did next; why I behaved so dreadfully. Or perhaps it was the fury in my heart, the anguish that Anthony and I were never going to be friends again, and feeling that probably I had never meant anything to him.

It all started when Mrs Prendeghast confided in me that she was embarking on a new career as a sex therapist.

'My husband was rather nervous at first, as you can imagine,' she crowed, 'but I said to him, it's the twenty-first century! *Everyone* has a sex therapist these days – it's more usual to have one than a dentist or a personal trainer!'

'So if Anthony and Kerry ever encounter any problems in the bedroom, you'll be able to sort them right out,' I said cheerfully.

Kerry, Morrison and Anthony immediately shot me that's-dangerous-territory-Lucy looks. But Mrs Prendeghast was delighted to be on her favourite subject.

'Oh, absolutely,' she cried. 'I remember that Kerry's first boyfriend, Damien, was a terribly lecherous young man—'

'Mom, you are so embarrassing.' Kerry cut in, covering her face with the dessert menu. 'You can't say this stuff, not in front of Anthony. He's British.'

'Oh, I'm sure Anthony's fine. Though you did mention earlier that for the last few days . . .'

Everyone sat up, ears pricked.

'Mom, Anthony's been tired,' Kerry interjected, a note of panic in her voice.

'Jet-lag,' Anthony said quickly.

I couldn't stop myself. 'I think Kerry and Anthony should share everything – we're all friends and close family.'

'*Exactly!*' Mrs Prendeghast said. 'See, Lucy's British and she's not a prude! Kerry, you don't need to be embarrassed, sex is an everyday topic of conversation – like weather, like gardening – and there is nothing wrong with not being able to get it—'

'I think it's time for desserts,' Mr Prendeghast interjected loudly. 'I don't know about you, but I'd quite like the pistachio ice cream.'

For a moment we all pretended to be staring hard at our menus. I reined in a wild, hysterical desire to laugh. I felt glad and naughty and awful all at once. I didn't dare look at Anthony.

'But,' said Grandma Rose, 'what was Virginia saying about Anthony not being able to get something?'

'It's nothing, Grandma,' Morrison said.

'But I want to know what she was saying,' Grandma Rose wailed. 'Just because I'm old and I can't hear, nobody thinks I'm interested in anything, but I am.'

'Oh, we know that all too well,' said Mr Prendeghast under his breath.

Ignoring Anthony's absolutely thunderous glance, I leaned over and whispered in Grandma Rose's ear. She went pink and then said, 'Oh, oh!' in a small, high voice, and then went back to perusing her dessert menu. A tiny smile tickled the corners of her crimped lips. Then she let out a giggle. And it was such a funny sight, seeing this elderly woman trying not to laugh like a naughty schoolgirl, that I exploded into laughter, which set her off too.

'What's so funny?' Mrs Prendeghast asked, rather oblivious to the chain of humour and humiliation she had set off.

'So, have you shown Lucy her bridesmaid dress yet?' said Mr Prendeghast.

And then, thank goodness, the subject had changed, and Grandma Rose and I managed to stop giggling. However, a new-found warmth had formed between us, a camaraderie that transcended our age gap. I felt glad of it, because I was aware that

I was behaving appallingly. I could feel Kerry's quiet rage and Anthony's seething astonishment. And worse, I was scared of how naked I had been for a moment: after all, why else would I behave so dreadfully if I didn't care so deeply for Anthony?

The conversation continued on the subject of the wedding preparations. Kerry shook off her irritation and blossomed again, raving happily about her dress and the bridesmaids' outfits and the food and the placements. Anthony, meanwhile, remained fairly quiet. I didn't dare look him in the eye.

'Will you be bringing a partner to the wedding?' Mr Prendeghast suddenly addressed me.

I looked at him nervously, noting the faint touch of acid in his voice.

'I was hoping Lucy and Morrison might have gone together,' said Kerry gaily, 'but now I'm not so sure they're suited. I mean, Morrison generally has gone for some very classy girls . . .'

I knew she had every right to insult me after my behaviour, but I couldn't help feeling stung.

'As a matter of fact,' I said, 'trying to matchmake me was a complete waste of time, though I appreciate the gesture. I'm bringing a partner.'

'You are?' Kerry asked.

Anthony looked up with a frown. Mr Prendeghast raised a dubious eyebrow. Mrs Prendeghast clapped her hands together.

'Well that's fabulous, Lucy. And who is the lucky man? You know, I thought Kerry told me you were single? Or have you managed to woo a man in the last twenty-four hours, you busy bee, hmm?'

'He . . . he . . .' I broke off, aware that if I didn't improvise fast it was going to come across as a totally made-up story. 'He's quite famous, actually, so I can't name him right now, in case the press get wind of his coming.'

'Well!'

'Wow!'

'I'm sure he's a very lucky man,' said Grandma Rose, smiling at me gently. 'I have a feeling that whoever grabs Lucy will have to be very special.'

Everyone laughed, and I blushed.

'You can say that again,' said Kerry in a low voice. But I hadn't been offended by Grandma Rose's remark somehow; there was love in her words, and insight.

Anthony didn't look at me once for the rest of the meal. We all had coffee and then said our goodbyes. Mrs Prendeghast said, 'It was so lovely to meet you,' though I knew it hadn't been really; she hadn't taken in an atom of my personality; she was too wrapped up in the World of Mrs Prendeghast. But thank goodness for it, I thought, or she might have seen the threat I posed to her daughter's happiness and locked me away until the wedding was over.

Outside, I found myself alone for a moment with Anthony, while Kerry was still saying goodbye to her parents in the restaurant.

Anthony turned on me at once.

'I'm sorry—' I began.

'Oh, *sorry*, are you? What the hell were you doing in there?' he hissed. I flinched at the fury in his voice. 'God, Lucy, we paid for you to come all the way over here and you could at least be happy for us, even if you don't want to be friends . . .'

And then Kerry came sweeping out, and to our joint horror, insisted on forcing us on to a nightclub. She didn't seem at all bothered by my rudeness over dinner; perhaps because she realised I'd done myself far more damage than her.

The club was an absolute nightmare. It was about the trendiest place I'd ever been to. In fact, it was so trendy it was ridiculous. It didn't have a proper name, or a proper entrance; just a door, cut into its silver paintwork, which we had to knock on. Kerry, depressingly, clearly knew all the right people, for when a cool black bouncer opened the door, she only had to flutter her lashes and he let her in at once.

Inside, the menus were silvery swans that glided over the marble bar top. They listed all sorts of cocktails, all named after famous writers. An Ernest Hemingway, for example, was a mixture of mint, rum and sugar; whilst a Jack Kerouac was vodka, orange and cranberry juice. I had the feeling nobody in this place had read a single page of either author.

'Er, I'll have a Lord Byron,' I said.

312

'Actually you might prefer the Jane Austen,' said Anthony eagerly. 'It's even got chocolate in, you might like that.' Then he broke off, frowning, checking himself as though he hadn't meant to be nice or friendly.

'I think I'll stick with Byron,' I said miserably, thinking, Oh God, he's never going to forgive me.

As we sat sipping from our literary gems, Kerry kept chatting away endlessly about the wedding. Thankfully, the conversation began to falter, and we took to staring at the dance floor. Nobody was moving with much energy. Perhaps they were all too terrified of sweating. All they did was sort of bend their bodies, clicking their nails and swinging their streaky hair.

Only one person was really dancing with any flare: a black guy in a red rollneck, who was swirling about with some snazzy moves.

'Oh my God!' Kerry squealed, slamming down her George Eliot. 'That's Drew! Can you believe it! I must say hello!'

She dashed off, flinging her arms around him. Soon they were dancing, Kerry undulating her body in sexy curves, leaning in close to him.

Shit, I thought, any minute now, Anthony's going to storm out. Or he'll walk up and sock Drew one. I felt shaky with disbelief – didn't Kerry realise how jealous Anthony could be?

But Anthony just sat there sipping his cocktail.

'Do you mind?' I blurted out.

'What?'

'This.' I waved at Kerry.

'What's to mind?'

'Well, aren't you jealous?'

'You taught me not to be jealous, Lucy,' said Anthony. 'I'm not going to mess up this time.'

I felt shocked.

'But Anthony, this is stupid. I mean, this is the other extreme – I think you *should* be jealous . . .'

'What's it to you anyway?' Anthony snapped. 'I thought you didn't care. I thought you didn't even want to be friends.'

I recoiled, stung. Suddenly I didn't want to be here any more. I'd said sorry, hadn't I? I was trying to make amends, and all he could do was insult me.

'What are you doing?' Anthony asked as I stood up.

'Look,' I said, 'the only reason I've come here is because of you. I thought we could still be friends. And I'm sorry if I was rude at dinner but I was just – just nervous. I don't know why you paid for me to come all the way here if you're going to treat me this way. I don't think I'm even going to come to your stupid wedding. I think it's better if I just fly home, don't you?'

'Lucy . . .' Anthony began, but I turned and ran out.

Outside, I hailed a taxi. As it swung away, I found myself bursting into hot tears of shame. I knew that I had been in the wrong; Anthony's words kept repeating over and over, lacerating my heart with a fresh slash each time. I didn't mean to hurt you or be rude at dinner, I kept apologising inwardly. I just couldn't understand why you were being so unfriendly. I can't understand what's happened between us.

Oh God, I wept, I wish I'd never come. What if I've ruined my friendship with Anthony for good?

iii) A very long talk with Anthony

A knock on my hotel door.

Now what?

I had got back from the club an hour ago, and now I was feeling rather sheepish and stupid. The truth was, I had backed myself into a corner. Deep down I really did want to stay and see the wedding, but my angry pride kept telling me I had to follow my threat through and start packing.

I had just put on my bridesmaid's dress again – with a masochistic sort of sadness that I wouldn't be wearing it, mixed with relief that nobody would have to see me looking this bad – when there was a knock on the door.

'Yes?' I called out.

Anthony entered. He did a doubletake at my outfit, then swallowed.

'Lucy, I think we've been having some kind of mis-understanding,' he said. 'Look, I really didn't mean to upset you.

314

I was so worried I was going to come back and find you'd left. I've been going crazy, ringing the hotel every few minutes to see if you'd checked out.'

'Really?' I asked in astonishment. Suddenly relief washed over me. Anthony did care; he did want me here. Then I said sharply, 'But you've been so mean to me. I mean – I know I was rude at the dinner, but only because you were making me so upset by being so cold!'

'Yeah, well, it's all a misunderstanding,' said Anthony. He broke off and looked over my shoulder. 'Is that a minibar?'

'What?'

'A minibar. Lucy, my head is thumping and I am dying for a drink. Fuck, Morrison is organising this stupid stag night tomorrow night that I don't even want, and now I've just had this row with you – I *so* need a drink.'

'Well, sure.' I laughed.

We took some gin and tonics out of the little fridge and sat on the bed. We chinked our bottles and grinned. Even without explanations, forgiveness was already starting to flow between us.

'So,' I said, my tone playful but also still rather hurt, 'why were you so mean to me?'

'D'you remember that night you came over when I was at work and you and Kerry had a chat together? Well, she told me you'd said it was better if we weren't friends any more. I felt pretty hurt – I mean, God, I should have spoken to you, I knew in my heart I should have. But there was no time, and Kerry whisked me off to the States. I didn't even think you'd turn up for the wedding. Kerry said you felt really hurt by seeing us together. She said you wanted space.'

'But that just isn't true!' I cried, my face flaming. Now my mind was made up. I opened up the 'evil bitch' box and flung Kerry firmly inside, slamming the lid down tight.

'I realise that now,' said Anthony. 'I had a talk about it with Kerry just now – well, it was a bit of a row, as she was very drunk. I've left her behind at the club. I thought I'd better come straight over and talk to you.'

'I still can't believe it,' I said. 'I mean, it was just a blatant lie.'

'Well, not a lie – she probably just got the wrong end of the stick.'

'No, Anthony,' I cried. 'She's *lying*. We *never* had that conversation. *Ever*.'

I waited for Anthony to erupt. To realise that Kerry wasn't all she seemed. To declare that the wedding was off. Instead, he let out a deep sigh and lay down on the bed, loosening his tie. I turned and glared down at him.

'Anthony – this behaviour – it's not on, you know. It really isn't.'

'I know, I know,' he sighed. He glanced at me. 'But I understand it.'

'What!'

'Well, Kerry's jealous. That's obvious. She's felt threatened ever since she met you. And I know it's awful, but I do understand it.'

Oh give me a break, I thought. Then I slumped inside. It seemed as though Kerry could let off a nuclear missile and Anthony would say, 'Well, she was just having a bit of P.M.T. that day . . .' This, surely, was verging dangerously on unconditional love.

I reached over to the minibar, pulling out another drink. I felt Anthony's eyes on me as I stretched over and found myself blushing. Then I shook those thoughts away: they were just my imagination.

'So, tell me about your mother,' I said, eager to change the subject. 'I'm so glad Kerry persuaded you to see her.'

'Well, it wasn't really Kerry, you know,' said Anthony, patting my arm. I remained very still, hiding the sensations he was provoking inside me. 'You were the first one to bring it up. And you were so right. I was angry, I admit it, but when I finally thought about it, and talked about it again with Kerry, I realised what I had to do. So I met up with her.'

'And?' I asked excitedly.

'Well, it was the wedding that made the difference. I couldn't not invite her – weddings are a time to be with family. So I got in touch and gave her a chance to tell me everything. And you know, I just feel so bad. I didn't realise how tough things were. She and my father met and fell in love and got married within the space of about six weeks – it was all so rushed, and they obviously weren't meant to be together.'

And aren't you repeating their mistake by marrying Kerry so fast? I mused, but Anthony seemed oblivious to the comparison.

'And I realised too that the reason she had an affair and left was

316

because she couldn't cope with Dad's infidelities. Apparently in India he was always chasing young girls, and it broke her heart.' I didn't realise she'd got pregnant either; I knew I had a half-brother but I never wanted to meet him. Now I think I might finally be ready – well, after the wedding.'

'Oh God,' I said uncomfortably. 'Well, I guess she reached a point where she couldn't stand it any more.'

'I know. She also said that when she left, she wrote me a letter explaining things, but I never got it. I don't think a letter makes everything all right – I still find it hard that she left me – but I also realise my dad didn't help. He blocked her seeing me when we first moved to America by not even telling her where we were. By the time I'd finished speaking to her, I actually felt more mad with Dad than with her. I went and had a huge row with him and I was ready to stop speaking to him. And then I just thought – fuck it. The past is past. If I carry on hating my parents like this, what good does it do them or me or anyone? They're human, and they made a mess of things, but at least I know that in marrying Kerry I'm not going to be like them. I'm not going to mess up.'

'Oh, Anthony,' I said, deeply moved. I was slightly tipsy now and I lay down on the bed next to him. It felt intimate and friendly.

'I think I might ruin this dress before we even get to the ceremony,' I said ruefully.

'It's a nice dress,' said Anthony, taking a swig of gin.

'No it's not.' I giggled, and Anthony giggled too, choking slightly on his drink.

'Well, I'm sure she meant well – it's probably quite hard to tell from the material and designs how something will end up looking.'

Men can be so naïve when it comes to the subtleties of female cattiness.

'Oh, sure,' I said, rolling my eyes. Anthony grinned, a sheepish, apologetic grin that said he could see that Kerry and I were never going to be the best of friends but there wasn't much he could do about it.

'Oh, Lucy, it's good to have you back,' he said passionately. I looked over at him and we smiled at each other. I held his gaze for just a few seconds too long; he dropped his eyes first.

317

I swallowed, fiddling hastily with the label on my bottle.

'So,' said Anthony. 'You said at dinner you're bringing someone to the wedding. Who's the lucky guy?'

'Oh, nobody really,' I sighed.

'Shame. We could have had a double wedding.'

'And he could have proposed to me in a chocolate shop,' I replied, my voice barbing with hurt. 'He could have bought me my favourite chocolate, and then told me he loved me.'

'Oh, Lucy!' Anthony put his hands over his face in embarrassment, groaning. 'When they brought that story up at dinner, I nearly died. The truth is—'

'You don't have to explain,' I said quickly.

'No, Lucy, I'm going to explain,' he said sternly, rubbing my shoulder. 'The truth is, I told Kerry the whole story of how I'd taken *you* to that chocolate shop. You see, we were having a discussion about the most romantic days of our lives, and when I told her about that day, she got, well, jealous, and insisted I take her there. And she seemed so happy . . .' his eyes grew wistful, 'it just seemed like the perfect moment to propose.'

'I see,' I said, feeling both assuaged and jealous.

'I hope you do understand,' he said. 'I hope it doesn't spoil our memory in any way, because it shouldn't do, Luce.'

He gently stroked my cheek, and the caress of his fingers was so unexpectedly tender that a baby bird fluttered in my throat and I ducked my head, play-pushing him away and turning it into a mock tussle.

We lay in silence for a few pensive minutes.

'D'you want to know something?' he said.

I made a faint noise.

'D'you remember the night we broke up?'

'Mmmm.'

'Well, d'you remember that we went to The House and they'd lost the reservation? God, I'd planned the whole night so meticulously and it just seemed doomed from the start . . .'

'Planned – what d'you mean by that?'

'Well,' he cleared his throat, 'I actually had a present for you, but because you broke up with me, I never got to give it to you.'

'Oh?' I perked up, wondering if he was about to produce some belated chocolate surprise. At least I would have something to comfort me when he'd gone.

'It was a ring.' He looked awkward, grinning hard.

'A ring?'

'I was going to propose.'

I lay in silence for some time.

'Lucy?' he asked, his grin beginning to fade.

I was unable to speak.

'Lucy? Are you OK? Are you mad at me?'

'No . . . why would I be mad at you?' I managed. 'But . . . but you told me you were going to break up with me.'

'Yeah, well,' he grinned sheepishly, 'I had to say that, didn't I? I mean, you made me feel like a total twat. There I was, about to propose, and there you were, about to dump me.'

'Oh, Anthony, I'm sorry, I'm so sorry . . .'

'No, really, it's fine,' he laughed. 'I will never, ever forget the pain I suffered that night – you crucified me, Lucy, if the truth be told. I mean, fuck, I feel embarrassed telling you all this, but I thought that it would be OK now that it doesn't matter any more. We've both moved on, and I've got Kerry now . . . but in a way, I kind of owe you one. I don't think I would have proposed to Kerry and I don't think I'd be sitting here now about to get married if it hadn't been for you.'

'Why's that?' I asked shrilly.

'You know the story, Lucy, I don't need to tell you. Before you I was Mr Big Commitment-Phobic. And then I got together with you, and to be honest, I never expected it to last, but it did, and I learnt that I could handle a big relationship – indeed, that I wanted one.

'I mean,' he said, warming to the subject, 'everything is about timing. I've realised that now. In my early twenties, girls were always trying to put a ring on my finger, but I was young and I wanted to travel and see the world and have a career. Most of the time relationships fail not because of a lack of love, but because people are at different stages in their lives. You know, like my parents – my father dragging my mother to India when she just wanted a quiet life at home – or someone who wants babies when the other wants to be free, or someone who wants to live in the city while their

319

partner wants to live in the country. I hit thirty and I was ready for marriage. I was a bit disappointed to find out I had such a hunger for it, to be honest. It all seemed so predictable. But that's where I was at. And you weren't, Lucy. You weren't at that settling down and marrying stage and you never will be – you're a free spirit! Whereas Kerry – she was at the same stage as me. Maybe if you *had* been at the same stage . . .' He lowered his eyes, swallowing.

'I . . . I . . . I feel like such a bitch – I dumped you and you were going to propose to me,' I said, unable to quite take it all in.

'Haven't you listened to a word I said?' Anthony laughed gently. 'I'm not telling you off, I'm thanking you. By dumping me, you gave me a kick up the backside. If we had stayed together we would have made each other unhappy – I'd be secretly wanting to propose, while you'd be secretly dreading my proposal. It made me pick myself up and move on.'

We sank into another pensive silence. While Anthony appeared to be revelling in the joys of fate, a rainbow of emotions was rioting inside me. I was still stunned. An urgent voice in me was yelling: *Tell him, Lucy. You have to tell him how you feel.* But I kept yelling back: *I can't, I can't! He is still marrying Kerry, after all.*

Then a thought struck me.

'What did you do with the ring?' I suddenly burst out.

'What?'

'The ring. You said you'd bought one.'

'Oh . . . yes . . .' He suddenly went red. 'I, er, got upset and threw it in the Thames.'

I narrowed my eyes at him. I knew him far too well to believe that. All his familiar lying signs – which nobody else, not even his mother, could ever pick up – were twitching across his face.

'No you didn't!' I cried. 'You gave my ring to her, didn't you?'

'Well, I . . .'

'You recycled my ring! Like toilet paper!'

'Lucy, you're being so unfair. You can't blame me – it cost two thousand pounds!'

We glared at each other with a mixture of outrage and laughter.

'Well, it is a very nice ring,' I said.

'You can't blame me,' Anthony repeated. 'You did dump me.' He looked anxious. 'You won't tell Kerry, will you?'

'Of course not,' I said, still spitting. 'But you know,' I added, unable to stop myself, 'I think you should be careful about her. She was flirting pretty badly tonight.'

'What d'you mean by that?' Anthony asked defensively.

Suddenly the atmosphere between us felt strained and harsh. I didn't want us to start arguing again; I couldn't bear it. I was still in shock from his revelation, too.

'Oh, I'm sure it's all just harmless,' I said quickly, smiling.

Anthony grinned in relief, though an uneasiness still lingered on his face.

'Well,' he said, standing up and checking his watch, 'I guess I should be going . . . Kerry'll be wondering where I am.'

'Yes, of course,' I said.

'I take it you're still not going to tell me who your mystery partner for the wedding is?'

'You'll just have to wait and see,' I said. I stood up, and was quite surprised that I was able to do so. I seemed able to laugh and talk quite naturally, holding the tears tight in the backs of my eyes, my pain entirely invisible.

But as I watched him walking towards the door, I realised how fragile my cool veneer was: a thin layer of ice that started to crack with despair when I saw he was going.

Say something! I told myself. *Say it!*

I can't, I argued back in terror. *It's too late. I've lost him. It's all too late.*

But he proposed to you once – you never know, there might be the tiniest shred of hope.

I can't, I can't, I'd make such a fool of myself.

If you don't say it now, when will you ever? It'll be too late . . .

'Anthony?' I called weakly.

'Yes?' He turned round, grinning.

'I . . . I . . .' My voice sounded as thick as treacle. 'I just wanted to ask if . . . if . . .' I was shaking with nerves, terrified that I was going to break down. 'I just wanted to say – well, I'm glad we're still friends. I'm really glad.'

'So am I, Lucy,' said Anthony, staring at me softly. 'So am I.'

He lingered for a moment, and then left, shutting the door gently behind him, and I exploded like a nuclear bomb.

321

iv) Lucy explodes

HE WAS GOING TO
PROPOSE
TO ME!

v) Time machine

The next day, I was in such a state of shock that I barely registered time flitting by. The evening came, and it was time for Kerry's hen night. But I just sat in my hotel room, churning, churning, churning.

That night – the night he had been meaning to propose – kept going through my mind over and over. Ever since, I'd kept feeling that the details had never fitted together properly to make a neat jigsaw; the edges had always been ragged. Now I understood why. No wonder Anthony had been awkward and moody; no wonder he'd told me to dress up; no wonder he'd gone so bonkers when they'd screwed up our reservation at The House. None of his behaviour made sense if he'd been planning to dump me . . .

But imagine, I thought. Imagine if we had got that reservation at The House. If we'd sat down and had a lovely dinner. And I'd decided to put off dumping him. And then he'd proposed . . .

I started kicking myself. But then I realised that it still wouldn't have worked. After all, if he *had* got to propose, things would have been even worse. Because back then I was Lucy the commitment-phobe. I'd have freaked. I'd probably have felt so awkward and guilty that I'd have said, 'Can I think about it?' And then it would have dragged out for weeks while I drove myself insane with insomnia, and Anthony insane with indecision. Then he would have finally snapped and forced me to make up my mind, and then I would have said no, and probably have felt too guilty to ever face him again.

I stood up and went to the minibar. I unscrewed a bottle of something, too dazed to register the brand, and swallowed it down. It hit my stomach in an acidic arrow. I winced and sat down again, staring at my reflection in the mirror. My cheeks were flushed, my eyes sparkling. I saw a huge smile slowly breaking across my face, at the same time as I felt hot liquid behind my eyes.

I lay down on the bed and grabbed a pillow, hugging it tightly. For a moment I swept all the complications of the present aside and let the joy of his revelation sink in. Anthony had wanted to propose to me! He hadn't chosen Kerry over me because I was ugly or boring or hopeless or a rubbish cook. I had been worthy of him, worthy of his love, of his first proposal. He loved me, he loved me, he loved me!

Or rather, *he'd loved me, he'd loved me, he'd loved me*.

I sat up, zinging with a fresh idea. Hang on, I thought, hang on. I could go back this time. It would work. I could wipe all of this out – Kerry, Byron, the awful dinner where I claimed to be the *Mona Lisa*.

I could go back to that night. Anthony could propose. And this time I could say yes!

I gulped. Uncertainty skittered through my stomach and I felt vexed. God, what was the matter with me? This *was* what I wanted, wasn't it? After all these days and nights of angst and longing and jealousy . . .

I'm scared, a small voice said, *of letting him down. What if we marry and I'm a useless wife? What if I'm not really the right one for him? What if Kerry is? What if fate arranged things so that we missed The House that night because Anthony is meant to be with her? What if I find I can't make him happy* . . .

My mobile shrilled. It was Kerry, no doubt wondering why I wasn't in the lobby, why I wasn't joining her for her hen night.

I had to be quick.

I ran over to my suitcase and took the time machine out. Adrenalin spurted through me; my mind became clear and cool, and I managed to put the whole thing together within twenty minutes. By the end, I was coated in a nervous sweat and shaking slightly with anticipation.

I climbed into the machine, pausing. I was about to put in the date when a thought crossed my mind . . .

'Lucy?'

Suddenly I heard pounding on my hotel room door. Kerry. Oh God, just fuck off, I thought furiously.

I turned back to the machine and keyed in the date: 2015.

It was the only way to do it. I would check out the future, and find out who Anthony was meant to be with . . .

I found myself in the middle of a large kitchen. It was gorgeous: stone floors, light slanting through lattice-patterned windows on to a large oak table strewn with a happy paraphernalia of magazines, newspapers, bills and recipes. A golden retriever lay in a basket, thumping his tail; at the sight of me he gave a little bark. I felt a glow of happiness inside. Is this where I live in the future? I wondered. This is the house I own? With this view from the window into a back garden that looks like Eden, flowers wafting clouds of scents? Wow. Maybe I do have some good karma after all.

Then, suddenly, I heard a voice in the hallway. I looked around nervously. Where to hide, where to hide?

'Anthony?' the voice was calling in the distance. 'Anthony?'

I dived under the oak table, hiding beneath a hem of lacy tablecloth. I watched a pair of legs stride into the kitchen: tanned legs in red stilettos. Immediately my heart sank. So I'd put on a bit of weight. So my fast metabolism had started to slow down. That was a bugger. I'd have to throw away all my chocolate the moment I got home.

Then another person entered the kitchen: I saw shiny black shoes and black trousers. The black shoes walked up to the red stilettos. A suck of pleasure as they exchanged kisses.

'Come on, honey, we should get going,' said the man's voice.

Anthony. I squinted nervously through the lace. When I saw him, my heart opened like a flower in the sun. Yes, he had a slight double chin, and that vein that protruded in his forehead had now slashed into a fork of stress, and those gentle lines fanning his mouth and eyes were now deep-rooted. But he had a new edge to him I hadn't seen before. He was stronger than ever. He had become a man.

'I'm tired, I don't know if I feel like going tonight . . . Oh well, I guess we should.'

Hang on. *That* wasn't my voice.

Oh God.

Oh no.

Kerry.

He was meant to marry Kerry.

I couldn't believe it. Why the hell had I decided to come and find this out? Ignorance is bliss; it would have been better not to know.

Anthony and Kerry left the kitchen and went down the hallway. I emerged from under the table blinking back tears, my heart dull. Suddenly I heard Kerry's voice in the hallway. 'Oh shit, I forgot to lock the back door.'

I was about to dive under the table again when suddenly the dog leapt up and barked at me rather savagely. The footsteps were getting closer and closer and I panicked. I flung open the back door and ran outside into the garden, diving under the shelter of a bush.

'Jesus – we even left it open.' I heard Kerry's voice floating out. 'I can't believe it, it's a miracle we don't get burgled . . .'

Her key scraped in the lock. I listened to the sound of the car engine revving up, thrumming louder, then fading away. Then I realised: *fuck.*

Now the kitchen door was locked. Which meant I couldn't get back to the original place where the time machine had flung me out. Which meant I was bloody well stuck out here for goodness knows how long while Anthony and Kerry were having the time of their lives.

Nice one, Lucy.

I crumpled under the bush. I just couldn't accept what I had seen. How could he have ended up with Kerry – *how*?

The chill began to prick my skin. I slunk out and went up to the kitchen window, standing on tiptoe to glance in. I wondered if I should grab a stone and smash the glass.

Then I jumped as a female entered the kitchen. *Great*, I wailed inwardly, *now Anthony and Kerry have a daughter* . . .

No. Wait. She was much too old to be their daughter. Actually, she looked very familiar . . .

And then a man entered. *Anthony.* Yes – Anthony! He came up behind the woman and kissed her neck lovingly. She swung round and kissed him hard on the lips. Oh God, surely Anthony wasn't having an affair? What excuse had he made to Kerry? Goodness, how awful . . .

Then the woman glanced out through the window and I twigged. I was so shocked that I lost my balance and went careering back, stumbling into the grass. I lay there watching the clouds chase each other across the sky, utterly dazed.

The woman had been *me*. So Anthony was having an affair with me . . . ?

But hang on – when I'd glanced in, the kitchen had looked different. It had been a lot more messy, the sink piled high with plates. And the dog had disappeared. Could it be . . . ?

Could it be that I was seeing an alternative future? Different realities?

The time machine was teasing me. It was telling me that the future was fluid. Malleable. It wasn't going to give me any easy answers; in fact, the only answer it seemed to be giving me was that I had to make up my own mind.

The trouble was, I still needed to get back home.

I figured that if I walked into the kitchen and encountered my older self, I might give her a bit of a shock. At the same time, I was fizzing with curiosity. All my life, I had always wondered about my future: *Where will I be in five years' time? Ten years? Will I live long enough to grow old?* I wanted to know if I had kids; if I had found out what job suited me; and most importantly, if I was happy.

I waited for them to leave the kitchen and tried the back door. It was open. Yes! All clear. Time to escape.

And yet.

I found myself standing in the kitchen, taut with alertness. Where were they? I could hear muffled giggles, voices floating down the stairs. I found myself taking off my shoes and placing them under the table. Tiptoeing down the hallway. I eyed the stairs, prayed they didn't squeak, and bounded up them softly.

In the hallway I stopped. I listened to the sounds and felt a blush burn across my face and singe the roots of my hair. As I edged towards the doorway, I wondered to myself if there was a name for this type of perviness, a new species of eroticism. I peered round the edge of the door.

Anthony and I were lying on the bed. We were naked, languidly entwined. Anthony was stroking me and staring deep into my eyes and whispering something. The sound of his voice said that this wasn't sex; this was lovemaking, lovemaking soaked in a decade of happy marriage, of coming to know every nook and cranny of each other's bodies.

Then he looked up and saw me and let out a cry.

I screamed.

And then I – the I on the bed – screamed again.

I turned and ran down the stairs, grabbed my shoes and dived into the time machine, where I collapsed, laughing.

Back in the hotel room, reality rushed back in all too quickly. My laughter faded. I was back to square one. Now what?

Somehow I just wasn't sure. Yes, I could go back and accept Anthony's marriage proposal, but every day I would have to live with the knowledge that I had stolen his future, that I had lied to him, tricked him, warped reality.

A depression swam over me. Suddenly I felt utterly helpless. I was in possession of one of the most powerful tools in the universe, I could play God with time, but I couldn't fix this. Kerry and Anthony were getting married tomorrow, and that was reality.

I went back to the time machine. I downed a speaking vial. I typed in a date. I just wanted to escape reality. I hit the button before I could change my mind.

Chapter Nine

Casanova

I don't conquer, I submit.

CASANOVA

i) Venice, briefly

The moment I climbed out of the time machine, I knew I'd done the wrong thing.

I was in a bedroom. It was dawn. Sunlight trickled in caresses through the shutters, running along the floor and up the four-poster bed. The sheets on the bed were rumpled over a dark figure. The figure rumbled with snores.

I was drawn to the window. The view was breathtakingly beautiful. Venice was laid out before me, a beautiful collage of waterways and ancient buildings. The sky and sea, both a divine shade of aquamarine, were like two brilliant mirrors reflecting each other's perfection. Suddenly I understand how our ancestors had once believed that the sky was part of the sea.

Normally when I landed in a new place my excitement was at its height, anticipation frothing inside me at the adventures yet to unfold. But now I just felt uneasy. *This isn't going to solve anything, Lucy*, I told myself. I felt sick inside, the same feeling I used to have when I swore not to touch chocolate and then shoved a bar into my mouth in a mad binge. *Get back into the time machine.*

Unfortunately, before I had a chance to summon it, Casanova woke up. He let out an explosive snore and blinked awake, shaking himself and then gaping at me in amazement.

'Have I died?' he asked in a frightened voice. 'Am I dying? Are you an angel?'

'I'm not an angel,' I said with a soft smile. 'So I think you're OK for now.'

He gazed up at me, drinking me in. I studied him. So. Here he was. The world's most famous lover.

Was he handsome? Not really. He had a big nose and a chunky face. He also looked somewhat tormented, his chin rough with stubble, stress lines thick around his mouth, and there was a look in his eyes that suggested life had recently been hard on him. Yet this only served to give him a kind of desperate, boyish vulnerability that suddenly made me ache to reach out and stroke his face. Yes, I thought, understanding then: he is irresistible. He has something far more powerful than looks; he has charisma. He made me want to love him right away.

And yet.

He wasn't Anthony.

'You're beautiful,' he groaned, catching my wrist between his fingers. 'Why, you're the most perfect maid I have ever seen.'

'I'm not your maid,' I replied, drawing back. 'I have to go. Anthony's getting married and there's nothing I can about it and coming here isn't really going to help.' I knew my words were a senseless babble but I didn't care; I had to go.

There was a loud banging on the door. I jumped. Casanova's eyes mooned. I sensed trouble. Time to make a hasty exit, I thought.

As I turned to summon the machine, Casanova pounced, taking hold of my arm and flinging me back on to the bed.

'I . . .' I gasped. 'I thought your style was to woo slowly.'

'Don't toy with me.' As I tried to rise, Casanova pushed me back down roughly, catching my wrists. 'Who sent you? Did *they* send you?'

'Nobody sent me. I'm innocent, I don't know what you're talking about.'

The bangs were getting louder. I looked straight into Casanova's eyes, begging him to believe me. He let me go, ran to the door and put his ear to the wood, listening hard. Then he turned back to face me, sweat pouring down his face.

'I escaped prison last night,' he said. 'And this inn was supposed to be a safe hiding place!'

'Why were you in prison?' I cried, though I had a sneaky feeling that the question ought to be: *Who did you seduce that you shouldn't have?*

'For no reason! It was utterly unjust! They stuck me beneath the Doge's Palace for a year! A year!' He paced the room, pushing open the window, glancing down at the drop. 'We shall have to escape through here!'

The banging at the door turned into crashes. Pieces of wood splintered and flew off in all directions.

'Quick!' I cried. 'No – not through the window! Here!'

Casanova turned to me, his eyes desperate. I grabbed his arm and yanked him to the centre of the room. As the time machine appeared, he let out a shocked gasp. The door caved in, men piled into the room . . . but we were away, flying through centuries, shell-shocked but safe.

ii) The end of the time machine

Back in my hotel room, the time machine landed with a groan, a cough and a clatter. This time not just one door fell off, but two. Steam rose in a black mushroom cloud from the front. This didn't look good.

'Oh God!' I cried. 'I think it's on its last legs.'

'*Che cosa state facendo?*' Casanova cried, dazed. He came up to me, gripping my shoulders, his eyes filled with terror. '*Dove sono? Siete una spia? Chi li ha trasmessi?*'

'OK – OK, I'm sorry – *here*.' I ran to the machine and pulled out the speaking serums. There was only one vial left. So if Casanova drank it, that was it . . .

I turned to him, torn between selfishness and kindness. Still, I thought uneasily, I can always write to Dr Schwartzman, and ask him to make some more potions. I can tell him all about my adventures . . .

But if he knows it really works, he might want it back, a voice pointed out. I ignored it, nobly proffering the potion to Casanova. He eyed it up, perhaps fearing I was part of a conspiracy to poison him.

'Look. Here.' I took a sip to assure him it was safe and then handed it back. Casanova downed it in one go.

'Wow,' he said, 'what the hell was that?'

I let out a giggle. His accent was pure New York. Well – I guess we were on American soil, so it made sense.

'Where the hell are we?' he asked, shaking his head, still utterly confused. 'I think this might be heaven – am I right?'

'Er, not quite. We're in the future. We're in 2005. I'm sorry, I know this might be a bit of a shock to you . . . but the main thing is, you're safe here. Nobody is going to put you in jail. Look – I suggest we both have a drink.'

I opened up the minibar, but it was rather empty after all the drinking I'd been doing. And I really didn't want to be sober.

Then my mobile rang again. I waited for it to switch to voicemail, then listened to the message Kerry had left. 'Look, Lucy, we can't wait any longer, so we'll see you there. At the Parrot Wine Bar – get a cab!' Suddenly I felt guilty, for her voice was concerned rather than angry.

I turned back to Casanova, suffering a twist of unease. After the fiasco of Lord Byron, the last thing I'd wanted to do was bring another famous historical figure back to the present day. Oh God, this was all such a mess . . . I ought to have known the time machine would bring nothing but more trouble.

'Look,' I said to Casanova, 'I have a hen night to go to.'

'A hen night?'

'It's an evening – with women only – to celebrate the night before a bride gets married. Not that I'm a fan of the bride in question. But anyway, I have to go, so it might be better, for your sake, if I took you home.'

'I'm not going back there!' Casanova cried. 'And end up in jail again?'

'Well,' I said, chewing my lip, 'I could just leave you here.' I looked at him and he gave me his best boyish glance. 'Or you could come with me,' I relented. 'I mean, look, I don't mind if you come, but suddenly leaping into 2005 is going to blow your mind, and I just wanted to protect you.'

Uh-oh. Wrong word. Casanova's masculinity was severely wounded.

'Protect me? I've been in prison for a year. I've fought duels! And you think I need protecting? You think I'm shocked by being in the future? One of the reasons that I was arrested was because of my occult abilities. I want to go out. We both need a drink. And *I*,' he finished grandly, with a twinkle in his eye, 'shall protect *you*.'

'Well, come on then,' I said. I had to admit, a rather wicked little thought was worming into my mind as to how interesting it would be to introduce Casanova to Kerry.

Then I paused uneasily. 'But – look – this is kind of embarrassing . . . I'm not saying . . . don't be offended . . . but I just thought I should make it clear that I'm out of bounds.' I giggled nervously. 'You can't seduce me, you see.'

Casanova looked more offended than ever.

'I hadn't entertained any intention of seducing you.'

'Oh.' I shrank to the size of a pea. 'Well then. Let's go.'

iii) Taking a gamble

As for what happened later – well, I blame Casanova entirely. It was his idea that we should hit the casino.

But first of all came the dreaded hen night.

On the way there in the taxi, my anxiety began to intensify. *This is silly, Lucy,* I kept telling myself. *You can't go around collecting historical figures and dragging them into the present. Just have one very quick drink and then make sure you get back home and into that time machine.*

The Parrot was a very snazzy bar. As we entered, I leaned in to Casanova, curling his arm around me.

'I thought you didn't want me to seduce you?' he teased me gently.

'Well the thing is, I kind of wanted to show Kerry that . . .' I waited for him to protest, but instead he grinned and kissed my temple.

And, I had to admit, it was worth it all just for the look on Kerry's face. We entered the bar just as she was arched backwards beneath an ice sculpture, vodka dribbling into her mouth. Catching sight of us, she spluttered and coughed. For the next five minutes she pretended she hadn't noticed we were there, chatting with her other girlfriends before sidling over.

'Lucy, you must introduce me to your lovely boyfriend!' She turned to Casanova, smiling up at him. 'This is a hen night, you know. You're not really allowed here!'

'I can see other men,' said Casanova, nodding. We turned to see a stripper standing on a table, struggling with his Levis, and Kerry giggled.

335

'Well I think I can make an exception just for you,' she cooed. Inwardly I began to seethe. Jesus. First of all she'd stolen the love of my life, and now she was going after my pretend boyfriend. Still, I thought, if I leave them together, perhaps she'll be so busy tonight she won't make it for the wedding tomorrow . . .

Then, to my surprise, Casanova said, 'Well, Kerry, we're just dropping in. I'm afraid we can't stay. We have another engagement. Have a good time, though. Behave!'

When we got outside, I looked at him in confusion.

'I could see you were pretty tense in there,' he said. 'I figured we might have more fun on our own.'

I blinked, struck by how sensitive he had been to pick up on just how I was feeling.

I wasn't keen on hanging out for much longer, but Casanova drew me into the bar next door. He still seemed completely unfazed by his new surroundings, though I saw his eyes darting all over the place, his pupils dilating with each new surprise, and I sensed he was just putting on a good act.

'So what would you like to drink?' he asked, touching the small of my back.

'Er . . .' I glanced around, aware of people giving Casanova's clothes odd looks. 'I'll just have a Coke,' I said quickly.

'She'll have a rum,' said Casanova. 'And I'll have one too.' Ah. He patted his white shirt.

'Don't worry, I'll pay,' I said, grinning weakly and handing him a twenty-dollar bill.

Casanova led me into a quiet corner. I took a sip of my drink. I'd never been a fan of rum. I felt taut, coiled up like a spring. Casanova kept making charming remarks; I replied with distracted *hmms*. All I could think about was how dreadful Kerry was, and yet Anthony was *still* marrying her. This time tomorrow the wedding would be over, and then what? Back to England, where I had no job, no flat. I found myself beginning to slide into a dark depression.

Casanova looked at me. 'Did you hear what I just said?'

'Er, no,' I admitted.

'I said you had better drink up or I'll have to kiss you,' he teased. 'And after all, you're desperate not to be seduced by me, aren't you?'

I quivered with alarm. I didn't want to be kissed by anyone except Anthony. I quickly downed half of my rum, then broke off and gave him a sidelong glance, realising how insulting I was being. Casanova, however, merely smiled a half-smile, as though quietly confident that my resolve wouldn't last.

I put my glass down on the table, chewing my lip. Casanova contemplated me.

'I think you should have another drink,' he said. 'Come on, Lucy, just the one?'

'Well . . .' Oh God, he was so charming, it was impossible to say no. 'OK. Just *one* more. And that's the very last one.'

Casanova went up to the bar. I couldn't help noticing that everyone was looking at him. At first I thought it was his crazy costume. Then I realised that it was the *women* in the bar who were watching him. A group of middle-aged women sitting in a corner were exchanging carnivorous glances and whispering, while a gaggle of teenage girls, who looked suspiciously underage, were giggling and shoving each other and saying, 'No, *you* go and ask him' – 'No, *you!*' The barmaid who had taken over behind the bar managed to lean forward when passing over his change so that he had the finest possible view of her cleavage. I couldn't help sitting upright with indignation. OK, so I didn't fancy him, I felt like saying, but he is here in this bar with *me*.

Casanova, who seemed relaxed at all the attention, returned to our table with the drinks. He smiled his goose-bumping smile again, a smile that whispered both reassurance and mischief. That said: *I'm going to make everything all right.* And: *I think you deserve to have a little fun.*

As he chinked his glass against mine, I felt my depression lifting.

'To a wonderful night!' he said. And downed his drink.

He thumped his glass down on the table, glanced around the bar, and allowed a momentary panic to pass across his face. He looked so confused, so vulnerable, that I touched his cheek.

'You're coping very well,' I said. 'I mean, it must be hard suddenly going two hundred and fifty years into the future.'

He smiled and nodded. 'I'm used to adventures far stranger than this. Drink your drink.'

I downed it. And suddenly the world seemed a much more rosy

place. The alcohol began to drown my pain, liquefy it into something vague and distant. And when Casanova suggested we get another round in – well, it wouldn't hurt, would it?

'A toast – to the wonders of rum!' he said.

'To the wonders of rum!' I agreed.

'So,' Casanova said, looking at me over the rim of his glass, 'would you care to tell me what's troubling you?'

'I'm not troubled,' I said jumpily, crossing my arms. Then I looked down, laughed sheepishly and uncrossed them. 'Actually . . . actually . . .' I swallowed. 'I'd prefer it if we could talk about you. I just want to forget, you know, all the stuff that's happening to me right now . . . Tell me what it's like being the world's most famous womaniser. Because I can tell you, you're still famous now.'

'I'm not a womaniser!' Casanova objected. 'I love women!'

'Oh, sorry,' I said quickly. 'I didn't mean . . . I just meant that you seem to have been quite successful with them, that's all.'

Soon Casanova was lost in amorous anecdotes that had me crying with laughter. But what was also fascinating was the sincerity of his passion. He certainly wasn't an Ovid; women were not boars to be caught in nets. He really did love the female sex; he was fascinated by our mysteries and contradictions and was determined to understand us fully. Then there were other stories: stories of his writing, his life as a spy, his success in inventing the lottery, which had made him a millionaire.

Suddenly I felt very drunk and very happy about it. Here I was, in a bar with a gorgeous, funny, sexy guy, and though I didn't want to sleep with him, hell, it was a million times more fun than Kerry's stupid hen party.

Once more we downed our drinks, eyes on each other, grinning.

'The night is still young,' said Casanova. 'I think we need to find some new entertainment, Lucy. Are there any casinos around here?'

'I don't know. I think we really need to go to Las Vegas – there are *zillions* of casinos there. I guess we could always use the time machine. But then we don't have any money.' I pursed my lips. 'Mind you, I do have some credit cards on me. I could live dangerously . . .'

'That sounds like another toast coming on!' Casanova cried.

Outside, I realised how very drunk I was. I couldn't even walk in a straight line, so Casanova kindly offered to support me. We walked arm in arm, giggling. As we reached the queue for the cash machines, several people gave us weird glances.

I emptied my bank account, taking out the last few hundred in my account: my month's rent and money for food and Lyra. Now I had a nice fat wad of notes to convert into chips. I hardly cared if the night bankrupted me; in fact, in part I wanted it to. I was furious with myself for messing up, furious at fate for not intervening. Now I just wanted to stick two fingers up at everyone, to give up, to tell the world where to go.

Back in the hotel, we clambered into the time machine, giggling. It was in such a decrepit state that I had to punch the button three times before it finally heaved us, with a great sense of weariness, over to the casino capital.

In the casinos everything was a blur of light. White lights above; the electric rollercoaster lights of fruit machines; the red orbs of cigarettes, burning embers of pleasure and decadence. People leant over tables, casual shoulders belying knotted stomachs. It was all so surreal, like being in a dream. We tried the fruit machines first, lost ten dollars and then won seven back on some winning cherries. As the money poured out of the machine in a frothy clatter, we whooped and hugged each other.

We stopped for more drinks at the bar. I was reaching the point where standing might soon become rather a challenge.

'We'll play poker next,' said Casanova. His voice was completely steady; he had the demons of alcohol under control.

'I don't know how to play spoker,' I said. 'I mean, spooker. I mean . . .'

Casanova smiled and tucked a lock of hair behind my ear.

'You watch and see.'

'I don't think I've got a very good spoker face.' I attempted to form one and ended up collapsing into giggles.

'Tell me, Lucy, seriously,' said Casanova, stroking my hair, 'why don't you want to be seduced? Why are you scared of love?'

I lowered my eyes, feeling melancholic again.

'It's so painful,' I said. 'I like the ups, but I can't survive the downs.'

'But that's love,' said Casanova, taking my hands in his. 'Yes, it can be painful, in the most pleasurable way. *'Even as love crowns you, so may he crucify you,'* he quoted. 'For love's task is to try to make our hearts completely pure, and make us better people. Love is . . . love is like a mother who scrapes the dirt from our hearts, and in doing so causes us grief . . . but in the end also brings us the ultimate fulfilment. If love was easy and painless, my dear Lucy, it would be dull. Don't you think?'

I raised my eyes and looked into his warm gaze, and smiled uncertainly.

After poker, we had a go at roulette. Our money was dwindling fast.

'One last bet?' said Casanova.

'Yeah! One last bet!'

Casanova tossed his chips on to number 24. Then he turned to me and cried impulsively, 'If I win, you have to marry me!'

'All right!' In my drunken state, I felt high with the whimsicality of it all. 'If number twenty-four wins, we shall be wed.'

The dealer closed off the bets; the chips sat, pregnant with anticipation, around the wheel.

I followed the path of the ball: in my inebriated state, colours swam and numbers doubled, tripled, quadrupled into figures vibrating and spangling with possibility. Then the ball began to slow and slow and trickle as though weary with the weight of expectation . . . 18 . . . 21 . . . 23 . . . I felt Casanova's excited grip tighten around my waist . . . 24 . . . I waited for a groan of disappointment, but it never came. The ball stayed put.

Number 24.

A big grin spread across Casanova's face. Several people cheered. Several muttered with jealousy.

Casanova turned to me and took me in his arms.

'So, my darling – will you marry me?'

I stared up into his eyes and thought of Anthony's face when he saw the ring flashing on my finger tomorrow at the service. I could outdo him. I could marry before him. I could damn well show him that I didn't care.

340

Somewhere in the back of all this swimming darkness, a sensible voice was pointing out the insanity of it all. But that voice was too quiet, too drowned out by alcohol.

'Yes!' I cried, flinging my arms around him. 'I will!'

I let out a scream as Casanova suddenly swooped down on me and picked me up in his arms. The crowds around us burst into cheers; soon the whole casino was watching us. I let out a shrieky giggle at the craziness of it all. For the first time since I'd come to the US, I really didn't care about anything or anyone. I was getting married!

He carried me to the cashier's booth, where he collected his winnings.

Then he scooped me up in his arms again and carried me out of the casino. Outside the night was black, the lights of the city sparkling like fireworks of celebration.

Did I have any moments of sanity, of sobriety, before we found a chapel? Yes, perhaps. But I was caught in a current of recklessness like I'd never been before.

As we walked up the aisle, a thousand thoughts jack-knifed through my mind. When you reach one of those moments that is life-changing, life-defining, it's as though the past rushes up to meet the present to explain it. I thought of Anthony and the very first time we'd met, on that plane, his smile and those dark circles under his eyes that I longed to gently stroke; I thought about making love in that Parisian hotel room, the taste of his chocolate gift still under my tongue and my heart pounding with love for him; I thought of that moment when I had turned him down and thrown away my future; I thought of what a failure my life was. After all, how do you measure success? By whether you're happy. And I realised now, more acutely than ever, that I had failed at that, that I was more miserable than I had ever been and after tomorrow I was probably going to spend the rest of my life being miserable. And that was why I was doing this: it was symbolic, the opposite of every girl's dream, to make a mockery of marriage, to treat it as a savage joke.

For as I walked up the aisle to marry Casanova, I knew I was doing all this for Anthony. If I hadn't been so desperately in love, I doubt I would have done something so ridiculously perverse.

As we came out of the church, the cold air hit me and I felt horribly sober. I suggested in a shaky voice that we should have a few more drinks to celebrate.

Very, very drunk now. Taxi. Urgh, feel sick, get into the time machine. Ooh dear, it's in a state. Back in hotel. Fuck, time machine's collapsed into pieces. Goodbye, time machine. In bathroom. Cool water on my face. Casanova behind me, stroking my hair. In my room. Look, that's my bridesmaid's dress, my horrible bridesmaid's dress. Casanova, with a glint in his eye, hands me a small knife. Go on, he says. I burst into a whoop. Slash, slash, slash. Oh dear oh dear. Goodbye, dress. My wonderful wicked wife, come here. Warm arms, but not Anthony's arms. Lying on the bed, kissing. Nice lips, but not Anthony's lips. Feeling sad, drawn deep into a well of sadness. Anthony has filled my heart, no room for anyone else. Room spinning. Everything going black. I'm married. Oh God. Blackness; sleep; yes, sleep, take me away from all this; good night, Casanova, good night . . .

I expect I made history that night: the only girl in the world who'd ever fallen asleep in the arms of Casanova as he attempted to make love to her.

Chapter Ten

Casanova and Anthony Brown

Real love is the love that sometimes arises after sensual pleasure. If it does, it is immortal; the other kind inevitably grows stable, for it lies in mere fantasy.

CASANOVA

i) The morning of the wedding

I woke up, aware of a heavy pressure on my rib cage and a disgusting taste in my mouth, as though my tongue had been coated with green slime. As I opened my eyes, the light pierced them like a dagger. I shifted the weight – which turned out to be an arm – and my brain, shocked at the slightest movement, seemed to stumble and crash about in my head like a drunk attempting to walk in a straight line. A voice inside pleaded that it was best to disappear back under the covers and hide in the dark cocoon of sleep. Only the pulsing ache in my bladder forced me to get up and negotiate the stretch of carpet from the bed to the bathroom. The time machine, sitting in the corner, was a black husk: burnt out and ruined.

So was my reflection in the mirror. I looked ghastly.

I went to the toilet in relief. As I washed my hands, I took care to keep my eyes fixed on them and not my face. Gradually I became aware of a few annoying little bits of green soap caught in my ring . . .

My ring.

I let out a cry.

I ran out of the bathroom, the water still gushing behind me, and jumped on to the bed, pulling back the bedclothes. Casanova's face was slack and peaceful in sleep. I found a hand – no, that was the wrong one. I searched for the other one, splayed across the pillow. There it was. On his third finger. *My* ring.

Oh, dear God!

Casanova blinked, stirring. He stared up at my horrified face and a smile stretched across his features.

'Good morning,' he said, 'my darling, darling wife.'

I burst into tears.

Casanova, as considerate as ever, ordered me some tea from room service. He stroked my face gently with the tips of my fingers.

It was such a sweetly consoling gesture, yet I still felt blank. It was as though my body was a ragdoll and Anthony was a magician, the only man who could wave his wand and bring it alive, make it pulse with life and passion and lust and sparkle.

'Lucy,' Casanova coaxed me, 'why so sad? I know our marriage was rather sudden . . .'

I put down my tea, fragmenting my reflection and slopping some into the saucer. I knew what I had to say – and it had to be said as soon as possible.

'Casanova – I'm sorry.' I pulled the ring off my finger. Halfway, it caught on a knobble of bone and I had to wrench it. I flung it into the sea of bedclothes. 'I shouldn't have married you,' I said. 'I'm sorry, I'm so sorry. But I think we're going to have to get a divorce.'

Casanova's hand slowly drooped away. He stood up. He walked into the bathroom. I heard the sound of running water.

I fell under the covers, curling up in a ball. My head lurched with pain; I felt sick with hangover and self-loathing. Just how bad could things get? Not only had I screwed up my own life very nicely, but now I'd screwed up Casanova's as well. He was meant to be the world's greatest lover and I'd probably turned him off women for good. For God's sake – what was I *thinking* of, dragging him forward to 2005 and *marrying* him? I had a feeling that in a year's time I'd look back on this and giggle. But in the here and now I had seen the hurt on his face, a hurt I recognised, a hurt Anthony had provoked in me . . .

Anthony.

And Kerry.

'Oh my God!' I cried. 'I'm supposed to be at a wedding! I'm supposed to be a bridesmaid – right now!'

What was the time? Half past nine. Not a total disaster. The ceremony wasn't for an hour. If I just yanked on the dress and got into a taxi round to Kerry's apartment . . .

The dress. I whirled round, praying my memory was false. But there it was. On the floor in a crumpled heap, like a pool of pink blood. I lifted it up and the sunlight streamed in through the slashes.

It was unwearable.

Tears filled my eyes again. *I can't go*, I realised. It was too excruciating. To suffer the love of my life's wedding with no dress, whilst my head was splitting and I was trying to obtain a divorce after being married to Casanova for less than twelve hours – it was beyond the limits of human endurance. I'd rather scale Everest than deal with this.

I went to my handbag, yanking out my mobile. The ringtone had been muffled by the bag; sure enough, there were three missed calls from Kerry. I deleted them without listening to them.

I can't face it, I thought. I can't face hearing her voice on the phone, screaming at me . . .

Instead I sent her a text. I told her that I was terribly sick and that I hoped she enjoyed her wedding. I pressed SEND, then switched off my mobile.

I pictured Anthony's face when he saw that I hadn't turned up, when he saw that his best friend had let him down. Then I climbed back under the covers and shut the world out.

ii) Casanova's words of wisdom

A little while later, I was aware of pressure on the bed as someone sat down. Then the sheet drew back from my head. I looked at Casanova. To my tearful relief, his face was full of compassion, not anger.

'My dear Lucy,' he said, cupping my face in his hands. 'Tell me what the matter is.'

'I'm in love with someone else,' I said. 'I'm sorry.'

'Who is he?' Casanova demanded.

'He's Anthony,' I said wearily. 'And before you challenge him to a duel or anything like that, he's actually getting married in –' I glanced at the clock '– twenty-five minutes.' I stared up into Casanova's eyes. 'I'm sorry if I've hurt you.'

Casanova sighed. 'The truth is, Lucy, I was a little drunk last night.'

'So it was just a drunken mistake for you too!' I cried indignantly.

Then I burst into giggles of relief – at least I was off the marital hook. At the same time, I felt a stab of misery – so a man could only marry me if he was drunk; was that how lovable I was?

347

'Last night,' Casanova reflected, 'I really did love you, Lucy.' His forehead folded into a frown. 'People have accused me of using women, of seducing them for sport, even of hating them. Nothing could be further from the truth. For this is my problem: when I meet a girl, I fall in love with her so passionately, so ardently, a flame flares up inside me and utterly consumes me. Whoever the girl is, I feel I will die if I do not have her, that no other woman has ever meant as much to me, that she is the pinnacle of her sex. But then – how fast it fades, how quickly it dies . . . the next morning, or a few days or weeks later, I look at her and see her crooked teeth, her crow's feet, her nagging voice, her flaws, and I am left with nothing but smoke inside and a congealed wick . . .'

'Maybe the time will come when you will meet someone and it will last,' I said. 'Or perhaps it's just not your path in life.'

'Well,' said Casanova, rather sadly, 'that is my story. And what is the story of you and Anthony?'

So I told him, the History of Lucy and Anthony. He interrupted me once or twice, curious to know whether Lord Byron was a better lover than him, and whether I considered Leonardo da Vinci to be more handsome, but he also listened with sympathetic attentiveness. After I had finished, he pondered for a few minutes, and then gave his verdict.

'It seems, Lucy, that your misery is a little false.'

'What do you mean, false?' I asked indignantly.

'Well, you are living in a fantasy of self-indulgent misery. Let us face reality: how do you know that Anthony loves Kerry more? He was going to propose to you first. For all you know, he may, at this very moment, be heading for the church wishing it was you who would be walking down the aisle. Why haven't you at least spoken to him, told how you felt? It seems to me he has no idea.'

'I . . . I . . .' I swallowed. 'I just feel I've missed the boat. I felt so stupid for mucking him about for so long. I mean, even if he did . . . if he did love me – well, I can't mess up his wedding, can I?'

'If you let him marry her, he may well mess up the rest of his life.'

'But what can I say – well, hey, Anthony, you're about to be married in fifteen minutes, and I've come to swear my undying love to you, and by the way, you might like to know I'm married too, as I

348

was very drunk last night. But let's not worry about that minor detail.'

'Exactly,' said Casanova, 'it's a minor detail. We'll be divorced by next week, and I shall have demanded all your savings and your best jewellery from you.'

I laughed and he touched my chin.

'Come on, Lucy,' he chided me. 'You must speak to him, or you are going to spend the rest of your life in a knot of regret.'

'You really think I should do it?' I quavered. 'Just go in there and tell him? Oh God . . . I mean, if he says no, it will be the worst thing that's ever happened to me. And if he . . . if he says yes . . .' I could hardly dare to hope. Then I bunched into a ball. 'Oh Casanova, I can't do it, I just don't have the nerve.'

'Lucy, you must take the risk. Jump off the cliff and love will catch you!'

'Well it's too late now anyway,' I said, feeling my mood slide back downhill again. Talking to Casanova had momentarily elevated me, but now I reminded myself of the cruelty of reality. 'The wedding will be starting, like, now. Oh God, I wish the time machine wasn't broken.' Suddenly time seemed like a prison; the present a rope around my neck, strangling me. 'Maybe I could fix it . . .'

'No, Lucy!' Casanova cried. 'You don't need the machine. You are going to get up and get dressed and we are going to that wedding.' And he hauled me out of bed, ignoring my screams of protest.

'I can't – there's nothing I can do. Let me *go*.'

'Well at least you can turn up. And at the very sight of you, Anthony may change his mind!'

'Oh yeah, yeah. Anyway, I've just texted to say I'm sick!'

'But imagine how dedicated you will look if you have battled sickness and still turned up!' Casanova said charmingly.

'But my dress . . .'

'Wear your little black number.'

I had a feeling he wasn't going to take no for an answer.

Ten minutes later, as we ran out of the hotel, my little black dress flapping about my knees, I found my stomach fizzing with excitement and new hope.

'So tell me,' Casanova asked casually as we dived breathlessly into a cab, 'will there be any beautiful bridesmaids? What?' he cried as I thumped him cheerfully.

iii) The wedding

The taxi pulled up at the church and we shoved a note into the driver's hand and tumbled out. I stumbled in my high heels, praying we weren't too late . . .

To my surprise, the oak doors of the church were still wide open. We edged in discreetly, to discover . . .

That nothing much seemed to be happening. The church was perfumed with flowers and the pews were a sea of pastel hats. But there was a fraught tension in the air, and I sensed at once that something was wrong. After all, I thought, checking my watch, the ceremony should have begun twenty minutes ago.

What if Kerry hadn't turned up? Or better, if Anthony hadn't?

Or worse – if something had happened to Anthony?

To my relief, I spotted him. He was standing at the front of the church. Seeing me, he frowned and then gave a little wave. I waved back, feeling quite concerned by his appearance.

So: Kerry was the one who hadn't arrived yet. But there still wasn't time for me to transform into a bridesmaid, and I just wanted to lie low and squeeze into a back pew.

Casanova, however, was determined to get a good view. He dragged me down the aisle, stopping three pews from the front. Oh God, there was Grandma Rose – she gave me a little wave, thank God. And – shit – there was Mrs Prendeghast! I ducked my head quickly, hissing at Casanova to jolly well *sit down*.

'Excuse me,' said Casanova, forcing a glamorous, Botox-faced woman in her fifties to squash up. She muttered crossly and her frozen face struggled hard to form a frown, then gave up in resignation, as though the last time it had succeeded in such a miracle was 1985. Casanova shot her a winning smile and, suddenly, adopted an aristocratic British accent.

'Good morning – goodness, what a pleasure it is to meet such a beautiful woman.'

She melted at once.

'Love your outfit,' she said, eyeing up Casanova's ruffled shirt.

'It was made for me by Manon Balletti,' said Casanova proudly, puffing up his chest and rippling the ruffles.

'Oh? I know him intimately. He has a boutique in New York, right?'

'Lucy, what are you doing here? Why aren't you with Kerry?' a voice cried.

It was Mrs Prendeghast. She came bustling up, her enormous peach hat bobbing.

'I'm sorry – I don't think I can be a bridesmaid today. I mean – I woke up this morning and I was feeling, er, terribly ill, and I did leave a message saying I couldn't make it . . . but anyway, then I kind of, um, made a miraculous recovery.' I laughed weakly; she didn't laugh at all. 'I mean, maybe I could join in when she gets here . . .' I trailed off sheepishly.

'I see. Well, I'm glad you had a nice night,' she said, looking me up and down and no doubt picturing me downing tequilas and getting laid – which admittedly wasn't too far from the truth. 'I shall contact Kerry now. I'm sure she's late for this very reason – she's probably waiting for you.'

I saw her go to the front of the church and talk quietly to Anthony. No doubt putting all the blame on me.

Anthony looked over. I expected him to be furious, but he just shot me a little grin. Now that I was closer, I could see that his forehead was shiny with sweat. His eyes were bulbous. He was as pale as a vampire. He looked awful.

'Damn!' Mrs Prendeghast cursed, switching off her mobile. 'I've tried Kerry three times now and she's not answering.'

Mr Prendeghast came up. 'Darling, have you rung Kerry yet?'

'Yes, darling,' she hissed. 'I was just telling Anthony that I've tried her *three* times. I knew I should have been with her this morning, but no, she insisted that she wanted to sort herself out on her own. Oh God, Charles, you're going to have to go over there and sort her out yourself.'

'Virginia, I think you ought to go. I need to—'

'Charles, I'm needed *here*.'

'But Virginia, I need to find a new vicar!'

351

'*What!*' she cried.

'What?' Anthony interjected, his eyes wild.

'What?' I muttered, nudging Casanova.

'What?' asked Anthony's mother, striding up and looking very cross.

'What?' Anthony's father chimed in.

'There's nothing wrong with the vicar,' Mrs Prendeghast said irritably. 'I spoke to him myself last night.'

'That was last night. He just called me to say he's feeling sick and he's sending a substitute.'

'A what! Good Lord, this isn't a game of football. We didn't pay five thousand dollars for a *substitute*. Oh Charles,' she said, her voice cracking, 'this wedding is just doomed . . .'

Mr Prendeghast pulled her into his arms.

'Virginia, it's going to be just fine.'

'Oh God, this is ridiculous,' Anthony's mother snapped under her breath.

'I don't mind a substitute,' Anthony said helpfully. 'Really. Anyone is fine. I just want to . . .' He trailed off, his words hanging in the air.

'Oh Anthony, you're being so patient, and it's all such a *mess*,' Mrs Prendeghast said, wiping her eyes and touching him on the arm. 'All right. I'll go fetch Kerry and Charles will sort out the priest. I think you ought to make some sort of announcement, don't you, darling – the guests are *waiting*.'

iv) Discussions in the vestry

'Excuse me, everyone . . .' Mr Prendeghast cleared his throat. When nobody quietened, he took hold of a book and slammed it against the lectern, then flushed when he looked down and realised it was a Bible. 'Excuse me . . .' Then he was off into suave business mode. 'I'd just like to assure you all that despite a few minor hiccups, the wedding will be going ahead. Kerry is on her way, but we are having a small problem with the fact that the vicar is sick . . .'

352

And on he droned. The guests exchanged sly glances and nervous whispers, unconvinced by his reassurances.

Anthony, meanwhile, stuffed his hands in his pockets and strolled into the vestry.

'Well, go on.' Casanova broke off from chatting up three different women in three different pews. 'Here's your chance. Go and speak to him.'

'I can't,' I whispered, my heart pounding, yet I found my feet were already carrying me forward.

'*Lucy!*' I was interrupted by Mrs Prendeghast, on her way out. 'Anthony needs to be left alone,' she said sharply.

'Actually,' a voice behind us said, 'I think it would be a good idea if Lucy spoke to Anthony.'

I jumped, and saw to my surprise that Anthony's mother was behind me. She smiled at me softly, threading her hands together fretfully.

'I'm terribly worried about him,' she said in a low voice. 'I think he could do with your help right now.'

'Thanks,' I said breathlessly, ignoring Mrs Prendeghast's furious gaze.

In the vestry, I caught Anthony off-guard; his face weak with uncertainty and confusion. He looked like a lost little boy. A deep wave of love and compassion overwhelmed me and I hurried forward and drew him into a hug. He hugged me back just as tightly and I felt the tension in his body.

'She's not coming, is she?' he said, drawing back.

'No, she'll come, she'll come,' I said, trying to cheer him up. He looked so sad I almost wanted her to arrive. I rubbed his shoulder. 'Anthony, are you OK? You really do look like you need some Nurofen or something.'

'It's Morrison's fault,' Anthony groaned, drawing out a handkerchief and swabbing his forehead. 'He organised the stag night from hell.'

'What happened?'

'Oh – the works. Beer. Stupid jocks. Music. Strippers. Fuck – I *hate* strippers. None of it was at all how I wanted to celebrate the night before my wedding. And then I woke up feeling . . .'

'Feeling?' I swallowed.

'I don't know – hungover. But there was also a bad feeling inside me. And now the vicar's ill. And Kerry isn't going to turn up. And I know she's been having doubts about the wedding . . .'

'She told you that?' I cried, trying not to sound too excited.

'Yes, but she said she was just incredibly nervous. And I'm nervous too – I mean, fuck, it's not every day you get married. I . . . What about you? You have to keep talking to me, Lucy,' he jabbered, 'to take my mind off all this.' He began chewing a fingernail and I softly slapped his hand away. 'Hang on,' he suddenly noted. 'You're not wearing your bridesmaid's dress. What's happened?'

'Well,' I said, gulping and twitching my hem with nervous guilt. 'I woke up feeling really sick . . .' I waited for him to get mad, but he seemed surprisingly calm. I took another breath. OK, here goes, I thought. Time to confess everything.

I decided I had to tell him the worst bit first.

'Last night I did something really, really crazy.'

'What?' Anthony blinked. 'You didn't murder Kerry at the hen night, did you? Is that why she's not here?'

I laughed slightly shrilly, punching him on the shoulder.

'Well, I went to the hen night with Casanova, and then—'

'Wait. I can't believe your boyfriend's called Casanova!' Anthony spluttered. Then he saw my face and his laughter dissipated. 'What? What happened, Lucy?'

I held up my hand. The light, fractured by the stained-glass windows, fell on the ring. Anthony looked stunned. He let out a splutter of incredulous laughter. Then he shook his head.

'I was drunk,' I gabbled. 'The drunkest I've ever been in my life.'

'Yes, but – you *got married*? Shit. Fuck. Look, you don't need to panic, Lucy. It's easy to get these things annulled. Kerry's family has got a really good lawyer.' He broke off, ruffling my hair affectionately. 'God, this is such a Lucy situation.'

Suddenly I felt a spurt of frustrated misery. Here was I, hopeless Lucy with her clownish marriage, and here were Anthony and Kerry, about to be so grown up and sophisticated with their perfect match.

'Hang on a minute,' I said hotly. 'Who says I want to annul it?'

'But you said you never wanted to get married. I always thought that . . .'

'Of course I want to get married,' I cried passionately. 'I wanted to get married and have a wonderful wedding and now I've completely screwed up with the wrong guy.'

'Oh, Lucy, I'm sorry. I didn't mean to take the piss. Oh God, come here.'

He pulled me into another rib-crunching hug. I held him tightly, and found I couldn't let go. I closed my eyes and nestled into the dark of his suit, breathing in his sweet scent, trying to imprint it on my memory, knowing this might be the last time that we would be together. Because I knew that I wasn't going to tell Anthony that I loved him. Casanova had pumped me full of false hope. It was crazy; Anthony was about to marry another woman. If I said anything, I would just make a total fool of myself; I could imagine him and Kerry on their honeymoon, giggling together, Kerry crying, 'Oh God, I can't *believe* she told you that – just before I turned up, too! She's crazy!'

As my hope faded into sad embers, a despair came over me. I knew that I was going to spend the rest of my life watching and waiting for something to go wrong with their marriage. Which was selfish and horrible of me, but I couldn't help it. I had a feeling that the rest of my life was going to pass by very slowly . . .

'This feels kind of weird . . .' Anthony whispered.

'Weird? Why?'

'Well,' he whispered, his breath warm and ticklish in my ear, 'you're married, and I'm about to get married. It feels, standing here, like we're finally going to go our separate ways . . . I'm going to miss you, Lucy, I'm going to miss you so much.'

I felt him rain a trail of kisses on my hair and I pulled back hazily. Our faces were very close; our eyes met.

'Oh Lucy, maybe I'm making a terrible mistake,' Anthony whispered, and placed a kiss on the edge of my mouth. His lips tasted soft and sweet. The kiss began to slide, oh-so-deliciously, to something more central. And then we were kissing. Gently, and then hungrily, drinking each other in desperately, his hands clawing my hair . . .

'*Anthony!*' Mrs Prendeghast rapped loudly on the door. Anthony quickly moved away from me, and a gust of cold air swirled about my body.

355

At first I couldn't hear what she was saying. The embers had flared into sparks that were flying about my body in dizzying tumbles. Hang on a moment, I wanted to yell, Anthony has just said he thinks it's a mistake. And he kissed me.

Didn't he?

Unless that was just a goodbye kiss. A kiss for old times' sake, an exes-for-ever kiss. But surely not, *surely not* . . . ?

Oh God. Casanova was right. I had to tell him. I had to tell him now.

'Kerry's here,' Mrs Prendeghast repeated. 'Kerry. Is. Here.'

'Oh . . . right.' Anthony sounded as though she'd just announced a man had come to read the gas meter.

'She's here!' Mrs Prendeghast repeated. 'I was driving out and she was on her way – she was just having some problems with, ah, traffic.'

No. I couldn't believe it. I turned back to Anthony. And found myself pleading silently: *Don't marry her.* Anthony stared back at me wide-eyed, as though uncertain how to interpret my gaze, as though hardly able to believe how it might translate.

'Well – I guess I should go,' he said finally, still staring.

I lowered my eyes in defeat. I had lost, and Kerry had won, in the Great War of Anthony, 2005.

'Well,' said Anthony, with one last, sad smile. 'I guess this is it . . .'

v) A new priest

But there was still the problem of no vicar.

I quickly edged back to my seat next to Casanova. Everyone was gossiping and peering back to the entrance of the church, where there was a teasing shadow of ivory dress: Kerry, waiting in the wings.

My head was still spinning. I thought of the questioning look in Anthony's eyes as I had left the vestry. He had *kissed* me with such passion. He felt something for me. Quite clearly. And what if I had just come out and said it? Just said, 'Anthony, don't do this, marry me!' Oh God, why had I chickened out? I should have ignored Mrs

Prendeghast; I should have demanded a few more minutes with Anthony.

My eyes darted to the front of the church, Mr and Mrs Prendeghast were arguing again; Mrs Prendeghast was practically in hysterics.

I thought: I could say it now. While they're arguing. I stepped forward to push my way out of the pew, but Mr Prendeghast suddenly picked up his Bible and bashed out a demand for silence once again.

'Excuse me. I'm afraid I have another announcement to make. The vicar is rather ill and the, er, substitute, seems to be caught in traffic. Now. This is rather embarrassing.' He made a steeple with his hands as though praying for divine help. 'If there is anyone in the congregation who has a licence to conduct weddings, we were rather hoping they might be able to step in.'

There was a resounding silence. Mrs Prendeghast pressed a peach handkerchief to her lips, choking back sobs of despair.

'Anyone . . . anyone . . .' Mr Prendeghast trailed off feebly.

I know this sounds terrible, but all I could think was: Oh, thank God. If the wedding was postponed, I could talk to Anthony, finally tell him everything.

'What qualifications does one need to marry them?' Casanova asked.

'You can't do it!' I snapped in a tense whisper. 'It's an American thing. You have to go and do a proper course – which you haven't done, mainly because they weren't invented in your day.'

But Casanova was already striding over to Mrs Prendeghast. He wiped away her tears with a lace handkerchief and clasped her hands in his, whispering something. Kerry's father tried to intervene, but Casanova barely registered him.

Mrs Prendeghast turned to the congregation, her red eyes now sparkling, and cried in a shaking voice, 'Everybody – I'm glad to announce that we have a solution! Kerry and Anthony will be married today, for Mr Casanova here is qualified to conduct the ceremony!'

There was ecstatic applause and whoops, and a little weeping too.

I wanted to join in with the clapping but my hands were balled

357

into fists, and when I let out a whoop it sounded more like the wail of a dying bird.

'Mr Casanova!' the Botox woman beside me chuckled. 'What an apt name – he is a dish!'

'He's not really called Mr Casanova,' I snapped sourly. 'He changed it by deed poll. He's really called Mr Smith.'

Oh God, why did Casanova have to ruin everything? Out of sheer desperation, I ran up to Mrs Prendeghast and cried, 'I'm sorry – I think there's been a mistake! Casanova didn't finish the course! So he really can't conduct this wedding.'

Mrs Prendeghast's eyes widened.

'Ah, Lucy,' Casanova sighed. 'We broke up, didn't we, before I completed the course? I realise you're bitter, but you need to move on.' He turned to Mrs Prendeghast. 'She's just hungover, her mind's a little confused.'

'Lucy, please go and sit down,' said Mrs Prendeghast icily. 'Now, Anthony – are you ready?'

I looked at Anthony and he stared at me. Once again our eyes seemed to reverberate with silent signals. But talking was now impossible; the organist had started the wedding march with a flourish. I had no choice but to slink back to my seat.

Mr Prendeghast scampered nervously up the aisle, as though hardly able to believe it was finally happening. And then, arm in arm, he and Kerry slid gracefully towards Anthony.

I couldn't take my eyes off her. She was looking lovely. She floated in her dress like a beautiful swan; the light glinted on the rosebuds in her hair and tinted her cheeks a radiant pink.

As she came up to the front of the church, Casanova's eyes gleamed. I looked quickly at Anthony. But though Kerry whispered something to him – presumably an apology – he merely frowned. If anything, he was looking even more ill; in fact, he was positively green.

They took up their positions in front of Casanova with nervous stiffness, like actors preparing for a curtain to go up. Casanova opened the Bible, smiling widely. Then, much to the surprise of the congregation, he reached out and shook hands with Kerry.

'I'm sorry about the other vicar,' he whispered. 'I'm Casanova, by the way.'

'Yes, I remember you from last night!' Kerry whispered back with a giggle.

The sound rippled and echoed through the congregation. It was a giggle of relief – the wedding was now on, even if the vicar was decidedly eccentric, and everything looked as though it was going to go swimmingly.

I felt panicky. This was it, this was it!

Oh God, I prayed, *please grant me a miracle. A bolt of lightning, hitting the church! Anything – just anything. I know . . .* My heart leapt. *Please can Casanova fudge the ceremony?*

Yes, *yes*! That was the answer. How on earth was his insane priest story going to hold up when he didn't even know the words to the marriage ceremony?

'We are gathered here today,' Casanova announced in a confident, booming voice, 'to unite Anthony Brown and Kerry Prendeghast in marriage.' He broke off to smile silkily at Kerry.

Oh God. I closed my eyes. Of course. The marriage ceremony back in Casanova's time was not much different to ours today. And how many ceremonies had Casanova gatecrashed, how many brides had he whisked away at the last minute from their unsuspecting grooms? Hundreds, probably. He must know the marriage ceremony by heart.

'As they pledge their constant abiding love to each other, let us remember that anyone who enters into this sacred relationship must learn to share a mutual love and concern for one another . . .'

He damn well did know it by heart.

'Love is one of the greatest of life's experiences,' he continued grandly.

The congregation swooned. Casanova broke off and – the cheek of it! – spun his eyes over Kerry's face, down her neck and to the scooped throat of her dress in an extremely appraising manner.

I looked at Anthony. *Go on,* I shouted inwardly, *sock him one for that!* But Anthony looked utterly dazed, as though he was in another world.

Casanova flicked his gaze over the congregation with a hopeful glint. 'If anyone should have any objection to the marriage, speak now.'

Suddenly Anthony turned and stared at me. I blinked. The look in his eyes was . . . pleading? Forceful? Or was it all my imagination?

I found myself jumping to my feet. I knocked on the pew. And then everyone was staring at me. Mrs Prendeghast turned and started flapping her hand in wild surreptitious gestures. Kerry scowled. Anthony looked as though he was going to faint.

'I . . . I . . .' God, this wasn't as easy as it looked in the movies. 'I just wanted to say . . . to say . . .' Oh God, what did I want to say? *Go on, Lucy, just say it. Tell him you love him. He loves you, you know he does, just have courage.* 'To say . . . to say . . . congratulations! Congratulations!'

I sat down, my face burning, my guts twisted in an agony of cowardice.

'Well, Lucy, thanks for that contribution,' Casanova said archly, and everyone tittered. 'I'm sure that was very clear.'

Anthony looked across at me, and I saw then that he knew. Why else would I stand up and make a fool of myself? But what did he feel? He just carried on standing there, letting the ceremony wash over him, looking increasingly stunned, and it was all going too quickly and now they were on the vows.

'Anthony Lewis Brown,' Casanova rattled off his name without even looking at him, his eyes fixed on Kerry, 'will you take Kerry Samantha Prendeghast' – he drew out each syllable, his tongue licking like a cat's – 'in all love and honour, in all faith and tenderness, to lie with her and cherish her in this bond of marriage?'

There was a long silence.

Then, once more, Anthony looked over at me. I looked back. And this time there was no doubting the look in his eyes. This time, I knew.

I felt my heart twist sharply and the air suck out of my chest. I screwed up every last drop of my courage into a tight ball. The rest of the church faded away into a blur as I pushed out of the pew blindly, ignoring their confused cries. I stepped out. I stood in the aisle, waiting for him to come down and meet me. Shaking with my daring, with my love for him.

'Hey,' said Kerry. 'What the hell . . .'

'I'm sorry,' said Anthony, stepping away from her. 'I'm sorry . . .'

'Well fuck you!' Kerry yelled. 'I didn't want to marry you anyway!'

Her words reverberated around the hushed church. For a moment Anthony looked shocked. Then he came down the aisle to meet me. He flung his arms around me and kissed the living daylights out of me. Finally we came up for air, and he gently rubbed my nose in an Eskimo kiss, pulling me against him, stroking my hair protectively, trying to shield me from the outrage around us.

'Well,' Casanova interrupted the cries of dissent, 'for God's sake!' His voice rose to a passionate shout. 'This wedding has been a farce from start to finish! What was a lovely, beautiful woman like you thinking of when you decided to marry such a cad?' He leaned down and grabbed Kerry and kissed her passionately.

She turned back to look at us with a smile that was half hurt, half triumphant.

'My darling, let us leave this haven of imbeciles!' Casanova cried, scooping her up.

Kerry let out a shocked, thrilled scream. As he ran down the aisle, carrying her in his arms.

They were halfway to the door before the congregation began to cry objections.

'Do something, Anthony!' Mrs Prendeghast cried. 'Stop them!'

But Anthony merely burst into laughter, holding me tight against him.

'Do something!' Mrs Prendeghast bashed her husband with her handbag.

The guests rushed to the church doors, forming a bottleneck of hats and handbags. Anthony and I followed them outside on to the gravel to see Casanova carrying Kerry jubilantly, like some fantastic piece of prey he had just ensnared and was taking home to eat for dinner; her wedding dress trailed in the gravel, turning from ivory to grey. Casanova spotted a taxi and waved.

As the taxi veered away, the Botox woman came up behind us.

'Well,' she declared, shaking her head, 'I could have warned them that you can't trust a man who goes around calling himself Casanova!'

vi) The wedding speech

'Come on,' said Anthony, grabbing my hand, 'let's go to Paris.'

'What!' I cried, stopping him.

'I've got the tickets,' he said. 'For the honeymoon. We could go instead.'

We were standing outside the church. Guests milled about us; everyone seemed torn between wondering if it would be more polite to go home and wanting to stay and see what other scandal might unfold next. So they hung about the graveyard, clustered in small pastel groups, hats bobbing, whispers floating: '. . . Kerry always was *unstable* . . . but then did you *hear* the rumours . . . according to Grandma Rose, they're not *sexually compatible*, would you believe it . . .' Every so often, people turned and gave us vicious glances. I hunched my shoulders uneasily, turning away from them.

'Mrs Prendeghast's delusional. She's convinced it's all still meant to be. She's just told me she's gone to look for Kerry to bring her back and talk some sense into her,' Anthony said. 'We have to leave just in case she succeeds!'

I burst into giggles and then looked up at him nervously.

'Anthony, are you sure you're not in shock? I mean – this has all been a bit much – a bit crazy – a bit unexpected – are you sure you don't need to just go home?'

Anthony gazed down at me, stroking my cheek.

'You know how I really feel? Relieved. Hugely, hugely relieved. Over the last few weeks I've been waking up every morning feeling miserable, without knowing why. Deep down, I knew she wasn't right for me. I've been trying to blot it out, but I just felt . . .'

'What?' I asked him.

'I just couldn't believe I was about to fuck up – either way. By going through with the wedding, or calling it off. I – just – I'm so used to getting everything *right*, Lucy. Normally everything I do, whether it's in business or my love life – I get it right. It works out. And today . . . I just fucked up . . . big-time . . . and I think,' he concluded, half-smiling despite the tears in his eyes. 'I think – well, there's a lot I need to say to you too, Lucy, but I don't think I can say it here and now. I think we need to get out of here. Please?'

362

I frowned suspiciously. There was still a splinter of doubt lodged in my heart.

'You're not just asking me as a rebound thing?'

'Of course not!' Anthony exploded. 'I am asking you because I really want to go with you. I can't think of anyone else I want to spend two weeks with.' He reached out and ran the tip of a trembling finger down the length of my face.

I turned to him, biting my lip in a wobbly smile. I gently brushed his hair back.

'Okay,' I said. 'Let's go.'

Anthony was so delighted that he picked me up and spun me round, laughing uproariously at the sky.

Several people broke off and turned to stare at him, and then more whispers started up: '. . . d'you think he's having a *breakdown* . . . ?'

'What about your parents?' I asked, as he hailed – with delicious inappropriateness – the bridal car.

'I'll call them.'

'What about the reception?'

'That's a good point.'

The bridal car pulled up and I slid in. Anthony turned back and clapped his hands.

'I'd like to invite everyone to carry on with the celebrations and to go to the reception for lunch and champagne! Go on! Go! Enjoy yourselves!'

Anthony dived back into the taxi, grinning.

'Mrs Prendeghast has paid for three hundred bottles of champagne,' he said, kissing my hair. 'And I'm going to make bloody sure every one of those bottles is empty by tonight!'

As the car pulled away, we both started to laugh at the impetuosity of it all, until soon hysterical tears streamed down our faces. I got the driver to stop at my hotel to pick up my luggage. As I got out of the car, Anthony pulled me back, gave me a kiss and told me to be as quick as I could. I kissed him back and promised I would run.

Run I did. Up the lift sailed and down the corridor I sprinted. Once in my hotel room, I managed to fling all my clothes into a case within the space of two minutes. As I lifted the bedclothes, my discarded wedding ring slithered off and hit the carpet. I picked it up and held it in my palm, musing that I could never, *ever*, have imagined that the day I got married, and Anthony nearly got married, could end like this. I suddenly noticed the time machine, a forlorn wreck in the corner. I checked my watch with a flash of panic – *shit, if I dismantled it now by the time I'd finished we'd never catch the flights.*

Then I let out a breath. What on earth was I going to need a time machine for when I had two weeks to spend with Anthony? I was cured of my addiction now, and I was only looking for it out of habit.

I went up to the machine and gently gave its dented metal side a kiss. A sudden spurt of happiness and freedom rose up inside me. All the terrible things that had happened over the last few weeks didn't seem to matter any more. Anthony and I were going to have a wonderful time together and the whole situation might be utterly crazy, but somehow I had a feeling that everything was going to work out.

Back in the taxi, Anthony was waiting for me with such bright eyes that I found myself grinning; I nestled against him and he put his arm around me, stroking my hair gently as the car slowly wove through traffic, and as we approached the airport the day began to die and bright lights of adventure tinkled across the night sky . . .

vii) The honeymoon

We spent the first day of Anthony's honeymoon mostly sleeping. Jet-lag and shock hit us like a sleeping pill and we found ourselves dozing deliciously, intermittently declaring that we would get up soon, and then soon became night and then morning again and we arose feeling fresh.

On the second day we ventured out gingerly, like soldiers who had been severely wounded in some war of love. Paris was strangely quiet; quiet and beautiful. Wreaths of morning mist slunk through the streets like grey cats, imbuing the shops and parks with a lovely mysteriousness.

By the fifth day, we were at peace. The wedding disaster seemed to have faded, swallowed up by the mist. Our mobiles had stopped ringing with messages from people wanting to interfere with our happiness. A bubble began to form around us; we wandered about dreamily, taking hours over lunch, sipping thick hot chocolates, talking things over. We laughed at how disastrous our weddings were; we sighed at how ridiculously life could turn out. But we didn't once mention the unspoken topic, growing bigger by the day, of us, and how our story might end.

On the last day, I woke up feeling slightly insecure. Time to go home now, and face reality. A divorce, no flat, and no job. And what about Anthony? I'd been hoping he might bring up the subject of us moving in together, but he hadn't even hinted at it yet.

We had lunch and then went for one last walk.

'Hey, look,' Anthony said suddenly. 'It's our shop. Patisserie Marie. The shop with the best chocolate in the world. Where I proposed to . . .'

'. . . Kerry,' I finished off. Suddenly I felt sulky with the memory. 'I don't really feel like going in.'

But Anthony was suddenly full of animation. Ignoring my grumpy protests, he ushered me inside.

The shop bell pinged as we entered. As we walked across the red and white tiles, dusty with spilt icing sugar, I forced back memories and bunched them tight in my heart. But smell is too great an evoker of memory. The scents of vanilla and honey, burnt sugar and cocoa brought back such a rush of feelings, I had to pay very particular attention to a box of Turkish Delight to conceal my face from him.

My misery was beginning to return. Anthony had proposed to Kerry in Paris. Was I just a rebound choice, a consolation fling? Just what did Anthony feel for me?

Why don't you tell him how you feel? a voice shouted. But I kept coming back to the same point: *But if he likes me, he should be the one to say. Why should I have to do the running? If he cares for me, he'd tell me.*

'Lucy, are you OK?' he called softly.

I ignored him. Then I heard him asking for the assistant. If he buys me the most perfect chocolate in the world as some patronising attempt to cheer me up, I shall kill him, I thought furiously.

'Lucy – fancy a taste of the best chocolate in the world?' he asked me.

'I don't want it,' I said, feeling him come up behind me. But as he held out the little box, I had to admit my stomach stirred.

'So,' said Anthony, 'if I proposed again, would you say yes?'

'No,' I said stoutly, staring down at the chocolate, glistening in tissue paper like a succulent jewel.

'If we come back in one year's time and I propose, would you say yes then?'

'I doubt it,' I said carelessly.

He turned away and I looked at him sharply. I waited for him to ask me again, but he was now busy paying for the chocolate. I watched him collect the change from the assistant, wailing inwardly: *Is he going to give up so easily?*

He turned to me and held the chocolate out, a curious smile on his face. I smiled back, taking a bite. I closed my eyes and it was heaven; a kind of *petit mort* for my tastebuds. Then I felt Anthony's mouth brushing mine, dusting my lips like icing sugar. I opened my eyes and swallowed, the bubble of bliss moving slowly through my heart and into my stomach.

'What if I were to ask you again, Lucy?'

I giggled and poked his chest.

'You,' I said, joking nervously, 'you manipulated me with all this. Proposing to me while I have the perfect chocolate in my mouth. You know me too well.'

'Well, isn't that why we belong together – because we do know each other too well?' Anthony asked, smiling, though his eyes were serious.

I felt tears in my eyes and I burst out: 'I'm frightened. We have such a wonderful friendship. What if we ruin it? What if in five years' time it all goes wrong?' I bit my lip, knowing this wasn't the sort of thing you were meant to bring up at this sort of moment. Great, Lucy, I thought, just blow the mood completely.

But I had spoken my true feelings.

'Lucy – if we crash and burn, we do. But we have to go for it, don't you think? Because I think we might just soar.'

He kissed me again and hugged me tightly, and I closed my eyes, tears running down my cheeks and mingling salty with the chocolate on my lips, and then, finally, I gave him my reply.

And a Half . . .

Exactly one year on, Anthony and I are getting a divorce.

No – I'm just kidding. In actual fact, dear reader, we've only just got married.

It took longer than I had thought to obtain my divorce from Casanova – the fact that no record of his birth could be found caused a number of complications. And then, I admit, I *still* had one or two flutters of doubt about tying the knot . . .

I suppose one of the reasons I'd always disliked the idea of marriage was that I'd always seen it as a set formula. You know: two people get together in their twenties, they both have great jobs, they marry, they have a kid, the woman gives up her job, they have more kids, they get bored, the man has a mid-life crisis and an affair with his secretary and they get divorced. I thought I had to tick all the boxes or else I was somehow defying social convention, and the marriage wouldn't be real. But after I moved in with Anthony, and had been living with him for a few months, I realised that you don't have to end up playing by the rules. You can make up your own rules. Anthony, having learnt his lessons about jealousy, doesn't stop me having male friends, and I don't stop him having female friends. Sometimes we take weekends apart. We make sure we have space, so that we can still be ourselves while being together.

Our wedding was divine. Casanova – with whom we are still in touch – offered to officiate, but we politely declined. Instead we went for an old-fashioned vicar, complete with glasses and yellow teeth and messy black hair, with an old-fashioned ceremony in a lovely church. I shall never forget how wonderful it was to walk down the aisle. I had been up all night, churning with nerves, but the moment I stepped into the church, I felt as though a great weight had been lifted off me. I saw the sunlight slanting through the stained-glass windows, as though ushering me on. I saw Anthony standing at the front, like the light at the end of a tunnel, with a shy smile on his face and a slight frown on his forehead, his eyes bright with love, and I knew then that marrying him wasn't going to be restrictive or a noose around my neck: that he was going to set me free.

Our vows went very well. Every so often I looked at Anthony and our eyes locked and I had to bite my lip because I felt as though I was going to burst into laughter out of sheer joy. And we were only interrupted twice by the screams of our daughter.

I forgot to mention that we had a daughter. She was conceived the night Anthony proposed to me in Paris. Anthony jokes that because I had just eaten the best chocolate in the world, I passed my bad genes on to our daughter and have created a monstrous chocoholic. And I admit that it is true that she does seem to scream longingly whenever I'm eating a bar . . .

Being pregnant was a little frightening. But my experiences in Roman times with Ovid and Tiryns had taught me a lesson. I swept aside all my doubts about whether I was ready to be a mother; I just appreciated what a great gift a baby was, and when she was born, it was the happiest day of my life.

We called her Ophelia Chloe Lyon-Brown.

Anthony and I have just returned from our honeymoon in Paris. We actually took Ophelia into the chocolate shop there and she stopped screaming and went all gurgly and quiet. Anthony looked at me and said, 'See, Lucy? Chocoholic genes. I rest my case.' Then he stroked her face with his thumb and I felt a flare of happiness inside. Seeing Anthony become a father has been just as wonderful as having a baby – the excitement of seeing him mature, of seeing the joyful pride in his eyes whenever he looks at her.

As for my career – I can assure you that I haven't neglected it completely. I spent a year trying to work out what I was going to do whilst getting fatter and fatter with pregnancy. I tried being a landscape gardener; I tried setting up a greetings-card company; I even tried becoming a professional chocolate-taster. Finally Anthony, who was being very patient, sat me down and told me I ought to just do something I enjoyed. I said that I liked writing, and he suggested I try my hand at a book. So I decided to turn my time-machine adventures into a story, and I recently decided that *A History of Lucy's Love Life in Ten and a Half Chapters* might make a very nice title.

But if it sounds as though my life is perfect now – well, it's not.

I still get restless from time to time. I have to admit that I couldn't quite bear to say goodbye to my time machine, so when we were in Paris I called up the hotel and asked them to pack it up for me. The burnt-out remains are now in storage and I am so proud of myself for not having touched it. But I admit that sometimes I still long to open it up and go off and have a fling with Andy Warhol, or Alexander the Great. Or I'm sitting in a coffee shop and a nice Italian waiter flirts with me and I feel temptation give a sudden naughty kick. A destructive, almost angry urge comes over me to just take his number, go off and have an adventure with him, carve out another future where I'm young and free and single and can do whatever I like with any man I like.

But then I remember Anthony and Ophelia. I stare into my coffee, feeling the steam caress my face, and I picture Anthony at home in the kitchen, wearing his silly apron with ducks on, cooking me the most sensational meal, occasionally breaking off to pull a silly face at Ophelia in her cot, making her gurgle and smile. And my heart leaps and I have to leave there and then without even finishing my drink because I just want to be back with him, bursting through the front door and giving him a big hug and a kiss. And then as I hurry home I think of how we'll eat and chatter about the day and then wash up together and then put Ophelia to sleep and watch a video, snuggled up like cats, best friends together. And I know that I have made the right decision and have sacrificed small, selfish pleasures for something much bigger – more scary, yes, – but also far more satisfying in the long run. And I know then we're going to be all right.

We're going to be all right because we've made a pact. We're never going to be bored. We're never going to stagnate or keep our emotions locked under the surface, pretending things are hunky-dory when we're secretly screaming inside. We're going to travel as much as we can. We've agreed that if we get bored of our jobs, we're going to jack them in and go off and be scuba-diving instructors or something equally wild. We're going to live life together, hand in hand, as one big adventure, here to be enjoyed together. And it's working. Every day we make an effort to surprise each other. Our most recent game has been notes, little love letters scrawled on scraps of paper, pushed into pockets on the way to work to pull out and read on the Tube with a secret smile. Yesterday Anthony's said: *Lucy means the world to me / She is as lovely as can be / And I hope she will forgive me / For being a terrible poet – as you can see . . . PS But though I'm never going to be Lord Byron, I do love you, Lucy!*

And this morning I tucked one into his briefcase that said: *You're the best man in the world. You're my ultimate fantasy. And even if Lord Byron miraculously turned up tomorrow and tried to sweep me off my feet, I'd still choose you . . .*

LOVE ETERNALLY

Deborah Wright

Steve is unlucky in love – he's shy and unable to bring himself to tell Dina, the girl he works with, that he loves her. On the night of his thirtieth birthday, he throws a party, drinks too much, falls in the Thames in a stupor on his way home – and dies.

But not quite. Steve comes round in the morning to find he's a ghost, unable to move on until he understands what relationships are about and what love means. He watches Dina as her life continues, and talks to her about what he's feeling. And, little by little, Dina begins to hear his voice . . .

Love Eternally is a romantic comedy about making the most of life, from the bestselling author of *The Rebel Fairy* and *Under My Spell*.

Other bestselling titles available by mail:

☐ The Rebel Fairy	Deborah Wright	£6.99
☐ Under My Spell	Deborah Wright	£5.99
☐ Love Eternally	Deborah Wright	£6.99
☐ Something Borrowed	Tina Reilly	£6.99
☐ Wedded Blitz	Tina Reilly	£6.99
☐ Lazy Ways to Make a Living	Abigail Bosanko	£6.99
☐ A Nice Girl Like Me	Abigail Bosanko	£6.99
☐ Playing James	Sarah Mason	£6.99
☐ The Party Season	Sarah Mason	£6.99
☐ High Society	Sarah Mason	£5.99

The prices shown above are correct at time of going to press. However, the publishers reserve the right to increase prices on covers from those previously advertised without further notice.

──────────────── sphere ────────────────

SPHERE
PO Box 121, Kettering, Northants NN14 4ZQ
Tel: 01832 737525, Fax: 01832 733076
Email: aspenhouse@FSBDial.co.uk

POST AND PACKING:
Payments can be made as follows: cheque, postal order (payable to Sphere), credit card or Switch Card. Do not send cash or currency.

All UK Orders	**FREE OF CHARGE**
EC & Overseas	25% of order value

Name (BLOCK LETTERS) . . . .

Address . . . .

. . . .

Post/zip code: . . . .

☐ Please keep me in touch with future Sphere publications

☐ I enclose my remittance £ . . . .

☐ I wish to pay by Visa/Access/Mastercard/Eurocard/Switch Card

Card Expiry Date ☐☐☐☐   Switch Issue No. ☐☐